SPECIAL MESSAGE TO READERS

This book is published under the auspices of

THE ULVERSCROFT FOUNDATION

(registered charity No. 264873 UK)

Established in 1972 to provide funds for research, diagnosis and treatment of eye diseases. Examples of contributions made are: —

A Children's Assessment Unit at Moorfield's Hospital, London.

•

Twin operating theatres at the Western Ophthalmic Hospital, London.

•

A Chair of Ophthalmology at the Royal Australian College of Ophthalmologists.

•

The Ulverscroft Children's Eye Unit at the Great Ormond Street Hospital For Sick Children, London.

You can help further the work of the Foundation by making a donation or leaving a legacy. Every contribution, no matter how small, is received with gratitude. Please write for details to:

THE ULVERSCROFT FOUNDATION,
The Green, Bradgate Road, Anstey,
Leicester LE7 7FU, England.
Telephone: (0116) 236 4325

In Australia write to:
THE ULVERSCROFT FOUNDATION,
c/o The Royal Australian and New Zealand
College of Ophthalmologists,
94-98 Chalmers Street, Surry Hills,
N.S.W. 2010, Australi

Madge Swindells was born and educated in England. As a teenager, she emigrated with her parents to South Africa where she studied archaeology and anthropology at Cape Town University. The author of numerous romance novels, her work has been translated into seven languages and has reached bestseller lists across the world. She currently lives in Dover.

TWISTED THINGS

Rescued after hours in the freezing water clinging onto the wreckage of her yacht, Clara Conner wakes up in Dover hospital. Patrick, her husband, is missing, presumably killed by the explosion that tore the *Connemara* apart. Clara becomes convinced that Patrick was murdered and that she was attacked. As she sorts through Patrick's business affairs, she realises that her husband had led a double life. He was involved with criminals and owed someone a lot of money. So when a mysterious man appears to be following Clara's every move, her fears for her safety grow — and that of her twelve-year-old son. Could this man be the attacker, and does he want to finish the job?

Books by Madge Swindells
Published by The House of Ulverscroft:

THE CORSICAN WOMAN
SUMMER HARVEST
SHADOWS ON THE SNOW
SONG OF THE WIND
SNAKES AND LADDERS
SUNSTROKE
WINNERS AND LOSERS

MADGE SWINDELLS

◆

TWISTED THINGS

Complete and Unabridged

CHARNWOOD
Leicester

First published in Great Britain in 2003 by
Allison & Busby Limited, London

First Charnwood Edition
published 2004
by arrangement with
Allison & Busby Limited, London

The moral right of the author has been asserted

This is a work of fiction and all characters, firms,
organisations and instants portrayed are imaginary.
They are not meant to resemble any counterparts in
the real world: in the unlikely event that any similarity
does exist it is an unintended coincidence.

British Library CIP Data

Swindells, Madge
    Twisted things.—Large print ed.—
Charnwood library series
    1. Boating accidents—Fiction
    2. Suspense fiction
    3. Large type books
    I. Title
    823.9′14 [F]

    ISBN 1–84395–437–0

Published by
F. A. Thorpe (Publishing)
Anstey, Leicestershire

Set by Words & Graphics Ltd.
Anstey, Leicestershire
Printed and bound in Great Britain by
T. J. International Ltd., Padstow, Cornwall

This book is printed on acid-free paper

Acknowledgements

With thanks to Jenni Swindells for her editorial and legal help. I would also like to thank Peter Archer for the information he provided. My thanks also to Shelley Power for her unfailing patience and editorial help, and to the Dover Lifeboat Association, Peter Foot and many Dover 'sea-dogs' for their technical advice, and not forgetting John Sokolsky for advice on youthful slang.

Prologue

She was lying face-down, spread-eagled over broken planks for balance, holding on as she rocked in the swell. She held her breath when the waves broke over her and took gasps of air when the raft bobbed on the surface of the sea. She gazed around, hoping to see anything, but there was nothing. The loneliest place in the world! She wondered why she was here and who she was, and how badly she was hurt.

Her fear was an image that stayed with her: an outstretched hand, an axe glinting in torchlight as it fell towards her, a dark shape in a balaclava wielding the axe. Someone wanted her dead.

She relived her trauma like the replay of an old movie.

She is falling, falling ever deeper. Above her a disc of golden light moves on the surface of the water, searching for her. She tries to swim away, but the light shoots around the water like a summer gnat. She has to rise, has to breathe. She breaks surface, gasping, and is instantly snared in the beam. A boathook strikes her shoulder hard, falls away, strikes again, tearing her anorak. She is tugged, like a fish towards the gaff. She struggles, fights, chokes as her head is pushed under the water, but the hook draws her inexorably towards the axe.

★　★　★

1

Shuddering, she touched the wound on her scalp, rocking the raft, almost upending it, longing to understand. Much later she saw a hint of light on the eastern horizon, a sullen mellowness like the sky before snow. She remembered the storm, the towering cliffs of water, the wind, the noise.

Her dark, tangled hair was hanging over her face. Her fingers, white and bloated from long immersion, were gripping the jagged edges of the slippery wood. She tried to move them, flexing her fingers. They looked familiar and that was comforting, but who did they belong to? She frowned as she stared at them.

In the dim light she saw letters on a half-broken plank. *Conne* . . . The rest was lost. Of course, *Connemara*, their yacht, but that was all she could recall. Remembering made her tired. She closed her eyes and drifted away.

'What does it mean, Connemara, darling?' *She is looking at a face well-loved, eyes of deepest blue, a strong jaw, laughter lines and a trace of grey in the blue-black hair.*

'Sea Wolf! She's well-named!' A deep voice, eyes glinting with pride. She feels proud, too. She has made Patrick happy after the bitterness of his retrenchment.

The image faded and her tears mingled with salt spray. She snapped back to consciousness and hung on to the raft. Sea and sky merged in the mist. She closed her eyes and let her mind drift aimlessly with no direction, like the raft.

She is standing on a box holding a bottle of champagne and she is laughing. 'I name this ship . . .'

'But it already has a name,' Jason whispers. She gazes into the eyes of her lanky young son. His reddish brown hair glints in the sun. She cannot ignore his anxiety at this slight inaccuracy. Jason is retreating from emotion and taking refuge in logic. She blames herself.

'I rename this ship . . .'

The image faded. She closed her eyes. 'Jason,' she whispered. 'I love you, darling. I'm trying . . . trying.'

She lay her cheek against the slippery wood and tried to extend the image, but it slipped away. She was sinking into a coma, but she no longer cared. The yacht was gone and she was alone. She could not begin to work out where she was. She wanted to drift into oblivion, but who would care for Jason? She had failed him once, but never again!

'Don't think! Just hang on. Help will come.'

Later she fell asleep and woke to find herself choking in the sea. The raft was hardly visible. With her last spurt of strength she kicked her frozen limbs towards it. She did not see the tanker gliding silently past, ephemeral and ghostly in the drizzle. It passed rapidly out of sight.

* * *

The Officer in Charge at Port Control had spent most of the night relaying messages to two patrol

3

vessels that were searching for the missing yacht, and to all ships moving through the Channel, instructing them to keep a look out.

When a passing tanker sent in a report of wreckage sighted drifting towards the Goodwin Sands, Distress Channel 16 on VHF Radio sparked into life as the exact position was broadcast to every boat in the vicinity, while an RAF rescue helicopter was dispatched from Norfolk.

Twenty minutes later the aircraft was circling the area. Visibility was poor, the sea was getting rougher and the crew didn't hold out much hope of finding a survivor. After an hour, when they had criss-crossed more than a square mile without a sight of debris, the pilot decided they should return to base. As he turned, the co-pilot pointed in an easterly direction.

'I thought I saw something in the water over there.'

The aircraft veered sharply to the east. At fifty feet a dark smudge became a makeshift raft, probably part of the wreckage they were searching for. A figure was lying on it, half-submerged in white foam.

'The swell is coming up against the Goodwin Sands making that disturbance,' the pilot called. 'We'd better be quick.'

He watched the winchman putting on his harness. Moments later he was swinging like a pendulum at the end of two wires, drenched by spray, holding his breath and clutching the second harness. For a split-second he swung over

4

the foaming waves. Then he dropped close enough to grab the raft and tip the body towards him.

The icy water shocked him. How could anyone survive more than a couple of hours in this? He spoke calmly to the woman. 'Relax. Everything's going to be all right. Easy does it!'

There was no reply.

It took only a minute to buckle on the harness. Clutching her to his chest, he gave the signal and they were towed up together. Still unconscious, she was wrapped in a space blanket. In less than fifteen minutes she was checked in at casualty.

Dover Post
Monday, October 25

SEARCH CALLED OFF

Dover Coastguards announce that they have given up the search for yachtsman, Patrick Connor, who, together with his wife, Clara, sailed out of Dover Yacht Harbour on the evening of Friday, October 22. Wreckage was spotted and recovered eight miles off Deal the following morning, but since then there has been no trace of the skipper. It is thought that the yacht foundered after an explosion, probably caused by a gas leak ignited during the storm when winds were gusting up to gale force. Clara Connor miraculously survived the blast. She was picked up by an RAF rescue helicopter early the following morning and is recovering in hospital. Members of the

Lifeboat Association confirmed that it is unlikely anyone could survive for more than a few hours given the temperature of the sea and wind velocity.

1

Something moves at the edge of her vision. She swings around too late to avoid the blow. Pain explodes inside her scalp and neck. Brilliant lights obscure her vision as she sprawls forward and for a moment she cannot move or talk. Time slows as she rocks in agony, feeling blood splashing on her cheeks. A dark shape looms over her, black against black, an axe glints as it swings towards her. Overhead the ebony sea, moulded by wind and tides into a preposterous wave, is curling, trembling, falling. She finds her voice, but her scream is lost in the crash.

The dream faded as she woke sobbing. There was something she had to remember. Something that spelled death. 'What was it? What was it?'

She could feel salt water burning her raw throat and nose. Shocked and bewildered, she touched the wound at the back of her scalp, rubbing the unfamiliar stitches with her finger. Where was she?

A door closed softly and she cringed. 'Who's there?' Footsteps! Light flooded the room. Jason, her son, was standing in the doorway looking upset. For a moment she felt confused, but then her love reached out to him. She had willed herself to survive for him.

Her tension drained away as memories of five days in hospital and her homecoming flooded back. Silly to forget. She looked around, drawing comfort from her familiar bedroom. Slowly her heart stopped pounding and the calm that followed was like a reprieve.

'Oh Jason. I thought . . . Were you downstairs?'

'No.'

'I heard someone.'

'Jock would have barked, Mum, but I'll go down and look. Stay there.'

'Yes. I'm sorry, love.'

She heard him checking the doors and windows before bounding upstairs, anxious to reassure her.

'Don't worry about anything. Relax and get better. No one can get past Jock.' She reached out and grasped his hand as he perched on the side of the bed.

'You're all right, Mum.' His voice croaked a little. 'You're safe at home. It's all over.'

It will never be over. He's coming after me. She was still in shock, she knew, and her fear was blotting out all other emotions. She forced a smile. 'Yes, of course.'

Jock sidled up to sit beside her, quivering with the force of his emotions. He was wide, black and ugly, a powerhouse of compacted muscle. Iron discipline prevented him from leaping on her; instead he licked her hands while intense love glowed in his eyes.

'It's great to be home,' she whispered, stroking Jock's head. She scanned her son's face and

8

dredged up a bright smile. 'Silly me. It was only a nightmare.'

Jason was a brown-haired, gawky boy, tall for his age, looking a bit like a stick insect with his long legs and skinny neck. A loving boy with a snub nose, a pleasant smile, soft brown eyes and never a sign of his extraordinary mathematical talent which embarrassed the hell out of him. She noted how short his pyjamas had become. She would have to buy new ones.

'You should be sleeping. School tomorrow. Where's Sib?'

'She had a date. I said we could cope. She needs a night out.'

She admired him silently, but with a touch of guilt. Since his father died he'd had to be an adult when he should have been a child and now he was entering his teens and she had a suspicion his voice was starting to break. It was all too fast.

'D'you feel a bit better?'

'Of course I do.' She reached out and hugged her son, smelling soap and toothpaste, and wondering at the breadth of his shoulders.

'You've been gasping and tossing around like crazy. Try not to think about it, Mum.'

'If only I could remember what really happened. I have these terrifying images and a sense of being touched by evil.' She broke off and clung to Jason's hand, unwilling to burden him with her trauma.

'Perhaps the nightmares are sort of filling the gaps when you were knocked out. You must get better fast.'

She squeezed his hand again, wishing she had kept her fears to herself.

'Go to bed, Jason. Sorry I woke you.' She smiled fondly at him. 'Everything's fine. Sleep well. See you in the morning. Go on! Off you go.' She closed her eyes firmly and turned away.

Jason wasn't fooled. Mum wasn't sleepy. He pulled up her duvet, switched off the light and called Jock as he crept back to his bedroom.

Sleep-fogged though he was, Jason couldn't shed his sadness. With Patrick gone, perhaps Mum would be happy, like she used to be. Three years with his step-father had almost wiped his mother out. She'd kidded herself that Patrick loved her, and perhaps he did in the beginning, but for the past two years he'd been putting her down. He was cruel, but subtle, and Jason had hated to see his mother bearing up bravely and pretending every incident was her own fault. He'd never understood why she'd married Patrick. Mum was the kindest person you were likely to meet. Birds were fed, foxes were given liberal hand-outs and Mum was about as 'green' as a person could get, recycling her waste in the right bins and growing their veggies organically. She couldn't even kill spiders. They had to be carefully prodded into jars and released at the end of the garden. She did her share of earth-loving. So why had she fallen for a git like Patrick?

'I'm glad you're dead, you bastard,' he whispered as he climbed into bed.

★   ★   ★

Autumn leaves falling past the window sparkled in pale wintry sunbeams. Clara could hear birdsong, and the scent of roses brought by Sib that morning was all about her. She heard gentle snoring close by and realised Jock was sleeping on the rug beside the bed. She felt pleasantly isolated from the world and her fears, but then she heard a man's voice. She frowned and tried to ignore the flutters in her stomach at the thought of facing up to Patrick's friends. Moments later Sib peered through the open doorway.

'Ah, you're awake, love.'

Flamboyant in orange pants and an emerald green sweater, pushing back her dishevelled Titian mane, green eyes glinting, she looked wickedly amused. She'd been flirting, Clara could see.

'Sib, I feel guilty.' She reached out for her friend's hand. 'It's time I let you off the hook.'

'I'm in no hurry to leave. Don't worry! I've got the routine taped. Jason's getting balanced meals and doing his homework. Jock's fine, but spoiled.' She broke off and frowned. 'Hell, Clara, I wish I could think of something succinct to soothe the agony.' Words were unnecessary, her eyes said so much.

Clara could feel tears pricking her eyes. It was good to have a friend like Sib. How many times had they nursed each other through illness and disasters? Years ago, when she was widowed while eight months pregnant with Jason, Sib had put her career on hold to move in and cope with running the household. She'd been a full-time nanny for the first few months of Jason's life until Clara emerged from her shock and depression and was able to take over.

'Bernie's downstairs. D'you feel up to seeing him?'

'I don't feel up to anything. My back feels like an over-wound winch and there's only a furnace where my stomach should be.'

She broke off as Bernard Fraser, Patrick's friend and lawyer, walked into her room and gazed around cautiously. Jock snarled sleepily. 'Oh, hell, Clara. Where's Jock?'

That was always Bernie's first question. He had a pair of shoulders that could stop a bull and the rest of the physical paraphernalia he'd needed to achieve a 4th Dan Black Belt and a chilling reputation. One would think he'd be the last man in the world to be afraid of dogs, but he was. Bernie was square, blond and weather-beaten. Not the type you'd like to cross. He looked like a docker, or a farmer, but he had good eyes, blue as cornflowers and they always startled her.

Jason called Jock from the doorway. 'Don't worry. I'll keep him in my room.'

'Thanks for coming, Bernie. I appreciate it.'

Bernie's anxious expression told her what a sight she looked with her white face, blistered hands and dishevelled hair sticking out around the bandage.

He thrust a newspaper into her hands. 'Glad you're awake, Clara. It's all there on page six, column three.'

She took the paper unwillingly. Her grief was

not for public consumption. Clara had no idea how long she'd sat trembling as she stared at the words, but she surfaced when Bernie put his hand on her shoulder and took the newspaper away.

'You knew all this. I'd never have shown you if I'd thought it would upset you.'

Liar! Bernie was very shrewd indeed. A successful, perceptive man and he never wasted his time, so what did he want?

'Don't worry. I'm all right.'

Bernie pulled up a chair and sat down. 'Tell me what happened. I want every last detail.'

She gripped the duvet and began to sweat as the dread came sidling back, making her skin crawl.

'I can't remember much. I can only tell you what I told the police.'

But she remembered her terror. She wondered if she'd ever be rid of it. She reached up and touched her head, wincing at the pain.

'Try! It's important. There might be something to help us find Patrick. The coastguard's stopped searching, but I haven't, I promise you. I have two boats and a helicopter out there.' He leaned forward, staring into her eyes as if the force of his will could restore her recall. She caught a whiff of aftershave and the musky male smell that was all about him.

Frowning with the effort, she forced herself to separate dreams from memories.

'There was a bad storm, as you know. Around midnight I grabbed my anorak and went up on deck.' That, at least, was one certainty because

13

she'd looked at the clock. 'I was hit on the head and I don't remember much more until I found myself hanging on to wreckage. I don't know how I got there or how long afterwards it was, but the sea was calmer. I felt cold and very tired.'

'But Clara, do you remember falling overboard?'

'It's so hard to explain. Images came later, more like dreams as I lay on the raft. I'm not sure they're real.'

'The police said you were blown or washed overboard. From the wreckage they suspect an explosion took place. Is that how it seems to you?'

'I don't know. When I try to think about it my head aches unbearably.' She sat up, gasping at the pain. 'Bernie, listen! Someone tried to kill me! I'm sure of that. And I keep having the same nightmare over and over. I see Patrick lying in the sail locker, his face pulped and smashed.' Her eyes filled with tears. 'God! I wish my mind would clear. All I have are these terrible images.'

'It was an accident, Clara. Nothing more. You've got to get that into your head. No one tried to kill you. All these bad dreams and images are just part of the concussion you suffered. You need to rest and you need looking after. Trust me.' Her scalp was hurting and itching, her face burning, and an all-pervasive languor was stealing through her body like a drug. She knew it was a cop-out. She gave in and closed her eyes.

'So what else do you remember?' he urged her, gripping her hand.

14

She looked up and caught Bernie unaware, saw the shock in his eyes and the intensity of his stare.

'I remember swimming towards the yacht and watching it sink with a hiss of steam and bubbles ... huge bubbles ... like the sea was belching. Then nothing but darkness, as if the *Connemara* had never existed. I felt so alone. I called for a long time. I felt so guilty. You see, I must have left Pat there to die, but I couldn't remember. I still can't.'

'You're overwrought. You have to get away from here, Clara. This place is full of memories. A change of scenery will do you good. Like a fresh start. I have a cottage at St. Margaret's Bay. You can stay there for a while. You, Sib and Jason, that is. We'll move you today.'

'Hey there. Wait a minute. I've been longing to get home and now I'm here at last I'm not going anywhere.'

He sounded stricken. 'I want to look after you. You and Jason, that is.'

'For God's sake stop patronising me.'

Bernie opened his eyes wide at her hostile tone. 'Trust me, Clara. A change will do you good. Then you can concentrate on getting better. Try it out for a day at least.'

'You're not hearing me, Bernie.'

Bernie stood up. 'You know where I am if you need me. Call any time, day or night. D'you have my mobile number?'

She nodded and watched him striding out of the room. Such a sudden departure, but then Bernie was always on a short fuse.

It wasn't anger, but fear that drove Bernie to leave hurriedly. He liked Clara. He always had done. She was straight and honest and absurdly loyal. She'd put up with Patrick's crap and kept on believing in him, even when she shouldn't have. He didn't know how to convince her of the slime she'd fallen into, without scaring her half to death. This wasn't her world. She came from a family where people did their duty and led good lives, worked hard for very little and slept safely in the belief that they were protected by the law. Patrick had opened the gates to the barbarians and now they could all be blown away. She shouldn't stay here. She should listen to him. For a moment he almost went back. He'd always fancied her, but despite her pain, her blue eyes had blazed with fury because he'd criticised her precious Patrick.

'If that's what you want, Clara, then that's too bad,' he muttered as he stepped into his car.

★ ★ ★

Sib frowned as she hurried back to Clara. 'Bernie says . . . '

'I know. I know. But I just can't see us coping in his cottage and Jason would hate it. It's too far away. Besides — ' She broke off, unable to explain her repugnance at being beholden to him.

'How about spending a few days with me? I have a bad feeling about us being here. You may

16

not be scared but I'm scared for you. Please, Clara.'

Sib was never afraid. She was one of the most self-possessed, courageous women Clare had ever met, but she knew from Sib's voice she was serious. It was that more than anything that persuaded her to give in, but not without some hesitation. Sib worked all hours painting and their presence would disrupt her routine. Despite Sib's carefully cultivated, frivolous image she was devoted to her art, yet she was equally loyal to her friends. Clara knew that she and Jason headed the list of Sib's priorities.

'If you're sure, but only after I've spoken to Jason, mind you.'

As she lay back on the pillow she wondered why Bernie had seemed so intent on getting her out of the house. But perhaps he was right. Perhaps she needed to get away for a few days. Was it really an accident as Bernie and the police said? Were all her nightmares merely the result of the blow to her head? She touched the scar and winced. If only it were true, but why was she so frightened?

Tears were burning her eyes, brimming over and trickling down her face and nose. She tasted their salt in her mouth. Strange anomalies came to mind as she tried to scan the past year with Patrick objectively.

Like most of life's traumas the beginning was hardly perceptible as it sneaked in like the first whispering breath of a hurricane. She was sitting at the dressing table brushing her hair, which was shining with bronze highlights in the early

17

May sunlight. Through the window she could see daffodils still in bloom, early tulips and blossom everywhere: apples, pears, and ornamental cherry trees, an impressionist canvas in pink and white with patches of yellow.

She could hear the shower running and Patrick whistling. She had tasted her first coffee of the morning, bittersweet and strong. She had been putting on her dressing-gown, enjoying the feel of silk instead of wool, looking forward to summer, when Patrick emerged naked from the shower. She heard his footsteps, smelled his deodorant and the warm soapiness that was all about him. She turned with a smile and that was when she first saw the bright blue and yellow butterfly, red-eyed and splendid, perched on Patrick's right shoulder.

'Heavens! What's that?'

'What does it look like?' He seemed half-ashamed of himself.

'It looks like a butterfly that a hippy might have tattooed on his shoulder.'

'That's right! You're witnessing the first step towards a new, hip Patrick.' When he looked round and saw her expression, his tone hardened. 'Poor Clara! You've missed out on the new scene. Must've passed while you were hunched over your PC.'

'It looks absurd.' She needed to hit back. 'You're being ridiculous.'

His eyes were gleaming with secret amusement, lips curling into a half-smile. Of all his expressions, that was the one she detested the most.

'I don't know what's happening to you, Patrick. I feel as if I'm losing you.'

'You can't lose what you don't have. You can't own people, they're not like houses.'

Cruel Patrick! The hurt had stayed inside like a small burning coal in her midriff, but she'd tried not to show this in the weeks that followed. By the end of August, Patrick was thin, muscled, tanned and his near-black hair, with only a few streaks of grey, was starting to curl around his neck. It was unusually warm and he'd taken to wearing brightly-coloured vests with jeans, a gold chain and an earring in one ear. She knew he spent hours at the gym and lately he only ate salad.

Clara took the tattoo in her stride and learned to smile at his corny cracks. She looked forward to the day when they would overcome the past and be a family again.

Reaching back in time, obsessively scanning her hopeful dreams and optimism, she was amazed at her sense of denial.

It was getting dark. Jason would be home soon. The birds were silenced, the wind had dropped, the world held its breath as if poised on the edge of an abyss. She felt cold sweat breaking out on her forehead and the palms of her hands. A sudden pain in her heart brought grief welling up from deep inside her. She stuffed a pillow against her mouth and pulled the duvet over her head. Her grief was bitter and very private.

2

Voices, movement, human interaction — Clara was vaguely aware of some kind of a domestic squabble. She had watched TV for almost an hour, but she had no idea what she was seeing. The room was dark except for the flickering screen. She stood up and poured herself a whisky, then decided not to drink it. It wouldn't solve anything and she hadn't eaten for days, not since they returned from Sib's house, although she had cooked for Jason. She was losing weight and her jeans were falling round her hips. It was Guy Fawke's night. Jason had gone with friends to watch the fireworks display at the castle and Clara was fighting off despair.

The programme changed. Dolphins surged through the Mexican Gulf, waves of spume on an indigo sea.

She was there, falling . . . falling . . . Down and down into the dark, safe water, intense cold numbing the pain in her head. Keep down! Swim away! Don't panic! Terror pierced her heart like a frozen shard of ice. A killer was waiting for her, leaning over the bulwark, shining a halcyon torch, reaching out with a boathook, his face hidden.

She gasped, gulped the whisky and waited for its merciful numbness to soothe her nerves. Sometimes she wondered if her mind was little more than a bog where every incident of her life lay festering. Images were rising like trapped air from their sinking yacht, great bubbles of images, but were they real?

Once again she relived her torment, trying to separate fact from fantasy. She remembered begging Patrick to return to harbour. The storm was worsening, the yacht might founder. Patrick's contempt had hurt. She moved on, retracing the night. Hearing again that awful keening, like the death agony of an injured beast.

It began as a low moan hardly distinguishable from the creaking boards of the bulkhead. She listened, pressing her face against the sail hatch as the sound increased in volume to a howl of unimaginable suffering, a primal cry of pain and despair, as if the victim had passed beyond the bounds of human endurance. Panic-stricken she battled with the hatch, trying to force it open, but it was locked or jammed. Using the full weight of her body, she pounded the stout wood with her shoulder, wincing at the pain. As the door fell open she saw a pulped face, the jaw hanging loose, teeth smashed and gone. She was unaware of the danger until a sudden, powerful blow to the side of her head brought a blinding flash and a numbing pain. Then darkness closed her mind.

Surely these grotesque images were real? Memories, not dreams? She had the wound to prove it. Feeling afraid of her fear, she switched off her morbid introspection and hurried into the kitchen. Light flooded the room bringing comfort as she gazed at the oak cupboards with the rows of china mugs which she collected, each

21

item in its right place. Order always reassured her. She switched on the kettle.

Clara had been a widow for a fortnight, but as yet she had not succeeded in coming to terms with Patrick's death. She felt desperate as she gazed at the two steaming mugs of coffee she had made, one strong and black with three sugars, which was how Patrick liked it. This morning she had laid his place at the breakfast table, much to her embarrassment. 'Idiot!' she said aloud as she tipped his coffee into the sink.

After the death of her first husband she had dropped into a deep bog of depression, shunning friends and staying home, neglecting herself and the house, and losing the desire to eat. She very nearly lost her baby. And then Sib had taken over and begun to bully her. Soon her cheerful optimism and her caring nature had brought Clara back to believing that the child she was nurturing was real and that she had a reason to live and be happy.

It was Jason's birth that had pulled her back to functioning level: the first time she held his hand, felt his small fingers tugging hers, saw his eyes gaze trustingly up at her, she pulled herself together fast. Her baby needed her. She could not allow that to happen again. She had to think of Jason. She made a promise to get out and mingle with people. She had not been out since Patrick's death.

Leaving Jock in the kitchen so he wouldn't be frightened by the bangs, Clara locked the front door and walked down the garden path. It was a cold but clear night, the moon particularly brilliant. She could hear foxes barking in the common and an owl calling in a neighbour's garden. She nodded and smiled when she passed an ancient labrador and its geriatric owner plodding uphill. A man was leaning against the lamp post. She called 'Good Evening,' as she passed. Strange that she didn't recognise him since she knew everyone in the road.

Pushing her scarf around her ears, she walked briskly to the park where the council were setting off fireworks. Trying to ignore a strange, jittery feeling, she sat on a tree trunk at the edge of the crowd and gazed up as the night sky erupted with brilliant colour. She felt vulnerable and targeted, but she was not sure why.

She glanced around surreptitiously, half afraid of what she might see. Sure enough, a man was leaning against the trunk of a chestnut tree a few yards off and he was staring at her. She felt a chill sweep through her as their eyes locked. He lifted his hand and something about his size and gesture took her back to the yacht, to the axe rising in an arc over her, falling — falling . . . With a sudden flash of panic she recognised the man who had been hanging around near her home. But why would he follow her?

She forced herself to get up slowly and walk towards the road, passing close to him, letting her eyes move sidelong, noting the black leather jacket worn over a dark grey tracksuit, his trainers and his black hair. He was staring straight at her and his expression broke her stride. Anger shone in his eyes. But why? She'd never seen him before in her life. Or had she?

Think positive, Clara warned herself, but the bleak certainty that Bernie had been right brought her arms out in goose pimples.

A deep shudder ran through her and she began to pant. 'Phew! Clara Connor, you're an idiot,' she said aloud as she neared the gate. There were dozens of reasons why he might be staring towards her. At the same time, Cowper Road where she lived was a long, lonely gravel track overhung with trees, a cul-de-sac and therefore the only way to reach her house. She decided not to take a chance. Fumbling in her bag for her mobile phone, she dialled the local taxi company.

Glancing back, she saw that the man was sitting on a bench not fifty yards off. Why had he moved so close, so fast? Clara shrank behind a bush and waited while icy drops from wet leaves trickled down her neck, and her toes began to freeze from the damp seeping through her trainers. She heard a dog barking in the park and the monotonous crack of fireworks. The smell of cordite was all about her. There was a distant murmur of conversation and faint music from a neighbouring house. The taxi arrived and drew up. After a while the driver switched off the engine and sounded his hooter. The seconds passed slowly.

'Move away! Go on! Leave me alone,' she whispered, but the man fumbled in his pockets and withdrew cigarettes and matches. While he stooped, with his hands cupping the flickering flame, she lurched out of the bushes and ran to the taxi. She had a last image of him standing astride the path gazing towards her.

Five minutes later she was home. She locked the front door and sank down behind it, her forehead damp with cold sweat. Jock came and sat beside her, whimpering slightly as he picked up her vibes.

Pulling herself together, she dumped her wet shoes on the radiator, grabbed the carving knife from the rack, put on her rubber boots and took Jock round the garden. She'd been silly, she decided, when she returned. He had probably mistaken her for someone else. A hot bath made her feel less tense. She went to bed and read a book, but she soon gave up trying to concentrate.

Who was this man who had followed her? She remembered how scared Patrick had been when he told her that he owed a great deal of money. Could there be a connection? She reached back to their last day together, sensing that she must remember every word Patrick had said

Just before dawn Patrick had returned looking exhausted from a week in France. To Clara he seemed like a man on a high-wire, keyed-up and rigid with tension.

It was six am when the telephone rang, waking them. She reached for the receiver, but Patrick's hand closed on her wrist, his touch conveying his tension.

She frowned. 'What is it?'

His mouth was pressed in a tight line, his eyes blinked too fast. 'Leave it. I don't want anyone to know I'm here.' He got up and pulled the plug out of the wall. When he put on his shirt she noticed that his hands were shaking. Patrick was always cool, always on top of the situation. What had frightened him so much? She insisted that he tell her.

'I guess I'd better spill the beans. I owe money to the guys I've been working with, so I'm not here right now. I'm expecting a large payment in a few days time, enough to clear the debt, so there's nothing to worry about.'

'And meantime?' Her voice echoed her alarm.

'I'll be in France.'

'Just like that!' She tried to get the censure out of her voice. 'So you're leaving again? Why didn't you tell me?'

'I came to fetch you, you goose.'

Suddenly he was clutching her, stroking her back and nuzzling her neck. 'We need a holiday together. Think of it as a second honeymoon! By the time we come back this mess will be sorted out.'

She sensed the tension behind his smile. He gazed anxiously at her. 'Say yes. Go on. Please, Clara.' It was really important to him. While her heart sang, she pretended to ponder. Let him sweat a bit. He deserves it.

'I'll have to ask Sib if she's free to move in.'

He relaxed and smiled. She was a pushover where Patrick was concerned and she knew it.

Remembering brought a lump to her throat. She covered her face with her hands and tried not to give way to grief.

She could hear seagulls calling plaintively. Perhaps a storm was brewing. Somewhere in the Channel the wreck of the *Connemara* was

26

resting on the seabed, drifting in the tide, broken and burned, a bad end for a brave yacht. Visions came of Patrick's body caught up in the wreck, crabs and eels moving in, eyes eaten, the flesh being stripped from the bones. At last she heard a car door slamming, the neighbours' kids calling goodbye, Jason's footsteps on the drive. The front door opened. Feeling relieved, she switched off the light and tried to sleep.

She woke later with a cry of alarm and lay still listening, waiting for her heart to stop hammering. What had she heard? She got quietly out of bed and tiptoed around the silent house, assuring herself that Jason was sleeping soundly and that Jock was in his basket, examining each window and double-checking the doors. They were still safe so far, she decided. Taking the carving knife from the rack once more, she took it back to bed and hid it under her pillow.

3

Clara had never been in debt, never been short of money, she'd always budgeted well and had just enough, but Patrick had changed all that. After a peaceful week spent at home Clara was recovering sufficiently to worry about their future and how to make ends meet. It was five a.m. and she was lying in bed totting up figures in her head. It didn't look good. She'd have to find a way to earn money fast or they'd lose the house. She had given up her work as a full time university lecturer when she married Patrick. Until then she had earned a good salary and their house was paid for. Patrick had changed all that. His incessant demands for cash, first to launch his tour agency and buy two boats, and then to save it from bankrupcy, had forced her to take out three separate mortgages on her house. Her current wage for part-time work at the local adult educational college was not enough to keep them, let alone make the mortgage repayments. She'd been writing a book on Celtic pre-history for the past year, but she'd spent the publisher's advance months ago. Backing Patrick with the cash he needed to set up his tour agency, after his retrenchment from the merchant navy, had cost her dearly. *So why not run the agency myself?* At first the thought scared her, but once she'd considered it she realised what a good idea it was. Why hadn't she thought of this before? Could she? Should she?

She was startled out of her introspection as Jock erupted in a fury of snarls and barks, racing from the study window to the front door and back. Clara switched on the light, grabbed her slippers and dressing-gown, and ran downstairs, but Jason was already outside with Jock, padding barefooted around the garden in his pyjamas.

'Hey. Come back inside.' Clara ran towards the street light, but the garden and the road were deserted. In the distance a car raced down Cowper Lane and turned towards town.

'He's gone,' Jason looked disappointed.

'Inside, Jason. At once. It was probably a false alarm.'

Jason shook his head. 'Someone tried to break in, but they hadn't counted on Jock.'

'You must never, never go outside like that again.'

'Come on, Mum, don't fret. I'm almost a teenager.'

'So what! We'll talk in the morning. Meantime, try to get to sleep.'

Jason grinned, patted the dog and went back to bed. Shortly afterwards he was sleeping soundly. Clara, on the other hand, wondered how to pass the time until breakfast. She made coffee and totted up her figures. She'd need a top salary to cover the mortgage payments, but she'd always thought the tour agency was a good idea and she still did, even though Patrick hadn't managed to make it pay.

At six-thirty she heard Jason get up, so she put

aside her fears, showered and dressed, and hurried down to make breakfast.

'Come and get it,' she called out, ten minutes later.

As Clara scooped the eggs and bacon on to Jason's plate, she felt bad about having to scare him, but she'd thought it all out and there was no other way.

'We must have a long talk, Jason. Correction: I'll do the talking, you do the listening. I'm slipping into fast forward as from today. No more moping. We need an income, I'm looking around for something.'

'I'll do a newspaper round. At least we don't have to pay rent.'

Clara felt herself flush scarlet as she crumpled back on the chair. Jason was fishing. She glanced at him suspiciously.

'I heard the fights, Mum. How much?' Tight-lipped and anxious he patted the dog.

'A hundred and fifty thousand pounds.'

'Oh, shit! But it's done now. We'll manage.'

She tried to explain, but she hardly knew how to begin. 'We had hoped that Patrick's tour agency would cover all our expenses — that is, once he got going, so I made this long term investment.'

She pulled herself together fast. 'Don't worry, I'll make the cash, but that's not what I want to talk about. On Guy Fawkes' night, I was followed to the park. This man, this stalker, or whatever he was, had been watching the house. He could be hanging around tonight. That might be what Jock picked up.'

'I was thoughtless, Mum. I shouldn't have left you alone.'

'Stop acting like you're Big Brother, will you? You're just a kid.'

Jason flushed and looked stung by her tone. Well, that was too bad. She wasn't usually this mean to him, but she wanted to send him somewhere safe. Boarding school seemed the obvious answer and he had to do as she said.

'Hey, Mum.'

'There's more! Just listen, Jason. Patrick admitted he owed money and said he wanted to disappear for a few days. And now this stalker or whoever he is . . . Well, he's here, isn't he? Watching us. Perhaps he wants his money. Maybe Patrick borrowed the cash and couldn't repay it all. Of course running a one-man business is never easy — ' She broke off and took a deep breath. 'The point is, I've decided to send you to boarding school.'

'Is that it? Is that what this is all about? You're wasting your time, Mum. I won't go. You're in danger, not me.' He scowled at her. 'Besides, where would you get the money to pay for an expensive school? Mum, listen to me. Don't break up our family. Can you imagine how I'd worry about you, stuck in school, not knowing what was happening?'

It was his woeful expression that threw her. 'I'll try to think of another plan,' she said, feeling defeated.

She saw the tension untwist on her son's face. Why should he suffer? She knew how much he'd hate going to boarding school. She would hate it,

31

too. She had married at nineteen and carried Jason during her last year at University. Perhaps because she was widowed, she and Jason had grown so close. All her adult life had been spent with him. How would she cope if they were parted? There must be another way.

'So what did this stalker look like?' Jason asked.

'Tall and skinny, but with large shoulders, dark and sort of foreign-looking. He was wearing a black leather jacket over a tracksuit and trainers. He smoked at lot. He was watching me and his face was full of hatred. Why should he hate me? He doesn't even know me.'

Jason flushed. 'I should have told you this — I didn't want to worry you — when you were in hospital, Sib saw a man watching the house one night. He left a pile of cigarette butts and an empty matchbox. I checked them with a boy at school and they were Serbian.'

'Oh! That's strange! The problem is . . . ' She shrugged. 'Lately I don't know what's real and what's imaginary. The doctor said that when you have concussion, or for any other reason you lose recall of a period of time, the mind replaces the gaps with other images and they become as real as . . . as reality. Oops! I can't believe I said something so dumb. I seem to be going one way.' She jerked her thumb towards the floor.

'Come on, Mum, don't put yourself down.'

She made an effort to cheer up. 'From now on you have to be careful. I don't want you cycling around on your own, especially after dark. I'm going to join a lift scheme.'

32

Jason was scowling to himself as he went upstairs to fetch his coat and satchel. He went off with a brief 'Bye,' without looking in her direction. Too bad if he didn't like it. She gave in far too often.

Clara heard her son's footsteps hurrying to the garage and then he was gone. He was trying to act so grown-up, but he was only a kid. He'd turn thirteen in December. She'd bought him a new racing bike which was hidden in Sib's garage. She frowned. Right now that didn't seem such a great idea.

Lately she'd been wondering just how badly she had failed Jason by marrying Patrick. It had seemed so right in the beginning, but by the time he turned twelve, the two males in her life were mortal enemies. She knew Jason despised Patrick, but he might at least have tried to get on with him. She understood his bewilderment because she had gone on this trip with Patrick. Jason's moral vision was still 20/20, no blurring between black and white, no concessions and no forgiveness. How could a boy like Jason understand the intricate relationship of two married people? Kids always saw the fights, but never the making-up.

Theirs had taken place at their local pub, the Royal Oak, and this had surprised her. On the rare occasions when they went out, it was never locally. Delayed by a supermarket queue she had raced back from Whitfield, hurried in a few minutes late and blundered against the wine waiter bearing champagne nestling in ice. As she sat down, Patrick's hand groped across the table for hers. Blessed relief set in. At times it seemed she danced on gunpowder it was so hard to keep the peace.

'What are we celebrating?' she whispered, not wishing to be overheard.

'Us.' He picked up his glass and said quite loudly, 'To us!'

A package slid across the table, a long, narrow box wrapped in gold paper with a glitzy bow pinned on it. He smiled his special smile that never failed to send her libido soaring. They were attracting attention, perhaps because Patrick was looking tremendous. Young girls habitually gave him the eye because of his sensual blue eyes and his reckless smile. Being tall, dark and handsome was almost extraneous.

When her hands had coped with the sticky tape, she saw a delicate gold bracelet, set with blue-green opals, lying in the satin box.

'I didn't expect ... Patrick ... it's so beautiful. Thank you, darling.'

He tossed the bracelet out of the box, as if used to handling expensive jewellery and fastened it around her wrist. There was a distinct hiatus in the surrounding conversation. Heads turned surreptitiously.

'I want you to forgive me, Clara.'

Clara felt a funny numb feeling in her stomach, while her mouth dried. No! Don't say anything. Just lie through your teeth. I'll believe anything!

'I got myself into a mess with another woman. She's very young and lovely, so I felt responsible for her. It's over now. She's found herself a rich lover, Vesno Mandic, an art dealer, and she's moved in with him. I went for the looks, not the person. Forgive me and I'll make it up to you.'

'I forgive you,' she said woodenly, wondering if unfaithfulness was more wounding than the mental abuse he'd been handing out lately.

'But Clara, you're not completely blameless. You spend too much time writing at home. I'm hoping you'll come on trips with me. We'd make a pretty good team. What do you say?'

She couldn't remember a previous invitation. Patrick had always been determined to keep her out of the business and off his yacht, but she said 'yes' because she loved him. So when the invitation to join him in a second honeymoon came, it was hardly unexpected, but how could her son understand?

She glanced at her watch. This was no time for daydreaming. Patrick was dead and she had to build a life for herself and her son. For a moment she felt dazed by the magnitude of her problem. Forcing her courage back, she grabbed a pencil and paper. Divide and rule, she decided. That was the best way. She would tackle her problems one at a time and never again allow them to unite and attack. Number one was their security. Tomorrow she'd tackle relaunching the business. She began to hunt through the Yellow Pages for a good security firm.

4

Her last student had left at last. Clara glanced at her watch. It was later than she had realised. She had spent an hour at her desk, correcting papers, returning phone calls, planning her next lecture and helping anyone who asked. It was a good chance to catch up because Jason was spending the evening watching films with his friends at a neighbour's house.

By the time Clara left the college and hurried towards the car park, it was half-past nine. Leaves spiralled in the wind, the air was crispy cold and smoke from a bonfire mingled with the scent of the sea. The illuminated castle on the cliffs glittered like a contrived backdrop to a heraldic play of ancient chivalry, too huge, too generous and too brilliantly designed to be anything other than make-believe in the utilitarian world Clara inhabited.

Walking towards her car, Clara became aware of someone loitering under a nearby tree. Her heart lurched as she peered towards the figure.

Robin Connor, Patrick's cousin, moved into the lamplight with a self-conscious swagger. 'Ah, Clara, fancy bumping into you. What are you doing here?'

As if he didn't know. He'd been waiting for her. She ducked the question. 'Have you been here long?'

'I was on the way to . . . ' He broke off. Whatever alibi he'd thought up was now discarded. He smiled beguilingly and shrugged. 'I have to talk. Can you spare the time?'

Clara nodded.

'There's a pub just round the corner. Let's go there.'

Why had she never noticed the resemblance between Robin and Patrick? Perhaps because she'd never much liked Robin. Despite his beige trousers and sweater, and the tailor-made tweed jacket, there was always something of a spiv about Robin. She'd seen pictures of him taken when he and Patrick were at naval college. Although tall he'd been the runt of the group, a skinny beanpole with hollow cheeks, spaniel eyes, and bone structure like a coat hanger. But they both had near-black hair from their Italian ancestry, squarish faces, and the same engaging smile. Five years of dedicated exercise had given Robin the body of a nightclub bouncer, but he wore Patrick's macho image like a hand-me-down.

He gripped her arm hard. 'Jesus, Clara. I can't come to terms with this terrible loss. Pat, of all people! He was so strong. I feel lost without him.'

Clara put her car keys in her pocket and linked arms with Robin as if they were old friends. Their social contact had been minimal, but their shared grief formed a bond. She blinked hard. Moments back she could have sworn she was listening to her husband, their voices were so similar. Patrick's voice was the first thing that had attracted her to him when she first met him.

As they walked along the pavement her mind drifted back. She'd been dancing with Doug Evans at a yacht club social when she heard a man's voice just behind her say: 'Mind if I cut in, sir? Clara and I are old friends, but I haven't seen her for years.' His voice was ultra deep, but soft, like a gentle growl, intimate and intriguing and she puzzled over his accent which had a faint foreign lilt.

'I've never seen you before in my life,' she whispered when Evans had bowed out. She wasn't going to tell him how grateful she was. She'd almost passed out with Doug's whisky fumes and her toes felt two-dimensional. 'How d'you know my name?'

His eyes had locked with hers for longer than they should. Then he gave a funny, quirky smile as his mouth curled up at one corner. 'I asked around.'

Robin's voice jolted her back to the present and her sadness. 'So how are you coping, Clara?'

'With difficulty.'

He pulled her arm tightly against his muscled torso.

'This is it.' He held the door open for her and she moved into a fog of smoke and stale beer fumes. It was a weary old pub, unchanged for the past half century or more; the clientele were poor but cosmopolitan and the dusty air reverberated with half a dozen Eastern European languages. They squeezed into a corner table. When Robin went to fetch their drinks, she slipped gratefully back to her compelling past.

Patrick was tall, fit, rugged and probably in his early forties. His black hair was cropped short and brushed back, his smile revealed humour and a sense of fun. Clara hadn't had any fun for a very long time. He was a good dancer and she was conscious of the scent of his aftershave and the way his eyes seemed to darken and glow when he looked at her. She felt captivated by his boyish grin. He was the master of an oil tanker, he told her, and he was currently on two months leave. He didn't normally socialise, but he'd sailed down with a friend to take part in the Prince of Wales yacht race.

Moments later the Commodore called, 'Will Captain Patrick Connor please come over here. We're about to present the cup.'

So he'd won. As Patrick strode to the rostrum, Clara stood up and said goodbye to Sib, who'd landed the guy she was after. Captain Connor was too much to handle: too male, too intent, too beautiful. Beauty was her Achilles Heel. It was years since she'd felt so attracted to any man. She knew she'd be his slave in next to no time. Looking back, she realised she'd been right.

Robin returned with a beer and a glass of wine. He sat down and lifted his glass. 'Cheers. Here's to the best bloody sailor in Britain. Pat was unbeatable!'

The macho image had been abandoned. Robin's shoulders slumped and he looked dejected. He put down his glass with a clatter.

'Clara, you have to help me. Help us both.

We're in trouble unless we find some missing cash. It's like this.' He shot her a sly glance and she guessed he was cooking up a suitable story. 'Patrick borrowed money from a group of businessmen. He died before he could repay them. Naturally they want their cash. Surely you know where Pat spent most of his time? Let's face it, he was never home. Did he give you cheques drawn on other banks? Foreign banks? Perhaps he left credit cards lying around. Believe me, in his work he handled a lot of cash. Make an effort to find out where it is.'

Clara ran her finger round the top of her glass, deep in thought. She believed Robin only because Patrick had told her that he owed money, but surely not a large amount.

'These businessmen you've mentioned. Who are they? I need to know what was going on. What are we talking about really? What am I looking for? Hundreds?'

'Add a few noughts,' he said roughly.

She gasped, feeling upset. 'Who told you this?'

'Pat did. I'm family, Clara.'

'But Patrick was almost broke when he died. How could he have all this cash?'

Robin flushed and looked evasive and this puzzled her.

'It's no secret, Robin. Patrick told me that he owed money, but that he'd repay it as soon as he could.'

'Come off it, Clara.' He glanced suspiciously at her. 'He wasn't short. Not Pat! I've seen him splashing cash around like he owned the mint. Wads of it! I went with him to buy his car and he paid cash for a Jaguar XK-120. Can you believe that?'

She flinched. Patrick had told her that he'd hired the car to impress potential customers. Could she believe Robin? Perhaps the time had come to go through Patrick's files.

'Pat was the middle-man in any number of deals and he was holding other people's cash at the time of his death. He didn't steal a damn thing. It's somewhere, but only he knew where. Could be in Europe. We have to find the cash and pay it back. It's up to us to clear his name.'

She frowned. 'Why are you so concerned with Patrick's reputation, Robin? Somehow your story doesn't ring true.'

He looked exasperated. 'Because he's my half-brother.'

Clara felt shock waves reverberate through her. 'What d'you mean, brother? You're cousins!'

'Poor Clara. You were way out of your depth. I could never work out why you married him.' He peered sidelong at Clara with a strange, triumphant glint in his eyes.

He doesn't like me any more than I like him, she thought. She leaned back and promised herself to look calm whatever Robin said, but inside she was churning with fear and hurt. Why had Pat lied to her?

'Pat always kept us apart. He liked to play different roles with different people, but not for too long. His name wasn't Connor, but Bonnelli. That's our mother's maiden name. This always bugged Mum. She was from Naples originally

41

and she wanted us to have the same family name.'

Her stomach clenched. How many more precious memories were going to turn to dust? Patrick had built up a facade and presented it to her at their very first meeting. So what had she fallen in love with — a fictitious image? And who had she married? Was her marriage legal? Dark thoughts were spinning around an apex of rejection.

'He used to tell me about his father, Sean Connor.' Clara gripped her glass and stared hard at it as she spoke. 'He was very strong and just, but rather hard on Patrick and he came from Shannon. Was that all lies?'

'No, but he was *my* father, not Pat's. Dad was a great romancer and he was homesick. He used to spend hours telling us about his home in Shannon. Pat sort of adopted Shannon, just as he adopted the name, Connor. Being brought up a bastard in a small, Catholic community was tough. We were born in Valletta, Malta. Patrick was two years old when Dad arrived in Malta. He was a shipwright.'

'But you were both here at naval college. Bernie said so.' She knew very well Robin was making the most of his powerplay, watching her squirm and enjoying it.

'I suppose I might as well tell you.' He gave a theatrical sigh. 'There was a scandal, involving Pat, and we decided to leave Malta.'

'What sort of a scandal?'

'Sure you want to know?'

He raised one eyebrow and leered at her. She

didn't answer. She was too busy trying to look calm.

'Some priceless relics disappeared from a local church. Pat was held by the police and questioned for days, but there was never any proof against him, so we left home. Dad gave us the cash to put us through Worcester Naval College.'

As Robin described the claustrophobic, love-hate relationship between them, Clara could hardly disguise her bewilderment. Robin was describing a man she had never known. So who was Patrick really? Robin's winner, or her business loser, forever taking on more than he could manage, failing so charmingly, and always so sorry for the cash he'd lost? She did not recognise this ruthless, successful role model whom Robin tried to emulate. She listened bemused as Robin described their escapades when they attended naval college together and joined the same oil company, culminating in their mutual retrenchment when management cut back on their fleet of tankers.

'We were dumped at the same time. We were all pretty bloody-minded at the time, but finally we all made it.'

Robin pursed his lips and ran his hand through his thick hair. 'I want to put a proposition to you. Pat's tour business was practically bust. He didn't make a secret of it, he had other resources, but that's no reason why the agency can't be developed. I want to run it for you. For us! I'll buy a half share. Name your price, within reason of course.'

Clara felt stunned. It was the last thing she had expected. Her mind raced around furiously trying to work out why Robin would want a loss-making tour agency. All her instincts were screaming no.

'I don't know what it's worth. Patrick didn't tell me much about the business. Besides, he said your trippers' boat, the *Dover Belle*, was doing well.'

'You're damn right, but we don't do much in winter,' he said dismissively.

'So why bother with a small tour agency currently operating at a loss?'

'Call it sentimental reasons.'

His evasiveness was infuriating her. 'Setting up that agency cost me a great deal of money, Robin. I had to take out a large mortgage. I don't believe you would build it up 'for us'. You want to find out what he's done with the cash he borrowed. After that you'd dump it.'

Robin's eyes narrowed while his mouth took on a sullen slant.

'Anyway, the business is not for sale.' She surprised herself with her brisk tone. 'I intend to run the agency myself.'

'You can't be serious. You know nothing about it.' He laughed derisively.

'Neither did Patrick when he began. Listen, Robin. I'm not convinced it was an accident that killed Patrick. I have these awful images. In my dreams I see Patrick beaten to a pulp, and then someone trying to kill me, too. I think someone else was on board the yacht that night. I want to find out what was going

44

on and just who Patrick was involved with. One of them killed him. Despite what the police think, I'm convinced it was murder.'

'You're crazy, Clara. You've had a bad knock on the head and these nightmares are the result. Take some advice from me — don't meddle.' Robin's voice was vibrant with menace. 'I know the type of people Patrick was working with. Criminals of the worst kind! You've seen enough Mafia movies to know how these guys operate. Let me take over the agency so you can stay right out of it. Just how much income do you need a month? I'll see you're not short. You and Jason. I don't want you two to be in danger.'

Sweat was breaking out on her palms and the soles of her feet. 'What are you talking about? Must I sell you the agency or take the consequences? Is that what you're saying?'

'You're a proud and difficult woman, Clara, and I'm worried about you. You could be hurt. These guys know how to do that. Can't you see I'm trying to protect you? You don't know where the cash is, so what are you going to tell them when they come after you? Far better to sell me the agency.'

Clara sat nursing her empty glass and her fear. She could no longer ignore the mounting evidence against her husband. He'd been involved with criminals, but no one wanted her to know what was going on. Why not? Her mind was a battlefield of warring emotions. Fury won. She found her voice with an explosion of sound: 'No. I won't sell! Get lost,

Robin. You're a bastard!'

Blundering towards the door, Robin knocked over a bar stool. She heard him swearing in Italian, just as Patrick used to. Then he was gone.

5

By eight a.m. the winter sun was sidling around the horizon and the sky was a delicate shade of oyster blue. Clara parked in Snargate Street and sat for a moment watching the cliffs sparkle in sunlight. She shut her eyes and concentrated: '*I'm just a robot, no feelings, no regrets. I'm here to do a job.*'

She intended to sort out Patrick's files and computer data. Perhaps she would find traces of the missing cash Patrick had supposedly borrowed.

The Connor Tour Agency was on the second floor of a five-storey building erected in the poverty-stricken post-war era after almost the entire section of the town lying beneath the west cliffs had been wiped out by shells and bombs. It stood roughly opposite to where the old Hippodrome had been. As she parked she was imagining the cobbled street of pre-war days, the gold and gilt exterior of the pint-sized theatre, the glittering lights and the echoes of a brass band playing the latest bawdy hits.

She dropped her box of cleaning materials and waited impatiently while the lift creaked to the second floor. Patrick's two rooms were at the end of the corridor and they overlooked the harbour.

The first thing that struck her was the mess. The curtains were filthy, the desk covered in

47

dust, and there were cartons and files lying all over the place. She wasn't surprised to find that the computer no longer worked. It had bombed out. She searched around to see if Patrick had a laptop stowed in one of the cupboards, but all she found were discarded files. She was soon sneezing from the dust.

Now what? Feeling exasperated, she scowled at Patrick's computer. She had once been told that it was possible to recover lost information from the hard drive with specialised equipment. After a moment's indecision she went through the Yellow Pages looking for Roger Burns, the computer dealer who had sold her Patrick's computer and installed the software for him. She found it and called him.

'I was sorry to read about your husband's death, Mrs Connor.'

Clara found it hard to cope with the halted condolences she was receiving from everyone. She mumbled her thanks and cleared her throat.

'I need to find a whole lot of data, but Patrick's computer seems to have bombed out. Our lawyer needs this material, plus the rest. Can you help me recover it?'

'We can but try. Best if you bring your hard drive to me?' He began to explain why some of the data might be lost. Clara listened impatiently. She had a class to teach later that day and she wanted to get on with it. Damn! Now she had to drive to Canterbury.

★　★　★

'As I mentioned to you this morning, Mrs Connor,' Burns said, pushing the Norton's Utilities' CD-ROM into the PC, 'some data is recoverable with this software. Whether or not it's been deleted is immaterial, just as long as it's been saved. Likewise, we'll only recover e-mail correspondence if it was saved.'

Burns keyed in and Clara leaned over his shoulder, watching the documents flash on the screen. 'There's masses of data here,' Burns said standing up. 'We'll have to save it on discs. The software won't recover the information in sequence and you won't get all of it. Instruct your computer to sort it out in date order. That's your best bet. I hope you find what you need.'

Clara stared in fascination as Burns keyed in to letters, e-mails, bank statements and faxes. From time to time he flashed a sympathetic smile at her.

The name *Valkyr* flashed onto the screen, plus a complete tally of the conversion work done as well as the various costs. Just seeing the name made her feel angry. Patrick had launched a company called Treasure Seekers Limited and bought a lobster boat, the *Valkyr*, for £20,000, from a French fisherman. Using cash from her second mortgage, he'd converted the vessel for salvage. He and his mates had spent months out at night supposedly searching the Goodwin Sands, but no one had ever seen any treasure. She'd never forget her anxiety as Patrick's demands for more cash diminished her resources.

Half an hour later Burns stood up and stacked

the discs. 'There you go! Rather you than me.'

Clara nodded in agreement. 'I guess I'll manage.'

Sorting would take care of her spare evenings for the foreseeable future, but what did it matter? Apart from teaching she had no engagements.

As Clara wrote a cheque for the excessive bill she wondered whether computer programming might be a viable future career. She glanced at her watch. There wasn't time to go home. She'd have to drive straight to the college.

★ ★ ★

It was late and Clara was tired after being delayed by students at her evening class. As she reached home and swung into the driveway, she saw the front door hanging open. There were no lights on.

Panic surged as she slammed on the brakes and raced into the house. 'Jason! Jason!' Her voice rose an octave. 'Where are you?'

There was no answering shout and no Jock. Had Jason taken the dog for a walk in the dark and forgotten to close the door? This hope was dashed when she saw Jock's lead hanging from its hook. There was a cold draught coming from the kitchen. She ran through the house and found the back door open, too.

Clara felt hollow inside as she stumbled into the garden. In the distance she saw Jason bending over a bush. She could see that he wasn't hurt. Relief brought a lump to her throat.

'Jason! What's wrong? What are you doing?'

50

'You're back. Oh, Mum!' He was sobbing as he spoke. 'Get the car out. Hurry. Hurry. Someone's poisoned Jock. He's dying.'

'I'll have to call first. There's no one there at this time of night.'

Moments later she got through to the vet's emergency number and arranged to meet him at the surgery. As she helped Jason carry Jock to the car, her son's expression brought tears to her eyes. Jock was only semi-conscious, his mouth open in a grimace of agony, his eyes rolled back into his head. He was covered in foul smelling vomit.

'Hurry. Shut the door.'

Jason squeezed in beside the dog on the back seat and sat soothing him. 'It's going to be all right, Jock.' His voice was breaking and it croaked from high to low. 'Lie still, boy. The vet will fix you up. Just try to keep still.' She heard a low groan.

'He's vomited all over the place. He's in a bad way. Oh Mum, d'you think he'll make it?'

No, she thought, silently thanking God that her son was safe. She tried to think of something comforting. 'If there's anyone who can save him, it's our vet.'

There wasn't much traffic. Ten minutes later she pulled up in Castle Street.

'Can you carry him in, Jason? I'll follow you.'

The vet came out to help. Jason and he could cope without her. She was shuddering violently and she felt light-headed. Delayed shock, she guessed. She took a deep breath and squared her shoulders. Jason would be inconsolable if Jock

51

died. But why would anyone want Jock dead? The answer was all too obvious. Because someone was coming after them and they wanted their guard-dog out of the way. She tried to pull herself together and spent the next ten minutes trying to clean up the mess in the car with paper towels.

She found her son crouched on a bench in reception, his face hidden in his hands. She put her arm around him and leaned against the wall, closing her eyes.

'He said he'll call us,' Jason whispered. Close to tears, he cleared his throat and looked away.

After a while Clara stood up and walked into the surgery. Jock was lying prone on a bench with tubes in his mouth and nose. 'Strychnine,' the vet said. 'It must have been injected into meat. I've pumped his stomach and administered an antidote. We might save him yet. He's an exceptionally strong dog.'

'We love him, we need him; he's Jason's best friend. Don't let Jock die.' She heard footsteps and turned to see Jason in the doorway looking haggard.

'You should go home, Mrs Connor, and take Jason with you,' the vet said tiredly. 'I'm doing all that's humanly possible. Call me in the morning.'

They drove home in sombre silence. Neither of them wanted to eat. They sat side by side watching television, until the phone rang at ten p.m.

Jason grabbed the receiver first. Watching him, she saw his face crinkle into a smile. 'He's over the worst,' he told her. 'He's going to be all right.' His eyes were brimming over as he bolted to his room.

What was she to do? Someone had tried to kill their dog and they would try again she knew. Perhaps she should put Jock in kennels until this was over? But could she put Jock into kennels while her son was at home and at risk? No, Jock must stay and guard him. She felt so afraid. If she had the cash she would pack up and take them somewhere safe and far away, but right now that was impossible. She had to make her business pay . . . and soon. Until then she couldn't afford to move anywhere.

She could feel her fear rising again. It came sneaking up like damp through the ground, turning her body to ice and panicking her mind. She went upstairs and rifled in her cupboard for tranquilisers. Breaking one in half, she swallowed it with a cup of coffee. Perhaps now she could face the night.

6

Clara sat bolt upright in bed. What had woken her? Perhaps it was her headache, which throbbed unbearably. Three a.m. she saw from the clock's luminous dial. She listened intently. The wind was rustling the branches of the almond tree, a car passed in the main road far away, a fox barked on the common. Nothing else! It was so cold. She snuggled back under the duvet and was almost asleep when she heard the single brief musical tone of her computer's e-mail being switched on. Her stomach lurched and she tasted bile in her mouth. Surely not. She must have been dreaming. Jock would bark, wouldn't he?

But Jock was at the vet.

She switched on the light and sat listening. It was dead quiet, but she knew she would have to go down and check. She reached for her dressing-gown and pulled on her slippers. A sharp, metallic crack downstairs sent her sprawling across the room to the window. Peering out, she thought she saw a movement, but it was so dark. Foxes or badgers perhaps? She had the impression a tall, dark shadow had slipped silently out through the gate. She couldn't be sure, yet her body seemed to know since waves of shock were moving over her skin bringing goose-pimples to her arms and neck.

Jason was sleeping, thank goodness. She took

the torch and crept downstairs. There was no sound or movement. She went into the kitchen, which was empty, and reached for the carving knife. The living room was deserted, too. Lastly she tried the study, but there was no one there. The computer was switched off, the windows closed. Had she imagined the noise? Then she saw that the window catch had been pushed up. But how? With a knife, perhaps. Could she or Jason have left it like that? Surely she'd locked the windows? She could not remember. It looked as if someone had broken in. The thought was chilling. She locked the catch and checked the other downstairs windows. Last of all she switched on her Mac. A message flashed onto the screen. *This computer was not switched off properly. Press return key to continue.*

It happened from time to time, but surely she had switched it off yesterday lunchtime? On impulse she switched to 'Recent Documents'. PPP and Internet flashed on the screen. Then she remembered sending an e-mail to Sib.

It was so dark. Beyond the privet hedge she could see part of the road, but it was half-concealed by an old sycamore tree rising from a pool of shadow, its leaves glistening in the street light. Then she saw a glow of light coming from under the tree. She waited and it came again, a stab of red that made her jump, as if someone had drawn deeply on a cigarette. She could hear her rasping breath in the silence and she fought to control it.

'For God's sake pull yourself together, Clara,' she said aloud.

A shudder ran through her as she peered out of the window and searched the flowerbed, but she couldn't see any footprints. The security company had quoted a two-week delay, so what was she supposed to do in the meantime?

She closed the window with a bang. Let him know she was awake. Again a pinprick of red stabbed the shadows. He was still there, smoking while he watched the house. It was so cold, so hard to think because her head ached. She'd been feeling better lately, but tonight the wound throbbed.

After a few minutes hesitation, she dialled 999. The policewoman who answered gave the impression that the general public were on a par with mental delinquents. Clara tried to sound reasonable, but as she told her story, the woman's manner made her feel paranoid.

'Has he tried to break into your house?'

'I think so. The handle of the window was pulled up.'

'Did you check that it was properly shut before you went to bed?'

'No, but I think it was. I'm sure the sounds I heard were the computer being switched on and then the window being slammed.'

'Did you see anyone trespassing in your garden?'

'A figure, like a shadow, moved through the gate, I think.' She didn't seem to be getting through to the policewoman. She could feel her skin prickling with suppressed temper as she fought against an impulse to bang down the receiver.

'Look here . . . ' Clara tried to explain and then broke off. 'Is there someone else I could speak to?'

'Relax, Mrs Connor. Is he still there?'

'Yes, I think so. It's so dark. For God's sake!' Clara searched for a way out of the morass she'd blundered into. 'He waited outside for a while. He's probably still there. I could see his cigarette. Surely stalking's an offence, so why don't you come and arrest him?'

'Of course stalking is an offence, Mrs Connor, but there doesn't seem to be much evidence of that. I'll send a car round to check out the street.'

Clara gave her the details. When she replaced the receiver, she saw Jason standing barefooted in the doorway. His mouth was downturned and his eyes glinted with fury.

'Why didn't you call me?' he muttered.

'I plead the Fifth.' She smiled to show she was joking, but Jason turned and ran upstairs.

Should she go after him? Clara stood staring out of the window, passive and indecisive, hardly able to think her head ached so badly. Finally she did nothing, but a small part of her shrivelled a little. She was Big Mummy, wasn't she? Always in charge, making decisions, nurturer and protector of her child, but Jason was firmly pushing her off her pedestal.

As she was pregnant when she was widowed she'd always had to be strong, coping with mumps and measles on her own, making decisions on what was best for her child, trying to be both a mother and a father to him. She'd tried never to show her fear or grief and later, when Patrick joined the family, she'd always taken Jason's side when they argued, even when she wasn't sure he was right.

She sighed. Jason was reaching puberty. Her thumbs-down response to his burgeoning manhood could lead to disaster. She had to let him cope, however frightening it might be.

Anticipating more nightmares, she had prepared the coffee filter for instant action, but it took two cups laced with honey and two painkillers before she began to feel well enough to face the day.

7

At eight a.m. the following morning, Detective Chief Inspector Peter Bates had a moment of misgiving as he glanced at DI Jonathan Fergus sitting opposite him. Bates hadn't slept much the night before and he felt intensely irritated by the inadequacies of his force versus the unprecedented rise in crime. The DCI gazed at his workload and sighed. Dover was in the grip of Mafia-type gangs smuggling liquor, cigarettes, people, drugs and only God knew what else, and fighting each other to boot. Add to that petty crime, prostitution, muggings, housebreaking, knife fights between locals and a flood of asylum seekers and he reckoned he was running the most understaffed station in England.

Consequently he'd applied for reinforcements and they'd sent him Fergus for his trouble, perhaps because the Inspector was originally a local lad. He'd started his career as a police diver and saved enough to go back to university and study criminology. Then his aunt had died leaving him a small inheritance which he'd used to gain more qualifications before joining the Canterbury force where he'd risen to the rank of Inspector within a few years. Bates put little store by theoretical knowledge and considered Fergus, at 35, to be the least qualified of his staff. Perhaps that was an advantage in this case, he pondered. You couldn't call this normal police work.

He looked up and noticed the Inspector glancing inquisitively at a picture of his wife taken so long ago that Alzheimer's disease hadn't been heard of. The young man shot a compassionate glance towards Bates. So his staff knew about his wife's dementia. He wondered how they had found out.

He cleared his throat. 'Sit down, Inspector. How tall are you? Six-foot-two? My neck aches from staring up at you.'

Fergus sat cautiously on the edge of the chair, hunched forward, elbows on the arm rests, fingertips pressed together. He looked more Spanish than Scottish, Bates decided. There was an air of gentleness about him which Bates found disturbing. He had a shock of curly black hair, cut very short, bushy black eyebrows, high cheekbones and a turned-up nose. He reminded Bates of an actor from way back, but he couldn't remember his name. Bates sighed. If he'd had any say in the matter, Fergus wouldn't be sitting there now.

'For your sins, Fergus, you are now handling most matters connected to asylum seekers. We have to keep a low profile on any disturbance. That's straight from Whitehall, via Canterbury.'

Fergus looked taken aback and then disappointed.

'A delicate situation, but right up your street.'

'Why is that, sir?' The Inspector looked suspicious.

Bates tapped a pile of folders. 'These are

60

yours, Fergus! All your cases put to bed with not one arrest.'

'But sir, they were all juveniles. No good ever came out of sending kids to prison and, besides, we'd be clogging up the judicial system. If you remember, I checked each one with you.'

The DCI slapped a file on the desk. 'Did you know that the law governing immigration is about to be changed, Fergus? Not before time. The word's got around that we're Mother Christmas and the Good Samaritan rolled into one. So far the cost to Dover's rate-payers is eleven million pounds. The government's promised to disperse them and they're looking for friendly county councils to help share the burden. If the asylum seekers became known as trouble-makers it might take years to lose them. Are you with me, Fergus?'

'Yes, sir.'

'Fine! Use your famous leniency to deal with whatever they get up to and try to persuade them to keep out of trouble. I've spread the word that anything pertaining to asylum seekers lands on your desk. Here's one for starters: a knife fight between immigrants and local youths in a brothel, which asylum seekers have set up with taxpayers' cash and intend to keep exclusively for themselves. Oh, and another one just came in. A woman complained to Sergeant Browning that someone has been stalking her, perhaps a Kosovan. Evidently he followed her to the park and later waited outside her house at night, or so she alleges. Browning took down the details and sent up a car, but they failed to find the man.

Coincidentally, the woman who complained is Mrs Connor.'

'Coincidentally . . . ?'

'Wife of the yachtsman who went missing when his yacht exploded. Go and see her. Perhaps there's a connection. Here's the Connor file.' He picked up a file on his desk and leafed through it. 'Because there was no corpse the inquest finding was deferred. Constable Jennings interviewed Mrs Connor at the hospital. She had a nasty gash on the head, but she survived six hours in the sea.' He slid the file forward and nodded dismissively.

Fergus stood up and hesitated, longing to have it out with the DCI. The phrase 'famous leniency' had hurt, but Bates was already considering his next problem.

★　★　★

The village called River, strung out along the banks of the River Dour, and nestling between chalk downs, was as tidy and law-abiding as any in Britain. There were no teenage gangs, no racial tension, no violence, no decay. There were few shops and no entertainment other than a few quiet pubs. Homes were well-kept, gardens blooming and residents' dogs were walked on training muzzles.

It was all too good to be true. Somewhere behind discreet lace curtains were the creators of the new and ruthless Mafia gangs that ruled the dock area. They lived Jekyll and Hyde existences, filing tax returns, living in unobtrusive homes, taking the kids to the park weekends, fitting into the modest routine of suburban daily living, while they hid their profits in Swiss numbered bank accounts, hired killers and trafficked in drugs and human cargo.

Soon Fergus was speeding to the top of Cowper Lane where he found the cottage tucked under the common, home to badgers, foxes and the Connor family. From here, surrounded by quaint bungalows, trees and flowering shrubs it was hard to believe that Dover's poorest area and industrial sites lay just beyond the next hill. It was so peaceful and rural. Beyond the cul de sac were farmlands stretching for miles over the north downs. He could hear cows lowing and, unexpectedly, a donkey brayed, startling him.

The boy who opened the door was long and lanky with brooding eyes and a bony face. He looked about thirteen, introverted, hostile and over-sensitive.

'Detective Inspector Jonathan Fergus.' He showed his badge. 'You're Jason Connor, I assume. I've come to see your mother. Is she in?'

The boy nodded briefly, his eyes registering his unease. Fergus remembered his own traumatic boyhood. There was always something to feel guilty about and the boy's attitude could mean nothing more serious than trying out pot with friends. Fergus gazed around the entrance hall which was bright, with a sunny, arty quality he didn't see often.

There was warmth and humour in the living room, a framed watercolour of nymphs lascivi-ously cavorting on a tropical beach, flowering plants in bright ceramic pots and books all over the place. Fergus approved of the room. He thrust away a sudden longing to have a home instead of the bare, but costly, digs he rented for eighty-five pounds a week where he could hear his landlady's snores all night long.

'Sit down if you want to. I'll fetch Mum.' Jason grabbed his Coke and backed out.

A woman's voice sounded from an upstairs room. Fergus moved to the doorway. Above him, Clara Connor paused on the stairs and patted her hair into place. She wore an old blue polo-necked jersey over stretch jeans and her dark brown hair was caught up in a ponytail. She must be all of 33, he realised. She looked younger, perhaps because there was something so vulnerable about her.

'Clara Connor?'

'Yes.' With an obvious effort Clara tore her eyes from his and moved towards him. As she approached he noticed the deep shadows under her eyes, her taut skin and haunted expression. She looked terrified, yet strangely she didn't seem to be a timid sort of person. He guessed she was unaware that she was chewing her bottom lip.

'I've come about the alleged stalker.'

'I thought . . . I called . . . Obviously you know that, but no one came. There's no end to it.'

She blinked hard and frowned. Enlarged pupils, shaking hands, dry lips! He noted all her terror symptoms and wondered if her fears were real or imaginary.

'No end to what?'

64

'This nightmare. Please sit down, Inspector.'

She seemed very distraught as she gave him the details, which didn't take long. Someone had poisoned their dog, but he was still at the vet's. She thought someone might have followed her, but she wasn't sure. A man appeared to be staring at her in the park, but again she couldn't be certain. Later, she thought she saw him in the garden, and the window appeared to have been forced open.

She shuddered. Her voice was low, but strangely compelling and there was something intriguing about her eyes. She might be lovely, he imagined, if she weren't under such a strain. He pulled himself together fast when he realised that he was only half listening.

Sighing inwardly, Fergus stopped writing and thrust his pen and notebook in his pocket. After five years of study he was lumbered with dead-end cases. The stalker, if indeed he was a stalker, could not be arrested, but only cautioned, because Dover's citizens wanted to rid themselves of their immigrant population.

'You must look after yourself, Mrs Connor. You've been through a terrible ordeal. I'm so sorry that you lost your husband.'

He seemed to have said the wrong thing. Her lip trembled, her face crumpled and she grabbed a tissue from her pocket and wiped away the offensive tears. 'Why am I crying? For God's sake! I thought I had myself in hand. I'm sorry.'

She was a woman who hated to let herself down, Fergus could see that. Crying was taboo. She was proud and very, very private, but the tears had a mind of their own and they were brimming over.

'What must you think of me?' Her voice came muffled through the sodden tissue. She pulled herself together fast.

'It's all right, Mrs Connor. Try to relax. I'll check out your stalker. Here's my mobile number. If anything frightens you or you think you see the stalker again, call me at once.'

Fergus left with strangely mixed feelings, hoping that this was the last he would hear of the case, but feeling worried about that sad, but lovely woman.

★ ★ ★

Clara could not stop shaking. How could she be such a fool? It was his kindness that had shaken her defenses. She went to the window and watched the Inspector's car drive away. She had never felt this alone. Never been this frightened. Something was terribly wrong, but how could she tell the Inspector about her dreams? Night after night she lay awake forcing herself to remember. She would retrace that last evening step by step until she climbed onto the deck. After that nothing! Just a vague memory of seeing the yacht go down and finding herself floating on wreckage. It was only when she slept that these terrible images returned to haunt her: Patrick half dead in the locker, reaching out to her; an axe swinging in an wide arc towards her; the towering waves. Were these nightmares real? She wasn't sure, so how could she tell the

Inspector? All her memories were surreal.

Dusk was settling in the valley. Purple clouds hung around the horizon. Birds were frantically gobbling fragments of peanuts to sustain them through the long, cold night. Jason was playing pop music in his room. Normality ceased there, for her head throbbed madly, and her shoulder was aching. How could these injuries be the result of the explosion? She wasn't burned at all. Her hair wasn't singed. She had fallen overboard before the explosion occurred, she felt sure of that. She stopped short and gasped as she remembered a voice in the wind: 'I'll come after you.' Surely that was real — or was her mind playing tricks on her?

Images were rising up as dark and fearful as the storm on the horizon. She couldn't bear more gloomy introspection.

Lately she was suffering badly from a sense of powerlessness which made her feel apathetic. No matter how hard she tried she could not remember what had happened on the yacht that night. Nor could she find out who Patrick had been working with, or what they were doing. Bernie and Robin said he owed money, but to whom? Why hadn't they asked for it? Just why were Robin and Bernie so uneasy? Who was watching the house and why? Too many questions.

Work was the answer. She hurried into her study and took out the discs filled with data from Patrick's old computer. Fragments, half sentences, entire paragraphs, words . . . She could lose herself in this mess for months at a time.

She set the PC to work, sorting the data into date order, but just how far back should she go? Begin at the beginning, she told herself. But when was that? Perhaps on his last but one birthday, which was when they purchased the PC, his birthday gift from her. On second thoughts she made it the day after, which was June 18, which was probably the first date on which the PC was used.

Her name flicked onto the screen — *Mrs Connor* — and this intrigued her. Fitting the sentences together was worse than a difficult jigsaw puzzle, but at last she found most of the message.

From: The Ambassador Hotel, Coral Beach, Eilat. Confirmation of your booking for Mr and Mrs P. Connor in a double room for five nights at $250 a night, commencing June 27. Bank draft of $1,250 received with thanks.

But how was this possible? Then she remembered that Patrick had supposedly been in Spain picking up a cheap fishing boat for his salvage operation.

'Bastard! Bastard! Bastard!'

She heard Jason calling from the front hall. 'Going down to the Co-op. Won't be long.'

* * *

It was dark when Jason came back on his bike. The telephone was ringing so he propped his bike in the porch, opened the front door and grabbed the receiver.

'Mum, it's the vet,' he called out. 'Jock can

68

come home. When can we go and fetch him?'

'Now,' she called sternly.

'Be right there.' He replaced the receiver and walked in the kitchen. Mum looked awful. Like she hadn't slept for a week and she was losing weight.

'Where've you been, Jason? You've been gone for hours.'

'Over at Jeff's place.'

'I don't want you going there, or anywhere come to that, without telling me.'

Now she was really over the top. Jeff was his best friend and he spent as much time there as at home. He only lived two streets away in Minnis Lane and his mum made super cakes.

'But Mum . . .'

'Don't whine. And don't stand there glaring at me. Put your bike in the garage and get in the car. I'm leaving the pie in the oven. Listen Jason, the lift scheme starts tomorrow, so you can forget your bike for the time being. You want to go to Jeff's, you ask me and I'll run you over.'

Mum was turning into some kind of a power-freak. Jason turned away and reached for the leash, just so she wouldn't see his face. Would things ever come right, he wondered? What would happen to them? Or to Mum? Depression tightened round his chest and pulled his stomach into a tight knot as he considered his mother's fears. Lately he was scared to go to school. Someone should be around to look after her.

8

Stepping out of the lift in her office block, Clara paused to admire Sib's dazzling montage of the castle, cliffs and scenic views with *Connor Tours* stencilled along the top. 'Thank you, Sib,' she murmured. The sign gave her a sense of excitement and then a thrill of fear. She had to succeed or they'd lose the house.

She walked down the passage, unlocked the office door and almost choked from the strong smell of paint and turps. Yesterday she and Jason had whitewashed the office walls while they waited for the new furniture and the computer to be delivered. Even more impressive were the piles of printed leaflets she'd written and designed about her planned tours. She opened the window wide and leaned out, breathing in cold, fresh air.

Her office overlooked the Wellington Docks, long since converted into a series of yacht basins, choked with costly yachts moored to pontoons. Ahead was the Hoverspeed Terminal from where catamarans raced to Calais and back, transporting thousands of trippers across the Channel. The sea was calm today, and the pebbled beach glittered in the sun. On the pier, anglers in boots and sou'westers hung out with their bait and sandwiches.

Dover was such a weird mixture of old and new, she thought, comparing the ultra-modern

P&O headquarters to the nearby Aycliff Fort, built to defend Dover in the Napoleonic Wars and nowadays used to sell junk furniture. The town had a chip on its shoulder, being a dismal shadow of its former self and poor relation to the powerful Western docks spread out under the castle. It was hard to see how they co-existed in close proximity; on one side of the castle a bustling, thriving, multi-million metropolis, on the other a jumble of sad streets and huddled Victorian villas. A cacophony of noise rose from the street below as massive lorries from Europe came to a standstill, bumper to bumper, caught up in a jam as they moved towards the motorway.

She slammed the window to block out the noise. Pushing the box of cleaning materials into the adjoining annexe, she sighed with distaste. She hadn't yet begun on this mess. There was a bad feel to this office, as if it echoed the deceit of Patrick's shady activities. Around the walls were heaps of sailing gear, files were piled in a corner and the large, recessed cupboard was filled with boxes. Patrick had used the room mainly for storage, she guessed, but the mess bothered her.

She began by emptying the cupboard. After a while she wondered whether she should ring Jason to make sure everything was okay. He was at Jeff's and they were supposed to be studying. Maybe not. She might make him look silly if she kept checking on him.

Hours later she heard the lift coming up. She glanced at her watch. Nine p.m. So she wasn't the only one working late on a Sunday night. The lift stopped on her floor, the doors opened and closed and the lift descended, but there were no footsteps. Switching off the light, she opened the connecting door and listened intently. She heard a creak halfway along the passage and then another outside the door. Rigid with fear, she watched the handle slowly turning.

Thank God she'd locked the door. But someone was tampering with the lock. Should she shout or scream? Would that make them go away? Her heart was thumping like a pneumatic drill as she heard the lock clicking and turning. The seconds passed agonisingly slowly as she watched the handle twist again.

Closing the annexe door softly, Clara grabbed her bag and torch and retreated into the cupboard, pulling the door to behind her. Feeling for her mobile, she rang the Inspector.

'Help me!' she whispered. 'Someone's breaking into my office. I'm alone here.'

'Where are you?'

Was that the Inspector? She wasn't sure. 'Connor Tours, Snargate Street,' she whispered and rang off. She could hear the sound of the outer door being closed. The sound hurt. Then footsteps crossed the office.

No longer trying to be quiet, the intruder opened drawers and slammed them shut. Stomach twisting, she heard him switch on Pat's computer. She'd taken all the recovered data home, thank heavens. What was he looking for? Eventually he switched off and walked towards the annexe. The door opened. She almost whimpered as the light switched on. She could hear breathing and the quiet shuffle of papers. She flinched as a pile fell onto the floor. He turned away and began searching the files, moving across the room towards her. Clara's body reacted with panic, her skin prickled and her throat constricted until she could hardly breathe. The tension was unbearable. She tried to think of anything she could use as a weapon, but she only had a torch.

The sound of his tread was like gunshots. He was close by. Too close! Pushing the door slightly open, she peered through the narrow crack. It was the stalker. Although his back was turned to her, she recognised the way his black leather jacket hung from his wide shoulders as if from a coathanger. Suddenly he straightened up, dropped the file and turned towards her. *He knew she was there*. Had he sensed her stare? She cringed into the cupboard, each heartbeat like a crash that must shatter her ribs.

He was creeping towards her. In the background she was dimly aware of a police siren, a door slamming, running footsteps. The cupboard door swung open. For a brief moment his eyes chilled her. Then he ran for the door.

★　★　★

Two startled faces were staring down at her: Detective Inspector Fergus and the caretaker, Mr Costas, a short, fat middle-aged man with hair everywhere except on his bald head.

'Mrs Connor, what happened?' Fergus's voice was hoarse. 'Thank God you're all right.' He helped her out of the cupboard and pushed her to a chair. 'I think you know Mr. Costas.'

She felt dazed. 'What happened? Where is he?'

She could still smell the stalker's garlic breath and see his eyes.

'Are you all right?'

'Why didn't you get him?'

'He left via the fire escape. I was more anxious to find you.'

Apprehensive and furious, she walked around.

'Don't touch anything,' Fergus snapped. 'I'll get the fingerprint team round here in the morning. Can you tell if anything is missing?'

'There was nothing much to take.' She felt amazed at how calm she sounded. Fury had taken over. She took a deep breath.

'So tell me what happened. Did you get a glimpse of your attacker?'

'Yes. It's the same man who tried to break into my house the night I called the police. There's someone after me, but you don't believe me.'

Fergus acknowledged her outburst with a cautious nod.

The caretaker paused in the doorway. 'I'm very sorry to hear about your husband, Mrs Connor. Is there anything I can do to help?'

She shook her head.

'Well, if you intend working late again let me know. Take care.' He nodded and left.

Fergus pulled out a chair and sat down. 'Tell me everything you can remember, Mrs Connor. Every little detail about him.'

She nodded and tried to remember the way he had looked and the stench of his garlic breath.

'I hid in that cupboard and called you. Thanks for getting here so soon.'

'This break-in appears to link the stalker to your husband. I want you to tell me about your husband's business.'

'His business?' Clara frowned. She'd always thought Patrick was battling to build up the tour agency. Now she knew better. He'd been wheeling and dealing, whatever that meant, but she was unwilling to admit this to the Inspector.

'Connor Tours was a one-man show taking holidaymakers on local tours. I suppose that brought in some cash. I hope so because I'm about to resurrect the agency. Besides that, Patrick owned a share of Robin Connor's boat, which takes out trippers in summer. They are half-brothers.' She broke off. Remembering Robin's story still hurt.

'Pat started a treasure hunting business. He bought a fishing boat, the *Valkyr*, converted it for salvage and launched a company called Treasure Exploration. He spent months searching the Goodwin Sands for old wrecks.'

'At night?'

'Yes. Mostly for secrecy, he told me, but why do you ask?'

'Just a hunch. And did he bring anything home? Silly things like teaspoons with a boat's name on it, a rusty bell, the sort of thing divers hoard? I'm a scuba diver. Mate of mine took home an entire dinner service over a hundred years old. I was with him when he found it. There's plenty of loot out there.'

His voice was dauntingly mild, but it was easy

75

to see what he was implying. She glared at him and shrugged.

'Patrick owed a great deal of money to business associates, but he said there was cash coming in to cover it. That's why he wanted to get away for a few days. Now his so-called friends tell me he stole money from gangsters.'

She slumped down, her elbow on the desk, pressing her fingers on her neck. God! It hurt so much.

'Everyone's bad-mouthing Patrick now, but they never said a word when he was alive.'

'Take your time, Mrs Connor.'

She sighed as she realised how little she knew about Patrick's affairs. 'It's pathetic now. The trip . . . well . . . it was supposed to be a second honeymoon. He even bought champagne. Some time ago we went through a bad patch. I suppose all marriages do, but Patrick had been trying his best to make up for the past.'

She frowned as Fergus demanded a minute-by-minute description of the storm at sea and the yacht foundering, or as much as she could recall. Remembering brought sadness. She was tempted to tell the Inspector about her dreams, but he wouldn't believe her, she decided.

'Let's get back to tonight.'

Clara tried to relate her fear as the footsteps came closer to the cupboard where she was hiding.

'Inspector, I've had enough. I want to go home. Surely you must be finished by now? I feel like the loser of a heavyweight boxing match.'

'One last question. Were you involved in your husband's business affairs?' He peered at her and she was suddenly aware of his kind eyes. They glowed with compassion, almost as if they had a life of their own. Fergus was trying so hard to seem impersonal and detached and not always succeeding. She knew he found her attractive, women could always tell, she supposed. Not that it mattered.

'I wanted to help him, but he wouldn't let me. He used to say: 'That's not how marriages work, darling.' I can hear him now.' She pressed her fist on her forehead. 'It was very effective in keeping me out of his way.'

She broke off. 'I can't talk about him anymore. Half the time I try to kid myself that it's over, that I can rebuild a life for Jason and myself. Then something like this happens and I realise I'm walking through a minefield and I don't know why.'

Fergus switched off the tape recorder and put it in his pocket. 'Would you like me to run you home?'

'Thanks, but my car's outside.'

'I'll walk you to it.'

Outside, as she gulped in the sweet sea air and heard the gulls and the splash of the surf, she felt braver. She was longing to cleanse herself of the lies and deceit. Not even a rusty teaspoon! Bastard! The Inspector seemed to think the treasure business was a front. He was probably right, too. But for what? She said good night and drove home.

'Damn you, Patrick,' she whispered. 'What

exactly were you doing and why couldn't you have told me?' She felt an overwhelming need to be free of the past and make a new start, but the past wouldn't leave her alone.

9

Constable Marion Jennings hurried into the office, smoothing her blonde hair as she smiled engagingly at Fergus. Amongst the functional steel office furniture, the beige decor and bare window frames, Jennings was the only vibrant being, reminding Fergus of a butterfly on a dissecting table with her discreet flashes of brilliance: jade earrings, emerald green scarf, scarlet lipstick and her cobalt blue eyes which he suspected were enhanced by contact lenses.

He had been sitting quietly at his desk, deep in thought, pondering on the enigma of Mrs Connor. She was a strangely mysterious figure, keeping much to herself. There were too many unanswered questions, such as why was she wearing a rubber diving suit at the time of the explosion? Or so the hospital had told him. It was the suit that had saved her life. What was her connection with the stalker and why was she so afraid?

Jennings broke in on his thoughts: 'Two local divers called in ten minutes ago asking for you, but switchboard put them through to me. They've found Connor's wrecked yacht on the Goodwin Sands with a corpse in the hull. Bit of a mess after four weeks' submersion I should think.' Her eyes widened in morbid delight. 'They should be here any minute. Bates said you can take the afternoon off, if you like, but try to

79

get the corpse to Forensics in one piece. Rather you than me.' She gave a theatrical shudder.

'Thanks. Tell them to hang on for five minutes.'

Fergus glanced at his watch and hurried out. The lift took too long, so he ran down two flights of stairs. On the pavement he paused and glanced anxiously at the sky, sniffing the wind: brisk, easterly and worsening. Crossing Park Road he went into the takeaway. He was starving. He grabbed a sandwich and ate it while he waited for his order. When he returned he found his two mates, Rolf Krantz and Peter Perry in the charge office.

'I guessed it would be you two.' He gave them both a clap on their shoulders and banged a bag of hamburgers and three cartons of hot soup on the counter.

The three of them had been mates since training days in the police diving school. Since then they'd gone their separate ways. Rolf and Peter had launched a local scuba diving school, but they still organised a dive together once a month, time and weather permitting. Fergus passed on whatever diving work he could and they always did a first-class job. He couldn't think of two men he'd rather be with in a tight spot. Peter was short and dark, with stern eyes, a gymnast's build and a lack of fear that was almost pathological. Rolf was taller with wavy blond hair and warm blue eyes that suckered the girls time and again, leading him into no end of trouble. Rolf was a man's man and his only love was diving.

'Eat fast,' Peter crammed his hamburger into his mouth and slurped his soup, swallowing it in noisy gulps. 'We want to get there when the tide turns around two-thirty. It'll be relatively calm and we'll have an hour or so of daylight. We definitely don't want to be fumbling around in the dark. It's going to be tricky.'

Fergus frowned. 'My gear's at home.'

'You can pick up what you need at the depot.' Peter threw his empty containers into the bin. 'We brought Rolf's camera for you. The lifeboat guys are raring to go. They're waiting at the wharf.'

They left shortly afterwards. Parking the firm's 4 × 4 at the end of the jetty, they lugged their gear down the steps to the lifeboat. The crew were in a hurry to get going. The coxswain, middle-aged and weather-beaten, was gazing anxiously at the eastern horizon. 'There's a gale coming up. I'd like to get this over and done with. I have a feeling we'll be called out again tonight.'

By one-thirty they were surging out of the Western Harbour in a Force 3 breeze, giving Port Control their destination. Hugging the coast, they passed the ferry terminal and changed course to avoid a small fleet of fishing boats with their swarms of gulls. As they cut through the waves at 25 knots into the major shipping lanes, they watched the weather anxiously. The sea was a deep slate grey with crests of foaming white on every choppy wave. The sky was dark with an imminent threat of rain, but a few errant sunbeams pierced the

81

clouds lighting the cliffs with an unearthly white sheen.

'Sure you got the right wreck?' Fergus was checking the controls of his gear.

'Of course. *Connemara* is written all over the place.'

'We knew Pat Connor from the yacht club,' Rob said. 'Perhaps that's why it threw me to see the corpse. He was a right sod, but a sailing purist. He never used gas. Never known him use the engine at sea either. The bastard stayed out two nights last May waiting for a breeze when he could have cruised back at any time. But this trip he had his wife on board and the gale was getting worse, so perhaps he thought he'd compromise for once. Bad choice as it turned out.' He broke off, looking depressed.

'If you boys have got your navigation right we're just about there,' the skipper called.

'GPS, mate.' Peter frowned as he stared ahead. 'Listen, you guys. I'm worried about the swell. It's pretty heavy and the wreck could be turned and buried in next to no time. As I see it, we should approach from the east, where the bows are bedded in an older wreck. That's the most stable part. You with me?'

Fergus looked round and gave the thumbs up sign, but Peter was ultra careful. His insidious voice, soft as a whisper, hadn't done yet.

'Furthermore, the hull is badly holed, more or less where the engine used to be. Whichever way the wreck rolls, that break should provide a quick exit. In case of trouble there are two more exits: the hatch from the stateroom, which has swung over to the west and is half embedded with sand, or a smaller break at the stern. The stateroom, which is roughly in the centre of the hull, is mainly intact. There's a table floating up against the deck and the corpse is on the port side of it. Or was. Let's hope for the best. Okay with you two?'

They nodded.

'How's visibility?' Fergus asked.

'About a foot inside the hull, so you'll need a torch and a headlight. Rolf will bring down the stretcher while you take your shots. I'll stick around in case you need anything.'

'How long will you be?' Peter asked Fergus.

'Not long. I guess ten minutes or so.'

'Give us the signal when you're ready. We'll transport the corpse up to the lifeboat and I'll get back as soon as the guys here take over. Mind your fingers. Some pretty big eels have taken up residence. I don't have to tell you to beware of the quicksands. Keep swimming.'

As they spotted the buoy Peter had tied to the wreck's hull, the sun broke through and the sea turned from slate to pewter.

'That helps,' Rolf said. 'Visibility is around 20 feet outside the wreck when the sun shines.'

Fergus stripped down to his vest and pants, and struggled into his suit and gear. Last of all, he adjusted his weight belt, clipped it round his waist and fitted his camera bag to his waistband. He felt a surge of adrenaline as he gazed at the sea. He couldn't wait to get down. After a last minute instrument check, he switched on his headlight, crouched at the edge of the platform

83

and toppled backwards. As he sank he watched the surface of the sea sparkling with silver bubbles. The dark shape of the lifeboat hovered over them looking like an airblown whale. A huge shoal of mackerel passed close by, followed by a solitary skate sparkling iridescent silver. Soles were slinking over the white sand.

This was his world. Sometimes he thought his soul would shrivel if he were unable to dive. He sank towards the wreck, letting more air out of the alternator until he was gliding over the sandy seabed. A quick swim around confirmed that this certainly was the *Connemara*, lying at 20 fathoms. It looked as if an explosion, followed by a fire, had sunk the yacht, although the hull and stateroom were mainly intact. He began to examine the wreckage more carefully. The burning was trivial, showing that the yacht had sunk soon after the fire began. From the holed engine compartment, he gathered that the fire had set off another explosion as the diesel ignited. The yacht lay snarled in a tangle of stout wooden beams, like ribs from an ancient corpse, a relic perhaps of an ancient trading ship and uncovered after hundreds of years under the sand. Soon the dunes would shift again to cover both wrecks for a century or more.

Fergus switched on his torch and swam through the hatch to the murky cabin. Everything that floated was pressed against the deck, the rest of the debris littered the floor including the engine which must have been carried forward by the rush of water through the holed stern. When Fergus shuffled forward in his flippers, sand and debris rose around him. The tide was changing, the swell strengthening and the wreck was heaving and groaning as it shifted in the sand. They didn't have much time left. Unclipping his camera, Fergus felt his way towards the port side of the hull where the cabin table had shaken loose from its screws and was hard up against the deck above.

Fergus caught sight of something moving in the darkness. He swung his torch around and almost yelped at the grotesque sight. Adjusting his headlight to a better angle, he studied the apparition, which appeared to be walking as it bobbed upright, feet dangling only inches above the deck. Fergus tried not to think as he gazed at the remains of what had been a human being a mere three and a half weeks ago.

He unclipped his camera, aimed and took the first shots. His flashgun captured the scene like strobe lights as he photographed the corpse from every angle, noting the smashed cheek and broken jaw hanging loosely, the missing teeth on the left side of the head, and the deep gash on the right side of the skull.

A dark shadow blotted out the dim light. Fergus spun round to see Rolf manoeuvring the 'body snatcher' through the hatch.

The explosion had holed the stern and destroyed the partition between the engine and sail compartments, and the rush of the sea had washed the engine and the sails into the cabin. He hunted around and found a wedding ring on the deck near to where the corpse had been floating. Searching for the missing teeth brought no success, but he found the ship's papers and the log, wrapped in oilskins, in the drawer of the desk.

Leaving the corpse to his mates, Fergus swam out to take a few more shots. He took a last photograph from above, before inflating his alternator for a slow ascent.

Back on the lifeboat, the wind had strengthened and the sea was rough, but still the cloying stench filled their lungs and penetrated every pore. One of the crew, a newcomer, was heaving over the side.

Shortly afterwards they were speeding back towards harbour where the undertakers were waiting with their hearse to transport the corpse to the mortuary. The three of them went back to the diving school to shower and change and share a bottle of brandy in the office.

Obsessed with thoughts of life and death and his own mortality, Fergus laughed too loudly and drank too fast.

Memo to: Detective Chief Inspector P. Bates
From: Detective Inspector J. Fergus
Date: 15 November, at 7.00 pm
Re: Disappearance at sea of Patrick Connor.

A body, which might be Patrick Connor's, was discovered at 10.45 a.m. today by Rolf Krantz and Peter Perry, joint owners of a Dover-based scuba diving school. They were exploring the outer perimeter of the Goodwin Sands for newly-exposed wrecks when they came across part of the *Connemara's* hull which had become snarled on an older, but newly-exposed wreck.

A corpse was found in the stateroom. As evident from the photographs, the right side of the face has been struck several times, fracturing and dislocating the jaw, smashing the nose and causing numerous fractures to the cheekbone while all the teeth on that side of the face are missing.

An underwater examination of the wreck of the *Connemara* verified the information given by Mrs Connor in her statement to Constable Marion Jennings on October 25, i.e. that an explosion aboard the *Connemara* holed the yacht and set fire to it, causing it to founder.

When there is a south-easterly gale in the Channel, it sweeps water into the Dover Straits causing a bottleneck. Currents running from 4 to 5 knots in the North Sea accentuated the hazardous sailing conditions, and it appears that a gas bottle fell and was damaged. Gas, being heavier than air, soaked down into the hold and the bilges, so that when Connor, or an unknown person, started the engine, a spark ignited the gas which exploded and started the fire. The fire ignited the diesel for the engine and a second explosion occurred in the engine compartment, holing the stern so that the sea poured in swamping the boat.

D.I. JONATHAN FERGUS

10

Inspector Fergus disliked driving to the mortuary. It was sited at the top of Coombe Valley Road, formerly Union Road that had housed the worst slum in Dover. Now it was semi-industrial, but some old villas had survived the bombs and shelling of World War II. A pub, the Primrose, which had stood there since Victorian times, still attracted the same rough and tumble clientele, loyal and headstrong, backing each other through adversity — and there was no shortage of that in this part of Dover, Fergus knew. The morgue had once been Dover's workhouse and it had lost nothing of its dismal appearance. Fergus parked and hurried inside to the waiting room.

For Fergus the smell of formaldehyde was synonymous with death. If he smelt one he would smell the other and he would see rows of icy coffins, hear the hum of the deep freeze engines and feel the cold penetrating his bone marrow.

The swing doors were flung open and Rob Miles, a South African pathologist, strode in, flicking off his mask. He was a long, lean man with a bony face, extraordinarily intense blue eyes and weather-beaten, deeply-tanned skin. He resembled an ancient patriarch from biblical times, an impression heightened by his deep voice, long surgical gown and flamboyant gestures.

'Let's get on with it, my friend, but wear one of these.' He handed Fergus a mask. As he held open the swing doors the smell worsened.

'The stench of death is one of nature's most remarkable feats.' Miles gestured toward the window as if nature was all around them instead of tarmac roads and rows of villas. 'It can summon vultures from a twenty mile radius, or cause the inhabitants of an entire village to abandon their homes and find fresh quarters. That's what it's all about, keeping the living from the dead. But you and I are going to have to breathe this foul odour.'

Miles grabbed an aerosol can and sprayed around the long, tiled, antiseptic room with its steel tables, whitewashed walls, harsh neon lighting, and a wildlife calendar of bushpigs and baboons hanging on the wall.

'Like that, do you?' Miles asked following his gaze. 'I took that photograph last year. The bush is my passion.'

A surgical table lay in the centre of the room under three garish neon tubes. Miles was gently withdrawing the white plastic sheet, revealing the bizarre tragedy.

As Fergus stared down at the corpse, blood began seeping out of the wounded flesh ringing the cuff and neck of the anorak. He shuddered.

'Don't worry. The blood's been congealed in cold water and the deep freeze. The corpse is warming, so the blood's flowing out of the wounds. It's normal and it won't last long.'

'It's the teeth that bother me most,' Fergus said softly as he bent over the corpse. 'I can't

89

work out what sort of a blow could have caused this much damage.'

Miles ran his fingers along the right side of the jaw. 'In the absence of any gums I can't tell you whether or not the blow, or blows, occurred at the time of death. Several blows to the left side of the head broke the victim's jaw, shattered his cheekbone and knocked out his teeth. A blow to the right side of the head inflicted this wound.' He pointed to the cracked skull. 'Two explosions, a fire, the boat floods and sinks.' He shrugged. 'I doubt there's anything here to excite a coroner.'

Fergus made his holistic scan of the whole corpse, or what was left of it, trying to get to grips with the man. He'd been powerful, big-boned and athletic, with a broad face and wide set eyes. The body was clothed in jeans, a leather belt, a sweater and an oilskin anorak.

'Scorched, but not badly burned,' Miles spoke into his tape recorder while rubbing his finger over the discoloured fabric. He slit down the side of the right anorak sleeve with a stainless steel knife. The scorched anorak and the jersey were peeled off in strips, followed by the trousers and thermal underwear until the bloated, silvery-white flesh was revealed, eaten away in places where the clothing offered entry. There was a small tattoo of a butterfly still intact at the top of his right arm.

'The clothes protected the skin from scorching, so the fire didn't last long. There are no burns under the anorak. All the exposed flesh

90

would have been burned black, but that no longer exists.'

'What's that by the way?' Fergus pointed to a stainless steel bracelet imbedded in the swollen flesh which had lain protected by the cuff of the anorak.

'A tag showing that the wearer was allergic to penicillin. The watch is still going,' he said, removing it. 'Remarkable, isn't it? Shows the right time, too. He put the multi-dialled watch with the broad black leather strap, together with the chain bracelet, on a small table by the wall to which Fergus added the ring he'd found on the cabin floor.

'The corpse was in his mid- to late-forties. He had been an athlete, a footballer or mountaineer, we can assume by the size of the biceps. He was used to hard physical work. Cause of death, drowning, despite the wounds.' He gazed at the head wounds with deep concentration.

'Have you informed the next of kin?' He turned and smiled sympathetically.

'Not yet.'

'Messy business. They'll be upset, whoever they are. Ghastly sight for a relative.' Miles was talking while he worked, already exploring the body's orifices. 'Well, I guess you'll want to be on your way. I'll be here for most of the night so if you want to know anything else give me a call.'

It was almost seven p.m. when Fergus reached his office in Ladywell, but three other detectives, including Jennings, were working at their computers. His printed statement for the DCI was lying on his desk together with the disc. He

91

glanced through it and typed in his corrections, adding a paragraph at the bottom:

Despite the force of the two explosions that shattered the vessel, I have the feeling that it is too much of a coincidence that flying debris could have struck the victim with such force several times on the left side of the face, knocking out the teeth and breaking the jaw and nose, as well as another blow to the right side of the head, particularly since there are no other wounds, scratches or bruises on the body. The damage seems to indicate a violent attack.

At least he had stated his concern. He left his report on the DCI's desk and went off to get some supper.

When Fergus returned to headquarters there was a message asking him to see the DCI as soon as possible. He glanced at his watch: eight-thirty p.m.

'Bates still around?' he called to Marion Jennings, who was sitting at her desk drinking coffee.

'He's working late like the rest of us.'

Fergus made his way to the DCI's office down the corridor. The door was open and he caught sight of him talking into the telephone. He looked bleak and tired. 'No, I'm sorry. I can't get home before ten. You'll just have to stay if you can't find a replacement.' He dropped the receiver with a sigh.

'Sit down, Fergus. Blasted part-time help want

to work to rule. They should try working here for a few days.' He picked up the report. 'Take a look at this!' He made a sweeping gesture towards a pile of files that was threatening to collapse. 'Here's a new one: a lorry driver has laid a charge of harassment against a whore who does the rounds. Evidently these women won't take 'no' for an answer and fight over the best prospects.'

Fergus, whose libido was causing him sleepless nights, wondered what it must be like to be 'fought over'. He'd heard the girls had their preferences, mainly for French and Italian drivers. Right now he didn't want to get involved. He felt exhausted after his long scuba dive. He needed to get to bed.

'My wife and I live in The Gateway, so we have a grandstand view from there.' Bates' eyes were glinting with fury. 'The lorries come lumbering off the ferries from the Continent, but when they get to the first traffic light along the A20 all hell breaks loose as the girls vie for business. Some of the newer pro's are asylum seekers and the locals don't want them around, so this one's for you, Fergus.'

He looked up and frowned. 'You're unusually quiet tonight, aren't you?'

'Tired, sir.'

'Join the club.' He tossed the folder aside impatiently. 'So you see, Inspector, we don't have to make more problems for ourselves by using our intuition. We have more than enough on our plates. The coroner will make his informed decision about Connor's death at the inquest.

Meantime, there's all this.' He gestured towards the files littering his desk. 'You understand me?'

'Yes, sir.'

'Time to tell Mrs Connor, isn't it? Take her down to identify the corpse.'

'Tonight?'

'Why not?'

'Miles is busy on the post mortem. He said he'll be working all night.'

Bates sighed. 'Well that gives you time to scout around the seafront. You see any trouble, book the women for disturbing the peace. Believe me, Fergus, Dover isn't a rest camp. Hardly the sort of place you're used to, I guess. Watch out for these ladies of the night. Scratch your eyes out if you give them the chance.'

'Sir!'

Bates grabbed the next file and scanned the contents. Noticing his obvious fatigue, Fergus gave up his intention of pleading for time off. Feeling hard done by, he strode out of the DCI's office and dumped the file on his desk.

Half an hour later he set off on foot into the drizzling night, passing the Town Hall, built at the time of the Crusades, crossing the cobbled Market Square towards the sea front. A solitary lorry rumbled by, but there were no loiterers except an old tramp and his scruffy white dog trailing round the bins looking for something edible. On impulse he crossed the road and handed five pounds to the old man. Turning the corner he walked along narrow dark streets, passing a large, open car park, which he reckoned might be just the place for pent-up drivers to take time off for a screw. Opposite was a squat old pub with walls of flint which looked as if it had stood there keeping its head down since the Napoleonic wars, evading shells and bombs and property developers.

Fergus hovered in the doorway. The Jam of Tarts seemed empty at first until he saw the owner flicking a feather duster over the pin tables in the shadowy, cavernous back room. There was no sign of any ladies of the night, however, so he ordered a coffee, relaxed into the corner and fell asleep.

When Fergus woke later, he lurched to his feet and hurried outside to search for loitering women. Four teenagers were standing on the corner, hair blowing wild and tatty in the chill north wind, shivering in their split-skirts and see-through blouses. He stood in the semi-dark, fingering his handcuffs and listening to the rain trickling down a blocked gutter in the grey building behind him. He could hear the roar of the multimillion pound harbour which never slept. He watched the lorries rumble past, filled with produce en route to wealthy markets, and he glanced back to the shivering girls, traditional flotsam and jetsam of a winners' world. He knew that he stood at the watershed of his life. If he failed now this failure would lead to more introspection and more self-doubts until he was running out of control. *Compassion or duty?* But were the two always set so irreconcilably against each other?

'So be it,' he said, as he turned his back on the ladies of the night and walked back to Ladywell where he had parked his car.

11

It was eight a.m, cold and overcast. Jason had stoically endured the humiliation of being driven to school by a parent in the lift club, Jock had been left with a neighbour and Clara had been about to leave for the office when she decided to spend another hour sorting Patrick's data. This was becoming an obsession. Every night she spent at least an hour on the files and she had sorted stacks of accounts and figures in bits and pieces and hundreds of e-mails to and from various e-mail addresses. Despite hundreds of communications, it appeared that there were four main entrepreneurs, including Patrick, who reported daily to each other about their business interests. Who were they and what exactly was their business? Shipping goods? She wasn't sure what was going on, but since Patrick was involved it had to be something to do with shipping.

She was still sorting fragments when she heard footsteps on the gravel drive. The bell rang. The moment she opened the door and saw the Inspector's serious expression, she cringed.

'What's happened? Is Jason . . . ?'

'I've come about your husband, Mrs Connor.'

She stepped back feeling alarmed. 'Have you found . . . ?'

'Scuba divers discovered the wreck of the *Connemara* with a body in the cabin. It has been taken to the morgue.'

He reached out and took hold of her arm as she turned pale. 'I know you must feel shocked, but, after all this time, surely you must have expected the worst. I'm sorry that I have to ask you to identify the remains.'

She shuddered and went to the window, playing for time while she pulled herself together. A squirrel was trying to prise a peanut out of the bird feeder. The nuts came out one at a time, but he wanted them in a hurry. Perhaps she should put some out in a box. He was still trying to gnaw a hole through the wire when the Inspector took hold of her shoulders. He was a kind man, she thought inconsequentially.

'You have to face up to this, Mrs Connor. There's no alternative. It won't take long, but it won't be pleasant for you. I'd better warn you that after almost four weeks underwater, bodily remains are generally unrecognisable.'

She shuddered and moved away from the window, wishing he would go away. Reality had started to detach itself. She was worried that she might forget something. Was the cooker off? Was the back door locked? Where was her bag?

'I'm sorry. In these cases, little things — birth marks, scars, or personal possessions, such as watches — are used to identify the body. We'll try make it easier for you and I'll bring you home as quickly as I can.'

'Just give me a few minutes to pull myself together.'

She checked the doors and windows and the cooker, fetched her coat and checked that she had her keys, moving with a strange sense of detachment. Like being in a bubble, she thought. For a month she had carried an image in her head: it was of a face beaten to a pulp, nose flattened, teeth smashed away, the jaw wobbling loose, his cheek battered to a shapeless mass. Surely these nightmares had no factual basis. She would soon know. When she came downstairs the Inspector was waiting by the front door.

He kept up a dialogue of small talk as they raced down a narrow leafy lane to the river with its reeds and willow-draped islands, while Clara tried to keep her attention on the ducks and swans. Anything but Patrick.

The view changed abruptly as they turned right under the railway bridge, past the defunct gas works and a few factories, to the mortuary, where Fergus parked.

The morgue attendant, young, blond and listless, ushered them into the examination room. Avoiding the trolley, he lead them towards a table where the exhibits were laid out.

'Would you come and look at these items please, Mrs Connor?'

Clara hardly listened to what the Inspector was saying. Drawn like a magnet to the corpse, she veered towards the steel table and tugged at the plastic sheet that slithered to the floor.

As the sweet, choking stench of death rose around her, suffocating her, she gazed as if in a trance at the half-rotted cadaver and the skeletal head picked clean of flesh. There lay the evidence of all she had feared and witnessed in her worst nightmares. She had hoped with all her heart that these images were nothing but a by-product of concussion, but here was the reality. It was all true. All her memories. Patrick had been battered half to death and it wasn't by the explosion. How could it be since she'd witnessed his awful wounds before the yacht blew up?

Was this all that was left of his beauty? The muscles of his neck had been full and strong, his face broad, his cheeks sharp and sloping, his eyes the deepest possible blue, fringed with black lashes, his hair thick and black and rugged. Gone now! His face, so beautiful and well-loved was eaten away. Christ! There was nothing left: a heap of fractured bones, flesh eaten and scarred, a skull's head. Patrick's fearless, devil-may-care, reckless spirit had quit the scene, abandoning his bones to fishes and crabs. So where was he? Had his spirit endured? Clara had only a few brief memories of a church-inspired heaven, nothing that could comfort her.

She heard sharp cries like a small animal makes and realised it was herself. The stench was like a living thing. Need to get out of here. Must try to move. Fergus was running towards her. She shuddered as he helped her to the sickbay and on to a stretcher bed.

'God! How horrible,' she sobbed. 'No, I'm all right. I'm all right.' She was only vaguely aware that the Inspector was rocking her to and fro. Fergus tried to take her hand but she pushed him away and stood up shakily. 'Please, go away. I think I'm going to throw up.' Moments later she was in the lavatory, her head over the bowl.

Clara knelt there for a long time, but she wasn't going to lose her nausea that easily. She would live with it for days, she realised. Eventually she got up and went out to sit on the bed again, rocking backwards and forwards, her arms crossed over her stomach.

After a few minutes, she pulled herself together and washed her face with cold water. She tried to stifle the buzzing in her ears and the feeling of not being there at all, but eventually she gave up and returned to the waiting room where Fergus and the attendant were standing.

'I'm so sorry, Mrs Connor. I'd hoped to prevent you from seeing such an awful sight.' He looked upset and this surprised her.

'Don't you understand? I see it nightly.' She put her hand over her mouth. 'Those awful wounds. I see them in my worst nightmares. So it's all true. You must see that.'

She took a tissue out of her pocket and wiped her forehead. 'I couldn't believe — I wanted to see for myself — I'm feeling better now,' she muttered. 'There isn't much left, is there? This is a terrible thing.'

'As the next of kin I need you to positively identify the corpse,' Fergus murmured. 'Can you manage to do this? We have to go back inside again. Perhaps you can recognise something else: his clothes and possessions, or any identifying marks.'

'I'm all right. Truly. Let's go.'

Fergus hung around looking inadequate and

falling over his feet. 'If you're sure. Would you like a mask?'

'Please.'

She put it on and pushed through the doors, walking firmly to the table.

'Yes, all those things belong to my husband. I bought the watch at the diving shop in Canterbury the Christmas before last. That was his ring and his tag which he wore as a bracelet to show he was allergic to penicillin. That was his gold chain and the medallion on a thong he had taken to wearing. I don't know where they came from.' But she remembered when she first saw the medallion and the earring and how shocked she had been.

'And the clothes?' Fergus asked.

'Patrick's. Everything is Patrick's.'

She hung onto her calm and asked the question that had been uppermost for a month: 'Just how did the right side of his face get so badly smashed, with the teeth gone and . . . everything . . . ? What is your explanation?'

Fergus shrugged. 'We can assume that the explosion had sent an iron bar, or something similar, flying against his face. His cheekbones and jaw are fractured, too. There was another blow on the left side of his head. Don't forget there were two explosions as well as a fire. Of course, we're waiting on the forensic report.'

Yet the wounds were sustained before the accident. Otherwise how would she have known about it? But could you call nightmares knowing? She frowned and clasped her hands together.

101

'And these blows killed him?' Her voice was hoarse and she cleared her throat.

'The pathologist believes that the victim died of drowning.'

She gasped and put one hand over her mouth.

'Did your husband have a tattoo of a butterfly on his right shoulder?' Fergus asked.

'Oh yes.'

She had to get out of there. She rushed to the swing doors, pushing through, hurrying along the corridor, by-passing the waiting room and out into the fresh air. She took deep breaths, leaning against the wall, feeling dizzy and loathsome. Would she ever get the stench out of her lungs? Fergus was right behind her.

'Well done,' he said, sounding ridiculously banal. 'We have to go into the waiting room to sign the papers.'

She walked back as if in a trance. 'I don't know how to start. Perhaps I should have told you before, but why would the police be interested in my dreams. But they are driving me crazy. The truth is — there's more to it than you realise.'

'Try to relax. Just three more minutes, Mrs Connor.'

'Don't patronise me. Just listen, Inspector. Night after night I have the same nightmare. I hear this noise. A terrible groaning. I go up on deck, I force open the hatch. And then — '

Fergus looked distressed as, in stops and starts, she poured out her images. 'Haven't you seen the corpse? Isn't it as I described?'

'It would seem so,' he said uneasily.

'Well then.'

'I'll fetch some water,' the attendant said. He hurried off.

'Something happened on the boat that night. I saw my husband as smashed and battered as his corpse is now.'

The attendant returned carrying a glass of water and two aspirins. She sipped the water and refused the pills.

'I wanted to touch him, to kiss him goodbye, but I couldn't . . . Just couldn't — I'll live with this for the rest of my life. He was a good sailor. The best! He wasn't careless. I'm so frightened, Inspector. What sort of a person can do such a thing? There's a cruel, sadistic killer stalking me and he knows that I saw him. That's why he tried to kill me. My son and I are in great danger. What are you going to do about it?'

'We'll do everything we possibly can, Mrs Connor, but of course the coroner will make his decision as to how your husband died.'

Watching Mrs Connor blurting out her fear and frustration, Fergus felt inadequate to cope. There was little he could do without a murder charge. Why hadn't she told him before? Had she made it up after seeing her husband's corpse? But why would she want to do that?

'I'll document your suspicions, Mrs Connor. In fact, I already have, but the verdict is a matter for the coroner to decide at the inquest. Until then my hands are tied. There are just a few formalities. Please sit down. If the corpse is that of your husband would you please say so and sign here.' He placed a form in front of her.

Clara sat down and buried her face in her hands. 'I positively identify the corpse, the tattoo and personal effects as that of my late husband, Patrick Connor,' she read from the form, her voice thick with tears.

'Please sign here, Mrs Connor.'

She took the pen and signed shakily. 'Can we go now?'

'Of course.'

The drive back was fraught with tension. Fergus tried to draw her out, but she ignored him. Ten minutes later he parked in her driveway.

'Mrs Connor, don't go yet. It would help if you could make a statement stating that you saw your husband lying on the deck badly injured before the explosion.'

'You mean I should lie?'

'No, of course not. I thought you might have remembered something by now.'

'Don't you think I long to remember? All I get are these awful nightmares.'

Fergus hurried to open her door, but by then she was already gone.

He started the engine and drove away feeling strangely empty. What did they really have as evidence for a murder charge? Her dreams and his intuition! Not enough to impress Bates. Nevertheless he would go back and write a report about Clara Connor's new evidence.

★ ★ ★

When Fergus arrived back at his desk the following afternoon, there was a terse note telling him to see the DCI at once. He wasn't particularly surprised.

'He's been yelling for you for the past hour,' Marion Jennings muttered. 'Something's got at him this morning.'

Bates was standing at the window looking at the street where groups of young men had congregated under the lights. When Bates glanced over his shoulder, Fergus saw that he looked exhausted. His white hair needed a wash, there were bags under his blue eyes and he seemed to be ageing daily. Lately he'd acquired a dispirited stoop.

'Sit down,' he said mildly enough. 'We're in the front line here, Fergus, and I don't want you to forget that. Dover's suffering from an identity crisis. Kent is in the throes of unparalleled change. It's like a massive building site. Here in Dover we're merging with European territory which includes a large chunk of North-Western France. Add to this, the asylum seekers and anyone can see we've got problems.'

Bates scowled over his spectacles. '6,000 illegals enter Britain each month, most of them via our town. Quite a few of them are hanging around below. Twenty if they're a day although they claim to be under eighteen. I've been watching them.'

Fergus got up and joined his superior at the window and studied the groups of dark-haired men whom the local girls seemed to find irresistible, although Fergus hadn't been able to work out why.

'It's getting worse all the time, but the point is,

you can't blame these people for trying for a new deal and a better life. So, Fergus, I have a vendetta of my own. I want to catch the criminals running the gangs that are bringing in these immigrants. They're very sophisticated indeed as far as making money is concerned. They're local and they're putting away millions in foreign banks. I want them arrested, brought to trial and put away. This must be your major case.'

'Yes, sir.' Fergus smiled with relief. At last he had something real to investigate.

Bates turned back from the window and sat down heavily.

'About Connor's death. The coroner in his wisdom has made his decision: 'Accidental Death'. He's about to release the body to the family.'

'But sir . . . '

'Dreams and intuition have no place in this office, Inspector. Let it go.'

Fergus picked up his file and hurried across the road to the cafe where he bought a carton of coffee and drank it hurriedly. Seconds later a burning pain in his stomach almost felled him. Was he getting an ulcer? He'd have to find a way to cope with tension. Would Mrs Connor feel relieved at the verdict? The thought made his nerves thrill with anxiety. Patrick Connor's death was no longer his concern, he reminded himself. He'd have to find a way to let go, but not before he'd checked out a few details for his own peace of mind.

12

For the next few days Fergus could not rid himself of the memory of Clara Connor, her eyes wide and frightened, as she described her husband's injuries. If her dreams were based on reality then Patrick Connor was attacked before the explosion, in which case she was in danger as the only witness to a capital crime.

Supposing Connor had been brutally beaten and left to drown when his attacker blew up the yacht. Where was Mrs Connor during the attack? Hiding? Watching? Helping? He shuddered. At the same time there was no mistake about her very genuine fear. Fear of what? The killer, or the law? If a killer existed, he must have left the yacht before the explosion. Had she heard an engine? It was just one of many questions that ruined his sleep. He felt uneasy about Connor's death and he decided to have one last try to get the DCI to open a murder docket.

Bates had recovered his poise and was looking a little healthier, Fergus thought, when he approached him in the gym at the health studio on the beachfront. Seeing him in shorts and a T-shirt he realised that Bates had been a dedicated body-builder for most of his life, until his wife took ill.

'If you're interested in joining, the office is down there.' Bates scowled and pointed to the corridor.

Not a very good start. 'The truth is, I wanted to talk to you about the Connor case.'

'There's no such animal. Listen, Fergus, this is where I come to relax, on the rare occasions when I get the chance.'

'I'm impressed, but I had to see you.'

'I can't imagine why you bother. The coroner has spent several days studying Miles' post mortem findings and statements from various shipping experts regarding the force of the explosion and the damage it might do. Connor's injuries were consistent with such an incident. He also had the medical report from Clara Connor's doctor, who pointed out that the mind will always fill voids with acceptable images which resemble real memories. You yourself reported that the heavy outboard engine landed up in the stateroom. The yacht was holed in several places. In any event we were lucky to find Connor's corpse in one piece. The verdict of death by misadventure prevents me from reopening the case without new evidence, even if I wanted to, but, Fergus, I don't. End of story. The corpse is being released for burial today.'

Fergus gave up and left. Finally he decided to check around in his own time. Another dive to the Connors' wrecked yacht might prove worthwhile, too, he decided.

The yacht club was almost deserted when Fergus arrived at seven a.m. the following morning. There was no sign of the club secretary, but he caught sight of the pudgy face and slightly protuberant blue eyes of Doug Evans, scuba diver, sailor and one-time drinking

108

buddy. Flamboyant and amusing when drunk, he was subdued and shy when sober and right now he was sitting mournfully at the bar with a cup of black coffee beside him.

'Mind if I sit down?' Fergus asked.

'Jon!' Evans leaped to his feet, his moon-face split into a broad smile while his purple cheeks glowed like beacons. 'I thought you were in Canterbury.'

'They sent me back here.'

'Dover hot enough for you? I heard there's been a few clashes between immigrants and locals up Folkestone Road.'

Fergus nodded and smiled which was his way of not getting sidetracked.

'Mind if I pick your brains, Doug?'

'Go ahead. Not that there's much of the grey matter left. Mainly pickled.'

Too true to be funny, Fergus thought, but he managed a grin. 'Coffee, Jon?'

'No thanks. I have another appointment.' He experienced a sharp sense of alienation from his old friend. Occupational disease, he decided. 'I went down with Perry and Krantz to retrieve Connor's corpse. Nasty business. I can't imagine why he didn't check the gas tanks.'

'It's a mystery, Jon. Patrick was a perfectionist. You know something? It's hard to believe he had gas aboard. He loathed it. Never cooked. He rarely started the engine to get to his moorings. He had to do it the hard way.' Evans pronounced his consonants carefully in his soft, Welsh accent.

'So where does everyone get their gas, Doug?'

'Any of the ships' chandlers, but probably

Jerry Watson's place down in Snargate Street, since the two of them were friends. It's called Harbour Heights Ships' Chandlers.'

'Did Mrs Connor ever come down to the yacht club? How much can you tell me about her?'

'She came along on social nights when they were first married, but I haven't seen her for over a year. She gave a party here on her husband's birthday. That was about eighteen months ago. Lovely woman. Too good for Pat.' Doug seemed bitter about it.

'How about sailing? Did she and her husband go out together?'

'Not that I know of. She used to sail, but she gave it up years ago. When she remarried a sailing man I thought we'd see more of her. Hell of a shame she should be widowed again, although this time she's probably better off.'

Fergus looked up with a flicker of curiosity. 'Why so?'

'Rumour has it that her husband lived a double life: in France with a young girl he was sweet on and in Dover with his wife. They say he commuted regularly across the Channel. I don't know how true this is. Ask Bernard Fraser. He's the one who told me.'

Clearly Evans had disliked Connor. Fergus was beginning to agree with him. How anyone could two-time a woman like Mrs Connor was beyond him. 'So where would I find Fraser?'

'He's a lawyer. He has offices off Market Square, or you might find him at his shipping agency in Townwall Street. Got his finger in a dozen pies. Greedy bugger!' Evans took out a handkerchief and wiped his forehead. 'Tittle-tattling isn't really my style, but since you asked.'

'Thanks for your time.' Fergus stood up. 'I'm up against a deadline, so I'll be getting along. Good to see you again, Doug.'

Did Mrs Connor know about her husband's affair? If so, she'd kept this information to herself. But why? This put an entirely new slant on the case. Apprehension surged. Deep in thought Fergus missed his exit and had to drive miles along the motorway before he could turn back.

★   ★   ★

It was mid-afternoon before he had the chance to visit the Harbour Heights Ships' Chandlers. Jerry Watson was in his shirt sleeves and overalls humping sacks around his warehouse. There was a strong smell of coffee, spices, fish and paraffin. Jerry was a tall man in his late thirties, deeply tanned and he'd kept himself fit, Fergus noticed. He flashed his capped teeth while his blue eyes stared unblinkingly. The effect was strangely unnerving.

'So what can I do for you?' He sat on a sack and rubbed his hands on his overalls while the scent of aftershave wafted around him.

Fergus introduced himself and showed his badge.

'I believe Patrick Connor ordered his supplies from you?'

'Ah! So that's why you're here. Terrible

111

business, isn't it?' His insincerity was obvious. 'Sure, he bought from me sometimes. So what?'

'Did he buy gas often?'

'Clara ordered the gas. He wouldn't have gas on board.'

'Did she often order their supplies?'

'No, never, and she never went on any of his trips before. At least, not that I know of. Not until the last trip, that is.'

Fergus felt stunned. Why hadn't Mrs Connor mentioned this?

'I queried it with her, but she insisted that the order came from Pat. I've heard the cock and bull story about the gas tanks leaking in the storm. Those tanks were bolted upright. Irwin, my driver, never fails to check. If Patrick had known he had gas on board he would have double-checked the tanks before starting the engine. He was a cautious bastard, but he must have been a sod to live with. He owed her a packet and he was having an affair.'

So Watson thought Clara Connor had murdered her husband. That was an unpleasant jolt. Fergus tried a few more questions without much joy. Five minutes later he took his leave and left, but Watson's words kept coming back into his mind. '*Clara ordered the gas. He wouldn't have gas on board . . . and she never went on any of his trips before.*'

He had a sudden vision of blue eyes smiling guilelessly. Could she be that good an actress? He felt an overwhelming need to find the truth, but Mrs Connor wasn't helping with her reticence and her secrets. He felt intensely irritated with her. Why was she holding back so much evidence?

★　★　★

A spate of muggings, shop break-ins and brawls kept Fergus working flat out. Three days passed before he was able to follow up the last of Doug's leads. He arrived at Bernard Fraser's chambers in Market Square just before lunch. Something about Fraser's bluff, hearty manner reminded Fergus of a bad actor mismanaging a role. He showed his badge, sat down uninvited and took out his notebook.

'I'd like to ask you a few questions, Mr Fraser. I believe Patrick Connor was a friend of yours. His corpse has been found in the wreck of the *Connemara*.'

Fraser switched to full alert. 'Yes, I'm going to the cremation. As a close family friend and Patrick's lawyer, I'd like to know exactly what you are investigating.'

'Mrs Connor has been followed and her dog was poisoned. There may be a connection between these incidents and her late husband.'

'I wouldn't be surprised.'

Fraser's relief at his answer was badly disguised. Fergus wondered what he'd been expecting.

'Pat was a ruthless bastard, the kind to make enemies. I tried to get Clara to move away for a while. I offered her the use of my holiday cottage, but she wasn't interested.'

'I heard that her husband owed a great deal of

113

money to unknown colleagues.'

'I heard something like that,' Fraser mumbled. He seemed to have induced a state of unnatural calm. Why would he need to, Fergus wondered?

'Did the late Patrick Connor have a girlfriend?'

Fraser laughed harshly. 'Did he? I would say so. Dozens of them, but lately he was shacked up with a girl hardly out of her teens.' There was a long pause. 'Okay, so he was my friend and client, but he treated his wife shabbily. We had a number of arguments about it. No sooner were they married than he wanted her house mortgaged to start him in business.'

'And Mrs Connor did that?' Fergus felt a deepening sense of sadness for her.

'Against my wishes, yes. Pat showered her with compliments every time he wanted something. He owed her a packet when he asked for a divorce. She wasn't keen. God knows why. Perhaps she thought she'd never see the cash if she divorced him.'

Yet Mrs Connor had said that she loved her husband. Why hadn't she disclosed that her marriage was on the rocks?

'Who's the girlfriend?' Fergus asked.

'I don't know. He kept her well-hidden in France. Bought her a house there.'

After a few more questions Fergus left feeling angry and disturbed. Connor's death was not quite as straightforward as Bates had hoped. He decided to have it out with Clara Connor there and then.

'What sort of a fool am I?' Fergus harangued himself as he drove up Cowper Road and turned towards the common. Patrick Connor's death was no longer his concern and his desire to do the right thing for the grieving widow was turning sour on him. Bates would have something to say about this waste of time. The DCI's words came back to him as he turned into the Connor's driveway:

'Re. Connor's death, the Coroner in his wisdom has made his decision: 'Accidental Death'. He's about to release the body to the family . . . Dreams and intuition have no place in this office, Inspector. Let it go.'

He parked behind the garage and walked to the front door, but when he lifted his hand to ring the bell he was disconcerted to see Clara Connor standing watching him from the window. Their eyes met, but there was no greeting smile. She stood motionless, scrutinising him, as if trying to appraise him.

He stared back and then made a tentative gesture as a form of greeting. She disappeared and moments later the door opened and he was startled by her melancholy expression.

As he stepped inside he hadn't the faintest idea what to say. What on earth was he supposed to be investigating? His voice seemed to work of its own volition: 'I spent several hours following up on your intuition about the possibility of your husband having been murdered, even though the verdict was Accidental Death. But still, I thought . . . ' His silence hung around them menacingly.

She stepped back and he followed her inside. The door closed behind him and Fergus found himself feeling acutely troubled as he followed her into the living room.

'You didn't tell me your husband had asked for a divorce.'

She shuddered at the mention of divorce and he gained the impression that it wasn't something she liked to remember.

'Ancient history, Inspector. Patrick had an affair and she . . . that is, the other woman . . . ' Clara broke off and sat down by the desk. 'She left him.'

Fergus could see that her pride had been dented and she was very proud.

As if sensing his thoughts, she said, 'I adored my husband, but I failed to make him happy.' She sighed. 'After she'd left him he asked me to forgive him. He said his feelings for her were well and truly dead and that he'd come to his senses. The usual thing that men say in such circumstances.' She watched him pensively and managed a slight smile. 'Of course, I agreed. I decided to put the incident behind me and never to think of it again. Later Patrick asked me to go on holiday with him. A second honeymoon. That was why we were on the boat together when the accident occurred.' She shook her head sadly.

'I don't believe he was ever very serious about her. I've been told she was young and lovely. I suppose my husband was grasping for his youth. He started to do such silly things: he slimmed

116

down, wore an earring in one ear, grew his hair, wore hippy clothes. Strangely enough, he seemed to be able to carry it off. He was a very handsome man. But it wasn't him . . . not the man I married.'

'Surely you were incensed that he bought a house in this woman's name, when he had not repaid the mortgage you took out to finance his business?'

'Who told you that? It was a rumour I heard, but I never believed it. Patrick was always broke. He wasn't a good businessman.'

'Jerry Watson told me that it was you who ordered the gas. Is that true?' Fergus pushed her.

'Patrick was busy. Perhaps I should explain. He said that certain people he owed money to were looking for him. He didn't want them to know he was in Dover, so he asked me to order the gas.'

She was very plausible and he had to admit that Fraser's information was only hearsay. Either way Clara Connor was in a no-win situation. Yet Fergus liked her. She had style and courage and she was a warm, sympathetic person, but he knew there was only one factor that should concern him — was she guilty?

13

Patrick had always been a loner, but no one would guess that from the crowds of mourners dressed in their darkest clothes who were gathering in groups in the shadow of the stark Gothic church, chatting and laughing quietly, their backs firmly turned to the graves. Together they formed a cross-section of River's well-heeled community, but appearances could be deceptive.

Clara shivered. Her courage was almost depleted and the day had hardly started. She was supposed to be grieving, not flinching at every sound and movement. Surely today of all days she should leave the terror at home, but since the discovery of Patrick's corpse she was now convinced that he'd been murdered. The thought that the killer might be out there, watching her, waiting for his chance to strike, dominated every moment of every day, even today. The killer was devious, patient and very evil. Was he here, dressed in a dark suit, his face wreathed in compassionate smiles? She knew he would come again. He had unfinished business to attend to.

Together with Sib and Jason, she was standing around in the driveway to greet the mourners before they went into the church. Rain was threatening, leaves were gathering against the wall and spiralling round the tombstones while overhead low black clouds flew in the face of the east wind. As the purple dusk gave way to darkness, the congregation began to file into the picturesque church of St. Peter and Paul in River for the service, prior to the cremation.

Standing tall at her side, she watched her son shaking hands with people they knew, nodding to others, wearing his anonymous expression, which was Jason's way of coping with Patrick's friends, whom he detested.

Sibyl was hovering slightly to the right of her, looking deceptively naive in her borrowed black suit. Black was not a colour that she normally wore, but in her inimitable way she had turned it into something exciting, her flaming hair flaunting life and lust. Cover her with a sack and she would still provoke admiration, Clara thought. Her warm hand was comforting and Clara was grateful for her moral support.

Bernie, tall and elegant in his dark mohair suit, paused in front of Clara, his brown eyes alert and questioning. 'You should have kept it small and discreet. I'd feel better if you'd go inside.' His voice carried like a stage whisper. Heads turned their way.

She scowled at Bernie. She was jittery enough without his help. 'We're coming soon. You go ahead.'

Bernie looked taken aback. He seemed about to make a rude retort when he thought better of it. He strode away looking furious.

'He who must be obeyed,' Clara whispered to Sib. She thrust away her fears as she walked arm-in-arm with her friend towards the church.

Piers Ferretti, Sib's father, was standing inside

119

the door handing out the Order of Service he and Sib had designed and printed in his printing shop. He was a short, wiry man with a clownlike thatch of fading red hair that grew around his bald dome. Piers was a man who laughed and joked a great deal and now that he could not, she was struck by the shrewdness in his grey eyes.

'Thank you for this, Mr. Ferretti. It's really beautiful.'

The front cover picture of Patrick standing on his yacht and waving goodbye was corny, to the say the least, but there was nothing wrong with the quality of the printing. She wondered where Sibyl had found the photograph. She'd never seen it before, which was curious.

'Sib, where did you get this photograph?' she asked as they reached their pew.

Sib seemed agitated. She frowned, stared at her feet and flushed deep red. Sib looked up and for a moment their eyes met. Clara read guilt and self-loathing, but that was absurd.

'I've never seen this photograph before in my life,' Sib said vehemently.

It was just one of those God-awful days, Clara thought, trying to keep her mind on the here and now. She looked around at masses of brilliant flowers filling the church with their heady scent.

'Thank you, Sib. I shudder to think what this cost you. You must have spent hours here.' She noticed Sib's tearful cheeks. That wasn't like Sib.

The choir burst into song: *For those in peril on the sea*. Patrick's closest friends: Robin, Jerry and Bernie, together with the black-clad pallbearers from the undertakers, carried the

120

polished coffin from the hearse and laid it by the altar. Clara tried not to look, remembering the gruesome contents at the mortuary. How could she reach the end of the sermon without breaking down? Perhaps by groping back through time and space to happier times.

Once her husband had loved her with all the deep sexuality of his Mediterranean blood. And she, in turn, had loved him with every ounce of her being. She'd been his wife, his sex-slave and his comforter, his psychiatrist when he was retrenched, his backer when he launched his business. She'd lavished him with all that she owned, and shared his hopes and dreams and his disillusion. She'd loved him every second of every day with the fiery intensity of her red-hot, passionate nature. He'd been so beautiful and nothing that he had done could take away her memories.

The choir was singing the last hymn: *God be with you till we meet again*, and the ordeal was half over.

★ ★ ★

It was starting to rain. The tyres whooshed on tarmac as Bernie sped towards the crematorium, while the windscreen wipers thumped a monotonous dirge.

By the time Bernie parked in the crematorium's yard beside the empty hearse, the rain had stopped. Miraculously the sun was shining briefly. Clara turned towards the garden where raindrops sparkled on leaves and the cobbled path shone like a burnished shield.

'You go ahead, all of you, please. I want to be alone for a few minutes.'

Looking baffled and misunderstood, Bernie hunched his shoulders and hurried to the entrance.

Beside the car park was a small wooded garden with a bench under a birch tree. She sat down and watched the sparrows darting amongst the shrubs searching for grubs. She needed her strength to get through the rest of the day.

'Mrs Connor,' a foreign voice said very quietly right behind her, startling her. She was immobilised by fear. Strong hands seized her shoulder and neck, pushing her hard against the bench. She tried to lurch forward, but he was stronger. She could scream, but the taped organ music coming from the chapel would drown her cries. He leaned over her, his breath flushing her face.

'Where is he? You know, don't you?'

'Who?' Barely breathing, she tried to slip away from his hands, but the fingers pressed harder, choking her. The pain was excruciating. She wanted to beg him to stop, but she could not speak.

'Tell me.'

The hands released her. She turned painfully, too shocked to be afraid, and gazed into her stalker's unfathomable eyes. His lips were drawn back into a bitter smile, revealing teeth that were held together with intricate steel dentistry. 'So you don't know after all. Be careful. The killer will come after you.'

Bernie was racing across the yard. For a few minutes the two men grappled each other in silence until the foreigner, who was stronger than he looked, pushed Bernie away and ran into the road.

'Keep away from Mrs Connor,' Bernie shouted. They heard a car's engine start up and the wheels squealing on tarmac.

'Come inside, Clara.' Bernie shrugged his jacket back on to his shoulders, straightened his collar and tie and pushed his hands over his hair. 'I'm sorry you got harassed by scum like that. I saw it all. I should have been faster.'

'He's the man who followed me and searched the office. What does he want? Why is he here?'

'Damned immigrants had it in for Patrick for all kinds of reasons.'

'You have to tell me what's going on.'

'I wish I knew and that's the truth, Clara. Patrick played things close to the cuff. Now let's get on with the cremation.'

Fear and grief vied for precedence as she walked into the crematorium. As she watched Patrick's coffin slide into the furnace she made a solemn promise that she would find her husband's killer.

14

The bills were piling up and the mortgage remained unpaid, but Clara had thrown all her efforts into relaunching the tour agency and each day brought several queries from travel agents and shipping companies. On Monday morning, when she opened her mail, she found her first firm booking from a local travel agency to take a party around the castle and cliffs later that week. There was a statement from the Harbour Heights Ships' Chandlers in Snargate Street, which said simply: 'To items purchased October — £3,000', but there were no details. And what had happened to the invoice? Here was a good excuse to question Jerry Watson about Patrick's colleagues. She called for an appointment and Jerry told her to come right round.

Once she'd got into her car and left her parking spot, she realised that it would have been as quick to walk, but too late; someone had driven into her spot. She drove to the end of the road and parked in the corner of Jerry's yard. Bathed in winter sunlight, Jerry was sitting in an enclosed garden at the back of the warehouse grooming three reluctant huskies. His blond hair shimmered in the light breeze and he looked fit and athletic. He would have been attractive, Clara thought, if it weren't that his astonishing blue eyes were set too closely together over a long nose. It worked for his dogs, but not for Jerry.

'Clara! No one told me you'd arrived. Meet Boris, Tanya and Natasha.' The huskies stared at her curiously.

'Beautiful dogs.' It was a fact, not a compliment.

'Yes. It's hard to believe how tough they are. Comes from all those generations pulling sleighs over the tundra.' His strong hands were working the comb through the dog's hair with light, but effective movements. He caught the brush in a tangle and Tanya winced, showing her yellow teeth, but flinched when Jerry lifted his hand. A control freak, Clara decided.

'So what can I do for you, Clara?'

'I came to see you about this account.'

Jerry reached for it, frowned and stood up. 'We'll have to go up to my office.' He tore himself away from his dogs with obvious reluctance.

Jerry's glass-enclosed offices were situated on a mezzanine floor, half-encircling the building, with access via hazardous steel steps. From his eyrie he could see every part of his large, open-plan warehouse.

'Here we are! Now what's your problem?'

Clara was stunned by his obvious antagonism. She could not recall any fights with Jerry. What had she ever done to him? She slid her statement across the desk. 'There are no details. I mean, really, what's it for?'

Jerry frowned and peered suspiciously at her. Paranoid, Clara decided.

'Surely this should go to Patrick's lawyer. Isn't he winding up the estate? I would have thought you had enough on your plate without this kind of thing.'

'I'm relaunching Connor Tours. To be honest I need an income and here's a ready-made business. Naturally I have to pay the accounts.'

'You're mad. The business isn't worth a damn. There's no goodwill. I know Patrick left you in a mess, with the mortgage and debts and I sympathise, but take my advice, don't make it worse than it already is.'

'No, you're wrong,' she temporized playfully. 'I've had dozens of inquiries. I'm offering ten new tours and this morning I received my first firm booking. That's pretty good, you have to admit.'

'Do you know how to run a business? Have you costed it properly? I suggest you stick to teaching history. At least you'll get a regular income.'

Clara couldn't help wondering why everyone was trying to keep her out of the agency, but this was no time to get offended.

'To be honest, I am. Most of the tours are historical. I've written a small piece about the vital role of the cliffs in defending Britain, covering the first rebuffed Roman invasion, and moving on to the role of the cliffs in the First and Second World Wars. So far I have sixteen tourists booked for Friday morning. I think it's going to work, so, Jerry, I really do need to know about this invoice.'

He reached for a file labelled 'Confidential' on

a shelf above him, leafed through it and handed a statement to her.

'This what you want?'

She checked that the totals matched and skimmed through the items: lifejackets, first aid kits, sea-sickness pills, anoraks, thermal vests, a hot water urn. Her stomach twisted as she considered the implications.

'I don't understand. Why would Patrick want these items?'

'How should I know? Everything was delivered to the Marina, as usual.' His voice had reached a hostility that went beyond politeness.

She could see he was lying. 'Why didn't you include the details on the statement?'

'Clara, this is how Patrick liked it to be. He checked the invoices monthly when he paid in cash.'

In cash! She fought off a surge of panic. Just how many people could you get on his yacht? Then she remembered the *Valkyr*, the lobster boat Patrick had converted for his so-called treasure hunting venture.

'Him and his partners?' she stammered. Her mouth had gone dry.

'Stop fishing, Clara.'

'Unfortunately this can't be paid until Patrick's estate is sorted out.'

'Naturally not. There's no hurry.' He took the invoice from her. 'If you hang on a minute, I'll check the statement with my accountant.' He left, carrying the file under his arm.

Clara pulled herself together while Jerry was gone. Silly to get upset. The gear had probably been for Robin. The invoice proved nothing.

After a long wait, Clara went looking for Jerry and found him in the accounts department. He was talking on his mobile with his back turned to her. She distinctly heard him say: 'Okay, I'll issue a credit note, as long as you cover me.'

Clara crept back. Five minutes later Jerry returned with a credit note for £3,000 which he flipped across the desk.

'It seems there was an error. The accountant sends her apologies. You don't owe us anything. It was someone else's statement. Would you like coffee?'

Someone didn't want her to know about the items on the invoice. But who? Who had Jerry been talking to? She decided to try another tack.

'No coffee, thanks. I must go, but first perhaps you can help me, Jerry,' she ad-libbed. 'Patrick told me he owed cash to certain business associates. He said he was expecting a large payment that would clear his debts. I'd like to settle, but apart from Robin, I don't know who he worked with. Do you?'

Jerry shrugged. 'Sorry, Clara, but I'm not aiming to put myself at risk. Patrick was bad news. He made a lot of money fast and he got in with a dangerous crowd. I don't want to tangle with those people. If you had any sense you'd keep out of it. Pat got what he deserved.'

The bastard! Her fury got the better of her. 'Really? I'd say you're making a fortune out of them. Just how many more blank statements are there up in those confidential files of yours?'

Her gibe had scored a bull's eye. Jerry's eyes glittered.

'Let me tell you something I heard recently. It's a rumour, okay, but it came from a reliable source. Patrick was bringing in a costly load of contraband when the customs' boat came after him, so he dumped the goods in the sea in sacks.'

'I don't believe that Patrick — '

He cut in on her. 'The contraband included three illegal immigrants. One was an elderly woman. She, her son and her brother were hidden in sacks, weighted with bricks and thrown into the sea through a raised hatch in the hold. Strange that, don't you think? D'you know of any boats like that? The son, formerly a university lecturer, bit his way through the sack, but he couldn't find his mother. That's how the story goes amongst our immigrant population.'

Clara gripped the arms of her chair and stood up. She could feel the blood pounding round her body. She felt very hot as she fought back an impulse to hit out at Jerry. She grabbed her handbag and blundered down the steps.

Jerry followed her. 'Strange business, that explosion. I didn't believe Patrick was dead until I went down to the mortuary to see for myself. Not much left, was there?'

She gasped and tried to banish the image of her husband's corpse. Jerry was being offensive.

'You look upset, Clara, but there's no need to play the grieving widow with me. I happen to know the truth about your marriage. Forget Patrick. You're better off without him.'

'Get lost, Jerry.'

Clara hurried into the fresh air feeling contaminated from Jerry's spite and longing to get away from him, but he followed her and leaned in through the car window.

'Don't tell me you didn't realise that you'd lost out, Clara. I heard you refused to give him a divorce until he'd paid you what he owed. You must have known you couldn't compete with someone half your age.'

She started the car, rammed her foot on the accelerator and lurched forward, tyres screeching. Jerry jumped back fast. Briefly she saw his shocked expression as he rubbed his elbow. 'Serves you right, you sadist,' she muttered.

Despite her shock, she noticed a blue Renault Safrane pull out from the car park opposite and coast behind her. It was the same car that had parked outside the church at Patrick's cremation. On impulse, she drove up the steep North Military Road that led to the local borstal, as the Detention Centre for Young Offenders was known. The car remained behind her all the way, not even bothering with subterfuge. She gained the impression that the driver was deliberately harassing her. Feeling incensed, she put her foot down hard on the accelerator and turned into South Military Road that plunged down a precipitous slope from the cliff-top to the town.

Madness, she thought later when she parked in Snargate Street. She'd been reckless, but the driver had remained behind her all the way. She couldn't see a sign of the car now. Feeling alarmed and still shaking, she hurried to her office.

15

Jason woke from a deep sleep to the sound of his mother thrashing around uttering cries like a lost puppy. Jock was padding upstairs whining uneasily and Jason listened apprehensively, wondering if he could safely get back to sleep.

Mum let out a yelp, and Jock jumped on to his bed and lay there growling.

'It's all right, Jock. Don't worry.'

But it wasn't all right and he doubted that it ever would be. Mum was running scared, haunted by her will-o'-the-wisp images. She was angry or sad or frightened most of the time. Lately he felt unable to cope with his mother's trauma and he was bewildered by her rapid changes of mood. She was losing weight and looking older, too. Yesterday she had shouted at him and burst into tears when he objected. He couldn't remember her ever doing that before. He longed for them to be happy again, like they used to be, before Mum met Patrick. She was pining for him and that amazed and infuriated him.

She didn't know the git like he did. The slimy bastard had been full of charm when Mum was home, but the moment she went out, he changed. He'd jerk his thumb and Jason would get lost fast, taking Jock with him.

All the time he'd been conning his mother out of the cash she'd raised from a mortgage, he'd been deceiving her. Surely Mum must have heard rumours of his affair?

He remembered when he had first found out about this other woman. He'd been working in the holidays as a deck-hand on Uncle Robin's boat, which he often did because Robin was generous with his petty cash. Robin got toothache one day and made an emergency appointment with the dentist, so Patrick had to take over at short notice. He brought the girl with him. She'd sunbathed in a tanga bikini on the top deck while Patrick took the boat to Margate and back with a hundred trippers. Jason spent the day dodging Patrick and watching her through Robin's binoculars. Fortunately Robin was waiting at the quay when they berthed, so the two of them left soon afterwards without seeing him.

They made no secret of their affair and from then on Patrick was hardly ever at home. She was a real looker; exquisite face and figure and flawless, velvety skin. He couldn't figure out why she'd want to be with a wrinkly like Patrick. Was it possible Mum had never known? And if she did, why had she kept quiet about it? Surely she must have wondered why Patrick was living in France four nights out of seven?

Jason heard another whimper. He climbed out of bed and crept down the passage. As he opened the bedroom door, his mother sat bolt upright, staring at the wall. There was something truly weird about the way she looked. Perhaps she was still asleep.

'Mum! Wake up. You're safe at home.' Her eyes

132

focused and her face slowly relaxed.

'Oh, Jason. I'm sorry I woke you.'

Jock came creeping in, laid his head on the bed and rolled his eyes mournfully. Jason sat next to his mother, leaned back against a pillow and dangled his hand over the edge of the bed until the dog sidled close enough for him to stroke his short, bristly hair. After a while he sensed his mother had gone to sleep, so he went back to bed and lay there shivering.

He felt so lost. Mum wouldn't be scared for nothing. Something bad was going on and she wasn't being straight with him. He didn't know what to do or who to confide in. Later he heard his mother get up and go down to her study. He was still wondering how he could help her when he fell asleep.

★ ★ ★

Clara waited until she thought Jason was sleeping before getting up and switching on the coffee filter. She sat in the kitchen sipping the strong sweet brew, trying to forget her dream. She had been sinking, sinking, in stygian black water, tied in a sack, unable to move or breathe. Oh God! Those poor people. She had thought of little else but that horror story since her visit to Jerry. It couldn't be true. Surely not.

She tried to shake off her repugnance which had become physical. After a second cup of coffee, she thought she might as well get on with sorting Patrick's data. This seemed to be the only way she would ever find out what had been going on.

As she pushed the disc into her Mac and saw the icons appear on the screen she felt a thrill of fear. Just what was she going to discover this time? For the past two weeks she had put in hours of boring collation every night. She had sorted stacks of accounts and figures in bits and pieces and hundreds of e-mails to and from various e-mail addresses. The bank totals were staggering. Deposits of millions, transfers in hundreds of thousands, like playing Monopoly, but all the money went the same way — to Sarajevo, where it disappeared and a throw of the dice wasn't likely to bring it back.

It was Jerry who had opened her eyes. She hadn't wanted to believe him, but here was the proof. Four men, including Patrick, were picking up so-called 'consignments' in Dubrovnik and transporting them by diverse methods: boats, lorries and a few were flown in, to Dover, or Deal, or Margate. The service included a week's accommodation in a safe house in Kent, which gave them plenty of time to declare themselves destitute and oppressed at home. From then on their fate was in the lap of the Gods, or the local immigration officials. The organisers communi-cated daily by e-mail about their business interests. Three of them were forever demanding that Patrick release their share of the profits. So was Patrick the keeper of the purse, like a club secretary? Or perhaps he handled the laundering of their profits? In Sarajevo?

Any number of fragments pointed in the same

direction. She keyed into one of them. It was an e-mail to Patrick with no trace of the sender. She'd found it days ago, but so far she only had a part of the message.

⋆　⋆　⋆

' . . . we have too many consignments waiting for shipment. More boats are required urgently. They are getting restless and there are other offers available to them. Shipped 20 on July 15.'

⋆　⋆　⋆

So what sort of consignments became restless? People, obviously. So far, apart from Patrick, the organisers remained hidden behind their e-mail addresses.

She remembered the expensive car Patrick had bought himself, claiming he had hired it to give the right image to his business. At the time they were so cash-strapped Jason couldn't even have bacon with his eggs. She tried to swallow her bitterness. She was the fool who had risked their home in order to set him up in business.

She keyed in to 'consignments' again, but only meaningless phrases appeared. She was jumping the gun. Until the material was collated by date and subject, there was little point in trying to make sense of it all, but she wasn't sure how to tackle such an undertaking. Several times she had tried to see the wider picture and get a system going. It was a painstaking, boring job, but she was fuelled by a deep determination to find out who Patrick's colleagues were and who he owed money to. Ultimately she hoped to find his killer and then she would hand the evidence to the police. She had to admit that the fragments were beginning to make sense. Somewhere in this mass of information lay the key to everything that had happened.

16

Clara was becoming obsessive about those wretched people who were dumped in the sea, imagining their anguish and terror. She tried to get a grip on herself, but failed. She couldn't accept Jerry's story. She had to see for herself if there was a well wide enough to push a body through into the sea. Patrick wasn't evil. Misguided perhaps, but not evil.

Jason was going to play table-tennis at a friend's house. He left at seven p.m. promising to be back by ten, which was enough time. Clara put on a tracksuit and an anorak and drove to the marina where the *Valkyr* was moored. The boat was still hers. Bernie was selling it, but so far there had been no reasonable offers.

She had never been on the *Valkyr*. That in itself was strange since she had lent her husband the cash to buy the lobster boat and convert it for salvage operations. Patrick had been so secretive. She'd thought it was because he was losing money and she'd been too nice to ask. *Nice!* That was her downfall, she considered briefly. If she were to believe Jerry, the boat had never been used for salvage, but was fitted out for smuggling immigrants and anything else that came their way.

It began to pour and she was drenched by the time she had negotiated the slippery wooden pontoons leading to the mooring. Flicking her torch, she mounted the shifting wooden gangway to the deck and looked around.

The hatch leading to the hold was unlocked. She opened it and gazed down into pitch darkness. Even her torchlight seemed feeble and inadequate, but there was a light switch outside the hatch. She pushed it down and two dim pools of light appeared on either side of the vast, shadowy interior.

As she climbed down, a strong stench of carbolic acid and vomit turned her stomach. The lower deck had been hosed down recently and wasn't yet dry. So who had taken the boat out? And for what purpose?

From the smell, she deduced that it had been packed with people. Someone was using the *Valkyr* for criminal practices. Did Bernie know, she wondered? The more she thought about it the more likely it seemed that Patrick's partners were still using his boat. It could be the men her husband owed money to. Or his killer? The thought shocked like an electric current.

In the dim light she saw benches lining the hold and a large padded box dead centre. She wandered around and found herself in a walk-in hatch built across the stern. It was piled high with boxes of provisions, first aid equipment, a heap of sacks, a pile of bricks — ! Her stomach lurched violently. Dear God! How can this be?

Jerry was right. This boat was kitted out for smuggling people. Had Patrick taken the easy way out only to fall foul of his colleagues? She cringed with shame. How could he? But perhaps he was innocent. What if he'd found out what

138

they were doing and they had 'silenced' him. The thought brought a shiver of terror.

Seconds later she froze as she heard footsteps on the quay. The boat lurched as someone came on board. There were at least three men. But who were they? Terror gripped her. For a few moments she stood paralysed. The foul air, thick with the stench of vomit, closed in on her. She heard voices, but none that she recognised.

The *Valkyr* shuddered violently. She heard the purr of powerful engines and the sound of the gangway being lifted and stowed away. Seconds later they were speeding out of the marina. She lost her balance and fell on to the padded box and remained there, crouched over her knees, listening intently.

This was her boat and they were trespassing. She should confront them and demand they turn back to the marina. But what if these men were gangsters? 'A bad crowd,' Jerry had warned her. She decided to stay in the hold. It might prove safer. She sat on the box to wait.

She was so cold. A band of ice seemed to be tightening around her forehead. She heard a splashing sound, like water revolving in a giant bucket coming from beneath her. Barely breathing, Clara got down on her knees and switched on her torch to examine the box. There was a padlock hanging open in a clasp. She removed it and pushed up the lid, revealing a well where icy, black water heaved and splashed below as the boat thrust through the waves. It was just as Jerry had said. Who were the men on the bridge? Patrick's partners?

She heard a strange voice talking from the bridge, giving Port Control their destination. Looking out of the porthole, she saw lights. They were passing the breakwater and moving into the Channel.

Footsteps were approaching. She was a fool to have left the hatch open and the lights on. Creeping to the stern she pushed herself behind a pile of boxes. Her panting breath was loud enough to give her away. She held her breath and almost choked.

A sudden lurch of the boat as it hit a wave head-on sent boxes crashing around her. The footsteps were coming closer. Her heart was threatening to explode in her chest and she could hardly breathe. Torchlight dazzled her. Someone muttered, 'What the hell? What are you doing here?'

'This is my boat and you're trespassing.' She was surprised how calm she sounded.

'Clara! What the . . . Hang on, I'll move some of this debris.'

Robin's voice! She almost cried with relief as she scrambled to her feet. Bottles and cartons were sliding over the deck as the boat lurched in the choppy sea. 'Mind out of the way, Clara. Go and sit down. I'll clear this up.'

Robin came back and sat on the bench opposite looking twice as swarthy in the dim light, but so much like Patrick with his black hair and fine features that it made her heart lurch.

'What are you doing on Pat's boat?' she asked.

'It's for sale, isn't it? I'm thinking of making an offer. This is a trial run.'

'So who's at the helm?'

'Mate of mine, Malcolm Key, a marine engineer. Of course, my offer is subject to Malcolm's assessment. Patrick worked this boat day and night. Packed them in like sardines.'

So it was true! Robin's casual words brought anguish, but she didn't have to believe Robin. He could be lying.

'Bernie gave the okay, by the way.' Robin looked out of the porthole. 'It's getting choppy. We'll take you back, unless you feel like a trip? We'd planned to spend the night in Calais.'

'No thanks.'

'You might as well stay down here where it's warmer. I'll tell Malcolm and be right back.'

There was a smash of surf against the portholes followed by a few big rolls as the *Valkyr* turned and headed back to the marina. Shortly afterwards Robin clattered down the companionway and sat beside her.

'Won't be long.'

'You can be frank with me, Robin. I know you helped Patrick. He told me,' Clara persisted

'I helped with the salvaging venture. That's why I want the boat. There's a fortune to be made around the Goodwin Sands.'

'Yeah, well, but does treasure smell of vomit, Robin?'

He glanced at her with a sly, moody, threatening expression that made her feel uneasy.

'Bernie's been renting out the boat. Didn't he tell you?'

'Yes.'

'Hang on.' He stood up and fetch a blanket

from a pile of cartons and put it around her shoulders. 'Can't have you catching pneumonia, can we? Now, talk! What on earth do you think you're playing at, Clara?'

'I came to see if there was a well in the hold. I was told — ' She broke off and covered her face with her hands. 'God! It's terrible! I was told that Patrick disposed of his contraband cargo, including three living people.' She choked on the last words.

Robin frowned. 'I've heard the same thing. Who told you about it?'

'The police,' she lied. 'Inspector Fergus to be precise. One of them survived by biting through the sack. I saw the sacks and the bricks over there.' She shuddered. 'I was hoping against hope that there was no such well on the *Valkyr*.'

'And now you've seen it. So what? Does it make a difference?'

She didn't answer.

'There's a cage down there for keeping lobsters alive, with a hatch that opens to the sea. Patrick bought the vessel from a Spanish fisherman. You should know since you paid for it. It's a standard design and there's plenty of them around. Why blame Patrick? At the same time it wouldn't surprise me if Patrick did this. He'd acquired a veneer of culture, but underneath he was a savage bastard.'

'Everyone's bad-mouthing him now he's dead. Funny that. He was your hero when he was alive.'

'He's still my hero, make no mistake, but it helps to be realistic. He got involved with people

142

he should have steered clear of.' His deep voice was strangely convincing. 'It's time we had a little talk, Clara. I know you think Patrick was murdered. Well, so do I. If I knew who killed him, I'd kill the bastard before he gets me. Patrick made some dangerous connections, but he kept them to himself. He was into the big time. Take some good advice from me. Give up playing the detective. Keep well away.'

Robin looked like a parody of a spiv: vicious, fearful and tricky. His eyes were shying from her gaze while his shoulders sagged. He was afraid, too, she realised, and his fear was catching. An icy chill gripped her.

'Listen to me, Clara. Even if you don't care about your own safety you need to look after your boy.'

As her confidence ebbed away, she had difficulty breathing. 'What do you mean?'

'If you keep probing into Patrick's business affairs, they'll get at you through your son. He's a great kid. Too good for them to maim or frighten. Believe me, anything could happen to him. He's at risk. You must see that. I want to protect him. But how? It would be so easy for someone to knock him off his bicycle. They'd do that *to teach you a lesson*.'

Was it a warning or a threat? She had no way of knowing. She felt hollow inside. 'What . . . what are you talking about? Are you one of them? Is that what you're saying? Are you threatening me with Jason's life?'

'Calm down, Clara. I'm simply warning you of the consequences of carrying on the way you are:

prodding and prying and poking your nose into things you'd be better off not knowing. I'm trying to tell you what's going on.'

When Robin put his arm around her, she was too stunned to push him away. Is he for real? Is it a warning or a threat? She had no way of knowing.

'Listen to me carefully,' he whispered. '*They* know what you're doing, but you don't understand what these guys are like. These guys are worse than you know. First they warn you, then they break limbs. They maim and torture. Jason's my nephew. I wouldn't like him to come to any harm. These smugglers employ psychopaths as heavies. What chance would a kid like him have?'

She wanted to say *he's no relative of yours*, but she couldn't speak. She seemed to have turned to stone. Her face was burning. Eyes stinging! She shook her head, hearing her rasping breath. Her mind was a battlefield, fear and fury warring.

She got her voice back with an explosion of sound: 'How dare you . . . how dare you threaten my son! How dare you try to control me with fear.'

She felt a lurch as the *Valkyr* touched the pontoon. Robin stood up.

'Let's go.'

On deck, an icy drizzle drenched her face and trickled down her neck. She waited as Robin swung down the gangway.

He said, 'Trust me! This is tough on all of us.'

Trust him? How dare he trot out that old

144

cliché! Robin was a fool. Nevertheless her hands were shaking and her knees could hardly support her.

'You know too much for your own good,' he called as she hurried down the gangway. 'Keep it to yourself. Think of Jason.'

She wanted to run, but the pontoon was slippery. She hung on to the rope ladder so tightly she drew blood from a finger. As she hurried to the car, she willed her fury to subside and her rasping breath to quieten. Once in the car, she put her foot down and raced home.

17

'I'm your lawyer, Clara. Let's say you've inherited me.' Bernie's deep voice was entirely accentless, as if he had worked hard to eradicate any trace of his background.

Clara leaned back into the leather sofa, observing Bernie and his office. The only thing that hadn't cost a fortune was the desk pad. Even his paintings were costly originals. Easy for him to sound so relaxed. He had no problems, whereas she had so many worries she hardly knew how to sort them out. She jumped up abruptly, walked to the window and stood staring down at the cobbled market square.

'Look here, Bernie,' she said over her shoulder. 'I'm short of cash. Have you had any offers for Patrick's car or his fishing boat?'

'A couple,' he said briefly. 'So far the offers are too low. D'you want an advance? The bank will cough up any time I ask.'

'I can wait, thanks.'

'And the rest?' There was a long pause. Then he said, 'Talk to me.'

'Leave me alone, Bernie. No one believes me and I'm not wasting my breath on you.'

'You seem to have wasted your breath on everyone else. I like to think I'm your friend as well as your lawyer.'

'Think on . . .'

'Jesus, Clara. What gives you the right to be so

off-hand?' Eyes glinting with suppressed fury, Bernie crumpled a sheet of paper and flung it across the floor.

'Fear maybe. Or tension. Or the fact that you're all ganging up on me and no one has any intention of coming clean . . . '

'Whoah! I presume you're here for a reason other than a slanging match.'

She wheeled round. 'Tell me who Patrick was screwing.'

'I don't know her name, but I heard that he bought her a house in Calais and transferred it to her name. Where do you think he was all those nights away from home when he was supposed to be working? Gossip has it that she's young and exceptionally lovely and that she left him for an art dealer. That is the total sum of my knowledge of Patrick's affair. Is that all you want to know? Does it make you feel better?' He stood up and put his arm around her shoulders, but she shrugged him off.

'You can't carry this on your own, Clara. Have you seen what you look like? Do you sleep nights? Let me help you. By now you should know who your friends are.'

'You? Are you my friend?' Clara asked in a tired voice. 'I should have known what was going on. Why didn't you tell me Patrick was using my cash to set himself up in smuggling? We'll probably lose the house.'

She walked back to the sofa and sank into it, closing her eyes.

'There's worse to come. Someone's following my car on a daily basis. Someone waits outside the house at night, but the police can't seem to catch him. The office was burgled. Well, you know that. Last month someone tried to break into our house, but Jock chased them off. Then Jock was poisoned. Patrick was murdered, *and the killer knows I saw him.* That's what this is all about.'

She broke off as Bernie's secretary brought in a tray of coffee and waited for her to leave before continuing.

'Now I hear from Jerry that Patrick was into big-time smuggling. Not only that . . . ' She almost gagged on the words. 'He murdered two immigrants. Tied them in sacks weighted with bricks and flung them through the hold. The son, who managed to save himself, is in Dover looking for revenge. Just what do you think I should do?' she asked in a tired voice. 'I've thought of telling the police.'

'Do nothing. You own the *Valkyr.* You paid for the conversion. Who would believe you were so naive that you didn't guess what was going on? Besides, Patrick's boat isn't the only one with a lobster hatch. It's common practice with lobster fishermen. Waste of time to check it out. Why did you? Why didn't you come to me?'

So Robin had told him of her visit. Robin had a big mouth.

'Robin threatened me,' she said sullenly.

'Perhaps he was warning you to stop prying. Leave it to the police. They're paid to take risks. There's big money involved in smuggling. If Pat got involved in this business it would explain what happened. Or what you think happened.

148

Let go, Clara. Promise me! Just let go.'

'According to Jerry, Patrick was into big time smuggling and making a fortune. He inferred that Patrick's friends were in with him, too. The truth is I heard him telling someone about an invoice he'd sent me for £3,000. It was you, wasn't it Bernie? You're one of them.'

Bernie paled and looked mean. For a moment their eyes locked, but then he made an obvious effort to calm down.

'Okay, so I was trying to help you. I'll recover the cash from the sale of the boat. You don't have to believe everything you're told, do you? Clara, cast your mind back to last July.' Bernie leaned back and crossed his legs.

She gazed blandly at him, determined to give nothing more away, but she couldn't help remembering one tearful summer evening when Patrick had demanded a divorce and left for France. She'd been appalled and almost incoherent as she called Bernie for an appointment.

'Pat wants a divorce, but how can he . . . ? What right does he have . . . ? The mortgage debt is in my name, but the business is in his name. I need legal advice or we'll lose the house . . . all my parents' cash . . . '

Bernie had rushed over. He'd looked so earnest standing in the doorway with a bunch of flowers in one hand and a bottle of wine in the other. The rain had flattened and darkened his mop of blond hair revealing an unexpected brutishness to his wide face and square jaw. He'd stepped inside the door, placed his gifts

149

reverently on the table and made a sudden lunge at her and she'd spent the next five minutes fighting him off.

'Pat must be mad,' he'd muttered sadly when she finally convinced him that he was wasting his time. 'You're the best thing that could happen to a guy.'

She hadn't seen him for months after that. Not until Patrick died.

'Are you listening, Clara? I said the girl Pat was shacked up with at the time was previously Jerry's girlfriend. They were about to get married and Jerry was very cut up about losing her.'

'Oh!' Clara took a deep breath and leaned back trying to disguise her relief. 'That explains a great deal,' she said eventually. She would have to reassess Jerry's accusations in the light of this information.

'So let's talk about the business,' Bernie said. 'How about selling Connor Tours to me? Get your accountant to name a satisfactory price and you're on. I don't like to think of you getting involved in slime.'

'I won't earn enough teaching to cover our expenses and the mortgage repayments. I have to build up the tour agency. I have no choice. Besides, I paid for it.'

'So you're still hanging in there. If there's one thing I've always admired it's your guts. But common sense? Well, I'm not so sure about that. I dare say Patrick owed money all round.' He looked sullen, as if unwilling to be thwarted again. 'You might find yourself being sued for it.'

'By smugglers, or drug dealers? Are you

150

kidding? I have to know who Patrick's colleagues were. You know, don't you?'

'I'm bound by legal professional privilege. But Clara,' Bernie lowered his voice. 'I'm so afraid for you and your indiscretions. I can't help you for the simple reason that I don't know. Patrick believed in reverse networking. Everyone got to hate the bastard.' He gripped her shoulders and gave her a half-shake. She was about to object, but looking up she caught an expression that shocked her. Bernie was frightened. But why?

'You're afraid? Patrick was afraid, too.'

'I thought I knew everything that went on in this town, but I don't know who Patrick's connections were and it's scaring the hell out of me. All I know is that he double-crossed some very dangerous men.' He pursed his lips. 'I don't want to frighten you, Clara, but Patrick did some money laundering deals with a Slav. Ex-military, ex-KGB and ex-links with the Russian Mafia. He was helping this Serb to auction part of his valuable art collection in London, but Pat hung on to the cash. Millions, are involved. Multi-millions! Last I heard, this man was in Dover looking for Patrick.'

'My God! How could Patrick be such a fool?' Fear flew into her face like a dark shadow and she struggled to keep calm.

It was dark outside by the time she left. She glanced at her watch. Four p.m. She had time to go home and do some more collating before her class. The picture was beginning to come together, but why was Bernie so afraid?

151

18

Mum had left a note pinned on the bookcase behind the front door: 'Lecturing late. Warm up the Kentucky Fried Chicken and chips when you get back from karate. Don't forget to walk Jock before you go. Back about eight. Love, Mum.'

They'd had an argument about his karate. Mum had wanted to alter her classes so she could run him there and back every Wednesday and Friday, and meantime he should give it up, she'd insisted. He'd refused, so eventually they'd reached an uneasy truce: Mum would reschedule her classes as soon as she could and meantime he must take care.

Jason took Jock for a jog to the park and back before cycling to town. The class was fantastic. DI Fergus was in charge. They had six teachers altogether, but the Inspector was by far the best although he had only just started teaching once a week. Jason was coming out of the gym when he passed two classmates, Ahmad and a friend, coming across the market square. Shy, hardworking boys, they kept to themselves and Jason was surprised when they smiled tentatively. Being recent immigrants, they were used to being snubbed. Jason grinned back. 'Hi, guys.'

He crossed the road and walked up the dark alleyway between an ancient graveyard and the car park. He was hardly aware of two men following behind him until he saw an obvious thug blocking his path. Targeting Jason with a malicious leer, he twirled his cosh. Jason turned and realised he was trapped. A jolt of fear gave him strength. Vaulting over the waist-high wall into the car park, he raced towards his bicycle.

They were gaining on him. Three obvious heavies against one boy. He'd be mincemeat. There was a stick lying by a car. Maybe he'd reach it — if he were quick enough. As he sprawled forward, the first one charged, kicked him hard and yanked him to his feet, his shoulder crashing into Jason's chest. Jason fell with flailing arms and legs half under the car. One of them pulled him to his feet and held him up. A fist crashed into his face and another into his stomach. Doubled up on the ground, he fought for air. It felt like a mortal wound. For a few seconds all he could see were feet pounding around him. They were kicking him to death.

After a few gasping moments of agony, Jason got his act together. He lurched to his feet and tackled the nearest goon, kicking up with his foot and crunching the heel of his hand into that hateful, bloated, crimson face. Another blow sent him staggering. Briefly, his two years of boxing came into their own, as he managed to get in a couple of blows which seemed to have no effect at all. It was then that he realised he wasn't alone. Ahmad was fighting beside him and he had a knife. Moments later Ahmad was writhing on the ground, clutching his knee and groaning.

Rage took over while his brains went into a coma. One of the toughs had his hands around his neck and he was throttling him. Stunned and

153

breathless, Jason almost fell as the powerful fingers tightened their grip. He struck out with his right foot and heard a grunt of pain. Above Ahmad's screams, he heard police whistles. An iron fist struck Jason's shoulder and his arm fell as if paralysed. Another blow to his forehead turned his world crimson. He was vaguely aware of a woman screaming and running footsteps fading towards the park.

Someone was dragging him to a pavement bench. He was lying there feeling dazed, watching Inspector Fergus talking to the people clustered around and listening to an ambulance siren. The ambulance arrived and he saw Ahmad being lifted onto a stretcher. He struggled to sit up and fight off his dizziness and nausea.

'Is he hurt badly?' he asked Fergus.

'He'll be all right. So will you.'

Jason stood up cautiously feeling amazed that his body was still functioning.

'In you get,' Fergus said.

'I'm all right.'

'Let's have a look at you.' He prodded Jason's ribs and peered in his mouth. 'Nasty black eye coming up. You'll be black and blue tonight.'

Jason hobbled to the ambulance. 'Thanks Ahmad,' he said, solemnly shaking his hand.

'What the hell's going on, Connor?' Fergus asked.

Jason winced with pain. 'I'm not Connor. I'm Jason Kent. Connor was my step-father.' He could taste blood in his mouth. 'Three thugs set on me. Ahmad, who was round the corner, ran back to help me. Am I free to go?'

'Look here, Jason. This is an unofficial talk, but I would like you and your mother to go into the charge office tomorrow to make a statement. Those thugs are guilty of ABH, and I hope we soon catch up with them. Meantime I want to straighten things out. No problems or charges for you and Ahmad, but I'd like to ask you a few questions. Have you seen these men before?'

'No. Never. But it wasn't a chance meeting. They were waiting outside the gym and they trapped me in the alley. They looked foreign to me, but at the time I wasn't thinking clearly.' He prodded his face and gasped with pain.

'Put some ice on your bruises when you get home. I reckon they were paid to scare you, not to hurt you. I'd watch out if I were you. Luckily I wasn't far behind. My car's in the parking lot here. By the way,' he said, as they walked around the corner. 'Constable Jennings is contacting your mother. Tell you what, I'll treat you to a Big Mac and fries. You deserve it. You'll be a regular Rambo one day if you'd keep up your karate.'

Jason glanced anxiously at his watch. Mum would create, but it was only half-past six. 'Well, thanks, but it's not necessary.'

'Gives me the chance to combine work and eating.'

'Then how can I refuse?' Jason said, suddenly feeling stronger.

★ ★ ★

The telephone was ringing as Clara returned home. It went on and on as she unlocked the

155

door and let Jock run outside before picking up the receiver.

'Hello.' She frowned as she heard heavy breathing.

'I'm hanging up,' she snarled.

'Clara! I have a message for you.' The voice came muffled, like a stage whisper, grating on her ear.

'Who are you? What do you want?'

'I want you to look after Jason. You've got a big mouth, Clara. Keep it shut. That way he'll be safe. Today was just a warning. Okay?'

'Today? For God's sake! No . . . ' A small click terminated the conversation.

'Jason! Where's Jason?' Sweat broke out on her hands and feet while shock waves were pulsing over her skin bringing her arms up in goose-bumps. Through a daze of fear she remembered her note to him.

Moments later she was calling the police, battling with her wobbling fingers. Then she remembered the warning and replaced the receiver.

'My son. They've hurt my son. Oh God! What shall I do? How can I find him?'

She ran to the car, dishevelled and frantic, and raced out of the driveway, careering over the rutted, gravel lane, towards town. Then her mobile rang.

'Is that Mrs Connor? Mrs Clara Connor? Constable Jennings here.'

Clara's stomach did a double somersault while she struggled to keep the car on the road.

'Inspector Fergus asked me to call you. Jason's

156

been in a fight, but he's okay. Just a black eye. He's having a bite to eat with the Inspector right now. The DI will see him safely home. You can expect him within the hour.'

The relief was so great Clara braked and howled.

★ ★ ★

MacDonalds was just up the road. Despite his bruises Jason was hungry. He tucked into a Big Mac and fries.

'Every time I see you, you're that much taller,' Fergus said.

Jason grinned shyly. 'Yeah! I hardly ever think of anything but eating.'

For a few minutes they wolfed down the food. 'Join me in another helping,' Fergus said.

'Thanks, if you're sure.'

Fergus got up and fetched the replacements.

'You used to work on Robin's boat at weekends,' Fergus said casually when he sat down.

'I still do. He pays me well to clean up after a trip.'

'I guess the trippers make a hell of a mess?'

'Seeing is believing.'

'Foreign, are they?'

'Well, I don't know,' Jason said cautiously. 'They come off as I go on.'

'But sometimes you went on trips with Robin.'

'Mainly in the holidays.'

'What about your stepfather. Ever go out on the *Valkyr*? Did Robin go along?'

Jason grabbed a chip and chewed it thoughtfully. Funny, he'd been starving two minutes ago, but suddenly it was hard to swallow. He pushed his tray aside. 'This meal . . . is it paid for out of your informers' fund?'

'No. Don't be silly.'

'Look! I don't know anything about Robin's business. He's always been a bit of an unknown. He came into our lives together with Patrick. You've probably guessed that I'm prejudiced against Patrick and his friends. I don't know of any illegal activities and I'm not sure I'd tell you if I did.'

'I'm sorry, Jason. Please eat your burger. I'm just trying to find out what's going on.'

After thinking about it, Jason thought he might as well finish.

'I would never regard you as an informer. But Jason, I don't believe you're the disinterested observer you make out to be.' He peered at Jason as if trying to scan his mind. 'D'you think your stepfather was treasure hunting at night?'

Jason shook his head. 'Smuggling I guess, but Mum doesn't know.'

'D'you have any proof?'

Jason flushed. 'Just a hunch.'

'If you hear anything bring it to me. Don't blab your mouth off. I have no doubt the locals running the smuggling rings are respected members of the community. You know the types: big houses, respectable businesses as fronts, kids at college, but make no mistake, they're killers. They've fought off the international drug gangs and hung on to their turf. That takes some doing. There's a lot of money at stake. Millions! I've known people kill for far less. Snuffing out a kid like you wouldn't give them a sleepless night, so if you think of anything at all, come and tell me. That's your safest bet.'

'I told you, I'm not likely to hear anything.'

There was a long silence while Fergus stared at him, one eyebrow raised. Eventually Jason shrugged. 'Okay, I get the message.' He stood up, resisting the impulse to yelp with pain. 'Thanks for the food. Be seeing you.'

'I'm taking you home, Jason. That's the least I can do for your mother.'

'I left my bicycle in the car park.'

'Are you fit enough to ride?'

'Sure I am.'

'Then I'll follow you.'

When he reached home he found he had seized up like an over-heated car. Nothing worked. He couldn't move. He made a monumental effort to get off the bicycle and stumbled to the front door.

'I'm fine,' he told Clara as he fell through the doorway. He waved feebly at the Inspector who reversed out and drove away.

19

Clara looked up and noticed that Jason was wearing his anorak and trainers. 'Where d'you think you're going?'

'To see Ahmad. He's still in hospital.'

'But the doctor said — '

'Come on, Mum. It's three days since the attack and I'm better. I'm almost thirteen. Remember?'

'How could I forget? You tell me so often.'

Nightly she rubbed Jason's ribs and back with Arnica cream. His torso was purple and black. He had to be one aching mess, but he wasn't going to admit it. He was a tough kid.

'You're always working at the computer, Mum. What are you doing?'

'Thinking up new tours.'

Clara hated to lie to her son, but until she handed over the information to the police no one should know about it, she'd decided. The attack on Jason had spurred her on to work harder.

She heard the lead being taken off the hook and Jock's excited whimpers.

'You will take care, won't you, Jason?'

'Sure.'

'Don't try to be a hero. If you see those thugs again, run like hell. Go into a shop and ask for help. Anything! By the way, you can't take Jock into the hospital.'

'I know that, Mum. I'll tie him up outside.'

'Someone might steal him.'

'I'd like to see them try. Relax, Mum. We're going over the hills so he'll get a good run.'

'Take care.'

She heard his footsteps running down the gravel lane. She wondered how any thugs could beat up a twelve-year-old boy and she felt contaminated by their cruelty.

She sighed and brought her mind to bear on her work. Keying into the 'banking' folder she got to work. All fragments containing the key words *bank, banking, sterling, deposit, dollars,* and so on, had been collated in date order. Sorting was a boring job, but her interest heightened when she realised that Patrick had changed to online banking in mid-'98. It was mind-boggling as massive deposits circled around eight different European and South American banks and then disappeared for good into Serbian banks.

About an hour later a letterhead flashed on-screen. The West End Safe Deposits Company, together with their address in East London. She had the date: 15th July 1999, the time and the letterhead. Now she needed the message.

She found it in three parts on another disc of that time and date. Within seconds she had the entire message on the screen:

★   ★   ★

Dear Sir, Due to escalating costs we regret to inform you that all our charges are being

161

increased by 20%. The rental of your box will be increased from £1,000 a year to £1,200, commencing on April 5.

* * *

It was addressed to the managing director of the Celtic Art Company, Netherlands Antilles, obviously an off-shore company. Was it Patrick's company? Or the group's? What kind of a name was that? Pretty big box, she mused. It must have held something valuable to pay that kind of rent.

'What sort of an idiot am I?' All she had to do was to write an e-mail and she might find out if the safe deposit box was still being used by the hoods.

Moments later she was typing a message.

* * *

'To the West End Safe Deposits Company: Dear Sir, Your latest communication makes no mention of a cheque for £1,200, sent to you on August 1. Kindly send an up-to-date statement of my account. Yours truly.'

* * *

Now what? Just what name had Patrick used here? Finally she wrote Patrick Connor, wondering if she would receive a reply.

So far all she had was Patrick's e-mail address: celtic@ironside.com, plus the e-mail address of someone who apparently appeared to be in

162

charge of the gang: starwalker@dockside.co.uk. Another member of team, who seemed to handle Channel crossings, operated from fiscal@clifftop.com. She had no idea who they were and since they were connected via the net, she didn't even know if they were in Britain, but from their knowledge of shipping and local officials, she guessed they were local and they had dozens of officials on their payroll.

Moving back a few months she was surprised to read that Starwalker, whoever he was, had been trying to recover a debt of £2.4 million. Patrick's excuse was always the same: the money was being laundered and they were getting high interest for long term investments in Sarajevo. Consequently they had to wait until the loans matured.

Had Starwalker killed Patrick because he hung on to his money? And who was this Starwalker? The date seemed to back up what Bernie and Robin had said. She knew it was vital that she find the identities of those hiding behind their code names.

Eventually she stood up and stretched. She was surprised to see that it was nearly dark. Time to make supper and she could do with a cup of tea. She got up and went into the kitchen. Jason should be back soon, she thought. Would the time ever come when she didn't have to worry about him?

As she began peeling vegetables she was remembering her student days. She'd been friends with an American called Rob Mason who was studying computer science. He'd been a whizz at hacking and he'd taught her everything she knew about data processing. At one stage she'd even thought of dropping archaeology and becoming a programmer. Hacking would be just the thing to get her into these computers, via their e-mail connections, but she didn't have the software she needed. She wondered if she could buy it in Canterbury. Clara thrilled at the chance of delving deeper into Patrick's criminal activities. It was only a matter of time now and she'd have it all.

★   ★   ★

It was cold and the cold made his bruises and torn tendons ache even worse. Jason limped along, half-trotting, half running in his efforts to keep up with Jock who was hell-bent on reaching the hills fast and choking himself on the leash. Because of those morons, a chore that was usually fun had become a torment. He was still hurting and he couldn't keep his mind off the attack. The thugs even invaded his dreams. Although Jason was the tallest boy in his class he'd been useless against grown men. His karate class training hadn't helped at all. His mother needed protecting and there was only him. Last night he'd dreamed Mum was threatened. He'd arrived at the eleventh hour to beat off her assailants, but he couldn't get close. Each time he rushed towards them he was tossed aside. The humiliating beating had knocked his self-confidence for six.

Jason groaned as he pulled himself up the

164

steep chalk hill, through groves of trees. This was the jungle part which he loved; crab apples, buckthorn, dogwood and chestnuts. Fox and badger tracks wound through the undergrowth, squirrels scolded overhead, magpies were squabbling, but Jason was obsessed with his problems. He sat on a fallen tree trunk and considered his mother's plight. He'd guessed why they picked on him, to teach Mum a lesson. Mum would do anything to protect him, he knew, even keeping her mouth shut when she ought to go to the police. She knew something. It was worrying her like crazy, but she wasn't likely to tell him.

If only his father were still alive. He'd never met his father, but sometimes, when Mum was out, he got out the photo album and studied the shots of a tall man with light brown hair, brown eyes and a ready smile. He looked a lot like Brad Pitt, Jason thought. Same square shoulders, same eyes. There were so many pictures: Dad on the lifeboat; Dad in the garden; Mum and Dad on the beach; and there were all the wedding shots. The loss of his father was an on-going pain to Jason, but he'd never told anyone, least of all Mum, how much he ached to see him, just once, to know exactly what he was like. Just to let him know how much he cared.

He bit his lip and fought back his tears. They needed Dad. If Dad were still alive he'd soon send those crooked smugglers packing. For a moment he was lost in his own, special daydreams where Dad lived and worked and came home nights, and played cricket and soccer with him at weekends, and made Mum smile all the time, like she did in the snapshots.

'Grow up Jason,' he growled, sniffing hard. Perhaps he should double up on his karate lessons. He was doing well, but not well enough. He felt unfairly prejudiced because of his age. Briefly he considered a knife like Ahmad had and then discarded the idea. Someone would get badly hurt and it might be him. He stood up, wincing with pain. Now where was Jock? He whistled and heard Jock crashing through the undergrowth. Moments later the dog appeared panting heavily and covered in mud. He'd have to wash him when he got him home.

'Come on, boy, come on.' He picked up a stick and threw it hard and the dog leaped in the air and came racing back with it. As they wrestled for the stick, his good humour returned.

Jock was panting happily by the time they took the white chalk path that lead through the bushes and down to the road. From here it was only a few minutes to the hospital. Tying Jock to a railing near the door, Jason went inside.

Ahmad was still under observation because of concussion and his damaged kneecap, but he was leaving soon. Jason could see how lonely he was when he arrived. It didn't take long before Ahmad was telling Jason about his family. Their name was Shamim and they came from Mazar-i Sharif, which had been one of the most liberated cities in Afghanistan. They had enjoyed a good life until the district fell to the Taliban.

As he talked, Ahmad seemed to shed some of his trauma.

'One night we walked out of our house with all

the spare cash my parents could raise. No goodbyes, nothing. We were unable to trust anyone. We drove as far as we could, but we had to abandon our car at the border. We paid ten thousand dollars to a professional smuggler to guide us across the border into Iran. The next morning we arrived near Herat, but it took us three weeks to find someone to take us to the Turkish border in the back of a lorry.'

Jason watched his friend and wondered at the change. He used to be so reticent and now he couldn't stop talking. He caught a glimpse of Ahmad's unhappiness at being pulled up by the roots and dumped in foreign soil.

'In Istanbul, my father paid twenty thousand pounds, the very last of our cash, for a passage to Britain for my mother and I.' His fierce dark eyes glistened with sadness and pride. 'The price included a month's stay in a safe house, but instead we found ourselves dumped and broke on Dover's seafront.'

Jason listened quietly, but his cheeks were burning. What kind of people profited from other's misfortunes and still sold them short? Patrick's kind?

Jason spent the evening studying for the next day's history exam. His mother came up to bed at half-past eleven. 'You're working late. D'you want a snack or a cup of coffee or something?'

'No thanks.'

'How's your immigrant friend?'

'Hey, Mum. He's my classmate, or friend, or anything other than that label. He has a name, by the way. It's Ahmad. He's getting better, thanks.'

'Sohreee! I'm glad he's getting better.'

She bent over him and kissed him goodnight, a habit from the distant past which had been lost and recovered and which embarrassed him greatly.

'Sleep tight, Mum.' He returned to his books.

★ ★ ★

Clara waited for Jason to go to bed before switching on her e-mail. When she keyed into in-coming messages she found there was one from the West End Safe Deposits Company. A surge of triumph ran through her giving her goose-pimples as she read it.

★ ★ ★

Dear Mr. Connor, We are at a loss to understand why you would have sent us a cheque for £1,200, since you no longer have a rental agreement with us. Perhaps your cheque was sent on behalf of The Celtic Art Company. However, we have no record of receiving this cheque. The latest cheque for £2,000 received last month from your company, was signed by Vesno Mandic and drawn on the Bank of Hong Kong, Geneva, on May 26 last. We'd like to take this opportunity of thanking you once again for recommending our company to Messrs. V. Mandic and M. H. Schmidt. Please advise us if you have further queries. Yours faithfully, Joe Jackson.

★ ★ ★

Clara let out a long, low whoop of pleasure. Vesno Mandic! Now who was he? The name seemed familiar. The fragments were beginning to make sense, but where did the cash go after Sarajevo? What had happened to the hoods' profits? After Sarajevo there was no further sign of the missing millions.

Running through the recovered data, she noticed that the name Vesno Mandic had been cropping up often. It was the only name she found on the files. A call to a friend at the college where she taught confirmed that it was a Serbian name. Could he be the man who'd been hanging around the house? She keyed in to 'find' and the computer came up with hundreds of fragments. She sighed. This would take days to sort, but she might as well start now.

Later she came across half a paragraph from Mandic dated March this year, addressed to Patrick.

★　★　★

Your laundering manoeuvres are time-consuming and hamper expansion. I have new plans and contacts. Set up a meeting in London . . . '

★　★　★

That was all, but it was enough. Had Mandic threatened to take over laundering their profits? She decided to go to Canterbury and shop around for the software she needed to hack into Mandic's e-mail system.

169

20

Sibyl shifted her body and stretched sinuously and dangerously. She was wearing an old t-shirt and blue dungarees covered with paint and she was lying on her back on a plank of wood straddling two ladders to paint a ceiling, her latest commission.

She glanced at her watch. She had to be at Clara's before eleven to pick up a party of tourists and conduct them round the castle. Clara had to see her bank manager urgently that morning. For Sib, this was a penance and nowhere near enough. Lately, Sibyl could never think of Clara without wallowing in guilt. This awful thing had come between them and Clara didn't know about it, which made it so much worse.

She and Clara went back a long way, to university days when they had shared dates and disappointments, and later a flat in Swiss Cottage. She'd always admired Clara for her courage and determination. She would make it, Sib felt sure. She expected nothing less of her friend.

As long as she lived she would never forget the way they met. On a skiing holiday, Sib had shot off a mogul into a deep snowdrift. She couldn't move, she could hardly breathe and her mouth was full of snow. In the distance she'd heard someone yelling curses. Something was scratching at the snow urgently, like a terrier after a rat.

Her world lightened as a small hole appeared to the left of her and hands that were blood-streaked began plucking at the snow around her face.

'Now don't panic because I'm getting you out,' a low voice with a London accent had growled in her ear. Sib had loved the voice ever since and the owner of it.

She gripped the side of the plank, swung her legs over and landed on her feet.

Shortly afterwards she was driving to Dover. There was a vacant parking place opposite Connor Tours' offices. Sib ran upstairs and arrived breathless.

'Clara. You look a sight. This is no way to impress your bank manager.'

'Yeah, right!' Clara looked up from the bank statement. 'I didn't realise you were standing there. I never can balance accounts. It's just not a talent of mine, and I feel awful. It's as if I have jet lag, but I haven't been anywhere.'

'Only to hell and back.'

'How trite can you get?' Clara grinned at her.

'You haven't eaten for days, have you? Have you seen what you look like? Visits to bank managers are one of the few occasions we still dress for. You can borrow my jacket. Come on, hand over your homespun.'

'I couldn't possibly . . . '

'Don't argue. You must. I have no doubt one of the trippers' kids will throw up over me.'

Clara smiled at last. 'They're not that bad. Honest! Thanks for helping me out. Let's go! I'll treat you to a snack.'

Sib couldn't help noticing that Clara looked much healthier after she'd gobbled a toasted egg sandwich and swallowed a glass of milk. She'd have to speak to Jason about looking after his mother.

'I feel heaps better now. Fit enough to fight for the cash I need. So how's the work going? Any new commissions?'

'A few. And I sold a painting.'

'Congratulations.' Clara got up and hugged her friend. 'You'll be famous one of these days. I always said you would. And socially. Are you having fun?'

'I've fallen in lust.'

'Not again.'

'The most irresistibly sexy guy, with dreamy brown eyes. You should see him dance. Oh Lord! Look at the time!'

She jumped up, grabbing Clara's keys. 'Good luck with the bank manager. Here's my keys. I'm parked right behind your bus.'

Sibyl had to speed to reach Dover's tourist information bureau by eleven. She found the group chatting and laughing with each other as if determined to make the most of the day. How will I bear those long dark claustrophobic tunnels, she wondered, as she packed them into Clara's mini-bus and set off up Park Road towards the castle

They were a diverse bunch: a party of six well-dressed, middle-aged Germans: quiet and alert; several bored Kosovan immigrants who had nowhere else to go; two Dutch grandmothers, Annalie and Marie, comfortable with

172

themselves and their white hair; and a loud, London couple. Their difficult, eight-year-old son whined perpetually. The Dutch grannies took an interest in the boy and before long he was sitting between them, sucking toffees and looking pleased with the attention.

Sib ushered her small party to the edge of the cliffs behind the castle and embarked on Clara's typed notes.

For thousands of years, this fertile little island has been the target of avaricious eyes, but the cliffs and our island defenders have beaten off countless would-be invaders.

An exhausting tour through a maze of damp, dark passages hewn out of solid chalk, brought them up to 1914 when the caves sheltered the local population.

Sib was feeling claustrophobic, but occasionally they passed short passages leading to the cliff-face where the light burst through doors which opened out onto a 500 foot drop onto jagged rocks and foaming seas. It seemed to Sib that the tourists were bored with the lecture, but intrigued by the castle and straggling all over the place, some anxious to quit the dark, damp air, others wanting to examine every last passage. Where were they all? She'd forgotten to count as they left the last room.

She heard soft footsteps some distance behind her. Had she abandoned one of them? She called into the darkness. 'Hello! Is someone there? Hurry up please and stay with the group.'

There was no reply, yet she could hear a soft tread creeping towards her. She decided to hurry

173

on and count the tourists, but when she turned away she heard footsteps gaining on her. She stopped and listened, peering into the shadows. A stone was dislodged and now she could hear heavy breathing. Something moved in the shadows. Darkness took shape and a tall, threatening figure in a balaclava moved silently towards her, hand raised. She screamed and ran.

★ ★ ★

'Where is our guide?' one of the Dutch women called to her companion. 'I thought I heard a scream.'

'She's behind us,' the boy replied uneasily.

'She should be here. I thought I heard something, too,' his mother whispered.

Marie turned back along the passage, hurrying as she saw light where before there had been absolute darkness. Annalie and the boy followed, and after yelling at him twice, his father brought up the rear.

All four of them saw a man run along the passage to a door marked *private*, and race through it. They ran after him, but the door was locked. Annalie was first to see their guide on her hands and knees at the open door in the cliff-face gazing into the void.

'It's all right, dear. Try to relax. He's gone. You're with friends. Let's get you back.'

The tourists helped Sib to her feet. She had a swollen lump on the back of her head, blood on her hands and her forehead was bruised. She was covered in chalk. No one believed her story of tripping over a hump. Annalie took over, driving the bus to Casualty to deposit Sib, and from there to the police station where the tourists made a joint statement before dispersing.

Calmed by a strong tranquilising injection, Sib was flying on gossamer clouds. Much later she did her best to ignore the handsome, Spanish-looking policeman with the unlikely name of Fergus, who wanted to wake her and ask silly questions.

'No, I don't know who he was. A serial killer I wouldn't be surprised. Perhaps a ghost from the hundred-year war. He appeared from nowhere and disappeared as suddenly. No, I'm sure it had nothing to do with Mrs Connor. Why should it? No, I wasn't sure what he wanted.'

Then Clara appeared in a white haze and all Sib could see were her pale cheeks and staring eyes.

'Sergeant Browning told me what happened.' She sounded panic-stricken. 'I'll never forgive myself for asking you to go. He meant to get me, Sib, and he got you instead.'

'Forget it! It's me he was after.' The gossamer clouds were disintegrating. Sib closed her eyes and tried to will them back, but it didn't work. She sighed. 'Did you get the overdraft?'

'Yes. Thank you Sib, but that's not important now. I'm so very sorry. How can you ever forgive me?'

It was getting monotonous.

'Look, Clara, I want to be alone for a while.' Sib buried her face in the pillow and pretended to be asleep. She couldn't face Clara right now. She felt too frightened.

21

It was a dark afternoon, with low rain clouds racing in from the south-east. Clara sat in the hospital waiting room in a state of numb anxiety becoming increasingly depressed. Eventually she walked back to Sib's ward. Dim beams of light took on the ghostly pallor of the white tiles and blanched Sib's rich colouring. She was still sleeping, but Clara longed to wake her.

The sister came in with a click of heels and a rustle of starched linen. She had short auburn hair and friendly brown eyes.

'Oh, you're still here, Mrs Connor. I expect Miss Ferretti will sleep for hours. Why don't you come back later? Don't worry! We won't let her out on her own.'

'You'll find it's not so easy to stop Sib, but do your best.'

She might as well go and fetch her minibus from the police station. At the Charge Office, Clara was directed to the detectives' annexe where she found the Inspector's office. This open-plan room with six desks overlooked the car park. DS Browning was the only detective there.

'Well, hello,' Clara said. 'We met at the hospital.'

The sergeant nodded coldly and left the office.

Clara gazed out of the window. She could see her minibus parked in the corner against the black flint walls of the town-hall. A grim view, made gloomier by the dim light.

'Ah, Mrs Connor.' Fergus had walked in silently behind her. He waved one hand towards a chair, but she remained standing. There were bags under his eyes which she hadn't seen before. He looked as if he needed a good night's sleep.

'It's just one darned thing after the next, isn't it,' he said.

She murmured non-committally.

'I don't believe in coincidences.' He scanned her with his strangely glowing dark eyes. 'Too many things have happened that concern you. Now this! What is the connection between you and Miss Ferretti, apart from your friendship? Who would want to do this to her? Even more important, how did they know she would be taking your place at the castle?'

'I don't know. I don't know. What's the use of talking to you? I've told you everything time and again. People stalk me, break into my home and my office, but you do nothing to help. Now Sib's been attacked.'

His eyes were very expressive, a disadvantage for gamblers and policemen, Clara thought as she read his guilt and compassion. She simmered down. 'Tell me what happened to Sib.'

He looked out of the window speculatively, before coming to a decision.

'Miss Ferretti was threatened and her attacker attempted to push her head-first over the cliff-face. She fought back and fell, stunning herself. Or so she says.'

'Oh my God! You see, they thought she was me.' Clara could not begin to describe how she felt: guilty and scared would have to do.

'No. I don't think so, Mrs Connor. Her attacker frightened her badly, but I doubt there was any intention to let her fall. Evidently the man wanted some information from her, but she won't tell me what it was. I want you to try to persuade Miss Ferretti to tell me what the man wanted to know. She said she thought it might be a joke. Birds of a feather, aren't you?' He smiled mirthlessly. 'You're both holding back on me.'

'I've told you all I know.'

Fergus pursed his lips and eyed Clara speculatively. 'There have been lots of things you haven't told me in the past, haven't there? Now I need you to think back carefully. Was there an inflatable on board the *Connemara*? Did you see a motor launch, or hear an outboard engine?'

'No.'

'Did your husband own an inflatable?'

'I don't know that, either. I don't think so. He never mentioned buying one.'

'You seem very sure there was a killer on board. How do you think he got on and off the yacht?'

'How should I know? But I know he was there. I saw him. He attacked me. I have the scar still.' She fingered her scalp where it was still tender. 'Why don't you believe me? I've also wondered how this murderer managed to get aboard without either of us knowing. Of course we were in the cabin for a while and the noise of the wind was intense. He might have approached the stern

178

and made fast. He might even have hidden somewhere on the yacht and been there when we set sail.' She shuddered with fright.

Fergus perched on the end of the desk and toyed with his pencil.

'Why did you go on this trip with your husband?'

'Is this relevant? Why do you want to know?'

'Please answer, Mrs Connor. I'll explain in a minute.'

She shrugged. 'When Patrick asked me to take him back he said we should spend more time together. That I must go sailing with him. Then this trip came up and he wanted it to be like a second honeymoon.' She stood up and stared out of the window, trying to dab her eyes without Fergus seeing. 'Can't we drop it? I've told you all this.'

Ignoring her, he opened a file and fumbled for some printed pages. 'Previously you told me that your late husband opened champagne when you were at sea together on the evening of the storm.'

'Yes.' She frowned. They'd been over that, too.

'Can you remember the brand?'

'Of course. It was Laurent-Perrier. My favourite.'

'But you didn't drink any?'

'I was feeling sick, but I did sip a little.'

'So what happened to the bottle?'

'I — I felt guilty. He'd gone to so much trouble. The champagne made me feel even more nauseous, so I hunted around for an old rubber bottle-sealer and put the bottle in the fridge. I was thinking in terms of a champagne

179

breakfast, but it's never the same, is it? Pouring flat champagne down the sink doesn't seem so bad the next day. Any more silly questions?'

'Just one. I retrieved the bottle. There was enough laudanum in the champagne to knock out an elephant. Was it meant for you, or your husband?'

She gasped. 'God, no!' Betrayal was like a dagger thrust. She felt dizzy and sank onto a chair. Then came another more urgent fear. 'Do you suspect me of drugging my husband?'

'It was there for one of you. You're alive and he's dead.'

'You bastard!' She felt appalled. Strange tingling feelings were racing through her bloodstream bringing a curious sense of self-loathing.

Fergus was watching her curiously. 'Let's look at it from another angle. You wouldn't give your husband a divorce and you had asked him to return the money he owed you. He must have felt trapped. Perhaps sufficiently trapped to look for another way out. So he asked for a reconciliation and you know the rest.' He gave a funny little nod.

'But neither scenario includes the killer we had on board.'

Fergus ran his hands through his hair. 'You're right, of course. Could a third person have tampered with the bottle? Was it opened and left standing when you weren't there?'

'No. Of course not. How do I know you aren't lying?' she flung at him.

'Here's the forensic report.' He slid some

180

papers across the desk. Hands shaking, she thumbed through them. Was it possible that someone else had tampered with the bottle? She tried to remember when Patrick opened the champagne.

She had been lying on a bunk feeling scared by the ferocity of the storm. She was cold and very sick and for once Patrick had been kind. He'd always been wild and reckless. It was part of his appeal. She remembered how his eyes had glinted with excitement.

Feeling stressed and upset, she travelled back in time and space to the last time she had seen Patrick conscious. She heard the deafening crash and felt the hull shudder as the yacht fell into a trough and met a wave head-on.

She remembered Patrick laughing. 'What a yacht! She's made for seas like this,' he said, caressing the bulkhead.

He gets a high from danger. We won't make it, Clara thought. She hung on to the bunk as the boat swooped down sickeningly and landed with a deafening crash.

'For God's sake, turn round. Sail back to Dover. Please, Patrick. We'll founder. We must try to make harbour,' she begged.

'Poor darling. The storm's not as bad as you think. Come on, sit up. I'll open the champagne.'

Patrick fumbled in his bag for a bottle and showed it to her. It was Laurent-Perrier, her favourite. 'Good enough for a second honeymoon, is it?'

'Let's save it for the morning, darling. I feel a bit queasy.'

'Nonsense. It's for now. It'll fix you up. Trust me!' He opened the bottle with a flourish and laughed as the champagne sprayed the floor.

How does he keep on his feet? she wondered.

Then he turned his back and fumbled around wiping the glasses. *Was that when . . . ?* She almost passed out.

She remembered he'd said: 'Drink this and you'll be on Cloud Nine.' Then he'd laughed and somehow managed to pass her a full glass. He'd carried his up on deck and at the time she'd thought it would be half full of brine and undrinkable.

'You bastard! Bastard!' she whimpered aloud. She had never felt this lonely and betrayed. There had to be another explanation. She had fallen into a light, restless sleep and woken to the sound of groans coming from above. Oh God. The laudanum had put her to sleep and that was when . . .

Fergus was leaning over her. 'Are you all right, Mrs Connor?'

She felt depression tighten around her chest as a lump settled in her throat. Suddenly it was hard to breathe.

'So it was drugged . . . The champagne . . . I sipped a little . . . I'd have gone down with the yacht.' She could feel cold sweat gathering between her shoulder blades and moistening her brow. She thrust the horror story into the bog at the bottom of her mind, but she couldn't avoid it. Her hands began to tremble and she felt sick. 'Yes. I'm all right.' She stood up slowly feeling slightly unreal. 'Can I go now?'

'I wasn't detaining you, was I? Here are your keys. Your minibus is just below in the car park.'

She scowled at him as she grabbed her keys and left.

★ ★ ★

Clara drove the minibus back to her garage and called for a taxi to drive her back to her car. She was trying to keep her mind blank as she drove once again to the hospital.

Sib was sitting on the bed dressed to go, wearing a scarf around her neck, swinging her legs and scuffing the floor with her shoes in a show of childish bravado. She was wearing jeans and Clara's woollen jacket with a raincoat over it. It was the first time Clara had seen Sib look her age. It didn't seem so long ago when they were both students. We go back a long way, she mused. Fourteen years.

'It's so damn cold here,' Sib said by way of greeting.

'Sib, dearest, so you're awake at last! I'm so sorry for everything. What happened exactly?' She caught hold of her friend's hands, rubbing Sib's cold fingers in her warm palms.

Sib snatched her hands away and stood up groggily. 'Can we get out of here? I want to go home.'

Clara felt herself flushing. She turned to the nurse. 'Can we?'

'As long as she stays home and goes to bed. She'll be light-headed from the injection at least until morning. Maybe longer.'

183

'Let's get out of here. I hate hospitals. I shouldn't have let them bring me, but at the time I felt dizzy. Shock, I suppose.' Sib fingered her neck softly and grimaced.

'Just look at your bruises. He nearly killed you. I'm so sorry. It's all my fault.'

'Cut the histrionics, Clara. It's over and I don't want to talk about it.'

Sib walked out of the ward into the passage, leaving Clara dumbfounded. Was it the pills, or delayed shock that was causing Sib's aggression? Or was Sib blaming her for causing the incident? Clara hurried after her.

'You're angry with me. Well, I don't blame you, but Sib, just think. Your life was endangered and that means I'm in danger, too. And maybe Jason. I need to know what's going on. Did he say anything? Have you any idea what caused the attack? Surely you must have recognised something about him.'

Sib scowled and pursed her lips.

Clara unlocked the door and closed it after Sib got in. She didn't know how to break the tension. Her story seemed to have made it worse. Sib had become even more withdrawn.

Clara drove out of the car park and took the London Road to Temple Ewell where Sib lived in a small, medieval flint villa backing on to the river. She parked and got out.

'How d'you feel?' Clara ventured, expecting another snub.

'I can see Fergus told you what happened. My head hurts like crazy. I don't think he intended to hurl me out, but I fought back and slipped. I

184

almost fell through the door. It was terrifying . . . '

'D'you need anything from the shop? I could
pop down to the Co-Op.'

'Thanks, but I'm okay.'

At the door, Sib turned and blocked the
entrance. Reaching out she took Clara's hand.

'Thanks for bringing me home, but now I
want to be alone.' She gave a strange, tense
smile. 'I'm going to sleep. Goodnight. Thanks for
the lift.' She was about to slam the door, but she
paused and her face softened.

'I wish I'd been a better friend to you, Clara.
You're closer to me than my own sister. Far
closer. You didn't deserve this, but now I need to
be alone.'

Clara was still trying to work out what she
meant when the door was firmly closed in her
face.

As she walked back to her car, Clara was
fumbling through her trauma to find a common
thread, but nothing made sense. What was it the
stalker had said? 'The killer will come after you.'
Had he picked on Sib by mistake? All she knew
for sure was that time was running short and so
far she had no idea who he was.

22

Jason found Sib painting a mural on the wall of a new tea room overlooking the river. Wearing paint-splashed overalls, her hair pushed into a shower cap, she was sitting at the top of a ladder, gazing at the blurred shapes with an expression of critical distaste. Flashes of iridescence seared his eyes as turquoise and blue merged in an underwater scene of frogs and fish.

'Hi Jason,' Sib called, looking over her shoulder. 'This is a surprise. So what do you think?'

'Looks fantastic to me.'

'And the colours?'

'Just great. I like that greeny-blue water. Same colour as your eyes.'

'Wow! Jason. That's not bad. Is that your very first compliment?'

'I'm practicing for a girl I know.' The lie bothered him.

She laughed and Jason leaped to her side as the ladder wobbled.

'So, why are you here?' she asked as she added a few more strokes.

At close hand Jason noticed how tense Sib looked. There were deep black smudges round her eyes and the freckles on her cheeks and nose stood out in startling contrast to her pale skin.

'I need some advice. I need to talk about Mum.'

'Would you like some tea and cake while you talk? It's on the house here.'

'If you're sure that's okay. Yes, fine.'

'I'm sure.'

Sib smiled and suddenly she looked like the old Sib. She was overweight, but the excess was piled up in the right places and that sort of made it all right. When she flung off her paint-splashed shower cap and shook her head, her dark red hair fell around her shoulders and she looked pretty, even though she was so old.

'Chocolate cake, Jason? It's the best one here.'

He nodded and Sib called the waitress to order tea.

'Are you supposed to be working, Sib?'

'According to whom, my doctor or my bank manager?'

'Good question.'

Jason gazed around wondering how to begin, feeling too inadequate to cope with this adult matter.

'What is it?' Sib prompted him.

Jason flushed. 'I have to ask you something. It's about Mum. It's like she's lost in a maze of terror. She hardly eats. She's tormented by recurring nightmares. I wish I could help her. Ever since Patrick died she's been like someone else — snappy, sort of bitter, sometimes really mean.'

'You can't expect her to be happy right now. She's just been widowed for the second time.'

'Yeah, I know.' He took a deep breath and let it all out. 'It's much worse since you were attacked. I wish you would tell her why. You

187

know, don't you? She suspects you're holding back.'

'I can't tell you, Jason. Besides, it has nothing to do with you, or Clara.'

'If you say so.'

When the cake arrived Jason realised how hungry he was. He didn't say much more until he'd finished it and drunk his tea. He took a deep breath. He had to do it. It was like letting yourself jump off the pier with your eyes closed, he decided. No, worse than that. He was leaping into unknown water.

'I know about Patrick and your sister, Gina,' he said in a rush. 'The trouble is I'm too young to know if I should tell Mum or keep quiet. It would be better if you told her. I guess this had something to do with the attack. Am I right?'

He watched Sib go very white and then very red until little drops of moisture shone on her forehead. She took out a tissue and wiped them away, smoothing back her hair with her hand. Jason tried to look away but his eyes seemed to be locked in on hers as the tears gathered and she bit her lip.

'How did you find out?'

He shrugged. 'Let's say I have extraordinary insight.' Then he grinned.

'This isn't a game, Jason. Now tell me how you found out?'

He sighed. 'The git brought her to Robin's boat one day when I was cleaning up. Robin pays me to help out sometimes.'

'Is that what you call him? The git?'

'I've got a few other names.'

'That bad?'

'Past tense. But I don't know what to do, Sib. I've known for months. Trouble is, Mum's never going to forgive me when she finds out that I knew.'

'Let's hope she never does. The affair was over before Patrick died. Don't tell Clara, Jason. That's best. Let her keep her memories.' Sib peered over her shoulder as if fearing that Mum would walk in on them. 'She'd be so hurt. She'd blame me for not telling her. Our friendship goes back a long way. I wouldn't want anything to come between us, especially right now when your mum needs a friend.'

'Okay, but Mum's very determined and I think she's about to find out. She keeps gazing at that brochure your father printed for the funeral service. Something about the picture puzzles her. She says she's never seen it before.'

'It was a mistake to use it. I told Dad, but he went ahead anyway. Gina left it lying around.'

'Don't you think it would be kinder to come clean. And was I right? Does it have something to do with the attack on you?'

Sib shrugged. 'I can't talk about it. And no! It would not be kinder to tell your mother. Listen, I'm going away for a while, Jason. All this . . . well, let's just say it's getting me down. To put it bluntly I'm a wimp and I'm running. I've accepted a part-time job teaching art in an Inverness school while their teacher is on a sabbatical. Now promise me you won't tell her about Gina.'

Jason kept a bland face as he considered Sib's

moral blackmail and his own failure to stand up to her. He couldn't look at her. Instead he gazed out of the window. Thick clouds had gathered and dusk had fallen like a shroud over the lake. A sudden gust sent a vortex of leaves across the tarnished surface. He shivered as he watched the willows bend before the chilling east wind.

★   ★   ★

Clara had been kept late at the college, so she had warmed up some ready-made curry and rice. She kept a few containers in the freezer for emergencies. Jason, home early for once, was hanging around the kitchen, a sure sign he was hungry.

'Did you know Sib's going to Scotland for a month, Mum? I saw her this afternoon. She's taken a temporary teaching post in Inverness.' Now why was Jason sounding so secretive, Clara wondered?

'Leaving? Are you sure? She hasn't called me since the castle attack. I still feel so guilty about it.'

The curry smelled good and she noticed her son's sigh of relief as she gave him all of it. Keeping him stoked up was a full time job.

'Sib's been so strange lately. It's almost as if she thinks she's harmed me in some way. Well, you know how expressive Sib's face is. Yet she was attacked, not me. I'm the one who should feel guilty, since I sent her there, and of course I do. I don't understand her, but there must be a reason for her odd behaviour. Come to think of it, she was a bit strange at the funeral, too. I wonder what's worrying her?'

Jason was engrossed in shovelling mango chutney over his food.

'Jason, d'you know what Sib said to me? She said: 'I wish I'd been a better friend to you, Clara. You're closer to me than my own sister. Far closer. You didn't deserve this.' Now I ask you, Jason, what was she talking about? What didn't I deserve?'

Jason shrugged and a strange, trapped look appeared in his eyes. 'Are you talking about the explosion and all that?' He gazed at the wall with great concentration.

'You're not listening to me. What are you thinking about, Jason?'

'Sorry, Mum? You were saying?' He looked up, feigning ignorance.

Clara wasn't fooled. Playing dumb was what he did when he didn't want to be cornered.

'How's the curry?'

'Great!'

Clara watched her son wolfing his food down. He ate enough for three and she could see how he was sprouting up and out. He was going to be even taller than his father who'd been well over six foot.

'Who do you think Sib's running away from: her attacker, or me?' she blurted out.

'You've lost me. Mum, can we talk about this some other time? I was trying to work out how to write an essay.'

'Of course. I'm sorry.' She frowned. Why was Jason putting her off? And why had Sib said:

'You're closer to me than my own sister?' Of course she was. She and Gina barely tolerated each other. They had nothing in common and there was a huge age-gap between them. Sib hardly ever gave Gina a thought. So why, at such a time, had she mentioned her sister? The implications were perfectly obvious, but Clara didn't want to accept them.

Something else had worried her since the funeral. Where on earth had Piers Ferretti got hold of that picture of Patrick rigging the sails on the *Connemara?* He was gazing at the camera with an expression of the utmost adoration. Once he had looked at her like that. So who had been taking the picture?

'How old is Gina?' she asked Jason out of the blue.

'What are you talking about?'

'For God's sake, Jason. Come on!' Her voice rose to an unbearable wail.

Jason blushed scarlet. Mumbling something incoherent, he fled.

Clara sighed. He was only a kid. Sometimes so grown up and at other times a real baby. She had no right to push her worries on to him. Just what sort of a mother was she?

'You come back and finish your supper this minute, Jason,' she called up the stairs. 'The inquisition's over. I'm sorry. Really, truly sorry.'

Jason came down looking as apologetic and as guilty as Sib. Clara pretended not to notice as she busied herself opening a tin of rice pudding and warming it in the microwave with some baked apples.

'D'you have a lot of holiday homework?' she asked.

'Not really. I might mess around on the computer. Mmm! Baked apples. That's great.' His expression lightened. 'Mum, listen!' He reached towards her, took her hand and squeezed hard. 'You worry too much. I'm sorry I'm not much help to you when it comes to love affairs, that sort of thing, but . . . ' He broke off and bit his lip. He'd almost blurted it out. He said the first thing that came into his head. 'How about watching a video? I could cycle down and get one.'

'Sure. Why not?

Clara stacked the dirty dishes in the machine, switched it on and sat down to consider what she knew about Gina. According to Mr Ferretti, some freak of nature had produced a woman who embodied perfection. Perhaps he was right, but Clara had never really noticed. Even Sib had said Gina was exquisite and Sib didn't like her sister. She was bitter because their parents, who were struggling financially, had spent part of their savings on drama lessons. As her father had put it: 'This sort of beauty belongs to the world.' It turned out that Gina had no talent for acting, and that she was lazy. She'd told her parents that a rich husband was the be-all and end-all of her ambitions. Patrick wasn't rich, so why choose him?

He wasn't much good at love affairs, Jason had said as an apology for not unravelling the mystery of Sib's strange behaviour. Everything was pointing one way.

Clara sat on a kitchen stool and lapsed into melancholy. What a relief to hear Jason pushing his bicycle into the garage. She couldn't have stood another minute of her masochistic imaginings. She made up her mind to confront Sib with her fears. Meantime she promised to put aside her gloom and enjoy the movie, but Jason had brought some weirdo video about vampires. Not wishing to hurt his feelings she sat and endured every minute of it, right to the inexplicable, clamorous end.

23

Clara had a splitting headache and was in no mood to go anywhere, but she felt deeply hurt and she wanted to have it out with Sib. She drove straight there after college, but it was almost nine p.m. by the time she arrived. Parking her car in the road, Clara hurried up the path and rang the bell.

Sib answered the door, looking hostile and wary. She was wearing a long, embroidered cotton blouse, souvenir from a shared holiday in Jordan, which brought back memories of scuba diving in the Red Sea, riding with Bedouins through the mountains and the long trail of Sib's robed suitors. Happier times, that brought a lump to Clara's throat. Without saying a word, Sib turned back into the living room, flung herself on the couch and lit a cigarette.

Clara walked inside and shut the door behind her. 'Jason said you're leaving.'

'For a term.'

Clara looked around at the familiar scene: sketches and half-finished watercolours lay on every surface and there was an oil painting of a fox pinned on an easel. She wanted to ask Sib why she was smoking again, but that would sound as if she cared.

Sib looked sad and Clara warmed to her, but the question had to be asked. 'You knew all the time, but you didn't tell me. Why, Sib?'

Sib exhaled loudly. 'Phew! For the obvious reason that you were better off not knowing.' Her husky voice was hoarser than usual.

So it was true. Her husband had deceived her with Gina and everyone had known, but no one had told her. Clara felt her spirit shrivelling.

'But Sib, you had no right to make that decision for me.'

Sib drew deeply on her cigarette. Her large green eyes gazing blandly at Clara. 'That's why you're here, isn't it? To shift the blame on to me. Well, if that's what you want, go ahead.'

Clara felt a sense of outrage at Sib's ducking and diving. 'You're not getting away with that. You always twist everything to become the martyr, but the facts speak for themselves. You betrayed me.'

'Listen here, Clara. Patrick betrayed you, not me. I merely kept quiet about it. Why don't you sit down, for God's sake? You're giving me the creeps hovering over me.'

Clara felt her hackles rising, which was her way of coping with aggression. 'Is there any place to sit in this slum you call a home? I don't want paint all over my clothes.'

Sib was on her feet in a single fluid movement, dragging the cover off a chintz armchair.

'Have you come here to hurl abuse at me, or is there something constructive you wanted to say?'

'I suppose you introduced them.'

'You're being ridiculous. You introduced them at the yacht club. It was Patrick's birthday party. Remember? I was in Wales on a job.'

Logic only made Clara feel worse. She felt as

if she'd swallowed lead. They'd only fought once before and they'd both suffered for weeks. She paced the floor as she recalled Jerry Watson escorting a willowy girl she'd mistaken for a model. She felt sick remembering how Patrick had thanked her for a wonderful evening. Had he danced with Gina? She couldn't remember. She'd been too busy organising.

'But that was eighteen months ago.'

'Yes. Just how long does it take you to find out something's wrong?'

'And all this time . . . Let me get this straight, Sib. You knew your sister was knuckling in on my marriage, but you couldn't be bothered to warn me. I might have salvaged something, but you just buried yourself in your precious paintings and let them get on with it.'

Clara had plenty more to say and her voice rose louder and harsher. She hated herself, but she didn't know how to stop. She had to wound, just as she'd been wounded.

A sudden gust of wind blasted the house and slammed rain through an open window. They both jumped and looking around saw the sleet smashing against the floor. Sib stood up and slammed the window.

'I only found out recently when they split. I swear it,' Sib tossed into the silence.

Clara felt deflated. She didn't know what to say.

'I didn't even know Gina was seeing Patrick. Okay, so I knew she had someone. Later she told me that meeting Patrick was like spontaneous combustion. That same evening . . . at your party

. . . well I don't know. Really, I can't see the point of this conversation.'

'Tell me,' Clara screamed.

'They went outside and made love in Patrick's car, there and then. Summertime we all went to Monaco on Patrick's yacht. That was your idea, too. Within weeks they'd moved into a house in Calais and Patrick commuted across the Channel to you. Later they moved to London.'

Clara heard her wail of self-pity and despised herself, which made her even angrier. 'Damn you, Sib. You had no right to withhold such a thing.'

'I would have told you at the time. Of course I would have, but I didn't know. My slut of a sister found it amusing: two houses, two totally different lives running parallel to each other. She swore he'd promised not to fuck you.'

'You're lying. I know you're lying.'

'You see, you didn't really want the truth. It hurts too much. Gina would never have told me while she was with Patrick. In April this year she phoned to tell me she'd left him. I thought you two might get together again, so I kept quiet.' Sib's voice was dead and expressionless. 'I knew you loved him.'

Clara could not answer.

'Look here, Clara, I don't care about my sister. She's a tramp. Available for the highest bidder, but I've been going through hell. Put yourself in my position. Gina was raving about someone new, an Italian art dealer. A rich, handsome, sophisticated man. Silence seemed the kinder way.'

'You think you know what's best for me? Well, fuck you, Sib.'

'He came back to you, didn't he?'

Remembering the laudanum in the champagne brought white-hot fury.

'Did you think I wanted Gina's leavings? I took the bastard back because I didn't know. I feel cheapened and dirty.'

'This isn't grief, Clara. This is anger and it's Patrick you're angry with, not me.'

Clara kicked against the fender until her toe ached. 'He stole for her. Can you believe that? He wanted her so much he turned to crime and put all our lives in danger.'

'Shh! The neighbours will hear.'

'Damn the neighbours!' She took a deep breath and struggled to calm down. 'Is there anything else, Sib?'

'Patrick came here and begged me to help him get Gina back.'

'And did you?'

'For God's sake!' Sib leaped to her feet and paced the room. 'No, I didn't. No! No! No! Damn you, Clara! Don't you think anything of me?' She picked up an ashtray and hurled it across the room.

'It was Jerry who attacked you, wasn't it? He wanted to know where Gina is living.'

'Yes.'

'Do you know where she is?'

'What does it matter?'

Clara almost choked and broke into a fit of coughing. It was so smoky. How could Sib do this to her lungs? She could hardly see across the room.

Oh God! She had to get air. She picked up her

bag and opened the front door.

'Don't go! Please! There's something else. I need to talk to you.' Sib's face was twisted with grief.

'I can't take anymore. Not tonight. Got to go. Got to think.'

As she slammed the door behind her she was still angry. She had to cool down. She turned her back, blocking out the hurtful sight of her traitorous friend and her sad expression.

★　★　★

Icy rain drenched her hair and ran down her neck and the frantic wind whirled around her, but Clara was hardly conscious of the night as she walked faster. Slowly and painfully she compiled the story of their marriage, examining Patrick's attentions and responses with a cold, analytical perspective, noting for the first time her own sense of denial. She had refused to accept that she was losing his love. Even when he asked for a divorce she had made excuses for him. He was overworked, too tense, and there was always the mid-life crisis. Why hadn't she faced the facts?

She remembered that April night so well it might have been yesterday. It was unseasonably hot, a balmy night, and Clara had longed for love. She put on her prettiest nightdress, brushed her hair, added an extra puff of perfume and snuggled up behind him, but Patrick turned his back and feigned sleep. She got up and tiptoed around the bed and got in on the other side

200

where she lay very still, stroking him gently, her mouth nibbling his jaw, his ear. He gave a brief exclamation and two powerful hands thrust her away. He got up and moved to the door. 'I can't go through with this. I want out.' His voice was hardly more than a whisper.

'Out of what?' she asked stupidly.

'I want a divorce.'

Fear hit her as intensely as a bomb blast. He couldn't mean it. She wanted to turn back the clock, just five minutes would do, if she could only reach back to the moment before he uttered that silly statement, which of course he didn't mean. He loved her. It stood to reason. How else could she have such intense feelings for him? Every part of his face was loved, his blue eyes, slanting downwards, which gave a slightly quizzical look to his face, his delicate features which belied his intense strength, his dark hair.

Gazing at him she tried to disguise her profound longing. She wanted to beg him to take the words back, but Patrick had pulled down the shutters, his lips were set in a tight line. It was a look she knew and feared.

'I know you don't mean that. I'm sorry I woke you. Forget it. Sex isn't important. We have far more going for us than that. I love you, Patrick.'

'I know you do. I feel a heel, but for me it's over,' he said quietly.

Rejection brought bitterness. 'How convenient now that I have no more money. Don't bother to talk about it again until you've repaid the mortgage.'

Patrick dressed, packed a bag and disappeared

for a week. When he returned he was remote. From then on, he spent more time away from home than with them. Business, he explained politely. Then came the time when he came home to ask for a reconciliation. The other woman had left him for someone else and he wanted a chance to make their marriage work. She hadn't needed much persuasion to try.

Now she could see that Patrick had never loved her, merely used her, and he had entirely abdicated all responsibility to Jason. They and their home had provided a convenient backdrop to cloak Patrick's nefarious undertakings with an aura of middle-class respectability. That was all. She could die of sorrow when she remembered how often Jason had been told off for his confrontations with Patrick. And how could she blame Sib for her broken marriage? How could she possibly think that Sib was disloyal?

Here she was stranded on a dark street on a winter's night lost in an emotional void of her own making. She had to retrace her footsteps and take the long road back to the world of feelings. Shame set in and with it a sense of unease, which gradually changed to a feeling of foreboding and then panic. She had to get back, had to make it up with Sib.

24

For the second time that night, Clara turned into the cul-de-sac leading to the river between narrow, terraced houses. She rang the old slave bell three times, but Sib did not answer, yet she was sure she heard footsteps creeping across the room. Then a door slammed.

'Come on, Sib. I know you're at home,' she called through the letterbox. She peered through. The light was on but there was no one there.

'Sib, it's me, Clara. I'm sorry. I came back to make amends. Please open the door — I'm wet through and freezing.'

She waited, but no one came. Perhaps Sib had a lover upstairs, but there were no lights shining through the windows. She should go home, but couldn't because she felt so uneasy. Instead she sat shivering on the top step, watching the leaves drift aimlessly to and fro in the wild gusts of wind.

The patio door slammed again. How strange. Sib told her that she had lost the key to the door. She'd asked Clara to get a spare set cut. They were in the glove compartment of her car. They kept copies of each other's keys for emergencies. Clara tried to ignore the panic fluttering in her stomach as she rang the bell again.

'There must be a reason for this,' she muttered. After one last bellow through the letterbox she went to her car to fetch a torch and Sib's keys. She returned and tried to unlock the door, but the key wouldn't go in. Strange! She couldn't reach the back unless she walked to the end of the row of villas and waded up the river. She reckoned she'd better do that, she couldn't get much wetter.

She was unprepared for the shock of the icy water, and the ankle-deep mud she sank into. As she reached down and fumbled for her shoes, a frog leapt out of the water, startling her. She went on slowly, feeling her way for firm ground, trying to ignore the small creatures that leaped and plopped around, while the sleet fell down her neck and dripped in icy trickles to her knees. She sneezed loudly. An owl rose from an overhanging branch and circled overhead uttering mournful cries. A shiver of inexplicable terror sent her splashing through the water and clambering on to Sib's patio.

Everything looked so normal. No doubt Sib had taken a sleeping pill and hadn't heard the doorbell. It was a comforting thought until she remembered the patio door slamming shut. But now it was locked. She unlocked and walked inside. Switching on the light, she blinked in the sudden glare.

'Sib!'

She went upstairs, cautiously opening the doors, but there was no sign of a lovers' tryst. The beds were neatly made, curtains closed, and a half-packed suitcase lay on Sib's bed. Searching Sib's cupboard, she found overalls and an old duffel coat. 'Heavens!' she muttered. This

204

took her back twenty years. Stripping off her wet anorak, jeans and jersey, she put on the overalls, a sweater and the coat and went downstairs to find a bag for her wet clothes.

She glanced at her watch. Ten p.m. She had left Jason a note, but perhaps she should call him. The phone rang a few times before Jason answered.

'How're you doing, Jason?'

'Okay. You still at Sib's?'

'Yes. Did you get my note?'

'Thanks. I warmed the pie in the microwave and ate it. Pretty good, too.'

'That's great. Listen Jason, I might hang around here for another half-hour. I had a fight with Sib. It upset me, so I went walking in the rain.' She paused and thought about it. 'For hours I suppose. Bit silly really, but the point is, when I came back Sib wasn't here. I thought I heard footsteps, so I waited, but she didn't come. I have Sib's keys, but I couldn't open the front door, so I waded along the river to get to the patio. I'm drenched, I can tell you. I borrowed some of Sib's dry clothes and I'm hanging in here until she gets back.'

'Listen Mum,' Jason's voice had gone hoarse again. 'Sit tight. I'll be there in ten minutes. Mum . . . listen . . . '

Clara stopped listening as she glanced towards the front door. Of course, she couldn't unlock the door because Sib's key was in the lock. Sib was in the house somewhere. 'Oh Jason. The door's locked from the inside. She's here some-where. Oh God.' Clara dropped the receiver.

'Sib . . . ' she whispered. 'Sib . . . '

She went upstairs slowly, forcing each step against a tidal wave of dread. The bathroom was empty. Almost rigid with fright, Clara went to each wardrobe in turn, pushing the clothes aside. She was panting as she crept downstairs to the living-room.

The sounds of the empty house were intensified by her own heightened perception: the bedroom clock ticking like a metronome, the vague sound of the neighbour's TV, the rain pouring from a blocked drainpipe, the creaking of the cooling central heating, a tap dripping somewhere, the sound of her heart beating like a drum.

There was only one door left, the cupboard under the stairs. Clara was sweating with fright as she moved towards it. She opened it a crack and felt a wave of nausea rise in her gorge at the scent of turps and a subtle perfume. It was so dark. She didn't want to see what was there, but she forced herself to pull back the door. One glance was enough. Sib lay sprawled over the bottles and canvasses, her head falling back, eyes wide and staring. Sib's face was as white as chalk, her eyes mirrored her last frantic terror and a crimson stain soaked her long embroidered blouse.

It wasn't Sib at all, just an empty shell. The fiery, passionate life force, the glowing, generous spirit had vanished. Gone forever!

'I'm so sorry,' Clara whispered as she crouched beside Sib and caught hold of her hands. 'Sorry I fought with you. Sorry I deliberately misunderstood. Sorry I took out my grief and jealousy on you. Oh Sib, who did this to you? How could this terrible thing happen? Who would want to kill you?'

★   ★   ★

Jason arrived some time later. Clara gazed blankly at the letterbox listening to his frantic voice. 'Mum, open the door.' He kept repeating the same words. She stared at the front door, lost in her thoughts.

Eventually she managed to cross the room and let Jason in. She tried to mouth the ugly words, but couldn't say them: 'Sib . . . ' she whispered. 'Dead . . . Over there . . . I think she was stabbed, but there's no sign of a knife.'

'You're as cold as death, Mum. Sit there. The police should have been here by now.'

'Police?'

'I called them. I was worried about you. Oh, Mum. I'm so sorry.'

Words couldn't help, Jason knew. He watched his mother shuddering violently and then he went upstairs and found a blanket and put it around her. She made an effort to recover, biting her lip and pushing herself upright. 'Just leave me be, Jason.'

There was nothing he could do for her. He went to the cupboard under the stairs and stared for a long time. There must be a clue. A subtle sensation was setting off reflexes of unease, but he couldn't get to grips with it. Mum was right. They were surrounded by evil. He sat beside her and tried to warm her hands in his. Before long they heard a knock on the door. 'It's not locked,' Jason called.

Detective Sergeant Browning walked in. 'What's happened? Are you all right? Are you alone here?'

Jason nodded and indicated the cupboard door. The policewoman peered in and then straightened up looking pale. She went outside and returned moments later.

'The rest are on the way. Have you touched anything, Mrs Connor?'

'Only Sib. I . . . I held her hand.'

Mum could hardly talk, her mouth seemed numb, as if she'd just come from the dentist. Shock, Jason thought, watching her struggling with the words.

Two uniformed police arrived and a few minutes later, DCI Bates arrived with Fergus.

Jason walked over to them. 'Good evening, Inspector. My mother's very shocked. She discovered the body and called me to call the police. I'd like to take her home now. She isn't well. I think she's in shock.'

Fergus left the cupboard and walked across the room. 'We'll need a statement from Mrs Connor first. I'll try not to be too long. Where can we go?' He looked questioningly at Browning.

'There's a small office upstairs. Bit of a squeeze.'

He went upstairs and called Browning to bring them up. When the three of them had squeezed into Sib's tiny office their knees were almost touching.

'So, Mrs Connor. Here we are again. Please tell me why you were here at this time of night and how you found the deceased?'

Jason groaned inwardly as his mother told Fergus of their argument over Gina and the way she had walked unseen into the stormy night, obviating any chance of an alibi and still unaware that she needed one.

A policewoman came up with a bag full of wet clothes.

'Those are mine,' Mum said reaching for them, but Fergus nodded and the clothes were taken away.

Mum frowned and looked uncertain. 'But I told you . . . They're mine. I was wet through from the rain and the river.'

'Forensic will confirm your story, I have no doubt,' he muttered.

Mum gasped and closed her mouth firmly.

'I must ask both of you to come down to the station first thing tomorrow morning and make statements. Meantime Sergeant Browning will drive you home.'

Mum got up looking more angry than shocked, which was a good sign.

'I'll drive myself . . . ' She stood up and paused in the doorway. 'You must contact Sib's father. I have his number in my bag.' She leafed through the pages, unable to see through her tears.

'What's it under, Mum?' Jason said, taking the notebook gently. Deciphering Mum's telephone book was always a creative exercise because nothing was ever in alphabetical order.

'Under S for Sib of course, see father — Piers Ferretti.'

'Of course.'

'I'm so sorry, Mum,' he told her when they reached the pavement.

'Don't talk. Just don't talk. I thought I'd reached rock bottom when Patrick died. But it's never rock bottom, is it?'

Mum's left hand reached out and squeezed his. 'Go carefully. I'll see you at home.'

A sense of impending doom hung over Jason as he rode home. He wondered how his mother would cope with yet another disaster.

25

Detective Inspector Fergus seemed cold and distant as he switched on his tape recorder, gave his name and rank and the time and date. Clara found the procedure intimidating. She had arrived at seven-thirty with Jason who had made his statement and left for school. She glanced round at the hateful room with its dusty, scratched table, four chairs and stuffy, over-heated air, sensing the vibes of desperation. Fergus, whom she had always liked, was assuming the guise of callous authority.

'Thank you for coming to assist us with our inquiries. You are free to leave at any time. Let's start from the beginning,' he said, without a glimmer of friendliness. 'Just how well did you know Ms Ferretti?'

'You want all of it?'

'Please.'

'Look,' she said with a hint of defiance in her voice. 'Sib and I were close friends for fourteen years. You can't expect me to begin to explain.' The pain of Sib's awful death and their fight over Gina was still frighteningly close. She knew she would never lose her anguish or her fear.

'Try your best.'

Tears burned her eyes. How do you condense years of close friendship into a short answer? She recalled how they met on a student skiing trip when she had dug Sib out of a drift, only to discover that night that they were both studying at University College, London. Later they shared a flat and they had remained close friends ever since.

Fergus frowned and flicked through his notes. 'Please tell me exactly how you came to be at Miss Ferretti's house at that time of night and what caused the argument between you?'

'I told you last night.'

'But this time it's official.'

'Why is it that I feel I'm a suspect?' she asked aggressively.

'You tell me, Mrs Connor.' Fergus looked up and gave her a fierce look as if quelling any rebellion.

Clara faltered and tried to remember what she had said the last time, while Fergus sat motionless on the other side of the desk. She felt exhausted by the time she had finished her story, but the policeman merely nodded.

'Why did you walk through the river to the back of the cottage? It doesn't make sense to me.' His voice had become expressionless. She might as well try to reason with an android.

'We've been through all this. You know very well why. Because there was no other way to get inside.'

'Please answer the question in detail, Mrs Connor. Tell us what led you to make a rather hazardous trip upstream in pouring rain and in pitch darkness.' He gazed blandly at her.

Clara tried to make her story more convincing, describing her unease, her premonition of doom when she heard the door slam shut, remembering that she had Sib's spare keys in her boot, the sinking feeling in her stomach as she waded upstream, but she couldn't begin to describe her skin-crawling fear and her disgust with herself for losing her temper with Sib. There was no reaction from Fergus. Resentment surged.

'Explain to us again why you were wearing Miss Ferretti's clothes, Mrs Connor.' Fergus retained his anonymous expression, but his eyes were watchful, as if he didn't know her. At first this had irritated Clara, but now he was frightening her. Do they teach them how to do that at police school, she wondered?

'Because I didn't want to catch pneumonia. That's why,' she snarled. 'I was wet through and freezing. This isn't fair.' She glanced at her watch. It was past nine. 'I need some coffee. I told you.' Clara struggled to remain calm in the face of the DI's lack of concern. 'I can't see the point of going over the same thing again and again.' Her mouth was dry and she was feeling badly shocked.

'We'll have a twenty minute break,' Fergus told Jennings. 'Show Mrs Connor where the rest room is and fetch her some coffee and a sandwich. Give her the menu. We have to fetch the food from the takeaway opposite,' he explained to Clara.

She fumbled in her bag.

'No, no. It's on the Force.' Momentarily his eyes scrutinised her anxiously as she left.

Twenty minutes later she was back in the office. Fergus arrived, picked up his notebook

213

and gave her a quiet nod.

'When you arrived the first time did you gain the impression there might be someone else in the house?' he asked, giving her some hope that he believed her. 'Did you sense someone's presence, or did Miss Ferretti appear agitated, or in a hurry for you to leave, or in any way reticent?'

'No. Not at all. But later, that is when I was sitting on the steps outside the front door, I thought I heard footsteps and then the patio door slammed shut. I was surprised because Sib told me she'd lost the key and she asked for my spare set back. That's why they were in my glove compartment, but I'd forgotten to give them to her. I went to fetch them, but I couldn't get the front door unlocked. Of course I know now that her key was still in the lock.'

Fergus gazed reflectively at her. 'Why didn't you tell us this in the first place?'

'Because you didn't ask me, I suppose.'

'Let's get this straight. Was the door locked when you walked upstream to the patio?'

'Yes. My fingers were frozen. I dropped the key twice before I managed to open the patio door.'

'Did you hear anything outside?'

She faltered, remembering the wind roaring and branches snapping, the flooding river splashing over stones, the night bird that had frightened her, but that wasn't what Fergus wanted.

'Nothing.'

'You must have felt very bitter for the

neighbours to have heard you shouting.'

'Did they?' She sighed. 'Of course I was angry.'

'That's what murder is; an expression of anger,' Fergus told her.

Her heart fluttered wildly. 'Stop twisting everything. You're browbeating me.'

'I don't think so. I don't understand why you should be so angry with your friend so long after your husband's affair was over.'

'It was a matter of loyalty.'

'Or was Sibyl Ferretti your husband's mistress and you had only just found out?'

She stared defiantly at him. 'You don't know Sib or you wouldn't say such a thing. Are you allowed to badger people in this manner? I had nothing to do with Sib's murder. I've told you that dozens of times.'

'The neighbours heard a scream at nine p.m. Where were you at ten p.m. Mrs Connor?'

'I don't know. Oh my God.' Clara covered her mouth with her hand. She felt hollow inside. 'That must have been when Sib was . . . was . . . ' She couldn't say the ugly word. 'I don't know where I was. Walking somewhere, I suppose.'

'Mrs Connor. I'm suggesting that at ten p.m. you opened the patio doors for your accomplice to gain entrance to the house in order to murder your husband's mistress.'

'I don't have to sit here and take this, Inspector. For the last time, I had nothing to do with Sib's murder. I loved her. I don't have an accomplice and I've told you all I know. I'm going.' She stood up and then hovered uncertainly, wondering if this would look suspicious.

'Please sit down, Mrs Connor,' Fergus said, looking accessible for the first time. 'Quite apart from this murder, there's something odd going on. I know it and you know it, too. Too many unexplained incidents all lead back to you. Need I list them? The death of your husband in very suspicious circumstances, your office burglary and the attack on you, the unknown stalker waiting outside your house, rumours that your husband was engaged in criminal activities; then Miss Ferretti is assaulted in the castle while standing in for you, and now she has been murdered. A string of rather strange coincidences, if there were no link between these crimes. I'm sure you agree. So in order to find Miss Ferretti's murderer, we are looking for the link or a common denominator, and all we have at the moment is you. Do you understand?'

'Yes,' she whispered, suppressing a jolt of fear. 'But I know who beat up Sib at the castle. Sib admitted it.'

'So you've been withholding vital evidence.'

'I forgot. Jerry Watson has a pass to deliver produce to the castle. They have an account with him. He wanted to know where Gina was living. He was engaged to Gina before she left him for my husband and he still loves her. Sib admitted this to me. Sib was a lovely, loyal, kind, talented person. Why would anyone want to kill her?'

'That's what we hope to find out.'

'Someone is moving in on us, Inspector. Can't

216

you see that? Why don't you help us? Oh, what's the use? I must go.' She reached for her coat and bag.

'If you like, Constable Jennings can drive you home,' Fergus said. He dismissed her without a smile or a handshake.

26

'Ah, Fergus, sit down. You seem to be getting nowhere fast on the Ferretti murder. The case is becoming increasingly baffling. There's no conclusive evidence in any direction. Any new leads?'

Despite Bates' calm manner, Fergus could sense his intense irritation. He wanted results fast, but it seemed to Fergus that there just weren't enough hours to get by. It was eight a.m. and Bates was enjoying his coffee and a sandwich while he issued his commands. The tantalising smell of the toasted cheese was almost unbearable. Fergus had spent half the previous night hiding in the shadows of the wind-swept, freezing marina waiting for incoming boats to unload their immigrants. It hadn't happened and at three a.m. he had given up and driven home, feeling depressed. Now he was tired and very hungry.

'So where have you got so far, Inspector? I've been expecting your report on the Ferretti murder.'

'Yes, I know, but so far I've drawn a complete blank. Everyone who knew Miss Ferretti has a watertight alibi and there's no reason to suspect Mrs Connor.'

'Except that she was there,' Bates cut in on him. 'She was also there when Connor died. I think she's guilty.' He took another long slurp of coffee.

Shock waves reverberated through Fergus. He leaned forward and peered at the DCI. He could hardly believe he was serious.

'I have nothing like enough evidence to make an arrest.' He scowled as he scrutinized Bates, wondering how he could convince him of the absurdity of arresting Clara Connor.

Bates put down his cup with a clash. 'There's a strong link between the two deaths, which is that Mrs Connor was the wife of one victim and the best friend of another, and she was angry and felt cheated by both of them. Furthermore, she was on-hand. I think she's guilty.'

'But sir, all the evidence points towards the murderer being male. The bruises sustained by the victim indicate that her attacker pulled her right arm behind her in a half-Nelson and pushed her into the cupboard. Miss Ferretti was a big woman and that takes some doing.'

Bates looked sceptical, but said nothing so Fergus carried on.

'There's another thing. Forensic tests show that there was no blood on the clothes Mrs Connor left in the shower. Yet the raincoat that we found hidden near the river had traces of the victim's blood. If Mrs Connor had been wearing it, not only would her clothes show some traces of blood, but they would not have been so wet.'

Bates snorted. 'You're grasping at straws, Fergus.'

The DCI was indifferent as to whether Clara Connor was guilty or not, Fergus suspected, but he understood his motivation. Dover's citizens, horrified by this cold-blooded murder, were pushing for the case to be closed. So was the Chief Constable. Rumour had it that Bates' job was on the line due to poor performance since his wife fell ill. He needed an arrest. Even the wrong one, Fergus thought treacherously.

Suppressing a surge of mutiny, Fergus felt an overwhelming need to get out of Bates' office. Like time and space, truth changed according to the viewer's stance. Bates wouldn't be convinced of Mrs Connor's innocence, because he didn't want to be. Fergus hurried across the road to buy coffee and a toasted cheese sandwich.

As caffeine and glucose surged into his blood stream, Fergus lost some of his tension and regained his confidence. He'd find the killer. He knew that, but it wasn't going to be easy.

He returned to his office, switched on his PC and keyed in for a new report sheet. As he filled in the date he was mentally listing the pros and cons. His intuition told him Clara Connor was innocent but he had to admit that some of the facts looked bad.

She had almost died from concussion and exposure after a night spent in icy waters after the capsizing of the *Connemara*, but that wouldn't convince Bates of her innocence. The DCI would argue that having drugged her husband in order to attack him, her plans went awry when the boat blew up too soon, knocking her overboard and destroying her inflatable. Assuming that she had such a thing.

He'd been through the pros and cons of Clara's guilt a hundred times. Two questions were bugging him. First and foremost, why was she off the boat at the time of the explosion and wearing a wetsuit? Strange thing to wear onboard. And then, why was she on the boat in the first place? Surely she couldn't be so naive as to think that her husband wanted a reconciliation?

He sat doodling for while, trying to think of more points in her favour. When he couldn't think of any, he searched for some other avenue of investigation he'd neglected. What about the stalker? He slapped his forehead in disgust. The man seemed to have disappeared. He might be able to provide some answers. He was an unknown quantity — and Fergus hated unsolved mysteries.

★ ★ ★

Fergus drove down Castle Street towards the market square, passing quaint Victorian houses converted into a mismatch of shops and offices. Deep in thought, he almost overshot his turn-off. He turned in time and drove into the car park adjoining Pencester Park. Here amongst the pay and display meters a Kosovan washed and polished local cars. He had always caught Fergus's attention with his amazing energy as he ran from car to car loaded with two buckets full of soapy water. His arms whirled like windmills as he sponged the chassis, while his eyes gleamed with zeal. His name was Vladimir Zlokovic and Fergus had checked him out with Immigration. Formerly a science teacher, he had joined the Kosovan Liberation Army and been caught and imprisoned in a Serbian concentration camp where he had been tortured. After eventually escaping, he had led his wife, three small children and an elderly mother, whom he had carried most of the way, over the mountain pass into Macedonia. He earned a small wage and ten percent of takings, but so far he had scarcely reached the breadline.

Zlokovic was at least six foot, with strong Latin features and dark eyes, but his face showed none of the warmth Fergus had expected from such a tale of family fealty. He was as expressionless as an animated robot and when Fergus introduced himself, there was a distinct lack of empathy.

'What you want?' His voice was very deep, like a growl from a grizzly bear. 'I have my papers. I do nothing wrong here. I obey the law, work hard and pay cash for everything.' He seemed concerned that he might lose all he had fought for.

'I only need some information,' Fergus said soothingly.

'No time, no information.' He hadn't once lost his stroke as he splashed the soapy cloth over the car.

'So what time d'you stop work?'

'Four, unless it rains.' He glanced briefly at the sky.

'No lunch break?'

'Depends.'

There must be a way to get through to him. 'Listen, Mr. Zlokovic. We pay informers in this country. This could lead to regular windfalls coming your way.'

'Windfalls?'

'Payments,' Fergus assured him.

He shook his head and pressed his lips together.

'And a possible kick up the ladder on the house waiting list.'

'Ah.' His hand missed a stroke and then continued. Fergus guessed he was getting somewhere. 'What you want to know?'

'I need to contact a man. He's Serbian, I believe, like yourself.'

Zlokovic snorted with impatience.

'I want to know his name and what he's doing here.' Fergus took out the photographs he'd sent Sergeant Browning to take of the man loitering in Cowper Road. 'The car's easily visible and so is the German registration number, but the pictures of the man are indistinct. Have you heard of him at all? Could you ask around?'

'Come tomorrow at noon. You want your car washed and polished?'

'Thank you, yes.' It was the last thing he wanted, but it seemed prudent to become a customer. Now he would have to hang around headquarters until he got his car back.

The windmills whirled faster as Fergus walked towards the park, haunt of immigrants and haughty gulls. Today it was occupied by a small travelling fun fair with shooting booths, bumper cars, roller coaster and a gypsy fortune teller, Madam Zorac.

Fergus was tempted to walk into her booth, but what could she say: 'You long for love, but you are surrounded with death and greed?'

223

Glancing up, he saw rain clouds moving rapidly in from the west and quietly swore to himself. He had worked through the weekend and he had the rest of the day and the evening off. He'd hoped to get in some diving, but the weather was against him as visibility would be almost nil.

He passed on to Ladywell, bought a carton of coffee from the cafe opposite and turned into headquarters where he tried to chat up their new, busty constable, Rosa Myerson, for half an hour, but without much joy.

★　★　★

It was pouring with rain and bitterly cold the next day as Fergus drove into the car park for his appointment with Zlokovic. Business was bad. No one wanted their cars polished in the rain and Zlokovic was hanging around the public convenience, the only cover he could find, looking gloomy. He was wearing a fleece-lined, dark leather jacket over a black tracksuit. The jacket looked as if it had accompanied him on the gruelling march over the mountains into Macedonia.

'You've been favoured,' he told Zlokovic. 'You're now number three on the housing list. At most, it's only a matter of weeks to wait.'

'My wife will be pleased. There are six of us in one room.' He sighed. 'I have some information for you.'

'Shall we go for a drink?'

'I don't drink.'

'Or coffee?'

'I have to wait for my son. He walks here from school. We should move around the corner. I don't want to be seen talking to you.'

There was an alley between the public toilets and a waist-high wall and beyond the wall was an L-shaped extension of the car park. It was private and Zlokovic lead the way. He leaned over the wall and looked haughtily at Fergus.

'How much are you paying me?'

'Whatever it's worth. You'll have to trust me.'

Zlokovic shrugged and thrust his hands in his pockets. He began to talk in his low, growling voice, almost as if he had learned the message by heart. Perhaps he had.

'Many people know of Peric Zimon, although he has few friends. He was once a lawyer with his own practice in Britain, but towards the end of the war, when news came of the atrocities, he returned to Kosovo to help the people fight for freedom. He was taken prisoner and badly tortured in one of the Serb's notorious prison camps. Eventually he escaped.

'He returns to Kosovo often and he travels Europe. He was seen in Dover yesterday. He says he searches for a lost relative, but no one believes him. Most of the immigrants assume he's a criminal. He has a British driving license, a new Mercedes bought in Germany and a driver, or a colleague. He owns or rents a house in London. No one knows his address. He has connections in high places.'

Zlokovic's English had improved dramatically as he forgot his reticence. Fergus wondered if he could find him a job as an interpreter.

A suspicion of a smile played around his lips as he gazed at the tarmac criss-crossed with white paint, marking empty parking bays.

'Why are you smiling?' Fergus asked.

'No barbed wire fences. That is why I smile.'

It seemed little enough to make a man happy. Fergus decided to keep that in mind for depressing days. He handed over a hundred pounds.

Zlokovic took the money, counted it and put it in his pocket, before saying: 'Was it worthwhile for you? If so, I have more information . . . '

Fergus sighed and reached for his wallet.

'He drinks at the Primrose pub in Coombe Valley Road and he often walks along the beachfront after dark. When he's in Dover, he and his driver, or friend, stay at the Belgravia private hotel, in Folkestone Road. He is a frequent visitor to the Albenor brothel which is nearby.'

Fergus handed over another fifty pounds.

'Thanks, Zlokovic. If you have any problems, call me. If the house takes longer than a few weeks, call me. I'll be seeing you.' He gave him his card.

'Wait! Another thing,' Zlokovic called after him. He waited for the cash while glancing at his watch. 'Right now Zimon is having a drink with Serbian friends at the Primrose. You'd better hurry.'

Fergus moved out of earshot, pulled out his mobile telephone and called Sergeant Browning.

'Remember the alleged stalker you took a few

shots of outside Connor's home? His name is Peric Zimon. You have his car registration number. Arrest him for stalking and get some assistance,' he told her. 'He might prove difficult. Oh, another thing. Keep it to yourself for the time being.'

It had all been too simple, Fergus thought uneasily as he walked to Ladywell. He'd been trying to get a Serbian informer for months without success. Zlokovic's message appeared to have been learned by heart. How would he know words like notorious and frequent? They didn't match his broken English. It was a set-up, but did it really matter? he asked himself, just as long as this could shed some light on the link between Zimon and Mrs Connor.

27

It was seven p.m. when Fergus arrived at Ladywell, following an urgent call from Bates. He knocked at the door and walked into the DCI's office. Bates was on the telephone to his home. His wife's nurse wanted to leave, but he had to work late — a familiar story.

Bates pushed a fax towards Fergus and carried on arguing.

Fergus sat down and stared at the order from Canterbury headquarters which read: '*Classified: Release Peric Zimon without questioning.*'

Zimon had kept silent during the interview, so Bates and Fergus had decided to leave him in the cell for the night to cool his heels. Now the matter had been taken out of their hands.

Bates replaced the receiver and sighed. 'Unbelievable!'

Fergus frowned at his superior. 'Any idea what this is all about?'

'You know as much as I do.' Bates shrugged.

'Who did Zimon call?'

'Our Interpol Liaison Officer at Scotland Yard.'

For a moment the two men sat silently considering the implications of this unexpected turn of events.

Bates picked up another file. 'You'd better go and let Zimon out. Take him for a drink. Try to pump him. I'll see you across the road as soon as I can.'

* * *

Remand prisoners were housed in the cells under the detective's wing in Ladywell. Prisoners were usually unnerved by the experience, but it would take more than this to dim the zeal in Zimon's eyes. He was athletic-looking, but too thin for his shirt collars, so presumably he'd lost weight recently. There was a strange smoothness to the right side of his face. Plastic surgery after burns, Fergus realised from the tiny crack-like scars around the patches. He looked like a deeply contemplative and disciplined man. When he uncurled to full height they were eyeball to eyeball, an unusual experience for Fergus. Zimon's Slavic-looking, high cheekbones and strong, regular features, were marred by the intensity of his compelling dark eyes. A fanatic, Fergus felt sure. But for whom or what was he carrying a torch?

'You are Mr Peric Zimon?'

'I am.'

'How good is your English? Do we need an interpreter?'

'Why should we? I'm sure you've been asked not to question me, but I can answer that question. I studied in England.'

Fergus tried not to show his annoyance. 'That helps. My Serbo-Croatian goes as far as *slivovitz*.'

'Ah, yes. There's a pub in Dover where you can buy *slivovitz*. A little raw perhaps, because it hasn't had time to mature, but it's acceptable. After all, your plums are excellent.' Fergus

229

wondered at his precise and only slightly accented English.

'How about vodka meantime? Come and have a drink with me. We'll collect your things on the way out. What exactly were you looking for in Connor's office?'

That was a bumbling one, Fergus thought, and it received the silent contempt it deserved. Fergus felt his irritation mounting.

'Whatever it is you're doing, Zimon, you seem to have *carte blanche* to burgle offices and stalk and attack local women,' he tossed into the silence. 'I'm amazed you got away with it.' Despite orders he could not control his anger at Clara Connor's ordeal.

'Yes, Inspector Fergus. I expect you were.' His face was as expressionless as a robot's.

The Sir John Falstaff was right across the road, but as Fergus ushered Zimon towards the entrance he was aware that the man could simply walk away. He probably would, yet so far he was still tagging along. Fergus hung back in the doorway to let Zimon go first. The Serb chose a table in the corner by the fire and sat motionless in one of the faded leather armchairs.

'Two double vodkas, ice and two lemonades,' Fergus ordered since he was on duty. He carried the drinks to the table. Zimon's fingers were kneading the soft leather, his face bland as usual.

'Cheers,' Fergus said.

'*Zivjeli!*'

'So what line of work are you in?'

'You want to pigeonhole me, Inspector. What difference does it make? I am qualified as a

230

lawyer. Correction! I was a lawyer. Then I joined the Kosovan Liberation Army.'

Fergus leaned back and tried to look relaxed although he was only too aware of his clumsy approach. 'Let me get this straight. You say you're here on a job?'

In the hiatus that followed Fergus cursed his crudeness while Zimon gazed at him in sardonic amusement. Conversation with Zimon appeared to be a non-starter. Fergus was searching around for a means to provoke a response when Zimon unexpectedly broke the silence.

'My last job would amuse you.' Zimon rested his chin on his hand and gazed into the fire. 'I was employed as a translator and legal advisor to the UN peace-keeping force setting up a Kosovan government in Pristina.'

This voluntary release of information staggered Fergus. His voice interested him, too: London, New York, Pristina, Paris also, maybe. It was all there in quiet intonations.

'So Fergus, tell me.' He leaned forward and laid his hand on the younger man's shoulder. 'What's the first necessity when a country has been totally destroyed? And I must admit, I did my share of the destruction.' He closed his eyes momentarily as if to block out visions. Fergus wondered if he were aware of the gesture.

'Law and order? A police force?'

'So says the policeman. No, my friend! Any country can get by without the likes of you, but its government can't survive without money. So the first thing to do is to set up a treasury department and tax the people. After a while I found myself involved in the unacceptable task of collecting taxes from the owners of destroyed farms and businesses. I quit! It seemed the only honourable move open to me.' Zimon seemed to be thawing out a little as he finished his first vodka.

'Listen, Zimon,' Fergus began cautiously. 'There's a certain overlap of cases. I'm on a murder inquiry and you might be able to cast some light on the background, without in any way prejudicing your security.'

'A murder inquiry? Yet you have released the corpse and it has been cremated.'

Fergus concealed a smug smile. Zimon was assuming he was talking about Connor and that the yachtsman had been murdered. Good! So there was a connection.

'True! I'll reword my plea,' Fergus said. 'I suspect murder has been committed. My superior doesn't, but I'd like to convince him.'

'I might consider a small barter. I can give you details of a double murder that's in your area of investigation.'

How did Zimon know what his area was, Fergus wondered.

'In return you might be able to help me. I am looking for a Serb from Beograd. You call it Belgrade. I traced him to Calais, but I've lost track of him since then. I have a few photographs here.' He opened his briefcase and took out an envelope.

At that moment Bates approached them, looking harassed. 'Bloody telephone. I can never get away from my desk.'

Together they examined the indistinct pictures of a Serbian army colonel standing up in a jeep, walking through a doorway and leaning over a pit where he was waving a baton. Fergus frowned and looked more closely into the trench.

'That's right. All those civilians had just been shot,' Zimon said softly.

'My God!' Fergus stared down at the photographs as if mesmerized. He shuddered and looked away and tried to lighten up. 'Sorry. Never seen him, or not that I recall. Would you like me to copy one of these images and issue it to our guys?'

'Thanks, but no. This must not get around. Colonel Vesno Mandic has absolutely no idea that he's a wanted man. I have no doubt he's living quite openly somewhere in Europe, enjoying his newly acquired wealth. Let's call it the spoils of war, to be polite. By the way, there's a rumour going round that he's having it off with Connor's woman. Of course that's only hearsay, but it came from a normally reliable source. It's known he had criminal business connections with Patrick Connor.'

Fergus felt shocked. If it were true it wouldn't look good for Clara Connor, but it explained Zimon's surveillance.

'How exactly do you figure in this?' Bates asked.

'I'm what you might call a bounty hunter.' Zimon was searching through his packed briefcase for an envelope. He found it and handed it to the DCI.

'Here's the case you might like to look into,

Chief Inspector. The affidavit has been signed by myself and the doctor in charge of Casualty. It concerns a Serb, a Dr. Gajic and his family, who came across the Channel illegally on the *Valkyr*, a converted lobster boat. When the coastguard approached the vessel these immigrants, plus other contraband, were allegedly tied in sacks, attached to bricks and dumped through the lobster hatch. Only Dr. Gajic managed to fight his way out of the sack and swim to shore. Here's Gajic's latest address.'

Bates swore quietly and handed the affadavit to Fergus. 'Follow it up. I have a longing to see these bastards brought to trial.'

Zimon wrote a name and address rapidly in precise script on a piece of scrap paper and slid it towards Fergus.

'The geography changes, but the cruelty never varies,' Fergus muttered.

Zimon tossed back his second vodka, stood up and nodded. 'Thanks for the drink. Be seeing you.'

Fergus followed him outside and swore as he watched Zimon disappear into the crowd looking like any other asylum seeker.

'You go through life with blinkers on, Fergus,' Bates snapped belligerently as they walked back to headquarters. 'There's a lot of evidence against the suspect. Let's assume that Mrs Connor was having an affair with this colonel. What if they joined forces to kill her husband, but then Sibyl Ferretti found out and threatened to expose them? So Mrs Connor went to Ferretti's house and distracted her friend while her lover entered through the balcony door, which she had already unlocked. How's that?'

Fergus scowed. 'In my opinion — '

Bates interrupted him. 'Add to that Peric Zimon's information that she's having an affair with this fellow and we have grounds for an arrest.'

He gave a self-satisfied smirk and a strangely Gallic shrug. 'That's only one of a dozen of scenarios. Arrest Clara Connor and pull her in for questioning. Keep the raincoat until last. I'll look in to help you. There's always a chance that she'll crack and confess.'

28

By day Clara worked on her tour business, sending out leaflets, and visiting publicity agents to woo passengers from the cruise liners and cross-channel ferries. She bought herself three new trouser suits, and made an expensive visit to the hairdresser. Fired by her determination to create a safe, secure home for her son, she succeeded in keeping her grief and fear at arm's length. By night she collated Patrick's computer data. This was her way of fighting back. Only in those frightening, vulnerable times between waking and sleeping, did her defences abandon her and she cried for her lost friend. Even then, she could never allow herself to cry for Patrick.

Clara now accepted that Patrick had been smuggling from the start. The tour agency had only been created to provide his cover. How could she have missed all the signs: cash payments for their bond, the housekeeping paid in cash, no evening chats about how the business was coming along, no business associates to entertain? Had she been blind, or what?

Three weeks had passed since Sib was murdered and so far there had been no arrests. Clara had her own theories: whoever had killed her husband and attacked her had killed Sib. It was a gut feeling more than anything else. She had yet to work out the killer's identity and motive. That would come. She felt sure she would find the clues somewhere in this mass of information. She waited impatiently for Jason's light to be switched off. At last she heard Jock's rhythmic snoring coming from his basket and Jason's light went off. It was time to get started.

Hacking had opened up all kinds of possibilities for Clara, enabling her to give free rein to her imagination, but it hadn't been as simple as she'd first thought. The hard part was finding a safe base so that the hacking could never be traced back to her computer. Last week she had waylaid a colleague at the college who taught basic computer usage and asked if she could sit in on a class. She had watched while the students typed in the class password and user name and yawned her way through an hour of basic computer training.

On Saturday she had driven to Canterbury to buy the special software she needed. Since then, using the school's user name as a base, she'd practiced hacking into dozens of operations and by now she had at least ten user names and passwords.

Her first priority was to trace the money laundering. She set about hacking into The Bank of Hong Kong's accounts. It took her half the night before she finally located the Celtic Art Company in the banks' files. She only found it by searching for Vesno Mandic. The company was one of four, she learned, under an umbrella holding company called Fick's Cordials, registered in the Netherlands Antilles. Mandic had sole signing power on all four accounts. Total assets amounted to seven million pounds sterling, which was about a third of the missing cash. The funds had arrived there by means of ten bank deposits from a Hungarian bank. Did that mean the money was washed clean? She wished she knew more about finance, but she could learn. From the bank's files she obtained Vesno Mandic's e-mail address. He also banked online.

Smiling softly to herself, she hacked into the West End Safe Deposit's e-mail account. It took over half an hour, but once that was accomplished, only a minute was needed to send Mandic a short message. Feeling pleased, Clara filed off, locked her discs and went to bed. She had exactly two hours in which to sleep, but it was worth it.

29

Was the stiff upper lip ever more than a disguise for numbed and stifled feelings, Clara wondered? She watched the mourners gather amongst the gilded statues and marble angels in the colourful Catholic cemetery, dressed in their darkest clothes, black bands round their sleeves, resembling a party of commuters standing at the platform. They had come to Sib's funeral out of friendship or duty and they were waiting around with baffled tolerance, feigning a little polite interest, knowing that death had absolutely nothing to do with them, the living.

Sib's father, Piers Ferretti, was the exception. His face was swollen, the tears were rolling unashamedly down his chubby red cheeks and his voice was hoarse.

Clara clutched Jason's arm, trying to banish the fury rising in her throat, whilst keeping calm. She had cried all night after finding Sib's corpse. Since then anger had replaced her grief and stayed with her. She would find Sib's killer.

When Clara stepped up to Piers, he clutched her, hugging her close and she felt his shuddering sobs start way down in his belly and move up to his mouth, she could even smell his grief, a strange sick-sour aura that was all about him.

'Gina's not here,' he muttered. 'I don't know where she is. She won't even tell her own father where she's living. She's abroad somewhere.'

'That doesn't sound like Gina,' Clara said, trying to provoke Piers into further confidences.

'Sib was set against her sister because she was living with a married man. It split the family and that's the honest truth, but Gina explained to me that he'd been brought up Catholic and wouldn't divorce. And anyway, the man's poor wife was about to die. Cancer or something. She wouldn't last out the year, the husband had told her. Then they were getting married.'

Clara struggled to conceal her outrage. For a moment she was so shocked she could hardly speak. 'When was this?'

'Oh, let me think. The last time I saw her was the end of July. He'd bought her a costly engagement ring. They'd set the date for the end of October.'

So Fergus was right about the laudanum. Clara's knees had turned to rubber and she found herself breaking out in a cold sweat. Momentarily speechless, she felt her anger uncoil while the first blows of a migraine fell around her temple. She took a deep breath and struggled to look calm.

After a few moments she'd taken control of her pain and rejection, but she couldn't get rid of her fury.

Glancing round she saw Jerry Watson watching her curiously, standing a little apart from the crowd.

'He's looking for Gina,' Clara whispered, as Jason took her arm. 'I want to talk to him. I won't be long.'

240

'Yes?' Jerry said rudely, pushing his hair out of his eyes as Clara approached.

'I'm surprised to see you here, Jerry. You're the person who attacked Sib. She admitted that to me. You wanted to know where Gina is.' Her words brought back the scene with Sib and for a moment she almost broke down. It was Jerry's smirk that pulled her together. 'I bet you know those castle passages like the back of your hand.'

'Yes. You're absolutely right. D'you know why?' he said, shocking her. 'Because my old man was stationed there. He was an electrical engineer in the army. They kept the place running right through the Cold War. I used to take him food and the odd beer. No one ever saw me.'

Clara hardly knew what to say. She'd expected a denial.

'Look, I'm not proud of what I did,' he went on. 'It got out of hand. She lashed out and hit me really hard. I over-reacted, but she had no right to be so unfeeling.' His eyes glinted with fury. 'I had to know where Gina was. I begged her to tell me, but she refused. She wouldn't even tell me if Gina was alive or in England. I've been going through hell, I don't mind telling you.' Jerry's voice was getting hoarse. 'That's why I'm here today. I'd hoped Gina would come.'

'I can't begin to fathom out your motive for wanting to kill Sib,' Clara went on, finding full scope for her aggression.

'Can't you? Well, as it happens I was winning the snooker championship at precisely the same time as Sib's murder. Luckily for me, I was there in full view of a hundred or more people all the evening. The police have been into it very thoroughly. I was their prime suspect, thanks to you. It was lucky that the championships were held that evening. I usually sit at home by myself.'

So that was that. Disappointment came like a physical blow. Feeling embarrassed, Clara turned to find Jason, but he was right behind her. Together they walked towards the grave where they waited in silence. At last the priest was coming, followed by the coffin carried by six pallbearers.

Footsteps were approaching over the gravel. It was Bernie. Clara sighed inwardly. Black suited him. He knew it and he moved towards her with the hint of a swagger. A cherubic smile curled his full lips while his blue eyes glinted with sensuous longings. He gripped her arm.

'Hello Clara,' he said in a stage whisper. 'I was hoping to see you. You'll be pleased to hear that your leaflets were very well received. I had lunch with Eddie Makin, manager of the local P&O Line, yesterday.'

'That's great, Bernie.'

'Makin said you write beautifully. He'll do what he can to create a special price around some of your tours with an all-in rate. The shipping company would pay you. They're very prompt payers.'

'Ah. That's what I'd hoped for. Thanks for your help.'

She looked up, forcing a smile.

'By the way, my offer to buy you out still stands, Clara.'

'I don't want your charity, thanks, Bernie. The business is worthless and I don't think this is the time or place to talk about it. Besides, I'm not selling.'

'Perhaps you have the odd fortune tucked away. Aladdin's cave under the floorboards. All the money Patrick stole must be somewhere?' His fingers tightened on her arm.

'I don't believe these millions exist. If they do, I don't have any of them. I'm broke. That's why I'm trying to make the agency pay. Don't worry, there's no bank statements coming in the post, no credit cards lying around, no gold nuggets in the drawers . . .'

A sneer of fury hung briefly around his lips. 'You're so bloody cocksure of yourself.' He laughed to dispel the unease. 'Clara,' he bent his head and muttered so close to her ear that his curls brushed her cheek. 'Please come and see me. I had an offer of £30,000 for the salvage boat. Do you accept?'

'Yes, of course.'

'Then you must come and sign the papers. Apart from that, I want to try to sort things out for you with the police. I've heard that there's a number of points that the DCI is worried about. Try to come during the week. Phone my secretary.' Another squeeze and he moved on, leaving her apprehensive.

It was so cold. Her feet were numb and her hands red and burning. She should have brought gloves, Clara thought regretfully. Dark clouds

243

were racing low overhead, driven by the chilling north wind, while leaves and small stones were dashing against the tombstones. Soon they would pile the damp earth over Sib. Life couldn't get much worse than this, she thought.

Clara felt a hand on her shoulder and glancing round she was suddenly jolted by the sight of Robin. She hadn't heard him approach, which was unusual. Clara's knees turned to rubber and she found herself breaking out in a cold sweat. Momentarily speechless, she felt her anger uncoil. She took a deep breath and struggled to look calm. To her annoyance he was smiling ingratiatingly.

'A terrible death.' His eyes were concealed behind his sunglasses, but his voice sounded hoarse. 'This sort of tragedy must never happen again.' His fingers were pushing into her shoulder.

'Don't look so startled. All I want is for you and Jason to be safe. I'm very fond of you both. Remember what I told you.'

She took a deep, rasping breath. 'Just one more bruise on Jason, Robin, just one, and I'll tell the police everything. While they're checking around they'll find a great many interesting things, so I'm warning you. Leave my kid alone, you monster.' She shook off his arm and turned to Jason. Together they moved back to the graveside.

Robin looked larger than life in the dim winter light. He stood sullenly staring towards her, a bearlike figure in tight and shiny black.

'The Brotherhood's here,' Clara whispered to Jason.

'Brothers! More like sharks in a womb where only one emerges,' Jason muttered.

Clara felt strangely vulnerable. Targeted! It was more of a sensation than a thought. She spun round and found herself staring at the tinted windows of a black car slowly cruising past the graveyard. It stopped momentarily and drove up on to the pavement where it parked. She waited for the door to open, but it remained closed. Someone was watching from behind the glass, but she couldn't see who it was. She shivered and hurried towards the car. She had to know, but as she approached, the car thrust forward on to the road. She stood still and watched it move toward the top street. It slowed and pulled into the curb. She hurried forward again, but the car shot into the road and swung around the corner.

She went back and stood beside Jason at the graveside. As Sib's coffin was lowered, Clara felt a profound and debilitating panic stealing through her limbs. Any minute now, she thought, I'm going to scream. She threw her flowers into the grave and turned away. She would make her excuses to Piers another time. She'd had enough for one day. 'Let's go,' she said to Jason. 'I have a great longing to be home.'

30

He had seen all he needed to see. The scene had
been memorised and filed for instant recall and
now he was soaring, floating, zooming through
green fields and copses of bare trees, watching
the crows and gulls circle and swoop as they
squabbled over pickings from the newly raked
earth. As the black Mercedes sped through the
Alkham Valley, the driver was in a trancelike state
as he listened to Khachaturian's *Spartacus*,
driving with fierce bursts of speed to the wild,
frenetic rhythms and slowing to the melancholy
lyrics.

At the approach to the M20, he braked. At
precisely that moment an image seared his
mind's eyes, shocking him. It was a woman's
face emerging from the sea, blood seeping from
her wound, blue eyes bloodshot and wide with
fear, but not panicking. She assessed the
situation, fought off the boathook and escaped.
And she knew! She knew! She had seen the car,
too.

He was hardly aware of the time passing as he
plotted to eliminate yet another problem.
'Problems are opportunities for correction,' he
murmured. He wasn't a killer, he knew, but he
had the strength of mind to do what had to be
done.

Snarled up in the traffic, he watched the bleak
faces of commuters hurrying past. By the time

he approached Mayfair he was over an hour late. Gina would be sulking.

His shared art gallery in Duke Street was run by a diminutive Bulgarian widow, formerly a professor of fine art in her country, who had sold so many items for him that he had been coerced into buying a controlling share of her business.

He hurried to the entrance and saw Gina through the window before she saw him. She was studying her nails and scowling. She didn't look up when he called to her. The manageress was beaming because she had just sold two of his ancient Russian icons for £30,000 each, she explained at great length. She was averaging three sales a week and showing a healthy profit.

'Listen, Vesno, there was a man here — well, I'm sure he was Serbian — but something about him wasn't right. You know what I mean? He said he was a collector, but I think he was military. The way he walked. His bearing. Many other things. Besides, he'd didn't appear to be wealthy. He spent a long time looking around and I was busy with another customer who made a purchase. Later I realised this man was photographing the icons — all the items on that wall. He said it would help him to make his final choice.'

Mandic shrugged. 'Why not? We have nothing to hide.'

Gina was still pouting on the *chaise longue*, her shining Titian hair falling over her purple seal-fur coat. She was by far his loveliest work of art, Mandic thought approvingly, and the most costly. He decided to cheer her up.

'Come on, let's go.' He guided her along the street, holding the umbrella over her to the Burlington Arcade, where she purchased a few cashmere jerseys, and on to New Bond Street where he nudged her towards the entrance of Veruccio's. Gina's large amber eyes were her emotional barometer. They showed a high pressure zone moving in fast and, with luck, it would stick around.

'How about a couple of new dresses to celebrate the icon sales?' He pushed her forward and she stepped inside, shrugging her coat into the arms of a waiting assistant. Turning to him, she smiled. It was a slow seductive smile that began when her lips curled at the corners and touched her eyes and the dimples on her cheeks, her breasts tilted, those provocative nipples hardened and her hips shifted voluptuously.

'Cocktail dresses,' she sang happily to the assistant.

Five minutes later they were ensconced in a changing room and the assistant was carrying in ever more outrageous models and offering coffee. As her footsteps faded across the showroom floor, Gina slipped off her dress with a sly glance and God's most sensuous creation stood naked except for her gartered stockings and dainty shoes, all too aware of her outrageous perfection.

He sat down, unzipped, and his member reared up, raring to go.

'Come!'

Her body scorched and squeezed him and he came with a muffled roar, only just in time as the attendant tripped along the passage with a tray of coffee.

Gina giggled.

'Was it good?' he asked her.

'The best. Need you ask?'

'Tell me! Am I better than Patrick? Is it better for you?'

'Please, don't say that sort of thing.' She looked stricken. 'I don't want to hear his name ever again. You promised.' In a rare show of affection she ran her finger down his cheek.

He had four calls to make that afternoon and Gina was taking forever to make up her mind, prevaricating over five dresses, so finally he bought them all. He had appointments with two map dealers and two galleries. Eastern European art was becoming rarer and prices were accelerating. He realised double what he had expected, so he could relax and enjoy dinner at Sheekey's, followed by a show.

It was almost midnight before they reached the tiny village of Nettleton. Their home was a secretive lair ten miles beyond the village, built on a hill, with access from a little-known road through a wood. Mandic operated the compli-cated electronic security system and the taxi swept through to their ultra modern Swedish-designed house. Money buys anything and everything if you offer enough, he thought, remembering the sale. The rooms were spacious, the ceilings high, the views extraordinary, and the decor was all white, which showed off Mandic's extraordinary collection of Eastern European art and maps. There were a few costly

Persian rugs scattered around and the furniture was modern and stark. Mainly he preferred open space and he could afford plenty of that.

'I have to work, but I won't be long,' he told Gina.

Mandic finished his accounts and switched on his laptop computer to check in-coming messages. His stomach tightened as he saw an e-mail from the West End Safe Deposits Company. Impossible! Only his Swiss bank knew this e-mail address. Yet somehow, someone had got hold of this information. His eyes skimmed over the message:

Dear Sir,
Unfortunately we have had a fire at our premises and although the safe deposit boxes are fireproof some of our clients are experiencing smoke damage to their goods. Kindly furnish us with a list of the contents of your box for our insurance company. We urge you to do this as soon as possible.
Yours truly,

JOE JACKSON, MD.

Mandic leaned back, his eyes narrowed with suspicion. Joe Jackson would never dare to ask for this info. Besides, other than a post office box, Jackson had no way of contacting him. Why refer to one box when he had rented two? It was impossible for anyone to discover his e-mail address. *Yet someone had.*

Feeling thoroughly baffled and incapacitated

by a sense of foreboding, Mandic poured a neat scotch. His hands were shaking and that annoyed him. He was painfully aware that this probe into his home base was as dangerous as cracks appearing in the Aswan Dam.

31

The morning was unfolding from its cocoon of white fog with a hint of blue overhead, the passing cars' headlights swinging like lanterns while the emerald green clifftops emerged from a lake of white mist like mystical islands rising from the sea.

Trying to clear her mind before her appointment with Bernie, Clara walked along the sea front and on impulse went down to the pebbled beach, her feet crunching and sliding as she watched the dismal debris and driftwood being slowly beached by the receding tide. She felt as blind as a mole as she tunnelled toward the roots of her own fear. She still carried an obsessive need to know what had happened on the yacht the night Patrick was killed. Lately her nightmares had worsened, but her memory lapse still plagued her.

She arrived ten minutes early and Bernie's secretary showed her into his office. Something was different. Now what was it? She scrutinised the decor and realised that the paintings had been moved around. Then she saw why: Roy Lichtenstein's landscape had been removed from its pride of place above the bookcase and replaced by Lucien Freud's nude. But a Freud, she wondered? This was into real money. Was it real? She was peering closely when Bernie walked in.

'Reproduction,' he said smiling, but from the way he said it she knew he was lying. But how could he create this sort of wealth? She caught her breath. Were they all in this together? She tried not to show her suspicions, but a shadow passed over Bernie's face. He walked towards her and put his hands on her shoulders.

'You have a very expressive face, Clara, but you have nothing to fear from me. You know how I feel about you.'

She gazed blandly at him, aware of his expensive aftershave, the scent of tweed and freshly-laundered linen. He stepped back frowning. 'Sit down. Here's the written offer of £30,000 for your salvage boat. Sign here if you accept. I must say it's a good price.' He pushed the documents and his pen across the desk.

'Thank you.' She signed. 'It's Robin, isn't it?'

Bernie flushed, looking disconcerted. 'I've been talking to the police, as you asked, but I don't have any good news, I'm afraid.'

She switched her mind to the business on hand and tried to quell her fear by pacing the carpet while she talked.

'I'm scared, Bernie, and by so many things. Dealing with the police is so confusing. One minute you think they're on your side and you're doing them a favour by 'helping them with their inquiries,' and the next they're plaguing you daily with their silly questions.' She laughed, trying to make light of her fears and morbid suspicions.

'I'm afraid they aren't on your side, Clara, whatever you thought. I asked Bates to let me know exactly where we stand.'

She pondered over the word 'we' while she stood staring out of the window.

'So where do *I* stand?'

He raised one eyebrow and his brown eyes glittered wilfully while he flashed a sardonic leer. 'Have it your own way. I'll tell you exactly what they said, but for goodness sake sit down. Fergus is concerned that you have not yet satisfied them on any number of confusing issues. D'you want coffee?'

'Just tell me.'

'They suspect that you might be involved with Patrick's Serbian partner.'

She gaped at him. 'Involved with who?' she said incredulously. 'Come on, Bernie. Don't pussy-foot around. What are you talking about?'

'I told you about the Serb, ex-KGB, who came looking for Patrick when he hung on to his cash.'

'But you said 'his partner'.'

'In a way that's true. They've had information that you were involved with this foreign man.'

'Involved in what way?'

'I suppose, financially and sexually.'

'How dare you repeat their disgusting insinuations? But Bernie, how do they know about him?' Not for anything would she admit to Bernie that she knew his name and his bank details.

'Well, they weren't insinuating anything. Just stating various suspicions. God knows who or what gave them this angle. Hey there, calm down. That's the police for you. They have to consider all possibilities. Don't blame me, that would be like shooting the messenger. Anyway, I told them you don't know this guy. None of us do.'

He leaned over the table and rested his chin on his hands so that his eyes were fixed on hers with a faintly belligerent expression.

'I'm not blaming you. It's just that . . . ' She stood staring out of the window, pressing her forehead against the window-pane. 'It's like being a shark caught in a net. Every time you move the strands tighten.'

'Their next query was why you asked your friend Sibyl to take your place coincidentally on the day when she was beaten up? They don't believe that this was a chance encounter or a last minute plan of her attacker. They feel that you tipped off someone.'

'That makes sense although it isn't true,' she said thoughtfully. 'Oh Bernie, what am I going to do?'

'This is no time for feeling sorry for yourself, Clara. Last of all: they don't believe that the murderer was able to enter Sibyl's house without help from inside, since there was no sign of a forced entry. The neighbours assure them that the patio doors were kept locked. At present the police have a reasonably open mind about you, so they're holding fire until they get the tests of your clothes back from forensic.'

'Do they have any theories as to why I would want to kill my best friend?' she asked bitterly.

'They suspect that it was Sibyl who was having an affair with Patrick.'

'But you put them right on that, didn't you,

Bernie? You know how it was.' She leaned over the desk, urging him to say yes with all the willpower at her command.

'Of course,' Bernie muttered unconvincingly.

'Did they mention the *Valkyr?*'

'No. Why should they?'

She shrugged. 'So the Slav is the red-hot favourite and I'm his accomplice.' She seemed to be lost in a nightmare of ludicrous proportions. 'It sounds very far-fetched to me.'

'Murder is always far-fetched. Hang in there, Clara. These are only theories. At this stage they've nothing on you, but evidently there were no fingerprints other than yours, Jason's and Sib's.'

'I wish I knew who my enemies really are. Perhaps you, for instance. You haven't been honest with me. You knew exactly what was going on, yet you let me stew in this mess while you pretended to be helping me.' She sighed. Seated behind his rosewood desk, with his Hirst, his Saville and his Ofili to say nothing of his Freud, Bernie could afford to look complacent.

'So what am I going to do about the police?'

'Nothing for the time being. Their inquiries may lead them in other directions, but you know what they're worried about, so get your answers ready.'

'If only I could remember what really happened. How about you, Bernie? Are you involved? Did Patrick steal your money, too? Just how many millions have gone missing?'

He stared at her blandly. 'I didn't kill Patrick, if that's what you're thinking, but whoever did has some unfinished business. You, for starters, who witnessed the crime. I've told you before you should move away, change your name, keep your head down until this is over. Why won't you listen to me?'

Something about Bernie's laboured advice got through to Clara. Suppressing a sudden shiver she reached out and took Bernie's hand.

'Is this Slav really so dangerous?'

'The worst.'

For a moment Bernie's suave manner deserted him and Clara caught a glimpse of terror in his eyes. He laughed deliberately, trying to recover his composure, but his voice was pitched higher and his hands shook as he repeated his advice and said goodbye.

Why would Bernie think that he was in danger? Long after she left she was still remembering Bernie's reaction to her question and the way he had tried to disguise his true feelings.

32

'Mrs Clara Connor,' Fergus said, unable to look Jason in the eyes. He heard the boy shout. 'No!' from right behind his mother. It was a cry of pure anguish and utter incredulity. Then their dog came rocketing forward. Jason hauled him off and thrust him into the kitchen.

'Mrs Connor, I'm arresting you on suspicion of the murder of Sibyl Ferretti.' He held out the arrest warrant for her to see.

Clara Connor stood her ground, calmly staring at him and for some reason Fergus felt like a small boy who'd just been reprimanded by his teacher.

'You do not have to say anything, but it may harm . . . '

'You maniac!' Jason yelled.

Mrs Connor was very quiet. It was almost as if she'd expected this to happen. The two policewomen, Jennings and Browning, were moving forward, expressions of quiet disapproval on their faces.

'Can I pack a few things?' she asked.

He nodded to Jennings to go with her as Jason grabbed his arm. 'You're making a ghastly mistake.'

Fergus couldn't stand the boy's pain. He turned away and waited until Mrs Connor appeared holding a small grip with an overcoat over one arm. She seemed composed as she whispered something to Jason and he nodded, tears brimming. Moments later she was walking towards the police car where Jennings guided her into the back seat and sat beside her. Browning drove towards the station.

'Is there someone you can call to come and stay with you, Jason?' Fergus said. He hesitated in the pathway, longing to say something comforting. 'Your Mum's not guilty. We have to explore every lead. She'll be back tomorrow, but you can't be left alone here, Jason. You got any friends handy?'

'Jeff's mum. He's my best friend and he's not far away.'

'I'll have to call her. What's her number?'

Jason shot him a look of intense dislike as he lead the way into the house.

★ ★ ★

Fergus was unable to see Mrs Connor again until she was lead into the interview room at seven a.m. the following morning. She looked so forlorn, a thin, sad figure in a navy trouser suit and white blouse, shoulders sagging, her hands shaking with nervousness. She hadn't slept, Fergus noticed. There were deep shadows under her eyes as if someone had taken kohl and slashed two deep black lines, her skin looked dull and her lips were swollen and red. He sighed. She'd done her crying alone in the night and now she was ready for the worst they could do to her. She had declined an offer to have a lawyer present which was typical, he thought.

Constable Jennings followed her in and sat beside the tape recorder. Fergus motioned to Jennings to switch on the tape recorder and he gave the time and date. 'This is an interview between DI Jonathan Fergus and Mrs Clara Connor regarding the murder of Sibyl Ferretti.' He cleared his throat and sat down wishing he were anywhere but here.

'Mrs Connor, I want to take you back to the night of the murder of your friend, Sibyl Ferretti. Tell me in your own words exactly what happened.'

She was trying her best. Fergus could see that. Two hours later he had not been able to find any contradictions and her evidence had hardly deviated from what she had said when he had questioned her on the morning after the murder.

'I regret the fight so much,' Clara said, when the tape had been switched off. 'Poor Sib. If only I could have half a minute with her. Just to say I'm sorry. That's why I went back. I felt so bad about the things I'd said. Sib's been wonderful. Until this time I could never fault her.'

'And this time?'

'I felt that she had no right to decide what's best for me. She should have told me what was going on.'

Fergus glanced at his watch. 'Twenty minutes break,' he muttered to the policewoman. He went across the road to buy a sticky bun and a carton of strong, sweet coffee before returning to the station to speak to Bates.

'She's not guilty,' Fergus said flatly. 'She couldn't be that good an actress.'

'Have you got onto her husband's death?'

'No. We've been going over her actions on the night of the Ferretti murder.'

'Where is she now?'

'Having a break. Jennings is with her.'

Bates smiled faintly. 'You don't have the killer instinct, Fergus. That's your trouble. You don't want to nail her.'

'Sir . . .'

'Oh, never mind, Fergus. I'll look in. I have a couple of calls to make first.'

Fergus waited for five minutes, but when Bates hadn't arrived he began again.

'Mrs Connor, the neighbours have sworn that you were shouting abusively and that you hurled something heavy against the wall.'

'But we've been through all this so many times. It was an ashtray and Sibyl threw it, not me.'

'Why was that?'

She sighed. 'I don't understand you, Inspector. What good does it do to go over the same ground so many times? Are you trying to break me down? Do you think I'm going to crack and confess to something I didn't do? I know you believe that I'm innocent.'

Fergus flushed despite his best intentions. 'Please answer the question, Mrs Connor.'

She sighed. 'My husband asked Sib to help him win back his mistress, Gina. Gina was Sib's sister. I asked Sib if she had agreed to help him. That was when she lost her temper and hurled the ashtray against the wall. She felt that I should have had more confidence in her.

She was right, of course.'

'Mrs Connor, it seems to me that both you and she demanded absolute loyalty from each other. I think you could kill in the face of treachery.' Fergus looked over her shoulder as he spoke, and this unnerved her. 'Did you kill Miss Ferretti because she was disloyal?'

'I didn't kill Sib. I loved her. She was the best friend in the world. Even when we were arguing I was sad about it. Why would anyone want Sib dead?'

'Someone wanted her dead enough to murder her.' A voice said from behind her, 'Perhaps it was you.'

Clara jumped and spun around. She hadn't heard anyone walk into the interview room.

'It's inconceivable! Sib never did anyone any harm.' Panic was sweeping through her and she was breaking out in cold sweat.

'She did you harm,' Bates said sternly. 'You told her so rather loudly, according to the neighbours.'

Clara didn't answer, but looked searchingly from Fergus to Bates and back again, aware that the rules had changed. She felt like a rabbit caught between two ferrets.

'Mrs Connor, how long did it take you to wash the bloodstains out of your raincoat?' Bates asked. 'It must have been quite a job.'

'Raincoat? I don't understand. What are you talking about?'

Bates nodded to Jennings who produced a plastic raincoat from a box. It was made of thin, clear plastic and it was intended to fit into a

262

small pouch which could be carried in a pocket, except that now it was lying in a sealed transparent specimen file.

'Have you ever seen this mac before, Mrs Connor?'

She flinched and gasped. Had they noticed? She sat up straight, smoothed her hair back and glared at both of them.

'How would I know? You can buy them in any shop and they all look alike.'

'Rephrase.' Bates scowled at her. 'Have you seen one like this?'

'Yes,' she mumbled. 'We have, that is, we *had* two like that. Maybe more. Last winter I bought two, one each for Jason and I.'

Calm down, Clara. Pull yourself together.

'This mac was found in the river. It had traces of Ms Ferretti's blood on it.'

'Oh my God!' Her mouth was dry, her lips parched. She checked an impulse to ask for water. 'So someone . . . the killer . . . came prepared. The murder was premeditated. How terrible!' She leaned back and closed her eyes. The statement had sent electric shocks stabbing at her stomach. Suddenly she could not stop shuddering.

'And where are these items now?'

'Oh, I don't know.' She returned Bates' stare, trying to disguise her panic. 'It's probably lost or torn. They don't last long and they're cheap and easy to replace. Jason used to keep his in his bike saddlebag.'

'So where is yours?' Bates replied with a hint of irritation.

'In my car boot I think. I haven't actually used it. They don't look too wonderful over a coat.' She sensed they had both picked up on her shock and fear.

'How did Jason get on with Miss Ferretti?' Bates volleyed back.

'He adored her.'

Bates turned to Browning. 'Check out the raincoats with Jason Kent, please.' Turning to Clara, he said: 'May I have your car keys, Mrs Connor?'

'The police took my bag, but the spares are in the coat cupboard.'

'Thank you.' Bates motioned to Browning who left.

'I'd like to run through your recollections of the night your husband died. Perhaps your memory has improved a little,' Bates said cynically. 'Mrs Connor, you state that you were hit on the head and blown overboard by the force of the explosion which destroyed your yacht, but you weren't burned or hurt at all, as your husband was. Not a scratch, we learned from your doctor, except a wound on your head. Don't you think it's strange that you were safely off the boat, wearing a protective rubber suit at the time of the explosion? Perhaps you were aware that the boat would be blown up, or are you claiming psychic powers?'

'I was cold. Jason's old diving suit was all I could find to put on. I don't remember clearly. I think I went up on deck and I was attacked there. I suspect that I jumped overboard. All I know for sure is someone tried to kill me and my husband was murdered.'

'Thank you, Mrs Connor,' Bates cut in on her. 'We agree on one thing at least, and we think it was you who murdered him, having drugged him first.'

'What?' she burst out.

'You see, Mrs Connor, you were there,' he added with a glint of triumph. 'And you were there again when Mrs Ferretti was murdered. A strange coincidence, don't you think? The jury will agree, I'm sure. Your first husband died at sea, too. I believe the insurance was, shall we say helpful at that time, as it would have been this time. Of course, you weren't to know that the premiums weren't paid.'

Clara tried to stay cool, but failed. 'Do I have to sit here and take this? Quite frankly I'm disgusted. Your questions have gone from ridiculous to obscene. My first husband died at sea saving the poor people whose boat was wrecked on the Goodwin Sands. He was awarded a medal for outstanding bravery. I was at home . . . six months pregnant. Don't you feel ashamed to make such stupid and cruel insinuations?'

'Murder is cruel, Mrs Connor, and so is drugging the champagne so that your husband would be unable to defend himself. Did you smash his face and teeth with the axe, or did you wait for your accomplice to come and do the job for you and blow up the boat?'

She stared at him dumbfounded while chilly fear touched her brain. She took a deep breath, thinking fast, knowing that she had to keep calm. 'These allegations . . . well, to be honest, they're absurd. What sort of an accomplice would leave me in the sea in mid-winter for six hours with an open wound when I was suffering from concussion?' She stared defiantly at him, her mouth sticky, her heart beating in sick thuds.

'You had a diving suit on. You were a former swimming champion.'

'I was champion of the eleven-year-olds. We swam five lengths.'

Bates looked embarrassed. 'Mrs Connor, it can't have been easy putting up with your husband's affairs,' he said, bouncing back on another tack.

'Affair,' she corrected him. Alarm sunk into her, numbing her mind. Was there anything they didn't know about her life? She felt her cheeks burning.

'You must have felt cheated when he borrowed so much money from you, and then asked for a divorce.'

'I was deeply hurt,' she acknowledged cautiously.

'With your marriage wrecked, your house mortgaged to the hilt and your husband's business running at a loss, I suggest that your husband's death was the only way you could possibly recoup your losses.'

Motive and opportunity! The words were knocking around in her head, while sweat rolled in cold trickles beneath her blouse. Bates regarded her silently.

'You mean from the insurance?'

Bates nodded.

'Then I'd check that the premiums were paid before killing him, wouldn't I?'

Bates ignored her comment. 'Perhaps you confided in your friend, Sibyl Ferretti, but later she threatened to go to the authorities, so you had no choice but to kill her, too.'

'No. That's not true.'

'So what is the truth?'

'That I went for a walk to cool off. When I came back she was dead.'

'Yes, and it was you who had killed her. That's why you had to cool off, but then you remembered the raincoat, so you came back to hide it in the river.'

'There's not a word of truth in anything you've said.'

Bates nodded coldly at her and walked behind her to the door. She glanced round in time to see him beckon to Fergus before hurrying out of the room.

She shuddered, feeling struck by the irony of the accusations. She had loved both of the victims dearly.

Fergus returned looking sick. The telephone rang and Fergus answered.

'You have. Good. Give the keys back.' Turning to Clara Connor he said: 'Jason was very co-operative and he opened the boot of your car. Your raincoat is missing. Jason's was in his saddlebag. Nevertheless, Mrs Connor, you're being released because of lack of evidence against you. Constable Jennings will take a sample for DNA testing and take you home. Please don't leave Dover for a while.'

'I'll get myself home.' She shot him a mean look, stood up and followed Jennings out.

33

Mrs Connor walked out quickly without saying goodbye, taking her sad, reproachful glances with her and leaving Fergus with an unpleasant aftertaste, like bile, in his mouth. She had looked wounded and that hurt him. She had counted on the police for support and protection and they had let her down. He felt a surge of mutiny against his superior. Bates was past it. They should put him out to graze. Anyone with an ounce of sense could have seen that Clara Connor was innocent. When, seconds later, Bates walked into the office, he felt obliged to say so.

Bates gazed at him with a strangely anonymous expression, his face showing no disapproval for once. Fergus on the other hand, was intensely irritated with the DCI.

'A waste of time. And suffering. She was hurting, make no mistake. All for nothing.'

'No, never. Not for nothing. We had to show progress.'

'Let me get this straight,' Fergus said to Bates. 'D'you call a wrongful arrest progress?'

'It's a case of elimination, Fergus. We went along with what Zimon told us. I think we both know she's not Mandic's woman. Not the type. So how did Zimon get it so wrong? Think about it. What was it that Zimon said exactly?'

Fergus opened his file. 'He said, 'There's a

rumour going round that he' (that's the Colonel) 'is having it off with Connor's *woman*. Of course that's only hearsay, but it came from a normally reliable source. It's known he had criminal business connections with Patrick Connor.' ' Fergus broke off and stood for a moment deep in thought. He'd been a bit dense. Why Connor's wife? Why not his mistress?

'That's it! It's his mistress.'

Bates grinned. 'Now you're talking. And Connor's girlfriend is the dead woman's sister.'

'Gina Ferretti.'

'It fits.' Bates slammed his fist into the palm of his hand, a gesture which normally preceded more work coming his way.

'We're both after the same man. You realise that, don't you, Fergus? If Zimon wins, Mandic will be whipped out of the country so fast we won't get a sniff at him.'

'Of course, they'll have — '

'They won't wait for extradition proceedings. Not those guys. Zimon will get him out the same way he arrived, in a small boat under cover of darkness. Make sure you get to him first, Fergus. We may have a temporary advantage, since Zimon doesn't know about Connor's affair, but it won't take him long to find out. Pull your finger out, Fergus.'

Fergus winced. It was an expression he disliked intensely.

'Aren't we forgetting a small matter of motive? What possible motive could Mandic have?'

'Don't waste time, Fergus. Worry about motive when you've found him. Zimon's close behind

270

you. D'you know where to look?'

'No, but I'll start off with the girls' father. Clara Connor gave me his address on the night Ferretti was murdered. We passed on the job of informing next of kin.'

'This time you'd better get out there.'

Fergus glanced at his watch. Almost one. No wonder he was starving. He might as well have lunch. He decided he had time to splash out on plaice and chips and apple pie. There was a place in Castle Street that grilled the fish totally to his liking and lavished real Devonshire cream on their apple strudel.

★   ★   ★

Strange eyes, Fergus thought as he shook hands with Piers Ferretti later that afternoon. They were large and ghoulish, the same colour as pewter, but ringed with dark smudges, like kohl, which gave him a theatrical appearance. Add to this his fleshy, down-turned mouth, his bald pate edged with a ginger fringe, and his boozer's nose, and there was a remarkable resemblance to a very sad clown. His eyes were bloodshot and Fergus could see how much he was suffering. This wasn't going to be easy, he decided.

'Mr. Ferretti, we are very anxious to question your youngest daughter, Gina — ' Resistance blazed in the sad eyes and Fergus hurried on, 'Regarding your daughter's murder, we've drawn a blank so far. We need more names. Your daughter might know of her sister's former friends.'

'I doubt that, but come in.'

Piers Ferretti lived in a modest, semi-detached house in Clapham. It had gone to seed, presumably since his wife died and his daughters left home, Fergus surmised. Once someone had filled the house with clutter: ornaments, souvenirs, vases, Toby jugs, family pictures. Now an endless variety of junk was gathering dust on every available shelf. Fergus, who was allergic to dust, could feel his nose twitching and his eyes watering.

Trying not to breathe, Fergus sat in a roomy armchair while Ferretti, with very little prompting, poured out the family history. The sisters weren't close, not only because of the age gap of thirteen years, but also because they were total opposites. Sibyl was his favourite, Fergus realised, but Gina was spoiled because of her beauty. They'd spent a fortune on her acting career, but she'd thrown it aside when she found a rich lover. Then she'd left him for an Italian art dealer and they lived abroad somewhere. He didn't know where.

'She's ashamed of her old father,' Piers Ferretti said in a splurge of self-pity. 'How about a drink? I have some excellent single malt scotch.'

'No thanks.' Ferretti gazed longingly towards the sideboard. 'But you go ahead.'

He shook his head and gave a wistful smile and Fergus hastened to bring his inquiry to a close.

'She doesn't even know that Sibyl was

272

murdered.' His voice wavered close to break-down.

'Has Gina called you lately?'

'Not since last Christmas.'

'Any postcards or letters?'

'Several postcards. Up there.' He pointed to the mantlepiece where several brightly coloured cards were poked amongst the bric-a-brac.

'May I?' Fergus examined a postcard from Greece. He read the usual message people send when on holiday. Most of the cards said much the same thing, but one from Sarajevo was interesting. Not a great art centre as far as Fergus knew and Gina expressed her annoyance at being stuck there for a week.

'Mr. Ferretti, what about credit cards, bank accounts, that sort of thing. Do you know if your daughter had any?'

'She had one card when she was home. I paid it, that's why I remember, but I don't know if she still uses it. She seems to have everything she wants provided. Beautiful clothes. He bought her an ermine jacket for her last birthday.'

'Were her credit cards under her own name? That is, Gina Ferretti? We can find no trace of them.' Fergus nudged Ferretti back to his inquiry.

'No. She adopted a stage name when she landed a few roles a couple of years back. Well, nothing much, but it was a start. We wanted her to carry on, but she met this man and that was that. She would have succeeded eventually.'

'And what name did she use?'

Fergus was filled by an overwhelming need to

get out of there. The smell of dust, stale cooking, old wine, and sadness clung to him.

'Gina Paloma. My wife and I weren't keen, but Gina loved it. She'll be calling in a few days time and I'll ask her then. If you give me a card I'll ask her to call you. Of course she'll be overwhelmed by this awful news. Horrible! Horrible! Who would believe it. My little Sib. She was such a lovely, talented girl.'

'You say Gina will be calling?'

'She usually calls on my birthday, no matter where she is.'

'And that is?'

'January the seventh.'

'What about Christmas and the New Year. Didn't she call you then?'

'She sent a card. It's up there.'

Fergus reached to the top of the cabinet. Not much to go on here. 'Wishing you joy and peace this Christmas, love from Gina.'

'Russian stamps on the envelope, but I've given them away,' Ferretti volunteered. 'The boy next door collects stamps.'

'When your daughter calls, I'd like you to ring 1471 and obtain the number of the telephone she calls from. Then contact me right away. Would you do that?'

Ferretti shrugged. 'Whatever you want. Now if you'll excuse me I have to get on.' His gaze shied longingly towards the single malt.

Fergus left feeling a little more hopeful.

★ ★ ★

It was six p.m. and Fergus could feel the promised night's frost as he drove towards Folkestone Road, focal point of the bed and breakfast establishments, where a former Professor of Mathematics from Pristina University, Kosovo, was currently staying.

Dr. Peter Gajic was fortyish. A thin, tall blond man with deep lines of fatigue on his freckled face and an expression of petulant intolerance, as if he were very close to the end of his tether. He paused in the doorway of his room, one foot tangled behind the other, as if unsure of whether or not he should let Fergus step inside.

'The police?' he asked worriedly. 'How did you find me?'

'Immigration,' Fergus lied.

'I'm not sure if I should say anything. I knew I should never have told the doctor. I was in shock at the time. I don't know if I'm safe in telling you this. Am I?'

'Your English is excellent,' Fergus complimented him, avoiding a direct answer.

'I studied mathematics at London University for a few years.'

'May I come in and sit down?' Fergus moved forward towards the only chair. 'For my sins I deal with matters pertaining to immigrants.'

'And your sins were?'

'Leniency, above and beyond the call of duty. I've come about your trip across the Channel. Perhaps you could describe exactly what happened.'

Gajic closed the door and sat on the bed.

'Since you already know, I suppose ... ' He sighed deeply.

'I left Calais on the night of October the tenth, with my mother and my Uncle Marko in a small vessel, having paid three thousand pounds to the skipper.'

'That is you and Emina and Marko Gajic?' Fergus asked, glancing at Zimon's statement.

'Yes, of course.' He had a curiously soft voice.

'Just outside Dover breakwater, coastguard or customs officials approached the boat and hailed us through a loudspeaker. The skipper raced down the companionway and suggested we hide in sacks. There was a pile of large sacks lying on the deck.'

Gajic broke off and began pacing the small room, from the bed to the window.

'Please carry on, Dr. Gajic.'

'I saw the skipper throw two large packages attached to buoys through a raised hatch in the hold. He pulled a long sack over my head and asked me to crouch down in the corner. I remember he said: 'These guys never do more than flick a torch around from the top of the companionway. You'll be safe if you hide, but if they find you, they'll send you back to Serbia.' I kept still and heard him pull two more packages towards the well. When I realised that the opening of the sack was being tied up I put up a fight and called out to my mother and uncle to resist. There was no answer. I panicked and kicked out, but felt myself being pulled across the deck. Moments later I was submerged in icy water.

'I was sinking fast, but I managed to keep my

head and reach for my pocket knife. I cut my way out and tried to dive down and feel around for my mother. It was so dark. I couldn't see the surface. When I found myself gulping air, I think I went mad. I screamed and shouted to the coastguards for help, but no one heard me. After that I dived time and again. Useless, of course. My mother was too deep to reach and there was no way of knowing where she was.'

He went to the window and stood there for a few minutes, his forehead pressed against the pane and Fergus saw his shoulders shaking. 'Eventually I managed to reach the beach and that's the last thing I remember. Later I was told that I had staggered to the road where a lorry driver picked me up and took me to hospital.'

Fergus studied the affidavit, trying to conceal his feelings. 'And you've never seen this skipper since?'

'No.'

'D'you know his name?'

He hesitated. When he answered there was the merest flicker of unease in his eyes. 'No.'

'But you know the name of the fishing vessel.'

'No. The name was obscured. That should have told me something.'

'Can you give me a description of the skipper?'

'Of course. He was well over six feet tall, black hair, blue eyes, slightly suntanned; women would call him handsome.'

'So Dr. Gajic, he murdered your mother and your uncle, and very nearly killed you, too. You must have thought about retribution? Have you looked for him?'

'No.' His mouth folded into a tight line and he stared at the floor.

'Well, at least you can identify the vessel. Come with me.'

Gajic took refuge in an obstinate silence all the way to the marina. He seemed to think he was running into more trouble, but when Fergus parked and lead the way to the *Valkyr*'s moorings he began to mutter to himself in Serbo-Croatian. A profound silence enclosed the boat as they mounted the gangway, broken only by the gentle lap of water against the hull.

It was the right boat. The hatch to the hold was locked, but Gajic was in no doubt about it. He sank down on the deck and burst into hoarse, painful tears. Eventually he stood up. 'Forgive me,' he said simply. He made the sign of the cross, bowed his head and mumbled what sounded like a prayer. Then he fled down the gangway to the quay, muttering all the way.

'And now?' Gajic asked, when Fergus joined him again.

'We go back.' Fergus put one hand on Gajic's shoulder. 'The man who did this terrible thing has died. His yacht blew up at sea. Let's go.'

Gajic shook himself loose. 'I need to walk.'

'All right. But be patient. The skipper was part of a larger gang. We'll catch all of them. I promise. I'll be in touch.'

Fergus went back to his car feeling depressed by the knowledge that murders like these took place too often in this business of human traffic and were seldom discovered. The motive was that most reviled of the seven deadly sins. Pure greed!

34

'Happy New Year,' Jason said when his mother came into the kitchen. She had put on her dressing-gown and brushed her hair, but she looked harassed. Her eyes were puffy and her face swollen. They had been out in the park watching New Year's Eve fireworks until late last night and maybe she hadn't slept too well.

'Hi! I need a cup of coffee to start the year right.'

'Just made . . . fresh and hot in the filter.'

'Thank you, Jason. Happy New Year to you, too,' she said gravely. 'What's that smell?'

'I burned the milk and made some toast. Yours is in the warmer.'

She sat down heavily and gulped her coffee. 'Wow! This is saving my life.' Jason watched her as she got up and poured another cup, ladling in the sugar.

'You look exhausted, Mum.'

'I'm still tired from the police questioning, but that was a week ago, so it's probably psychological. I feel deprived of a night's sleep that I'll never make up. Never, ever, because it was so unfair.'

Jason wished he could think of something to say that would ease her burden. He said: 'Fergus knew it wasn't you. He looked so guilty when he took Jock and me round to Jeff's. I guessed they'd release you, but I was so scared for you

279

left all alone in the cells.'

'I felt claustrophobic. I wanted to shout and kick down the door. I thought I'd go crazy. It's so wrong to leave someone shut up alone for twenty-four hours. I couldn't sleep, the bed was hard, I had no pillow and I almost froze to death. After that I began to think about our lives. I wondered if there's an evil force that truly exists? It's almost as if we've been targeted. But why? Then I thought about you.'

'Thanks, Mum.' He tried to hide his smile.

'I worried about you all night long. I haven't taught you anything about morality.'

'Of course you have, by example.'

'But do you ever think about things like this?'

Jason nodded without commenting, feeling embarrassed and resigned to any weird behaviour his mother might impose upon him.

'It's tough to be a mum in this day and age, isn't it?'

'I'm trying to be serious.'

'I'm serious, too. You better get off that decaying soapbox before you do yourself an injury. Hopefully you've done a good enough job to prevent me from becoming a psychopath, despite the TV.'

'You're just a kid. Why can't you act your age?'

Jason got up to fetch some more coffee. 'I'm almost a teenager. You have crazy ideas about age. I'm as good as adult, give or take a few years.'

'Like five. Oh well, put it down to thoughts on a New Year's morning.'

'So! What else did you think about?' Jason

poured his coffee and carried the biscuit tin to the table sensing it would be a while for his mother's homily to be over.

'That sleuthing is a bit like archaeology, and I'm well-trained in that direction. It can be a boring job. You search for hours, or days, or even months for a fragment of bone and painstakingly glue it to the next fragment and slowly you piece half a cranium together. So I'll just keep on digging up the past. I haven't got far yet.'

'Maybe a couple of teeth.' Seeing his mother's warning glance, Jason struggled to be serious.

'The most probable reason for someone wanting Sib out of the way is because she knew something. But how could she know anything about this business. Unless . . . ' She closed her mouth firmly.

'Yet she was scared, Mum, and she was leaving Dover.'

'True.'

How guilty Mum looked. He wished he was older. He longed to protect his mother.

'Mum, listen! Since it's a holiday, let's take Jock over the cliffs. We haven't had a walk together for ages and I think it will help him to recover.'

The truth was his mother looked hollow-eyed. She'd never truly recovered from the accident. Fresh air and exercise might do her good. He'd cancel his date with Ahmad when Mum wasn't listening. He'd have to go to the movies without him.

'I'm sorry, Jason. The truth is I have to work on the computer. Can I take a rain-check on it?

It will be fun,' Clara said.

She wanted to say: 'Later! when this incredible mess is solved and our lives are no longer in danger,' but how could she frighten him?

★ ★ ★

Early next morning, when Jason had gone out to meet his friends, Clara switched on the computer and sighed. She was tired. What did she have really? Two e-mail addresses: starwalker@dockside and fiscal@clifftop, plus a stack of theories. But what did she know for sure? She decided to jot down the facts.

Two men were hidden behind these e-mails, identities unknown. And they, together with Vesno Mandic and Patrick, had formed a gang that controlled a criminal network of routes across Europe bringing 'consignments' into Britain. From the wording in the e-mails, and from the equipment Patrick had purchased from Jerry's company, and Jerry's own accusations, she knew now that they were smuggling illegal immigrants as well as drugs.

They used dozens of informers and employees, and she had the names of most of them. They paid them well, but the profits were staggering. It seemed that about £12 million had gone missing. Patrick had been blamed and murdered because of it and even Jason was threatened. Clara suspected that the £7 million in Vesno Mandic's Geneva account was part of the missing cash, although she had no proof of this. The rest might still be in the washing cycle,

282

somewhere in Eastern Europe. She had no way of knowing. If she was right, did that mean Mandic was the killer? Surely her first priority must be to reveal the identities of the men hiding behind these anonymous addresses.

Various ideas had occurred to her: What if she hacked into Starwalker's e-mail and sent a message to Fiscal requesting a meeting and vice-versa? But on second thoughts that was too dangerous. If they knew each other well, and presumably they did, they could simply pick up the telephone and confirm or query the meeting. No, she had to think of something better.

So what if she hacked into Mandic's account to request a meeting, using the missing millions as bait? But the hoods might think it was a trap. They might not pitch. Besides, they'd be able to contact Mandic and they probably would. Then Mandic would learn that someone was hacking into his account, and that was the last thing she wanted.

So what was so dear to their hearts they would come to the meeting place *alone*, without contacting each other? Clearly money. But how could she tempt them? What would they want more than anything else? According to Robin, the gangsters wanted their profits, and badly, which was a reasonable guess since it was the sum total of two years criminal activity. Yet she couldn't think of a reasonable bait for her trap. Lately her head seemed to be stuffed full of cotton wool.

After a while she got up to make fresh coffee.

283

As she stood by the filter waiting for coffee to drip through, an advertisement in the local rag caught her eye. 'Rent-a-Container. *Cheap and secure damp-proof storage for valuables and all items. Total security with easy access to Dover harbour.*'

She grabbed the scissors and cut out the advertisement. A minute later she was on the telephone requesting the company's e-mail address and the name of the MD. The telephonist seemed only too pleased to supply this information.

It was easy to hack into the firm's e-mail, since no password was required. She was on a roll as she typed out her message:

To Starwalker@dockside.com

Your private e-mail address was passed to me confidentially by Mr Patrick Connor before his death. He stated that should the container rental remain unpaid for a period of two months I should contact you privately and hand over the contents of the container to you. We should also be obliged if you would pay the overdue rental when you call to collect the above items.

Yours faithfully
Trevor Dobson, MD.

She sent the same message to fiscal@clifftop.com.

Wow! She got up and paced her study. 'This is it!' she gloated to herself. Clara reckoned they would both race there just as soon as they checked their e-mails. They would never pass up a chance to find the missing millions, but it was unlikely they would contact each other and risk having to share the loot.

35

Clara left a note for Jason: '*Gone to see prospective clients. See you later.*' Wearing two jerseys, an anorak with a hood, sunglasses and Wellington boots, she felt equipped to cope with the damp and chilling north wind. More to the point, she doubted anyone would recognise her, at least not from a distance.

The container company was situated a few miles past the mortuary, at the end of Coombe Valley Road, at the edge of a small industrial estate, set against the hillside. Clara parked her car out of sight at the end of the cul de sac and walked back to the container depot. A high wire fence surrounded two acres of land filled with rows of containers. The office, a small, wooden structure, with a sign proclaiming *Do It Yourself Storage*, over the entrance, was just beyond the security gate, where a guard sat reading in a wooden hut. He didn't look up as she walked past.

Hot air enveloped her as she entered the large, open plan office, where a busty, blonde receptionist got up, smoothed down her tight and shiny mini-skirt and came to the counter. She listened impatiently while Clara explained that she was storing her furniture for a year and she needed details of prices and security. The blonde pushed a bundle of brochures towards her and returned to her desk to file her nails.

'Thanks. I'll study these and come back shortly.' The girl didn't reply.

Phew! That was easy! Clara went outside and walked to the end of a row of containers and perched on a pile of planks to study the literature.

Five minutes later, a car raced into the yard without pausing at the gate. The security guard looked up, waved his hand, and returned to his newspaper. The car was parked behind the office and a tall, overweight man with crew-cut black hair and a short beard hurried in. Clara took out her binoculars and watched him walk past the counter, nod to the receptionist and sit down at a desk in the corner. Trevor Dobson, M.D., she assumed. She thrust the binoculars into her pocket and got up.

She was frozen and her head was aching with the cold. Hurrying back to her car, she switched on the ignition and sat shivering with the windows closed and the heater on. The windows fogged over, which was fine. She wiped a hole with her fist and drove down the hill, where she parked outside the fence.

Half an hour passed. The temperature dropped to zero, low clouds threatened snow and the damp north wind roared and whined, splattering the containers with sleet, while gulls shrieked their anguish, circling low overhead. Clara shivered and kept an eye on the car park.

A black car drove through the gates and drew up near the office. Clara took out her binoculars, focused and gasped.

Bernie! She couldn't believe it. But on second

thoughts, hadn't she always suspected him? Her mind was darting around, trying to find an out for Bernie, but the facts spoke for themselves. She pulled her hood lower, her heart pounding. What a fool she had been to confide in him. Not once, but dozens of times. She'd trusted him with liaising with the police on her behalf. She'd poured out her heart and told him everything Jerry had said. Oh you blind, trusting fool, Clara!

She still couldn't believe it was Bernie. Perhaps there was a perfectly valid reason for Bernie to be there. She could see him on the other side of the office with the M.D. bending over a computer. They were arguing and she could guess why. But guessing just wasn't good enough.

Clara got out of the car and walked to the reception, pulling her hood forward to cover her face. She was just in time to hear the manager say: 'You can see for yourself there's no message sent by me. I've never heard of you or your friend. It must be a hoax. Really, this is not my problem and if you'll excuse me . . . '

Bernie swore loudly and turned on his heel. He was coming straight towards her. Clara leaned over the brochures as she whispered a question about damp and dry rot. The receptionist was getting impatient.

'We've never had dry rot,' she snarled.

Bernie was dialling his mobile as he passed close behind her. She let out her breath with relief.

' . . . bone dry because they're watertight. We've never had a complaint . . . '

She strained to hear Bernie. 'Hi Robin. It seems we have a problem? I received a garbled message . . . ' There was silence for five seconds. 'Jesus! Exactly the same. I don't like this. Where are you? Uh huh! Just stop. Get the hell out of here. It might be some kind of a trap. Do a U-turn, for Christ sake, and go. I'm leaving now . . . ' His voice faded as he hurried to his car.

Bernie and Robin! Triumph surged! It had been so simple. Why hadn't she guessed before? Perhaps because she knew them so well.

'I have to go,' she told the receptionist. 'I'll think about it.'

Thankful for the gloom, she hurried across the yard. Purple-black clouds gathering overhead were as dark as her mood. She should be happy. She'd won, hadn't she? But Bernie? And Robin? It hurt! Patrick, too. She'd fallen in with a gang of criminals and murderers. Bastards!

As she hurried through the gate she saw a police car approaching. It parked a few yards back. Footsteps were coming her way and they were gaining on her.

Don't panic. Keep walking. It's nothing to do with you. A hand grasped her elbow. She could feel hot breath on her cheek.

'So what was all that about, Mrs Connor?'

It was Fergus's voice. She turned slowly. 'Oh, Inspector Fergus. You startled me. What are you doing here?'

'I'll ask the questions, Mrs Connor. Why are you always around? How did you know that Bernard Fraser and Robin Connor would be racing up here so early on a nasty winter morning?'

'I can't see that it's any of your business what I'm doing, but the truth is — ' She broke off and scowled, unwilling to lie. 'It's a purely domestic matter.'

'I guess you could call it domestic. After all, Robin Connor is your brother-in-law and Bernie Fraser is your friend and lawyer. You own the boat that was used to smuggle in immigrants and occasionally to drown them, so perhaps you are in with them, after all.'

She gasped and tripped in a sudden panic attack. 'You can't believe that. Surely you can't believe I would . . . Oh God!'

'This is a strange place to hold a gang meeting, Mrs Connor. Luckily for me, I had a man tailing Robin Connor and he called me as soon as he recognised your car.'

'Is that what you really think?'

'I think you'd better start talking. You set them up, didn't you? Brought them both rushing out here, but that's only guesswork and I can't imagine why, unless of course you'd like to enlighten me.'

'I'm trying to find who killed Patrick. Maybe Sib, too. Someone has to. You don't seem to be very successful, Inspector.'

'And you think that one of these two men killed your husband?'

'Oh God! No! I don't think that. I don't know what to think. They were involved. That's all I know.'

'Involved in what?'

She opened her car door. 'I think you know, Inspector. You were following Robin Connor. Presumably you have a reason.' She broke off and leaned against the car. 'I feel . . . sort of shaky. Bernie's my lawyer and in a way a friend. I trusted him. I confided in him. It was such a shock to see him arrive. And then Robin.'

'I'll drive. You look sick. We have to talk, so get in. Browning can fetch me later.'

Clara leaned back and closed her eyes, calculating the pros and cons of handing her data to the police. Would the hoods suspect her when Fergus moved in on them? And would this put Jason in danger? There seemed to be danger in whatever action she took. Eventually she opened her eyes and saw that they were almost home.

The Inspector drew up in her driveway and leaned back. He sighed and spoke without looking at her. 'I find it strange that you figure so prominently in my two most important cases: the murder of Sibyl Ferretti and finding the leaders of the smuggling gang. It's time to be frank, Mrs Connor. There's any number of charges I can pin on you. You're an intelligent woman, you must know that. Obstructing the cause of justice is just one of them.'

'There's no need to threaten me. I was going to tell you everything just as soon as I found out who Skywalker and Fiscal are. You must understand that I only had their e-mail addresses. Now I know who Patrick's partners are. But somehow I doubt those two are killers. There's another unknown person — a Serb.' She

291

broke off as she sensed Fergus's tension. 'I'm not making sense. You can have everything, but it'll take a while to explain. Come in. I'll put the coffee on.'

The Inspector glanced her way and she saw his concern. 'Is Jason still on holiday?'

'Yes, but he's out with friends.'

Clara went inside and let Jock out for a run. He liked the Inspector, which was strange. He'd hated Patrick.

Fergus patted the dog absent-mindedly. 'You have a great son, Mrs Connor. He's the best in the karate club. How's he doing at school?'

She sighed. 'He's some sort of a mathematical prodigy, but totally dumb at art and music. Tone deaf. It's such a shame.'

She broke off, remembering Michael, Jason's father, who was always singing, but you could never recognise the tunes. Lost in daydreams, her subconscious took over, measuring the coffee into the filter, pouring the water, putting mugs on the tray, taking the sugar out of the cupboard. She splashed coffee on to her hand and the sting brought her back to the present. 'Damn!' She mopped up the mess and took the coffee into the living room.

'Begin at the beginning. It makes more sense.' Fergus stood up and gazed out of the window while she explained how she had retrieved the data from Patrick's bombed-out computer with specialised equipment.

'Are you some kind of a computer expert?'

'Not exactly. I almost studied Information

Technology once, but finally chose pre-history. Bear with me.' She sorted the discs into order. 'You'll see the picture clearly when you go through these files. I knew nothing about this until I recovered Patrick's data from his computer. You must believe that. At first I found it quite shocking. Jerry Watson told me Patrick was smuggling when I went to see him about an account. At the time I didn't believe him, but it's all here.

'It seems that Patrick was responsible for laundering the profits, but he soon became too greedy to part with the cash. He kept making excuses while the deposits were transferred to secret places. Then a fourth partner, Vesno Mandic, took over, and part of the profits have landed up in his Swiss account. Patrick was so scared those last few days.'

'He had good reason to be, Mrs Connor. He may have learned a little more about the background of one of the men he double-crossed. This Mandic, was previously a Colonel in the Serbian army. He was an ex-KGB liaison officer in the old Cold War days and he's known to have killed and tortured thousands of innocent people. I can't tell you more than that. I'm afraid I'll have to appropriate this data of yours.'

'No. I'm giving it to you. But first I want to know why you haven't caught up with Mandic. You know very well he's the man who's been stalking me. Surely you should have caught him by now.'

Fergus looked reluctant. He rubbed his chin

and squared his shoulders, while his eyes avoided hers.

'You can trust me,' she soothed him.

'Clara . . . Mrs Connor . . . you have to understand that I can't tell you certain facts for security reasons. But I can reassure you that the man who was stalking you is not Mandic. It wasn't difficult to find him, since he's well-known in local immigrant circles. I even arrested him, but we had to let him go.'

'Did you forget about his assault and burglary? I think I have the right to expect justice.'

'I can't tell you anymore. I shouldn't have told you anything.'

Clara could hardly control her anger. 'You're using me. I'm the bait, aren't I? Perhaps I'll contact the media and tell them my story.'

Fergus sighed. 'Don't use police methods on me.' He eyed her speculatively. 'I'm going to tell you something in total confidence. This man, this stalker as you call him, is a kind of bounty hunter currently acting for the United Nations. You have nothing to fear from him. He's looking for Vesno Mandic. He had reliable information that — in his words — 'Mandic took Patrick's woman', so naturally he assumed . . . '

'Good God!' A memory nagged at her. She was sitting at the Royal Oak with Patrick when he'd begged for a reconciliation. He'd said: '*I got myself into a mess with another woman. She's found herself a rich lover, Vesno Mandic, an art dealer and . . .* '

She felt shattered by her realisation. She almost blurted it out, but something prompted her not to tell Fergus. At least, not right now.

'Mrs Connor, I'm confidently expecting to find and arrest Vesno Mandic shortly. Mr Ferretti is assisting me. I have to find him before Zimon does. When I have him, you will be called in to identify him. Once you are face-to-face with him, I feel sure you will remember the attack on the yacht. As soon as he is charged I'll be able to provide you with witness protection. In the meantime, please be careful. You have my mobile number. Call me at any time. Have you any idea where he is?'

'I have his e-mail address,' she said reluctantly. 'It's in the files. I think the best thing would be for you to take the files back to headquarters. You'll need a team of experts to work on them. There's so much data.'

She could see that Fergus didn't believe her, but he'd see. She handed him a box of discs and said goodbye hurriedly.

36

Fergus had been hardly able to disguise his satisfaction when he left with Clara's computer research, but Clara felt distracted and confused. It was all over, so why did she feel so afraid? She had to be alone. Had to think. She went to her office and sat doodling at her desk, willing herself to be calm. Everything was connected. She must have the answer, it was just that she couldn't see it. There were too many unanswered questions, for instance: why was Mandic preventing Gina from seeing her family?

The answer came to her after a few minutes reflection: Because Sib provided a direct link to the only eye-witness to Patrick's murder? Even the police considered her husband's death to be an accident. Momentarily shocked, Clara could hardly believe her own deductions. Slowly she pulled herself together.

Of course! She banged her forehead with her fist. Fool! She should have realised weeks ago. She didn't need a crystal ball to guess that Sib had found out where Gina lived, *and Gina lived with Vesno Mandic*. Perhaps Sib had written down the address somewhere. She still had the keys to Sib's front door. She decided to go there at once and search through Sib's records. Piers had not yet packed up his daughter's effects. One of these days he was going to ask her to do it, she felt sure.

But what if she found Mandic's address. What then? Naturally she would tell the Inspector. Fergus would apprehend and arrest Vesno Mandic for the murder of her husband and she would be called to identify him. But would she recognise him? What could she really remember?

She forced her mind back to the night of the shipwreck, seeing the light glinting on the hook as it swung towards her face.

Suddenly it seemed so real. So terrifying. The impact of the wave had been unbelievable. Flattened by tons of water, breathless and only half-conscious, she was swept overboard. Falling, cartwheeling, she was thrust down and down, twisting and turning, unable to reach the surface.

Must reach air. Must fight back, but the undertow had been too powerful to resist. Then, unexpectedly, she was tossed to the surface in a bubble of spume.

Moments later she was floundering in the waves, battered and incapacitated, watching the boathook moving closer. A dark figure leaned over the side, reaching for her. She was safely out of reach, but drifting closer. 'Have to get away . . . have to swim . . . might drift back.'

She heard a voice in the wind: 'I'll come after you.' The killer's voice had brought new energy. Galvanised into action, she had forced her arms into a slow crawl, moving away from the boat.

Assuming Mandic was the killer, would he be released on bail? And would witness protection save her from him? She thought not. He would come after her, and maybe Jason, too. She shuddered.

Hadn't Fergus said that Zimon would attempt to smuggle Mandic out of the country? Surely that would be a safer choice for her? Suddenly she knew what she had to do, but first she had to find Mandic's address.

★   ★   ★

When the door swung open Clara sensed the sad atmosphere of Sib's abandoned home. A strong smell of paint, turps and linseed oil brought a vivid image of her dearest friend lying dead in the cupboard. She fought to dismiss her intolerable memories. She had a job to do.

Flashing her torch, she found the fuse box and turned on the mains. Bruised light from Sib's old street lamp flooded the room. She switched on the house lights and stood waiting for normality to return, but she still felt unequal to the task. Sib's possessions were all around her. Piers Ferretti intended to hold a furniture sale and put the house on the market, but he was still holding back.

Every garment reminded Clara of happier days: a rucksack from their camping holiday, the mohair blanket Sib had kept on her bed when they shared a London apartment. They'd even shared their clothes occasionally. She recognised the crimson cape she'd once borrowed for a party. Blinking back her tears she groped for a tissue.

'Stop snivelling, Clara. Get on with it,' she muttered.

By eight p.m. Clara's back was aching even worse than her head. She moved to Sib's tiny, upstairs office and invaded her desk and chair. It felt wrong to leaf through her friend's diary and invade her privacy, but she had to. Sib's handwriting was surprisingly bold and efficient and she doodled around every page, not just any old scribbles but exquisite little flowers and birds, obscuring half the messages. She'd always done that. When they shared a flat it was infuriating, but later on quaint and endearing.

She reached November the eleventh, Sib's last birthday, and sadness zoomed in again. Sib had written a telephone number on her birthday page and highlighted it in red. On impulse, Clara took her mobile phone out of her bag and called the number. The ringing went on and on, but at last someone answered:

'Hello.'

'Can I speak to Mary Sherrington?' She quoted the first name that came into her head.

'This is a public telephone,' a husky, male voice replied.

'I'm sorry. Someone gave me this number. Where exactly is this booth?'

'In the main street of Nettleton, outside the florist. Hang on!' There was a short silence as she heard footsteps. Then the door slammed shut. 'I don't see anyone waiting around.'

'Okay, I'll leave it. Thanks a lot.'

As she replaced the receiver, a jolt of excitement brought goose-pimples to her arms.

November the eleventh was Sib's birthday and she'd written down the number of the public telephone booth in Nettleton. What was it Piers had said? Gina always called him on his birthday and presumably she called her sister on her birthday, too. Then Sib had checked back on the caller's number.

So far it made sense, but why would Gina use a public booth? Perhaps because she couldn't ring from home? Because Mandic had told her not to contact her family? Could he have this strong a hold over Gina?

Eventually Clara located Sib's tax file and leafed through the paid receipts. There was a bill from a courier service: for transporting a painting to Nettleton. Somehow Sib had found Gina's address and sent her a painting. The pieces were falling into place. Sib had tried to reach out to her sister with love and a gift but unbeknown to her, she had zoomed through Mandic's defences. Clara searched for the memo sheet on Sib's diary and found the date of Piers Ferretti's birthday. It was in three days time. Would Gina ring from the same public booth? Should she go there and follow her home? And would Fergus get there first?

What was it Fergus had said? 'I have to find him before Zimon does.' Did he realise he'd let the name slip? And before then: 'He's well-known in local immigrant circles.'

It was time to find Zimon.

37

It was two a.m. and Clara was exhausted. Wearing a tracksuit and trainers, she had brought her sleeping bag and a pillow to the settee where she intended to wait out the night. Was there anything else she could have done, she wondered? She had left messages at all the places where the immigrant community gathered in Dover, even Immigration, their brothel and a mosque. Jason and Jock had been taken to Jeff's Mum, Marie, to stay the night. It was a reciprocal arrangement which helped them both with dates. There was nothing else to do now but wait.

At four a.m. a car drew up outside Clara's home. Creeping to the window she saw the stalker and cringed. He looked more like a poet than a United Nations' agent, she thought, watching him move into the light. He was tall and painfully thin, but he gave the impression of power, as if he drew it from another source. It was something to do with his fanatical eyes. She hurried to the door and opened it before he rang.

'Mrs Connor,' he said in his surprisingly soft voice. 'You've been trying to contact me. Well, here I am.' He squeezed past her into the living room. 'Please shut the door. It's safer. And pull the curtains'.

He stood in the hall until she had pulled the

living room curtains. Then he gave a funny half-bow and one side of his lips curled in a smile. He'd been beautiful once, before he was burned and God knows what else, she realised, taking in the scars and his taut, shiny skin. And then of course there were his eyes. All the pain in the world seemed to be mirrored there.

'Permit me to identify myself. I am Major Peric Zimon, of the Kosovan Liberation Army, recently lent to the United Nations Peace Keeping Force. In peacetime I'm a lawyer.'

He took a small wallet out of his pocket and handed it to her. It identified him as part of the UN Peace Keeping force in Kosovo. It didn't mean much, she decided, but he had a frank smile and candid eyes and she decided to trust him.

'Please sit down, Major. I have to talk to you.'

'I was very surprised to receive your message. Correction — messages!' He smiled and one side of his face crinkled like parchment. 'Just how many did you leave around?'

'Too many I suppose. We have to talk. Now I know why you were following me, but before — well, let's just say that it was very frightening. I wish you'd told me. I could have helped you. Inspector Fergus told me that you're looking for Vesno Mandic.'

'Did he? I thought it was confidential. Never mind. I was going to tell you myself; I think you deserve an explanation. Do you think you can keep this to yourself?' He scrutinized the room as if needing time to make up his mind.

'My task is to round up those who have committed war crimes, specifically genocide, and bring them to trial. Colonel Vesno Mandic heads my list. He's a Serbian national, although his mother was Italian, and he's wanted on a number of charges including genocide. He had business connections with your husband and we traced him as far as Heathrow airport in October.'

His voice trembled slightly as if he were unable to control his passion. For what, she wondered? Justice, or revenge?

'And then?'

'We thought that you had some sort of a connection with him.'

'You were following the wrong woman, Major. My husband was having an affair. Last May he told me it was over. His girlfriend had taken up with an art dealer. Only yesterday I remembered the name. It was Vesno Mandic.'

'And do you know who the woman is? Or where she is?'

Zimon was looking impatient. Clearly he was in a hurry.

'Yes. But first I have some questions for you.'

He looked stunned. Perhaps he was too used to giving orders.

He said, 'There's a contract out on your life, Mrs Connor. Mandic wants you dead. Remember Guy Fawkes night? I wasn't the only one following you. Help me to find him quickly. You don't have too many options.'

She felt hollow inside and very unreal. Shock, she supposed. Zimon's fervent brown eyes locked with hers, but she wasn't going to give in just like that.

He said: 'I have photographs here which I would like you to look at.' He thrust a handful of pictures at her that he had pulled from his briefcase. He seemed to have taken over.

Clara rifled through them and almost gagged at the shots.

'Interesting pictures!' Zimon laughed harshly. 'They show Mandic at work. He loves his job. He's a brutal psychopath who found full scope for his sadistic nature in the Serbian secret police, and before that, the KGB, in collaboration with the Russians. He's built up an enviable art collection, but everything was stolen from those who could no longer accuse him.'

Watching Zimon's expression, Clara believed him.

'Have you seen this man before?' Zimon asked.

'No. I'm sorry.'

'And that night on the yacht? Didn't you see your attacker?'

'He wore a balaclava and it was dark, but if I saw him again — maybe.' Clara shivered and pulled her cardigan tightly around her.

'Let's consider his situation,' Zimon was watching her warily and she sensed his tension. 'As far as his former colleagues are concerned, Mandic has simply disappeared. He has no reason to fear that there's a warrant out for his arrest. We kept the inquiry quiet. He thinks he's safe in England. We have no doubt that he's openly building up his investments, using the cash he received for the stolen art. He has no reason to resort to subterfuge. He has only one danger and that is you. He must assume that you saw him and can identify him.'

'Yet I'm still alive?' She frowned.

'I'll be frank with you,' Zimon said. 'Keeping you under surveillance has saved your life.'

She shuddered as she thought of Jason. That's what this was all about. Protecting Jason.

'There is only one way for you to be safe,' Zimon said, avoiding her eyes. 'That is to help us to put Mandic where he belongs. I think you've worked that out for yourself. That's why I'm here, isn't it?'

She nodded. 'Fergus wants Mandic for questioning in connection with the murders. Until they charge him he's at liberty to go where he likes. Furthermore, if he's charged right away, he might get out on bail, perhaps pending DNA tests. Naturally he will wish to eliminate the only witness to his crime. Fergus offered me witness protection, but somehow — '.

'No one can guard your safety twenty-four hours a day, unless they move you both away, change your identities and your names. It would mean a complete disruption of your lives.'

'Yes.' She sat back reflectively. So far he hadn't said anything she didn't already know. 'If you succeed in detaining Mandic, what will happen to him?' She needed every last fact to make her decision.

'We intend to arrest him and get him to trial in Kosovo. He'll be executed, I promise you that. We have many hundreds of witnesses who have suffered bitterly at his hands.'

He wouldn't look at her. Instead he inspected the pictures on the wall, and then his glance took in the table and the vase. Anything but look at her.

'We need to set a trap and I want to use you as bait. You are already at risk,' he assured her sternly. 'It can't get worse than it is.' Then he sighed.

Clara forced herself to relax. She didn't have to fall in with his plans.

'There's no point in trying to frighten me,' she said more calmly. 'I think I know where Mandic lives.'

Zimon's distrust was almost tangible. She could feel it fanning around her.

'I was about to ring Inspector Fergus. It seemed the right thing to do, but then I thought about Mandic out on bail, knowing there was only one person — ' She broke off and made an effort to keep calm.

'Yesterday, I went to Sib's house. No, I must start at her funeral. It was then that her father told me that Gina always calls him on his birthday. So I checked back to Sib's birthday in her diary. I'm not making sense, but look here.'

She went to the table and opened Sib's diary. 'I brought this from Sib's house.'

Zimon got up and leaned over her shoulder as she ran through the pages, showed him the telephone number and the statement from the courier. She explained how she had called the public booth.

'I believe Sib found out where Gina made her

306

calls, just as I did. As you can see, she then employed a detective agency to find her sister. It wouldn't be very difficult to find her once you know the village. Gina's the sort of woman people notice.'

His lips pursed thinly, but his eyes were sizing her up. 'So you know Gina Ferretti personally?'

Clara sighed. 'I once spent a holiday with her.'

'Our best plan would be for you to persuade Gina to lure Mandic to some secluded place where we can arrest him without witnesses.'

Clara sat silently considering the problem, licking her dry lips nervously. Just what was she getting herself into? The whole idea seemed fraught with danger and more for Gina than for herself.

'Gina won't listen to me. Besides, she's very young. What if she tries and fails? She can't act. He'd kill her if he found out.'

Clara wondered why she was worrying about Gina's welfare.

Zimon shrugged. 'You underestimate her and yourself.' He paused to let this advice sink in before adding: 'Once she learns that he murdered her sister you'll have no difficulty with her. It's up to you to tell her. She will cope with the deception. She's a woman, isn't she?'

What was that supposed to mean? Clara could feel the sweat crawling down her back in icy trickles. She couldn't remember ever feeling this lost and afraid.

'I want to think this out, Major Zimon. I'll give you my answer in the morning.

Zimon left with bad grace, looking furious.

Not expecting to sleep, Clara lay in bed with her earphones on, but dozed off in the early hours of the morning while listening to *Porgy and Bess*.

★   ★   ★

She was struck viciously on the side of her head. Dazed by pain she could hardly see. Terror surged as a tall, black shape loomed in the darkness blotting out the sky. She swung up the axe she was holding which caught the next blow, sending a pain like an electric shock zooming up her arm. In that split second she saw his eyes. Immobilized by shock she let him grab the axe from her and saw him swing it towards her . . . Then the wave crashed around them.

Clara woke feeling terrified. Evil was out there, stalking her and it wasn't a dream. To Clara it seemed that her worst nightmares had become reality. That awful imagining she had shut out of her mind was moving in on her, zooming closer, demanding recognition.

Pushing back the duvet, she stepped quietly on to the carpet and crept to the window moving the curtains slightly. There was someone out there watching the house. She felt this so strongly. She shivered with cold, but remained staring towards the road. A figure stepped out from under the tree and stood in a pool of moonlight looking up and down, and she knew from the shape of the man it was Zimon.

So he was expecting someone, as she was. He would come, as he had promised — as she'd always known he would. Putting on her dressing

308

gown and carrying her slippers for quietness, she crept downstairs.

She sat in the dark study examining her sense of denial that was almost pathological. She had shut out her fear, so now the slightest crack in her defences could release an irresistible force. Compacted terror! She saw those eyes again and cried out.

The balcony door crashed open and Zimon blundered in.

'What happened? Are you all right? What did you see?'

'Nothing. I'm sorry.'

'But look at you. You have experienced a trauma, yes? You remembered something?'

'Yes and no.' The words were whispered softly through dry lips. 'Do anything, anything you can to get this evil out of my life. I've made up my mind. I'll do whatever you want.'

Only later she vaguely remembered Zimon telling her she was in shock. She drank the cup of sweet tea he made for her and listened while he outlined his plan to her in great detail, going over it time and again. Marie was taking her son to school, she told him. Jason would only be home by three p.m. She could be back by then. She promised to try to get some sleep before morning.

38

It took two hours to drive to Nettleton and Clara indulged herself with gloomy introspection all the way. Almost two years had passed since that wretched sailing trip to Monaco and it had taken her far too long to suspect the truth about Patrick and Gina. She should have listened to her intuition. She hadn't wanted to go in the first place.

'We must celebrate,' Patrick had said, the moment the *Connemara* became theirs. He'd held her close and kissed the tip of her nose. 'You need a break so we'll take a holiday. Let's face it, you work far too hard. Hopefully I'll be able to change all that.'

Joy surged, but caution won. 'Honestly, Pat. We can't afford a holiday right now.'

It wasn't the cost of the trip that bothered her, but the cash they would lose if neither of them were working. After weeks of persuasion, she had taken out the first mortgage to set up Connor Tours and buy the yacht her husband craved. When Patrick spilled out his dreams they seemed to make sense, but when she was alone the thought that he might fail brought sleepless nights.

'If we can afford to live, we can afford to sail. It doesn't cost any more. Don't be parsimonious, darling.'

The taunt hurt and she gave in.

They needed a crew and, since Jason refused to come, Patrick suggested Sibyl and her sister. She remembered his words: 'Gina seems a nice kid and right now she has nothing much to do. She'd probably jump at the chance of a sailing holiday.'

Naturally she did, and Sib was persuaded to come along, too.

They set off from Dover in a brisk, easterly wind, but the weather improved and by the time they sailed into the Mediterranean they were tanned and carefree. Patrick larked around with Gina showing paternal qualities she'd never guessed he possessed. He taught her to sail, navigate by the stars and use the expensive navigation equipment they'd purchased. Clara smiled and wished like crazy she'd insisted that Jason come along, too. It might have broken the barrier between the two men in her life.

When they put into Monaco's harbour, Clara and Sib went shopping every day, but Patrick wouldn't leave the yacht unguarded. Gina said she hated shopping and would far rather lend a hand with cleaning and cooking.

'Patrick has a way with youngsters. Have you ever seen Gina so happy?' Clara confided in Sib.

'Something seems to have transformed her. She's a perfect bitch at home. She's nineteen, by the way.'

'She looks younger.' Plaits, freckles and a skinny figure made Gina look around Jason's age. Patrick, on the other hand, was forty-six, so Clara put her suspicions aside. The five-berth cabin put paid to their sex life, but Patrick was marvellous about it. For obvious reasons, Clara thought with hurtful hindsight.

Obsessed with memories she drove straight through Nettleton and had to make a U-turn. Stiff with tension she parked and locked the car. Temperatures were plummeting and black clouds were gathering overhead, as dark as her mood.

The public telephone booth was only a few steps from a mock Tudor tearoom. Clara went inside and chose a window seat with a good view of the street. The comfortable smell of toasting buns, confectionery and roasting coffee made her task seem ludicrous and brought a longing for normality. Why was this happening to her and Jason? Perhaps she should have put her trust in the Inspector.

Clara ordered coffee and sat fretting and worrying whether she would have to wait all day. Shortly afterwards, the sight of Gina swerving across the road in a white Jaguar convertible brought dread stirring in her bowels. As Gina hurried past, Clara caught a glimpse of her perfect profile and her thick hair rolled up at the back of her head. Her long, shapely legs, clad in ultra-high sandals, were visible almost to her thighs, the rest of her was hidden by an extravagant white ermine coat with a large, turned-up collar.

Just look at her! She wasn't real! Why should someone who looked like her want to steal her husband?

Gina was smiling as she dialled, tapping her fingers impatiently. She began to talk with

312

vivacious gestures, but seconds later she crumpled, leaning back against the glass as if unable to support herself.

Eventually she pushed open the door of the kiosk, and stood on the pavement looking lost. When she hurried to the car, Clara ran after her.

'Gina, we have to talk.'

'You! Oh God! Not you.' Her expression changed from grief to horror. 'I have nothing to say to you. Keep away from me.' She jumped into the car and turned the ignition key as Clara slipped into the passenger seat.

'Get out or I'll call the police.'

'Good. The police want to talk to you about your sister's murder. I assume your father has told you. You weren't at the funeral. How can you do this to him? Your father needs you, Gina.'

'Damn you! That's not why you're here. How did you find me?'

The car took off with screeching tyres and swerved dangerously. Glancing sidelong, Clara saw Gina's eyes glinting with fury, while her teeth bit into her bottom lip.

'I didn't. Your sister found you. When you called Sib on her birthday she jotted the number of the public box in her diary and hired a private investigator. You know Sib found your address. After all, she sent you a painting. Look here.' She fumbled in her bag. 'I have the invoice from the courier service if you're interested.'

'Oh God, no!' Gina couldn't hide her shock.

'Did you receive it?'

'No,' she whispered, shaking her head. 'Clara! Please listen to me. It isn't safe for you to be

313

here. Besides, I don't have time. I have to meet Mandic in London at an auction. I can't be late.'

'Then hurry! Drive off the road somewhere. We have to talk.'

When they passed a barn selling animal foodstuffs, Gina swung violently left and skidded to a halt in a cobbled yard behind the building.

'Get out now. Please don't come back.' She reached over and pushed. 'It's for your sake as much as mine. You can call for a taxi in the store.'

'No, Gina. Not so fast. I came to warn you. You aren't safe.' She had passed the point of no return. Gina would tell Mandic and he would come after her.

'Listen, Gina. Vesno Mandic's not an art dealer. He's a very dangerous man, an ex-Serbian army colonel — a killer and a war criminal. He's wanted for genocide.'

'A war criminal!' Gina began to laugh quietly. 'That's ludicrous! Vesno, a wanted man? That's rich!'

Clara had never witnessed hysteria before, but Gina calmed down abruptly. 'Thank you for telling me, Clara. You should go now. Please.'

'What's wrong with you, Gina? *He murdered Patrick*. You loved Patrick once, and so did I. I saw the killer on the boat. I saw Mandic.'

'Is this some kind of a vendetta, Clara? Do you still love Patrick?'

'I did love him. Dearly! But then you came into our lives. It's hard to talk about it, even now.' Gina was looking hostile and she wished she could avoid the 'other woman' syndrome.

'Patrick planned to scuttle the boat in the storm and leave me to drown. He drugged the champagne with laudanum.' Conscious of Gina's shocked expression, she elaborated. 'The champagne was to celebrate our reconciliation. We were supposed to be having a second honeymoon. Fortunately, I was too sick to drink much, so I'm still alive. Of course he didn't know we had Mandic on board and neither did I.' She broke off and shuddered.

'Go on.'

Clara glanced into pebble-hard eyes that were bright with suspicion. 'While I was below, Mandic smashed Patrick's face with an axe, but he was still alive. His face was pulped, teeth gone, half of his jaw hanging down, but he could still reach out to me. I was so shocked and horrified that I didn't see the danger. Mandic came from behind and tried to kill me with the axe, but a wave smashed down and I was swept overboard.' She broke off and swallowed. She could feel the terror starting to creep up on her.

Gina had recovered. She was a hard case, Clara thought, watching her. Would anything get through to her?

She said: 'Tell me about my sister's murder. I have to know everything.'

'Oh, Gina. I'm so sorry. I found her lying in the cupboard under the stairs. It looked as if she'd put up a bitter fight. She'd been stabbed in the back. It was someone who knew Sib's house well. He had a key to the patio door, too. He must have waded up the river, and unlocked the door to creep in unnoticed. He knew where to

315

hide Sib's body. Has Mandic been there before?'

She stopped in mid-sentence as Gina cried out. She flung open the door and raced across the yard to the trees. By the time Clara caught up with her she had collapsed on a fallen tree trunk.

'Get up, Gina.' Clara hauled her to her feet. 'Gina, listen to me. You always look like you're on the catwalk. Be normal if you want to stay alive.' She brushed the moss off her fur coat. 'That's better. Pull yourself together or you'll land up like Sib. Let's sit in the car.' She led her back.

'Does anyone know you're here?' Gina gave her a funny, sidelong glance and Clara's stomach stirred uncomfortably.

'I was sent.'

'Damn you, Clara.'

'An agent from the UN is after Mandic. He wants you to lure Mandic to a deserted place where he can pick him up quietly and get him out of the country. He's to be taken back to Kosovo.'

'What's the use? He will kill me,' she said in a small, hard voice. 'Just as he tried to kill you.'

'Do you want to live with your sister's murderer?'

'Do you expect me to answer such a question?' Gina spoke in a hard, flat voice. 'All right. I'll do whatever they want. But hurry.'

Clara hesitated. It had been too easy. Besides, Gina's sudden change of attitude had been inexplicable. She wasn't at all convinced that Gina intended to go along with their plan.

Zimon, who had bugged Clara's car and followed her since early morning, chose that moment to speed across the yard towards them. She left at once, as they had arranged.

★ ★ ★

Clara had plenty of time to plan her future as she raced home. Gina would never be able to pull it off. She wasn't that good an actress and Clara felt sick with fear.

By the time Jason arrived home she was halfway through packing their clothes.

'We're leaving Dover,' she told him. 'We're no longer safe. I'm putting the house and business on the market, but we're not waiting that long. We'll be gone by the end of the week, if we can.'

'What about Jock?'

'He'll come with us, naturally. It's not up for debate, Jason. We'll stay in Scotland until you finish school, or until this business is over and done with.'

'But why now? And what about Inspector Fergus? Couldn't he provide a guard?'

She turned on him fiercely. 'We have to look after ourselves. Call it intuition if you like, but I think we ought to get out of here just as fast as we can. Maybe as soon as tomorrow night. I'll try my best.' She saw the mutiny start up in his eyes and she grabbed his arm.

'I'm talking about our lives. D'you understand what I mean? I'm talking about staying alive. Now quit arguing Jason and start packing.'

39

The London auction house was overflowing and, from his seat on the aisle in the third row, Vesno Mandic watched the tension hotting up amongst the well-heeled crowd as they outbid each other for his Russian icons and priceless old Kosovan family jewels.

When Gina walked into the room there was a sudden change in the atmosphere like an electric charge. Heads turned. Moments later admiration and malicious envy were zooming in on her like angry wasps and the stings hurt, he could see that. Unsure of her beauty and her person, she faltered, immobilised by her own uncertainty, sensing the vibes but not understanding them, a lost girl. Yet he was there to reassure her and guide her, the creator of her astonishing new life, giving her everything she had ever longed to have. And he adored her, which made it all the more deplorable that she had disobeyed him. Her defiance had almost unmanned him. He feared the mysterious deviations of the female mind. Their pristine urges to be mastered and protected were forever conflicting with their laboured bid for liberty and equality.

He turned and beckoned from his aisle seat, urging her forward, smiling encouragingly. She was trembling. Surely not because she was late?

Of course she was beautiful. Perfectly beautiful to be precise, but it wasn't her beauty that turned heads. He'd never been able to plumb the source of her seductiveness. Some sort of signal she sent out seemed to charge the air with high-powered vibes, transforming balding, middle-aged men into stags in season. She was a witch, there was no doubt about it. He smiled to himself and turned his attention to the bidding, but then a strange feeling of uneasiness came over him. He felt hostile stares zooming in on him. Something was wrong.

With silent snarls and looks that could kill, two middle-aged peers were bidding for a small but exquisite Pissarro which had just come on the market. They'd been giving him snooty looks all morning while they outbid each other for his rare old Eastern European maps. All these grey-suited types with their public school backgrounds raised their eyebrows at his beige suede shoes and coat, his tan mohair trousers, and his black polo-necked cashmere jersey. They didn't like his thick black hair cut to shoulder length, nor his shoulder bag. Foreign, they thought to themselves, hippy type. He could read their minds. He beckoned to Gina and when at last she came tiptoeing towards him, contempt changed to envy, part of Gina's alchemy.

The bidding was rising to reach a ceiling at £1.5 million. 'Any advance on one and a half million pounds from his lordship? Going, going . . .'

The peers faced each other like a couple of fighting cocks, comb-red complexions.

He knew he should leave at once, but pride led him to hold up his hand and nod.

'One point eight million to number thirty-one,' the auctioneer called out looking pleased. 'Come along, gentlemen. An exquisite piece and a valuable investment.'

Visible angst threatened to veer out of control as the two peers turned querulously towards him. They put up their hands as one.

Mandic gave a two-fingered gesture.

'Two million? Is that correct?' The auctioneer smiled tightly.

He nodded.

There was a perceptible moment of silence. The auctioneer recovered first.

'Thank you, sir. This is more like it, ladies and gentlemen. At this price it's a wonderful investment. Any advance on two million?'

There wasn't and he guessed that after a suitable pause the Pissarro would be knocked down to him, but by then he had Gina firmly by her right elbow as he guided her towards a door beside the stage. They knew him well and the auctioneer nodded as he left.

'Let's go. We'll pick it up later.'

'Don't you have to pay?' she whispered.

'He owes me more for the icons and the portraits.'

This major triumph put him on a high, but his former uneasiness soon settled in. Someone had been watching him, but why should they? Gina was strangely tense and aloof. He sensed a widening of the chasm that had lately formed between them and he was afraid for her. Gina was his soft underbelly. He'd wanted her and he'd taken her, or bought her, and he feared the consequences of his dangerous obsession. She could never go free. But possibly he was imagining her coolness. He glanced sidelong at her exquisite profile and sighed. Cohabiting with a living work of art wasn't always easy.

They were walking towards New Bond Street when the idea came to him. It wasn't even original. They'd done it before. Perhaps that was the point. He could compare her reaction with her first impromptu rapture.

'We got a wonderful price for the icons, Gina.'

'But you spent it on the painting.'

'A wise investment. I feel like celebrating. Come on.' He pushed her towards the entrance of Veruccio's, but she hung back, looking afraid. Again uneasiness stirred.

'Don't tell me you can resist a new dress?'

She shrugged aloofly, but he took her arm and pushed her towards the open door. 'We'd like to see your latest cocktail dresses.' He recognised the under-nourished, beady-eyed assistant, hiding behind her facade of brittle sophistication like a hermit crab peering from a borrowed shell. She was the one who had scowled at him last time.

She called a girl to hang up their overcoats and lead them to the gowns.

Gina flitted from one dress to the next, handing the designs she liked to the woman who hurried to hang the gowns in the fitting room. But her heart wasn't in it, he could see that.

They were ushered into the usual beige and gold compartment, walled with mirrors, with three gilt armchairs and a carpet thick enough to sleep on. Mandic sat down. 'We'll call you if we need you.'

'Would you like coffee?'

'Yes, please,' Gina said before he could say no.

Phlegmatic as always, the assistant backed out and closed the door.

Mandic leaned back and thought about the future. When he'd finished selling his extensive art collection he might buy an island in the Aegean. Somewhere hot and free and very, very private.

When he next looked up Gina was standing naked except for her gartered stockings. She was bent forward as she wiggled into a tight, backless satin gown. He stood up to help her with the fastening, pressing his hand over her mound to push her buttocks hard against his thighs.

'No,' she hissed. 'Coffee's coming.'

'I know.'

He fastened her dress and she whirled around watching the flared satin and tulle skirt billow around her legs. 'What d'you think?'

'Only for walking barefooted on the beach. You need an island to go with it. I was thinking of buying one, but as yet . . . ' He shrugged apologetically.

'What about the yacht club do?'

'Too casual.' He pulled down the zip and reached for a midnight blue creation in jersey silk. She tried another. And still more.

'So far they don't do you justice,' he said. There was a click and clatter of crockery on a tray. A young girl came in and placed the tray on a gilt table before leaving silently.

'Remember last time,' he said, trying to ignite their previous joy.

'She almost caught us.'

'Who cares?'

Why was she trembling so? She was a mess of quivering lips and sullen eyes as she shook her head and ignored his need. He waited, moody and silent. He knew he was no longer in control of her. He'd guessed as much, but now he knew for sure. He tucked this information into the back of his mind. He would have to deal with it.

'Do you still love him?' he asked her.

'Who?'

'Patrick, of course.'

'I love you.' She looked round uneasily as she dressed, sensing a trap.

'Patrick was a fool. I despised him for wasting his life. I was glad when I killed him.'

Blue eyes opened wide with fear. 'Don't ever talk like that again. It's crazy talk. I don't want to hear his name. Not ever. I never want to think about it. Besides, you didn't kill him.'

Now she looked terrified and he wondered why. She could not suspect. She didn't even know. He had forbidden her any contact with her family. Right from the start this was an essential part of the deal and she had agreed, but she had let him down. She had given their address to her sister. He hated to be conned. He closed his eyes remembering Patrick who had been duplicitous, promiscuous and evil. He had atoned with his life. It was fitting.

He stood up, restless and anxious to leave. 'Choose a dress, or two if you like. Let's go.'

She couldn't decide, so he bought all four. Anything to get out of there.

* * *

They went on to the yacht club at St. Katherine's Wharf where Mandic had a mooring, although his yacht was currently being refurbished at a shipyard in Tyneside. It was almost midnight by the time they drove through Nettleton. Fifteen minutes later they were home. Gina had been strangely silent all the way, gazing blankly through the windscreen. It was as if she was growing away from him minute by minute. He dreaded the ultimate consequence of her disassociation. Strange how the things he feared the most were hastening towards him. He had to search around for conversation which was new.

'So when are you wearing the new dresses?'

She shrugged. 'You tell me.'

'There's a party coming up at the club soon.'

He hated parties, hated socialising, but he knew he had to make the effort. He dreaded the awful desolation of life without Gina. As they parked and walked through the connecting door into the entrance hall, Gina wouldn't look at him.

'I'm tired and my head aches so I'll take a couple of aspirins.'

A convenient pretext. She went off without kissing him, no offer of coffee, no excited chatter about where they'd hang the Pissarro. Once again he was struck with a deepening sense of foreboding. Had someone got at Gina? Or was there another man? She could never leave him. He could not allow her to go. Yet he wasn't a killer. He sensed that his first murder had type-cast him and he would never escape.

40

Eight p.m., River, Dover.

Clara concentrated on sifting the flour and kneading the dough. She was making biscuits, anything to keep her mind off Gina and Mandic. She was too tired to do any more packing. What was going on with Gina? Had she blurted everything to Mandic? Come to that, was she still alive? Whatever had possessed her to think that Gina could fool her lover? She was young and naive and he was old and cunning. He'd killed thousands of people and amassed huge wealth. He'd double-crossed his own partners in crime and murdered Patrick. He was a wanted man and therefore desperate. He could be driving to River right at this moment.

She had locked the windows and switched on the burglar alarm and she listened anxiously to every sound outside: a passing car, the hoot of an owl, even the wind seemed like a portent of doom. Earlier, when Jock had growled she had flinched and almost screamed. Letting the dog out set off the alarm which brought Jason grumbling downstairs. Jock chased a fox and disappeared, returning half an hour later looking pleased with himself. The burglar alarm was reset and Clara tried to relax.

Jason was watching TV. He should be doing his homework, but Clara didn't have the will to insist. Jock had stopped panting, stretched out in front of the fire and was soon snoring. She glanced at her watch. Two minutes past eight. Only two minutes since she checked the last time. It was exactly four hours since Peric Zimon had visited her to explain their plan. She was to drive to Nettleton in the morning where she would be hidden with Zimon's guards until they captured Mandic. She was needed to identify him. Other than Gina, she was the only person in England who had seen Mandic. Zimon only had photographs. But what exactly could she remember?

She tried to fight off the dreaded images, but they were flooding into her mind. She could smell the sea, feel the cold, hear the crashes as their yacht headed into the storm. She was spinning back through time and space to that terrible night. Would she ever forget those awful groans that woke her and brought her up on deck?

Scrambling up the companionway, she flung open the hatch and gasped as she stared into a solid wall of water racing towards her. She hung on as the wave pounded the yacht. Surely the groans were coming from the sail locker, but how was that possible? She battered her shoulder against the hatch and saw the hinges loosening.

Between waves she slithered into the engine hatch, grabbed an axe and a torch from the rack. It took only seconds to prise open the locker door which fell forward with a crash.

A hand reached out from the darkness and she saw Patrick's glittered in the torchlight. He was alive. 'Thank God,' she sobbed. 'I've got you. We'll make it, darling. I'll get the boat back to harbour.'

She tried to stop sobbing as she shone the torch over his head, almost gagging at the deep wounds. He was unrecognisable, his face a swollen, crimson pulpy mess, his jaw hanging loose, teeth gone.

Who had done this to him?

At that moment she was struck viciously on the side of her head. Dazed by pain, she could hardly see. Terror surged as a tall figure loomed over her. She swung up the axe which caught the next blow, sending pain like an electric shock zooming up her arm. Her attacker grabbed the axe and swung it towards her. Behind him a massive wave toppled over the bows. Her scream was lost in the crash as the wave hit the deck, knocking him sidelong and washing her overboard.

It had been so fast and so dark. How could she possibly identify this man? If only morning would come. Courage always returned with the first light. She glanced at her watch again. Only three more minutes had passed since she checked the last time. Impossible. Her watch had stopped. She glanced at the kitchen clock, but that too showed five minutes past eight. God! The night would never pass. Alone and miserable, she shaped the biscuits and put them in the oven.

The plan was madness. How could she identify a man she had never clearly seen? Yet somehow she knew that she must. If she failed now she would endanger the lives of Jason and herself and Gina, too.

Nine p.m., Ladywell police headquarters, Dover

Fergus and his team of detectives and data processing experts were assembled in the briefing room. Looking weary, but optimistic, they had been sorting Clara Connor's computer data around the clock.

DCI Bates walked in and sat on a chair near the door. 'Hope I haven't kept you,' he murmured. 'Carry on.'

'Sir.' Fergus stood up and pointed to the blackboard. 'To fill you in on the background, a mine of information was recovered from Connor's old computer by Clara Connor, but only a part of it was sorted. Basically Mrs Connor was preoccupied with finding the identities of her late husband's partners. However, this information will enable us to apprehend the Dover-based gangsters responsible for smuggling in thousands of illegal immigrants.

'Yesterday our computer team intercepted an e-mail to Bernard Fraser, the owner of Fraser's Haulage Company, which is based in Milan. It stated that twenty-five 'consignments' left Rijeka, Croatia, at dawn. They were on schedule according to the Croatian police who, by the way, have been very helpful. Presumably they will travel along their usual route, via Milan and Lyon, to reach Calais at midnight tomorrow, where they will be transferred to one of two boats for the Channel crossing.

'Basically they have Robin Connor's trippers' boat, the *Dover Belle* and the late Patrick Connor's *Valkyr*, which has now been purchased by Robin Connor. Depending on the weather, they should reach the marina in the Western Harbour, Dover, around three a.m. tomorrow morning.'

Bates scowled at Fergus. 'Let's hope those Croatian guys didn't give the game away. Carry on then.'

'Sir. The gangsters have a team of drivers and dozens of freelancers in their pay. The list of names is still being sorted.'

'How far have you got with the money laundering?' Bates asked.

'Well, it's rather interesting. When Connor first tried his hand at laundering their profits he met up with Colonel Vesno Mandic, an ex-Serbian army chief, who was touting for cash on behalf of Serbian banks, and offering ultra-high interest rates. Connor seems to be out of the smuggling picture now, but it's business as usual for the remaining partners.'

'The timing's important,' Bates stood up and paused in the doorway. 'These criminals are in constant communication. One slip and they'll go to ground. I'd like to see you for a moment, Fergus.'

'Okay, guys. Back to work,' Fergus called. 'Is there anyone who doesn't know exactly what he should be doing right now? Reports in by seven p.m. this evening. Okay? See you all back here then.'

Fergus caught up with Bates in the corridor.

'What news on the Ferretti murder case? Have you caught up with Mandic?'

'We're getting there. As you know, Gina Ferretti, ex-girlfriend of Patrick Connor, is rumoured to be living with Mandic. According to her father, she always calls him on his birthday, which, coincidently, is today. I saw Ferretti before the New Year and persuaded him to check back on her number when she calls. It turned out to be a public telephone booth in Nettleton, which is an up-market village north of Hemel Hempstead. Ferretti also gave me the name she uses on a credit card. As you know we drew a blank checking on Gina Ferretti, but her father told me she uses her stage name, Paloma. Now we've found that several purchases have been made at a florist in Nettleton. I have two men checking all house purchases in the area for the past six months. We should have the list first thing tomorrow morning.'

'You'll have to hand the matter over to the Buckinghamshire force.'

'Yes. I've given them the background in the meantime. I've also given them the results of Forensic's DNA tests on shreds of cloth caught on a nail in the cupboard where Ms Ferretti was murdered. And, believe it or not, a hair.'

'Could be anyone's.'

'Of course, sir. We'll see.' Fergus was feeling optimistic and he wasn't going to let Bates put him down over this one.

41

Midnight at Calais

Twelve uniformed police, lead by Inspector Jean Henriot, tried to keep warm as they waited in the back of a closed minibus overlooking the busy Calais harbour, opposite a fresh produce warehouse. Lights shone from dusty windows and from cracks around the main gate. Inside, two of Henriot's best undercover detectives had managed to cadge piecework unloading produce. The Inspector looked anxiously at his watch and shivered. It was five degrees below freezing.

He glanced down and saw a tripper's boat chugging towards the quayside. Taking his nightscope monoculars he read the name, the *Dover Belle*, and gave a grunt of satisfaction. Minutes later the boat touched the quay. A man roped the bollard and the gangway went down. After that the boat swayed gently in a light swell.

Five miles away on the road from Lille, a Renault Magnum refrigerated truck rumbled towards Calais. The driver, Louis Bastide, glanced at his watch. He was five minutes late, so he put his foot hard down on the accelerator.

Shortly afterwards he pulled up outside the dockside warehouse. Steel sliding doors opened and closed behind him as he drove inside. Lights blazed and Pierre, the foreman, came running forward, beckoning to him. Bastide drove slowly after him to a bay near the back. He switched off to a loud hissing of released, compressed air.

Bastide climbed out stiffly and hurried to the latrines. By the time he returned the crates of frozen pork sausages had been unpacked revealing a door to an inner container. Bastide climbed in and unlocked the door, but jumped back as the stench assaulted his nostrils. Something had gone wrong with the air supply.

'Come! Quickly, my friends. There isn't much time.'

Twenty-four exhausted, dehydrated men staggered out stinking worse than swine. They were lead off to the showers and latrines at the back of the warehouse.

'You leave in five minutes,' Bastide called after them.

The foreman came up to him and put his hand on Bastide's shoulder. 'We're in trouble. One of them is still there.' His voice betrayed his fear.

As Bastide shone a torch on the body of a middle-aged man, he felt no compassion, only fear.

'Hey you,' Pierre called to the hired hands. 'Stack the crates at the back.'

As soon as the packers were out of sight, the two men hauled the corpse out of the truck and dragged it to the side, pulling a pile of sacks over it.

The immigrants were filing back, their faces haggard after their ordeal.

'Okay you guys, let's go.'

* * *

The Inspector sighed with the relief as a side door of the warehouse swung open. A thickset man in corduroys and a leather jacket emerged, looked around cautiously, and beckoned. One by one, twenty-four immigrants filed out and followed him across the road, down the ramp and onto the quayside. Ephemeral as grey wolves drifting past, they moved up the gangway of the *Dover Belle* and disappeared from view as if they'd never been. Only the driver seemed substantial as he sauntered back, hands in his pockets, whistling jauntily to himself, anticipating his coming meal.

The Inspector watched impatiently. He saw the boat shudder as its engines revved up, he saw the driver enter an all-night restaurant and he saw with dismay the warehouse lights switching off.

'Go, damn you, move,' he whispered to the skipper in pent-up fury. Slowly the boat drew away from the quayside. He waited another minute and reckoned it was safe to move in fast. Aided by their two colleagues inside, the team took control of the warehouse, handcuffed the manager and workers and searched them for mobile phones and guns. The dogs went in. Moments later, frenzied barking pin-pointed the hidden cargo of drugs and the corpse.

Bastide flinched as two men entered the cafe. He could smell pigs a mile off. They beckoned to him and he stood up, shrugging into his leather jacket. Banging a few notes on the counter, he swaggered past the proprietor, avoiding his glance. When he saw the ambulance and the police cars, his red face flashed a deeper shade of cerise, his blue eyes turned bloodshot and his hanging jowls quivered.

'You're in big trouble, Bastide,' the Inspector said. 'One of the immigrants died so we're talking manslaughter, on top of the rest. I had a couple of plain-clothed men inside. You were photographed carrying the corpse out of the van. Co-operate with us and it might help you. It's the big guys we're after.'

'Naturally I'll do whatever you ask. I'm a law-abiding person, an innocent victim caught up in this fiasco.'

'Do you know this man?' The Inspector showed him two photographs of a thickset man with a shock of blond hair, deep blue eyes and an engaging smile.

'I've seen him once or twice. He owns our outfit. A Brit.'

It was not his fault the fools had been rumbled. Bastide felt no guilt, merely a great anxiety to save his skin. As he talked, the Inspector listened in amazement. Twenty minutes later, Inspector Henriot called DI Fergus on his mobile.

'We've got them, Fergus. Well done! Several kilos of coke as well as the immigrants were found in a sealed container behind boxes of frozen sausages. Not surprisingly, one of the poor sods died. This has been a very smooth operation and the driver's singing. The *Dover Belle* left fifteen minutes ago with twenty-four asylum seekers on board. I'll be in touch tomorrow. Good luck.'

Two-twenty a.m. St. Margaret's Bay

Bernard Fraser woke in his penthouse apartment overlooking St. Margaret's Bay, to hear loud knocking at the front door. He pulled his tartan mohair dressing gown over his wine red silk pyjamas and turned on the landing lights. Peering through the viewer he was amazed to see Detective Inspector Fergus standing there. Dozens of unpleasant possibilities raced through his mind, but none of them reached anywhere near the scope of the disaster that was about to engulf him.

'Bernard Fraser,' Fergus said when the door was open. 'I have a warrant for your arrest on suspicion of manslaughter.'

'Manslaughter?' Fraser gazed at Fergus in a daze.

'Plus the rest, but this will do for the time being.'

'You must be mistaken,' Fraser said, pulling himself together. 'I'm a lawyer. Perhaps you're looking for one of my clients.'

Ignoring the question, Fergus read him his rights.

Fraser's mind was racing round furiously. The police seemed very sure of themselves. Had someone informed on him, he wondered? His legal mind was toting up his probable fate. He could get up to fourteen years for smuggling immigrants into Britain, not forgetting the manslaughter charge and the sentences could run in succession. If so, he'd be there for life. He knew the judges took financial gain into account when considering the length of the sentence. Gazing desperately at his paintings, Persian rugs and all the costly paraphernalia with which he liked to surround himself, he wished he'd pulled out earlier and kept his cash in a Swiss bank

Three forty-five a.m., Dover's Eastern Harbour.

Inspector Fergus and Sergeant Browning were leaning over the railings of the car park overlooking the Marina, part of the Western docks. They could see the white cliffs shining with a ghostly radiance and above them the massive castle looking macabre and forbidding in the searchlights. A dull roar and a reflected glow of lights came from the Eastern Harbour below the battlements, but in the Western Harbour, nothing moved. It was dark and quiet, except for the sound of the waves splashing gently on the pebbled beach.

Browning pointed as she saw a dim light bobbing around beyond the breakwater. They waited in silence as the light moved closer. It was approaching the Western docks. Hope intensified!

Minutes later the boat sailed past port control and moved in the direction of the Marina. Fergus felt exhausted, but his dark eyes glowed

337

with anticipation as the vessel came into moorings.

'Listen,' Browning murmured.

Fergus heard the unmistakable sounds of a gangway going down. In the moonlight they could see figures moving along the pontoon towards the quay. Moments later the scene was lit as brilliantly as a film set from searchlights on the quay. Two launches sped across the harbour, their lights trained on the *Dover Belle*, leaving foaming white wakes behind them.

The file of men paused, huddled together and waited. Then a voice called through a loud-speaker: 'Come this way please.' It was repeated in French and Serbo-Croatian. The asylum seekers continued falteringly up the steps and onto the pavement in Snargate Street, where a group of immigration officials, a minibus and uniformed police had materialised as if from nowhere.

Fergus waited until he saw the skipper, Robin Connor, handcuffed and led away to a police van before taking off for a few hours rest.

Eight a.m., Immigration Department, Dover.

June Holman, dedicated humanitarian and full-time executive at the Home Office in Dover's Eastern Harbour, tried not to show how tired she was after days of questioning asylum seekers.

The man sitting in front of her looked as if he'd suffered badly. His arms were sinewy from hard manual labour, his brown eyes were ringed with deep shadows, most of his face was obscured by a thick black beard and he smelled of death. She knew that he'd come off the *Valkyr* and that he'd been waiting at her desk for three hours while his companions had breakfast and slept.

'Family name?' Her question was automatically echoed by Vladimir Zlokovic, their new, part-time interpreter, speaking in turn in Serbo-Croatian, Italian and German.

'Shamim,' the man replied. He spelled out the word. So he spoke English well. That was her first surprise.

'First name?'

'Danilo.'

'Place of origin?'

'Mazar-i Sharif, Afghanistan.'

'Do you have any documentary evidence to support your claim for political asylum?'

He reached into his pocket and brought out a poster. It was faded and torn, but she could recognise the eyes. It duplicated the name on his passport, she learned, when Zlokovic found an Afghan interpreter, and it put a price on his head, dead or alive. She studied the poster. Shamim had lost at least 20 kilos.

'Occupation?'

'By training I am a doctor, a specialist pediatrician. My wife and I were heavily involved in women's emancipation, so when the city fell to the Taliban I was a wanted man. We had to get out fast.'

June frowned. 'And now?'

'My wife and son are here. They have received right of residence.'

His name rang a bell. 'What are their first names?'

'My son is called Ahmad and my wife is Aida.' He seemed to savour the words as if he found pleasure simply in saying them.

June searched through the pending document on her computer. She found what she was looking for and leaned back looking sad. 'Ah yes! Your wife has given us a great deal of documentary proof that you are in fact, a bona fide asylum seeker. You might say she's been haunting us, Dr Shamin. Had you come over on the ferry with your passport and asked to be interviewed by the Home Office at Port of Entry you would have been granted residence straight away.'

'But my passport was confiscated by the authorities.'

'Yes. Nevertheless, by making an illegal entry you have breached our Immigration Laws. It will take six months for your case to be seen. Meantime, I am granting temporary admission to Britain, pending the outcome of a further investigation. You must report to the local police once a month.'

It took only a few minutes to print out the necessary documentation.

'You are free to go,' she said, smiling faintly.

Dr. Danilo Shamin waved and gave a small, polite nod. Overcome by emotion, he couldn't trust himself to speak.

42

Gina glanced at her watch. It was almost eight a.m. and inexplicably Mandic was still in bed. He was acting so strangely this morning, going out of his way to charm and amuse her. He couldn't suspect her, could he? A shudder of dread ran down her spine and she glanced around swiftly. He was propped against the headboard, gazing at her through sensual, half-closed eyes. She knew that look. It was all right.

'Come back to bed. It's too early to get up.' He grinned lewdly at her.

How had she ever thought him sexy? He was a monster. Gina dredged up an answering smile and rifled through the drawer for her sexiest underwear. Her composure slipped away and she collapsed on the bed feeling utterly lost. She was terrified. Surely he would notice? Had Sib been afraid, she wondered? Or had she been fierce and aggressive to the end? Oh God! I don't want to be hurt.

She said, 'I can't. I'm late.'

Mandic's expression abruptly changed. Lately mercurial moods raced over the surface of his face like a *son et lumiere* display, but the demand never varied:

'Come on, baby. Let's see if you can do the trick again.'

'I told you, I'm late.'

'Is it the Tate or the National Gallery that's waiting impatiently for your masterpiece?'

He always put her down. Whatever she did was no damn use. Only screwing. That's all she was good for. Not that it mattered any more. That was past tense. Right now he was making her very, very frightened. She mustn't show her fear. That would be the end, but she felt so powerless. He always seemed to read her thoughts. He blinked and she saw his jaw clench. A muscle twitched, a sure sign he was furious, yet he was hiding his feelings. Suddenly she couldn't stop shivering.

'Listen here, Vesno!' She was panting slightly as she put on a show of strength. 'I need something that's just me. Something private. Something that makes me feel good about myself. That's why I paint. Sib wasn't the only one in our family with talent. Why are you trying to spoil it for me?'

She dragged on a tight, sexy skirt and a see-through chiffon blouse.

'Don't I keep pushing you up? Aren't I always telling you how lovely you are?'

'I can't claim credit for my looks. I want to achieve something that's mine. You should understand.' But he wouldn't and couldn't and she knew that. Not that it mattered anymore. Suddenly she was quivering as her fear became physical. Her bowels squirmed and gurgled. Had he heard?

'Don't I make you happy anymore? Come here, baby.' He climbed out of bed and sat naked at the end of it.

She felt herself trembling. That look! That wild, sexy, predatory look! It used to grab her. Now it terrified her. She'd fallen in love with a bloody psychopath. She'd known he was dangerous and that had thrilled her. *But the bastard murdered her sister!* Part of her wanted to run and never stop running, but most of her wanted to see him dead.

She wiggled her skirt up, drawing her black gartered stockings over her long tanned legs in smooth, sensual movements. Naked underneath except for her stockings, she saw his eyes narrow with suspicion. This sexy, evil man, who dominated her mind and her body, would kill her without mercy if she threatened his security. How could she ever have hoped to deceive him?

'So why aren't you wearing knickers?' There came that furtive, sidelong glance again.

'You know why. Knickers leave ridges.'

'So why wear this skirt? For painting? In a field? In January? You must be crazy.' His voice was steeped in doubt. Right from the start, even when she had loved him madly, he'd never trusted her, perhaps because deep inside he felt himself to be unlovable.

'The others dress up.'

'And you say they're all women?'

'Mainly women. There's a couple of old men, but they don't always turn up. One never knows.'

'So where are you painting this time?' He tried, but failed, to sound disinterested. She could hear the tension in his voice.

'The old bridge past the barn and . . . Oh my! Just look at the time. I'm late.' He would follow her. He was hooked. Inexplicably she felt overcome with sadness. She wrapped her arms around him. 'There's never been anyone like you in my life.'

'So why does that sound like an epitaph on a tombstone?'

She felt appalled at her blunder.

He hung on to her. 'Don't go. I have such a bad feeling today.'

Was he psychic now? She stood up, hoping he would not feel her trembling. 'I must go. It's important to me.'

'And the teacher?'

'What about him?'

'Tell me about him.'

'Ugly, but sexy. He's a sculptor. Looks the part, too. Like a Spanish terrorist. I'll be back about lunchtime, but don't wait if I'm late. I'm on a diet anyway.' She glanced in the dressing-table mirror. 'How does my hair look? Okay?' She examined her nails. Fumbling for her lipstick, she smoothed it over her lips, glancing sidelong at him before shrugging into her red French duffel coat. He didn't trust her. Good! He was jealous and he would come.

★   ★   ★

He almost burst out laughing. Every gesture and movement she made, the sly slant of her eyes, her mouth curling in triumph, all that and so much more gave her away. He'd always been able to read her thoughts. Once he'd imagined he was psychic. Now he knew she always

344

signalled her intentions. She wasn't bright. As for getting a lover. What a laugh! She hated sex and gave it grudgingly. Not 'gave' but 'sold', he reminded himself. Hers was not a giving nature. Had they paid her, or threatened her? Frightened her perhaps? Or had they told her about her sister. He took his handgun from the drawer beside the bed and pointed it at the back of her head. Killing her would be like slashing a work of art, but what choice did he have? Do it now, he warned himself.

Gina swung round. Riveted with shock she could only stare, her eyes almost bolting from their sockets. He saw spittle gathering at the side of her open mouth. She recovered, swallowed and wiped her mouth with the back of her hand.

'What are you doing?' she asked coolly. He had to give her credit for her courage.

'Playing the fool.' He thrust the gun into his pocket.

She ran to him, throwing her arms around his neck, nuzzling her lips over his cheek, but still panting with fright.

'Listen to me, Mandic. We should go. Clara was in the village. She was looking for you.'

Clara! His stomach gave a painful twinge. Killing her was something he had hoped to avoid, too.

'D'you remember you said you would buy an island in the Indian Ocean? Let's do that. Let's live there. I'd love that.'

She was talking too fast, her voice pitched too high and her smile too false.

Bitch! He should kill her, but she could buy him time.

'You're late, aren't you? I'll come by and see how you're doing.' She almost passed out with relief. Stupid bitch! Yet he loved her still.

★ ★ ★

Gina arrived early and started to worry that there might be a downpour. What idiots would sit out in the tall wet grass painting a bridge if they could hardly see for rain? Besides, the water would wash the paint away, wouldn't it? Surely Vesno wouldn't buy this? She put up her easel, clipped on her sketch pad and shifted her seat, trying to ignore the cold damp penetrating her boots.

She glanced over her shoulder, scanning the trees and the oast-house at the top of the bank, but there was no sign of anyone. She seemed to be quite alone. Perhaps no one would come.

Gina felt very cold and her hands were shaking so much it was hard to hold the charcoal. She felt overwhelmed with a premonition of her own demise, as if it were she who were about to be trapped.

Moments later she caught sight of an old black car bumping down the slope towards her and her stomach somersaulted. The car was being reversed into a gap in the bank by the fence. A white-haired man got out slowly, incapacitated by his frailty. He opened the boot and took out a wicker basket filled with painting paraphernalia. Hoisting his easel over his shoulder and balancing his folding chair, he made his painful way down the slope towards her. This wasn't part of the plan. This wasn't a scheduled painting lesson, so who on earth was he?

Gina tried to smile, but her face and body had *rigor mortis*, except her hands which were making up for the rest of her. The old man walked around, studied the bridge, and put down his easel and chair some distance away from her. As he walked slowly towards her, Gina found she was holding her breath and this was making her dizzy.

'Good morning. I am Major Zimon. We met yesterday. You don't recognise me, I'm pleased to see. You can call me Percy.' He pulled up a chair and flopped beside her as if exhausted by his brief excursion. 'Listen carefully. If there is any shooting throw yourself face-down on the ground. While we wait we must play our roles. The view is better over there. Let's move you over.'

Did it matter? She was filled with dread as she trudged through the marshy ground.

'I have four men in the ditch,' he muttered. 'Two trained marksmen in the oast-house and more hidden under the bridge and in the trees. They are all excellent shots and trained fighters. There is no danger.' She looked around with a new, heightened perception, smelling the damp earth, the herbs along the bank, hearing the river splashing over stones and the purple clouds gathering overhead. She knew she would never go near a river again.

'Relax, Miss Ferretti. I can hear a car

347

approaching. Try to be calm.'

A green car bumped down the slope. A woman in trousers and an anorak got out, picked up her gear and floundered through the muddy grass. She said, 'Good Morning,' gravely to both of them in a heavily accented voice, before setting up her easel nearer to the road.

'Sergeant Anka Huic,' Zimon said. 'Please call her Joyce.' He turned anxiously to Gina. 'Were you this frightened at home?'

'No! I was fine then, but he will come soon. He was very suspicious of me because I wore these clothes. He's a very jealous man! But I made a mistake. I described our teacher, and, of course, he isn't here. He'll suspect something's wrong. He's very intuitive.'

'What does your teacher look like?'

'Long hair, gypsy looks, early thirties, ugly, but compelling.'

'Did you describe him this minutely?'

'Wait a minute! I think I said: 'Sort of ugly, like a Spanish terrorist, dark and gypsy-like,' but I gave the impression he was sexy.'

'Did you say he had long hair?'

'No . . . no, I'm sure I didn't.'

'Good! Then I can provide such a person.'

Zimon ducked behind his easel and muttered into his mobile. Minutes later an old Ford Sierra bumped down the slope and parked. A man in his early thirties climbed out and walked over to them.

'This is Major Stepanov, but you can call him Juan.'

'So what d'you usually do?' Juan said quietly

348

without a trace of an accent. 'D'you gossip? Laugh? Or work together in silence, as you are now?'

'We talk,' Gina said in a high-pitched tone. 'Sometimes we laugh. The teacher walks around and makes rude comments as he passes. Sometimes he draws on our work.'

Juan leaned over Gina and put in a few lines. 'Like this?'

As she caught the musky smell of the man, a thousand nervous impulses were urging her to get up and run. She willed her body to stay calm, but with every second that passed her tension heightened.

★ ★ ★

By ten-thirty, Mandic had filled the boot of his new, second car with rolls of paintings he had hurriedly packed. The pain of losing most of his precious works of art was almost more than he could bear. He could salvage a few things, but not the sculpture, nor the house. All was lost because Gina had betrayed him.

Abruptly he brought his mind to bear on more immediate matters. Running to the shower, he turned the tap on hard, stripping off his clothes and leaving them in a heap. A thrill of power ran through him. He was on a high as he ran barefoot to open his walk-in safe. At the back were two, white plastic German-made suitcases, kept hidden and packed. Working fast, he dressed in German-made clothes and thrust cash and jewellery into a case before carrying everything to the bathroom where he put on gold-rimmed spectacles and his German-made watch and hurried downstairs.

He wasted a few precious moments standing in the driveway regretfully. Sunlight glittered on the surface of the swimming pool and behind it, his handsome, Swedish-styled house seemed to beckon to him. The scene was compelling, the lines of the house designed in perfect symmetry, a vision of concrete and glass set amongst the trees. He turned away and pressed the button to open the garage doors.

Was it joy at outwitting his enemies that was cramping his muscles into a state of painful tension? Excitement had brought tears to his eyes and a lump to his throat. Nothing else! He had enough cash hidden around Europe to set him up in a hundred different lives. He could buy up any one of a dozen cash-stricken boatyards in Eastern Europe and make another fortune. Perhaps he'd buy the island he'd been promising himself. He made a point of listing his prospects and totalling the cash he had hidden around.

But then, frightened by the pointlessness of a future spent roaming Europe without Gina, his enthusiasm faded. On impulse he returned to the hall and scribbled a note on the table. 'Gone to find an island. Wait.' That was more than enough.

Moments later, Helmut Schmidt, German tourist, complete with driving license, passport, identity documents and two hundred and fifty thousand dollars in cash, sped down the

350

driveway in a small, German-registered Audi. It was almost noon when he drove onto the M20, towards the Channel Tunnel and a new life. He knew he'd feel better when he quit England, but he had a small matter to attend to in Dover first.

★ ★ ★

Around eleven a.m. the sun peered through the morose clouds and lit the bridge momentarily before sinking into indigo mists. By then, Gina was chalk-white and trembling violently. Tears were streaming down her cheeks. Zimon handed her a large handkerchief.

'Patience, Miss Ferretti. How long do your classes last?'

'Until half past twelve,' she murmured.

At noon a light misty drizzle began and her sketch was soon buckling and curling while her hair was wet through. She wanted to go, but where could she hide? She sat in a daze of apathy. She was as good as dead, she reasoned.

At twelve-thirty, Zimon straightened up and folded his easel.

'We've failed, Miss Ferretti. He isn't coming. Not your fault. You played your role well. Thank you for your co-operation.'

His eyes expressed his suspicion and Gina felt herself flushing heavily.

'We'll help you to pack your things.'

'And now? What happens next?' Gina caught hold of Zimon's arm. 'He must have suspected me. How can I go back?'

He frowned impatiently. 'We'll follow you to

351

your home and get him there. Colonel Vesna Mandic is a wanted criminal. He will be debriefed and flown to Kosovo as soon as possible to stand trial for war crimes including genocide.'

'And if he escapes?'

'There is absolutely no possibility of that. Relax, Miss Ferretti.'

'What if he's not there?'

'We'll find him.'

★　★　★

Clara was waiting under a canopy of pine trees with a Kosovan army sergeant to keep her company. She had watched a squirrel scratching around for hidden nuts, and heard the magpies squabbling. She had seen Gina arrive and the players assemble one-by-one to play out their roles, but it all seemed so unreal. The true reality was Jason, at school.

She went with him into the long hall for morning prayers, and mentally tailed him to his classes: Maths and English, but she had forgotten what came next and this bothered her. She tried to remember his timetable, and work out when he would be out in the school grounds, alone and defenceless. Would he stray too close to the road during break or sports? Where was he now, she wondered, feeling dazed with fear as she watched the class pack up their painting paraphernalia.

Jason left school at three. But no! Wait a minute. Today was Friday and they finished early. He would be off the school premises by one-thirty. And then?

She tried to comfort herself. Who would want to hurt a twelve-year-old boy? Answer: anyone who wanted to control her, and she was a witness to murder. That's why she was here. They wanted to pin her husband's murder to Mandic's long list of crimes.

What madness had prompted her to imagine that Gina could lure Mandic here? He must have found out. A worse thought came: perhaps Gina had warned him. Doom seemed to be settling like a black cloud over her son and her home. Nausea welled up inside her.

Soldiers were marching all over the field and a truck was racing towards her. Zimon got out and walked towards her and gently tugged her arm.

'It didn't work. We shall follow Miss Ferretti home. If he is in the house she will signal to us by coming outside on some pretext. We'll get him then. Otherwise — ' He shrugged.

Otherwise he could be waiting for me in my home with Jason held hostage and powerless to help himself. She wanted to cry out for help, but how would that help Jason? There would be a shoot-out. Jason would be hurt. Oh God! Not that! She had to go home alone.

She seemed to be watching herself from some distance behind. A double agent, on the stage and in the audience, too, but which one was she really?

'Don't worry. We'll get him,' Zimon called.

His words sent the last shreds of reality skittering away.

The sun came out and she felt its soft warmth on her shoulders. She could hear the river gurgling, closer now, and the wind sighing through the pines.

'I have only to put one foot in front of the other. It's a simple procedure. My car is not far away. Left foot, right foot. And again. I must get home.'

Later she couldn't recall walking back to the vehicle or the long race to River. But she knew she would never erase the memory of the note she found on the hall table: '*If you want to see your son alive wait here for my call.*'

43

It was six p.m. and after snatching only two hours of sleep, Fergus had worked through the day. He was on a high. They'd won and suddenly all the extra hours seemed worthwhile. Bates, on the other hand, looked tense and exhausted, Fergus noticed, as he walked into his office.

'So you got those two bastards, Robin Connor and Fraser?'

'Yes, sir. Both were caught with possession of large quantities of drugs. The Croatian manager in Rijeka spilled the beans and so did the truck driver. Add to that the manslaughter charge and we should be able to put them away for years.'

'This is a very odd business, Fergus,' Bates said, as he fingered his subordinate's report into Sibyl Ferretti's murder. 'Are Forensic positive that the strands of fabric caught on the nail in Sibyl Ferretti's cupboard match those of Mandic's torn trousers?'

Fergus, who had too much to do, was tired of the inquisition.

'Absolutely sure, sir. The evidence suggests that he murdered her.'

'You say you questioned Gina Ferretti this afternoon and she swore that Mandic had left the country.'

'So she said.'

'You sound as if you don't believe her?'

'Well,' he hesitated. 'She was in a bit of a state

355

and I don't think she really knew where he'd gone. She'd thrown some clothes into a suitcase and she was leaving. Believe it or not, she gave me the torn trousers. She told me Mandic had stolen the spare keys to Ferretti's home and he was out on the night of the murder.' He didn't add what else she'd said. That Clara Connor had warned her of Mandic.

'She wouldn't say where she was going. Only that she wasn't coming back and we could contact her through her father. She looked terrified. Evidently he pulled a gun on her earlier this morning, but pretended he was joking. She begged me to walk her to her car and drive behind her as far as the motorway.'

'You've put out a search and alerted Interpol, I assume.'

'Yes, sir.'

'He's gone to ground. We'll never find him.' Bates slapped the file on the desk in a rare show of temper. Fergus felt annoyed: his superior had mentally dismissed him and picked up the next file before he was out of the door.

His mobile was ringing. Fergus fished it out of his pocket.

'Inspector Fergus? Peric Zimon here. I got your message about the forensic tests. Thanks.' It was a bad line and Fergus could hardly hear what he was saying. 'I thought I had Mandic this morning, but he slipped through my fingers. He's left his home, probably forever. I'm worried about Mrs Connor. I think he might suspect that she helped us to trap him. I think she needs some protection.'

'I'll get right over there,' Fergus mumbled.

He felt shocked as he hurried to his car. So Mrs Connor had thought the Serbs a better bet for her safety. He blamed himself for letting slip Zimon's name.

★ ★ ★

There were no lights shining in Mrs Connor's house and at first Fergus thought the family had gone out. He rang the bell, expecting the usual explosive aggression from Jock, but heard only a whimper from just inside the door. Despite the silence, he felt that Mrs Connor was at home.

He knocked and called out: 'Mrs Connor.' Eventually he heard her footsteps dragging across the bare hall. When she opened the door, he saw that she was wrapped in a sleeping bag. All he could see were her swollen eyes. Reaching for his torch, he flashed it around and saw packing cases piled up against the walls and the rug rolled up on one side. Jock was curled in his basket, too upset to snarl. She'd been sitting in the dark next to the telephone for hours by the look of her. She was scared and frozen.

'What's happened? Where's Jason?'

She grabbed his torch and switched it off.

'Listen to me. I want you to go away. It's important. Do you understand what I'm saying? Go away.'

'I want to help you,' he muttered. 'I came to tell you that Forensic have produced the evidence that will convict Mandic of Miss Ferretti's murder. He killed her.' There was a long silence. 'So you're off the hook.'

She shrugged and glanced beyond him to the garden, searching the shrubs and hedge with anxious eyes. 'You must go now. For God's sake.' She leaned forward and pushed him.

'Mandic's got Jason, hasn't he? What does he want?'

'Me, I suppose. But I'm waiting to hear. He said that if I called the police . . . If he sees you here . . . ' She broke off and shuddered. 'If you value Jason's life, just leave and don't come back.'

Feeling shocked and overwhelmed by the tragedy, Fergus stepped back as the door was slammed in his face.

Deep in thought, Fergus got into his car and drove down Cowper Road. Sooner or later Mandic must make his move. He might call Clara Connor to go to him, or arrange to meet her somewhere, or drive up to her house. In any event, one of them would have to pass this way. It looked as if Mandic could be easily taken, but if he arrested him, he might never find Jason. There had to be a better plan. He parked under a tree in a driveway and prepared for a long wait.

★ ★ ★

Jason was trying hard to be brave. He was about to turn thirteen and therefore practically an adult. Men never cried, but the pain in his head was hard to bear and his wrists felt as if they were on fire. Even worse was his fear for his mother. He might never see her again and he

358

knew how sick with worry she must be. He had only just regained consciousness, but he had a vague recollection of being thrown down a hatch into the hold of a ship. He had no idea what was going on but he knew he'd been a fool. He hadn't even put up a fight.

Returning home from school, he'd rushed to the back garden to let Jock in, but strangely Jock was in the shed, growling furiously. While he was undoing the bolt, someone had hit him hard on the back of the head, knocking him down. Moments later a rag soaked in chloroform had been thrust over his mouth and that was the last thing he remembered until he found himself lying in the hold of a ship, his hands bound behind his back, feeling as sick as a dog, with tape over his mouth. He felt dizzy and he was scared to move.

★ ★ ★

Stiff with tension and tormented by her fears for Jason, Clara sat by the telephone willing it to ring. Around three-thirty a.m. she heard a car turn into Cowper Road. It was getting closer. Who would drive here at this time of night? It must be him. Her stomach twisted in painful spasms as she heard the car turn into her driveway. The engine was switched off. The door slammed. Footsteps were approaching. He was mounting the steps.

'Help Jason, God help Jason,' she muttered in a swift, impromptu prayer. Immobilised with terror, Clara watched the door handle turn.

Someone had unlocked the door. *Someone who had a key.* Her first reaction was to lurch forward and push the bolt home, but what was the point? He had Jason.

She flinched as a man stepped into the hall, while her senses cringed with recognition. Then fear hit her like bomb blast. *Fear of knowing!* It seemed that all the horrors of the past weeks were confronting her. Her vision took a snail's route to olive shoes that were highly polished. Mohair trousers of slate grey. A green and white checked shirt worn under a black anorak. Square shoulders achingly familiar and that strong, tanned throat.

She looked up into blue eyes of glittering fury and gave a single, high-pitched scream. In that split second of horror it seemed that she had always known.

'Patrick!'

'Himself!' She gasped with pain as he clamped his hand over her mouth and pressed his knife against her throat.

'No hysterics, Clara.'

At that moment, Jock raced in fast. As forty kilos of snarling fury leapt for Patrick's throat, he drove the knife into the dog's chest. Jock snarled, spraying blood over the carpet, but whipped round and slunk towards him looking mean.

'Call him off if you want Jason to live.'

'Basket, Jock,' Clara said and the dog limped off growling.

'You don't look quite as surprised as I'd hoped.' Patrick smiled, pushing his knife into his pocket. 'Well, this is unexpectedly macabre, isn't

360

it? Together again, but one of us passed over. Like a seance!'

To Clara it was like seeing a nightmare become reality. As he leaned over her she smelled his aftershave and the cologne he used and remembered the strangely familiar scent in Sib's cupboard on the night she was murdered. Why hadn't she realised then? She had denied her own senses right up until this moment. She shook her head feeling dazed and ashamed of her memory loss. All because she couldn't bear the painful truth: *Patrick had invited her for a second honeymoon in order to murder her*. He had planned to rid himself of two major annoyances at the same time.

Just how many weeks had he spent planning Mandic's murder, she wondered, remembering the dieting, the tattoo, the earring and the long hair? He needed to look like Mandic in order to pass off Mandic's corpse as his own. He'd fooled them all.

'Where's your computer?'

She could hear Jock panting as she lead the way to her study and switched on the light.

'Hmm! I see it's your office again.' He glanced around. 'Switch on and hack into my e-mail.'

'I don't know how to.'

'You know. Don't waste time. Jason's trussed up like a Christmas turkey. He might even suffocate.'

His eyes showed her the pointlessness of pleading. It was bad luck that she'd kept copies of all the computer data she had given to Fergus.

There lay her entire research into Patrick's affairs.

'Do the police have details of these deposits?' Patrick asked, leaning over her shoulder and pressing his knife hard into her back.

'No.'

She heard the soft padding of paws on the carpet. Jock limped in with blood over his chest.

'Basket, Jock.' She pushed him off gently and the dog left looking forlorn.

Patrick glanced at his watch and back to the computer. 'Be quick,' he muttered. 'Do this for me and I won't harm you or Jason. I want you to transfer all the funds that are on your files into these accounts.' He handed over the names, account numbers and sort codes. Now she saw that Patrick had established several accounts in Eastern Europe in the name of Helmut Schmidt. Her stomach lurched. How could Patrick let her live when she knew these details?

'It'll take a while. Patrick, please. I know what you're going to do, but Jason is just a little boy. Your step-son. He doesn't know anything. You mustn't hurt him.'

'It's up to you. If you do what I want I'll see he's okay.'

It took twenty minutes and all the while she was seeing Jason trussed up, hurt and very, very scared.

'Finished.'

'Open up the console,' Patrick's hateful voice whispered.

'How would I do that?'

When the knife dug into her neck, Clara

sullenly fumbled in the drawer for her screwdriver and opened the casing.

'Destroy the circuits. Use the hammer. Be quick.'

It wasn't as easy as she'd expected, but at last her PC lay in ruins.

'Okay, let's go.' Patrick sounded relieved.

The knife was never far from the back of her neck, as they went downstairs. The street was empty and Clara's heart sank as she realised that she and Jason faced the prospect of no reprieve.

44

The wind had dropped, but a dense, drizzling mist was drifting in from the sea. There was a strong smell of ozone and the dismal sound of the foghorn from the breakwater a mile offshore. Visibility was down to twenty metres as they hurried across the road and down the steps to the marina. Clara, half-frozen with fear and cold, lingered on the top step, glancing round longingly, but there was no help in sight, the road was deserted.

'You first.' Patrick pushed her on to the pontoon and pointed towards the *Valkyr* tied at the last mooring.

She clutched the rope guideline. 'Where's Jason?'

There was no answer. A dismal foreboding settled on Clara. Dread had turned her legs to lead.

She mounted the gangway and paused to glance around. Behind were the harbour lights. The castle, bathed in the floodlights, shimmered wanly through the mist. Before her was only black sea and sky.

Flinging open the hatch, Patrick thrust Clara on to the companionway. The lights from the Western Harbour were the last things she saw before descending into inky darkness. She stumbled on the companionway, as the hatch slammed shut. She heard the bolts slide home and now the darkness was absolute.

'Jason! Jason,' she called softly. Only silence and a strong stench of disinfectant and vomit greeted her.

Oh, dear God! What now? She heard a strange sound. 'Mmmm, mmmm,' far ahead. Her eyes acclimatised to the darkness and she saw faint glows from the portholes. She crept to the hull and moved towards the stern.

'Jason?'

'Mmmm!'

She burst into tears of relief as she ripped off the tape and hugged her son tightly to her. 'Jason! Oh, thank God!'

'Ow!' He struggled out of her arms. 'That hurt. There's a penknife in my pocket. It's sharp. Don't cut yourself — or me. Be careful, Mum.'

Unable to see, she did cut herself sawing through the ropes binding his wrists and ankles. 'Bastard! Bastard!' she muttered. She straightened up. 'We've got to get out of here. Can you stand? Stay close to me,' she whispered. 'There's a lobster hatch into the sea. We can escape through it, but we have to be well away before he starts the engines or we'll be mincemeat. He's installed a powerful engine. Feel around for a square, padded seat. It's near the stern. Hurry!'

The hold seemed vast and they had to feel their way in the dark. She crawled around and heard Jason call softly. 'Over here.'

Clara made her way towards his voice and they fumbled for the catch, snagging their fingers, swearing softly, sweating with urgency. The lid was pushed aside and now they could hear the sea splashing against the rim of the well below them.

'Oh for a torch,' Clara whispered. 'There's a sort of a cage to hold lobsters. The bottom unhinges. I'm sure it's closed now, but there must be a catch to open it from the inside. We mustn't get trapped underwater. We have to find out. Stay here. Don't follow me, I'm coming back.'

Clara sat on the rim and dropped head first into the sea. Kicking down into stygian darkness, she lost all sense of direction, twisting and turning. The metal cage was all around her. She reached the bottom, or was it the side? But now her lungs felt close to bursting. That was panic, she knew! Fumbling around in freezing water, her numb hands almost missed the bolt. She managed to draw it back at last and the gate fell away from under her. She sank down, grabbed the sides and began to hoist herself up.

Her heart lurched as the boat throbbed and vibrated, giving a jerk like a nervous, tethered horse. She heard a sound like thunder as the propellers revolved and a maelstrom of water knocked her hard against the cage. Blasted by noise and pressure, she hung on while she was sucked inexorably towards the sharp blades.

She dug her fingers into the grid and fought the momentum, hauling herself up, hand over hand, using every last ounce of strength. She couldn't get a grip with her feet, so she kicked off her trainers and dug her toes in, feeling her way up the slippery, slimy metal grid. As the boat thrust forward, the pull of the water almost tore her away time and again.

Her lungs were bursting when at last her fingers touched wood. Moments later she broke surface, panting, choking, taking huge breaths, half-sobbing as she filled her lungs with precious air. Then Jason was helping her over the rim. She fell on the floor and lay prone until she stopped gasping.

'Jesus, Mum! I've never been so scared,' Jason whispered. 'Just listen to the propellers turning. Sounds like jet propulsion.'

'We wouldn't stand a chance if we tried to swim for it. At least, not until he switches off the engines.'

Clara was shivering violently, so Jason took off his coat and rubbed her vigorously.

'I was so frightened for you, Mum.'

She folded him in her arms, rocking him gently. 'We'll think of something, Jason. He'll have to stop the engine when he comes down to . . . that is, when he comes down here.' Clara's lips were so numb she could hardly speak. 'As soon as the engine stops we must jump through the hatch and swim for it. It's our only chance. You know that as well as I do. We know too much to live. I'm the main source of evidence against him and he has a gun and a knife. Shh! Listen!'

The boat was slowing. Her heart was thumping wildly. They heard Patrick identifying himself as Robin Connor and giving Calais as his destination to Port Control. Moments later the boat moved past the breakwater, into the Channel, rising and falling gently over calm water.

Clara stared through the porthole. She saw only an occasional flash of irridescence, for the rest of the sea and sky merged in a cimmerian canvas.

'It's five a.m.' Jason said, switching on his watch light. Clara sat beside him and put her arms around him. They lapsed into silence, hugging each other as the boat chugged deeper into the Channel.

Apathy came stealthily as if from nowhere, settling into her bloodstream and her joints, numbing her mind, leaving her weak and resigned to her fate. Why fight? The odds were stacked against her. She felt overwhelmed by this evil man's power and his cunning plans. Even Sib had been conned by him. Hadn't Patrick begged her to help him regain Gina's love, merely to spread the rumour that his mistress had left him for Vesno Mandic? Remembering their reunion lunch, when she'd accepted his expensive gift, made her feel sick. She, too, had believed that Gina had left him for a rich art dealer. They had all believed him. Even Bernie and Robin. But Sib had taken steps to find out where Gina lived. It was only a matter of time before she followed up with a visit and recognised Patrick, despite his new image. Or had she already guessed? Sib had threatened his safety, so he'd murdered her.

As Clara's anger exploded, apathy vanished.

Somehow she must tackle Patrick before he shot them. It was dark in the hold, but there were two dim lights. The switch was outside the hatch at the top of the companionway.

'We must break one of the lights,' she muttered. 'Patrick will switch the lights on before he comes down. When he's exactly halfway down, you must break the other light. You'll have to be quick. Then I'll tackle him. He'll be shooting wildly in the dark so we must keep down.'

'He has a torch.'

'Of course. But he needs one hand to steady himself as he climbs down the companionway and another to hold the gun. Besides, he won't be expecting sudden darkness. Let's feel around the deck for something useful.'

Clara picked up what felt like an old tiller and smashed the plastic cover of one of the lights, breaking the bulb. Jason had found a yard of discarded chain.

'Listen. D'you hear that?' Clara heard the fear in Jason's voice. 'It's the foghorn from Varne Bank lighthouse. We're seven miles from land and there's a thick fog. We wouldn't even know if we were swimming round in circles and the sea's icy.'

'What choice do we have? We must have courage.'

Abruptly the engine stopped. There was an eerie silence. All they could hear was the sea lapping against the boat as they swayed in calm water. The foghorn sounded again. Stomach churning, Clara gripped Jason's knife and the tiller. She heard footsteps and felt the slight list of the boat as Patrick came down from the wheelhouse.

'He has a gun, but he'll be shooting blind.

Remember to keep down, Jason. And keep very quiet.'

Dim light from the one remaining lamp flooded the hold as the hatch opened and torchlight flashed around, on Clara curled up on the bench and Jason leaning against the bulk-head under the light, his eyes closed.

Patrick thrust the torch in his pocket and came down very slowly.

Clara watched him cautiously. Just let Jason do it right. Count his footsteps. One, two, three, four . . . Do it fast. Now!

Jason leaped up and swung the chain at the lamp which splintered with a crack. Sloe-black night fell like a shroud over them all.

Patrick swore. Five shots in rapid succession sprayed the bulkhead.

Where was Jason? Was he safe? Clara was close enough to hear the sound of Patrick's laboured breathing. A beam of torchlight flashed around the deck. Clara slammed the tiller down hard on Patrick's right hand. She saw the gun spin across the deck as she sprang towards him, thrusting the knife into his neck. The torch fell and went out, but Patrick was still on his feet. She had failed.

45

A sound like thunder dazed her. It was racing towards them at breakneck speed, vibrating through the *Valkyr* until Clara's head seemed close to exploding with the noise. A siren sounded from overhead. Simultaneously came the shock of a massive collision. Timbers were splintering around them. A violent lurch sent her sprawling across the hold. They seemed to be airborne. Clara was pushed down and down onto the deck, unable to cry out or get up. A split-second later they were falling and turning over and she was propelled through the air, landing with a thump against the hull. Where was Jason?

'Jason,' she screamed.

The grinding, tearing and snapping of timbers was like a bomb blast that went on and on, while the *Valkyr* was tossed back into the sea. The boat fell with a crash on her port bow and keeled over. Clara was thrown head over heels the length of the hold, landing bruised and shocked on the bench. The thunderous noise became louder as the boat spun, buckled and up-ended. Icy sea-water pressure-sprayed through the smashed hull.

Clara's world switched to slow motion giving her time to plan. A collision! Something big had capsized them and they were sinking fast. Must find Jason. We have to get out or we'll be trapped and drowned.

371

A powerful searchlight swept over the boat. The beam shone through the lobster trap, which was above them now, and swept on. It was pitch dark again. The water was cascading around her and Clara was swept off her feet. Shocked by the icy cold, she forced herself to swim frantically towards the hatch, screaming out: 'Jason, Jason! This way.' She felt breathless from pushing away the smashed beams that jostled and thumped around her. Dear God! Where was her son?

It was all happening too fast. Clara felt confused. There was no pocket of air to keep the stern afloat, because of the well. The tow from the sinking boat would drag them down too deep to survive.

She turned and reached out blindly, yelling: 'Jason! Jason!' She collided with a body. Hands grabbed hold of her. 'It's me. It's me, Mum.'

'We have to find the well,' Clara shouted. 'It's over there. Kick hard.'

A split-second later the hold was submerged and they found themselves trapped under the pitch black water. There was no way to tell where the hatch was. Clara kept her grip on Jason's collar as she kicked out. Miraculously the searchlight swept over them again, lighting the well which was diagonally above. Clara made for the light. Clasping Jason, she kicked her way to the surface.

★ ★ ★

On board the tanker, the *Onorato*, the watchkeeper was talking to the coastguard on his

VHF Radio, Distress Channel 16: 'We've hit a small boat, possibly a fishing vessel. It was a glancing blow, but we're cruising at twenty-two knots and the boat capsized and sank. Position 51 °, 03′ North, by 01 °, 24′ East. Good luck.'

As the message came in, the officer in charge at Port Control contacted a search vessel. Then he remembered he had grudgingly lent a Patrol Vessel and crew to Inspector Fergus to apprehend a fugitive on the *Valkyr*, so he radioed the position to him, too.

★ ★ ★

Morning had broken on their strange and silent world. The sea was as flat as a mirror, pewter-grey and glistening, while the fog had taken on a strangely surrealistic, white glow. It was all around them, so that they seemed to be swimming in a small oasis, surrounded with billowing white cliffs of fog. Jason caught sight of the tiller and grabbed it. It seemed like a good omen. A chunk of the bulkhead as big as a door floated by and Mum caught hold of it.

'Get on it, Jason,' she said.

'No, you must.'

'I think you need it more. Climb on.'

'We'll both hang on,' he agreed, grabbing the side. They were floating half-submerged in calm water listening to the foghorn which seemed to come closer as they drifted towards the Varne Bank. It was cold and they were wet through. Jason knew that they wouldn't last long. 'Keep kicking,' Mum said.

There was no warning, only a ripple as something dark moved below the surface of the water. It came up fast, surging out of the water like a massive elephant seal. Madness shone in his eyes. His face was swollen and bruised, the skin raw. He lunged forward, seized Jason's neck in his powerful hands and pushed his head underwater.

Stunned by the attack, unable to breathe or see, Jason wrestled with the hands, trying to free himself. The pain was intense and Patrick was stronger. Jason held his breath, trying to sink like a stone, dragging Patrick deeper. How long could he last, he wondered? As long as the git could. Maybe longer.

They were rising again and Jason was blacking out. The grip on his neck loosened abruptly. Then the hands fell away from his throat. Jason broke surface and splashed around choking and gulping. 'He'll be back,' he muttered. 'And soon. He'll finish me off and then he'll kill Mum. Where's the tiller? Got to have a weapon.'

Tense and scared, he waited for Patrick to rocket out of the sea and lunge into the attack. The tiller was gone and so was Mum. The raft was right next to him. Was she lost in the fog? Had Patrick surfaced and dragged her down?

'Mum,' he yelled over and over. Frantic with fear, he listened intently.

He dived down and swam around underwater. Peering into the gloom he could hardly see a foot in front of his face. He gulped seawater as he almost collided with the dark shape of Patrick's body. Jason was choking and backing off fast when he saw there were two shapes entwined just under the surface. Mum had the tiller under Patrick's chin, his neck was twisted back strangely. Her knees were round his waist. It looked like a lover's tryst, only Patrick was limp.

He got out fast and hung on to the raft. He wanted to vomit, but he couldn't.

Then Mum surfaced slowly.

'Don't panic. Just keep talking. I don't want to lose you or the raft in this fog. Count sixty seconds, five times. Loudly! I want to make sure . . . ' She sounded very stern.

Five minutes could last an eternity, Jason reasoned. Tingles of unease were running through his frozen body. His mother was the nurturer, giver of unconditional love, font of life. He'd seen Mum shed tears over a frozen bird. There and then another piece in the jigsaw of life fell into place. Behind the soft eyes, and fragile hands lurked the primitive Eve who would kill to protect her loved ones.

Mum was drifting away, he could hear by her voice. He stopped counting. 'Five minutes,' he yelled. 'Where are you? Talk to me!' The sound hardly carried through the mist.

'I'm coming.' Mum's voice was hoarse. 'Patrick has drowned and I'm moving his corpse away. Keep calling. I can't see a thing.' Moments later she surged towards him in a brisk crawl. Jason shuddered and tried not to remember what he'd seen. She was shivering violently as he pulled her half on to the raft. She hung on to his hands, her face so white and her eyes so scared. He wondered how long she could last? Possibly forever, he thought, trying to reprogramme his misconceptions.

'It's like the end of the world,' Mum was saying, gazing around her. 'As if there's nothing else but this oasis of calm sea and clear air, and beyond only those towering walls of mist circling us. I have the strangest feeling someone up there is watching over us.'

Not right at that moment, he hoped.

'Are you all right, Jason? Perhaps you should move around a bit, keep your circulation going.'

'I'm fine.'

'They'll rescue us, of course. When Patrick made me transfer his cash, I managed to send a message to Fergus. I guessed he'd take us out to sea.'

'Of course.'

'We need a better raft.' Her eyes searched the debris. 'What's that white thing bobbing past?'

Jason held his breath as he saw a white plastic case bobbing past, half submerged. He dived towards it, unzipped the fastening a couple of inches and peered in. The bag began to sink as the air escaped.

'You're right. Someone up there is looking after us.' He zipped up and hauled it back, pushing it towards his mother. 'It's filled with bank notes. I think they're dollars.'

'Heavens. It must be part of Patrick's loot. With luck it will repay the mortgage he borrowed.' They struggled to push it on to the raft.

'If anyone asks, say it's my school gear.'

'School gear? Here?' His mother was smiling

softly. Perhaps with relief. She didn't have to be scared any longer. She'd survived and won. She reached out and took hold of his hand.

'He was going to kill you. I was so frightened.'

'Let it go, Mum. It's ancient history.'

She touched his cheek, running her hands round his jaw, letting her fingers drift around his ears and stroking his sodden hair like she used to when he was a kid. Her eyes beamed naked, unashamed love.

'Shh! Listen!' She looked round urgently. 'D'you hear something?'

'No. Well, maybe . . . Hang on . . . '

'Jason!' a voice came faint and tinny through a distant loudspeaker. 'Clara!'

It sounded like Fergus's voice echoing eerily through the mist.

'Over here,' Jason yelled.

No one answered.

Now he plainly heard someone call out: 'There's a body in the water.'

Shouts and the sound of splashing echoed around, giving no clear sense of distance or direction.

'Jason!'

'Over here,' they bellowed. Seconds later a boat loomed through the mist, the black silhouettes of the crew looking twice as large as life.

'We made it,' Clara said as she slithered off the wreckage. Strong arms hauled her into the boat.

We do hope that you have enjoyed reading this large print book.

Did you know that all of our titles are available for purchase?

We publish a wide range of high quality large print books including:
Romances, Mysteries, Classics
General Fiction
Non Fiction and Westerns

Special interest titles available in large print are:
The Little Oxford Dictionary
Music Book
Song Book
Hymn Book
Service Book

Also available from us courtesy of Oxford University Press:
Young Readers' Dictionary
(large print edition)
Young Readers' Thesaurus
(large print edition)

For further information or a free brochure, please contact us at:
Ulverscroft Large Print Books Ltd.,
The Green, Bradgate Road, Anstey,
Leicester, LE7 7FU, England.
Tel: (00 44) 0116 236 4325
Fax: (00 44) 0116 234 0205

Other titles published by
The House of Ulverscroft:

WINNERS AND LOSERS

Madge Swindells

It isn't until her grandfather's accident that Samantha Rosslyn realises that Woodlands, the family-owned brewery, is in deep trouble. To raise cash, Sam decides to sell an ancient family title, but the proposed sale attracts a young American historian, whose presence brings unexpected complications. As Sam struggles to pull the company round, her sister becomes involved with a campaign to publicise the plight of animals kept in battery conditions, her grandfather teams up with some wartime comrades to fight off a threat to the brewery from organised crime, and Sam's best friend is desperately trying to avoid an arranged marriage.

SUNSTROKE

Madge Swindells

A fund manager for a London merchant bank, Nina Ogilvie vowed that love would struggle to have a place in her life. She has reaped the rewards and become one of the City's most brilliant — and most heartless — operators. When her firm decides a sojourn in South Africa is just the break she needs, Nina finds the Cape's beauty piercing her professional defences. Caught up in a romantic whirlwind with Wolf Moller, a wealthy German, she becomes pregnant and sacrifices her career for a man she deeply loves — but barely knows. Two years later, Wolf disappears with her beloved son, Nicky, exposing the reality of a man wanted by both Interpol and the CIA . . .

SNAKES AND LADDERS

Madge Swindells

Marjorie Hardy has brains, courage and beauty — but these assets aren't nearly enough when she falls in love with Robert MacLaren, heir to a Scottish whisky empire. Her family is poor and her accent and upbringing are totally wrong for Robert's calculating stepmother. Finding herself alone and pregnant, Marjorie makes up her mind to keep her baby and fight for her daughter's rightful inheritance. Her dream sets her off on a long, tough road of business. She reaches the top, becoming co-owner of a highly successful publishing company — but now she must choose between ambition and love.

FAMILIAR ROOMS IN DARKNESS

Caro Fraser

Harry Day was a national literary treasure, revered for his poetry, novels and plays. But his personal life has remained something of a mystery. When Adam Downing, a young journalist, is appointed his official biographer, he finds that Harry's life holds an abundance of secrets. But Adam is torn between wanting to protect Harry's reputation and his instincts as a journalist, which drive him to tell the truth at any cost. Even at the cost of losing the admiration and friendship of Harry's beautiful daughter, Bella. For Harry's biggest secret of all involves Bella; and Adam is well on his way to falling in love . . .

THE HOTEL RIVIERA

Elizabeth Adler

'Imagine a sunny, sea-lapped cove, gift wrapped in blue and tied with a bow like a Tiffany box, and you'll get the feel of my little hotel. It's a place made for Romance with a capital R. Except for me, its creator.' Lola Laforet doesn't have time for love. Her disreputable husband has disappeared, the police consider her a prime suspect and her beautiful home and business seems to belong to an ex-arms dealer. Lola doesn't go looking for danger, it just seems to walk through the door. And when it walks through the door in the form of the delectable Jack Farrar she knows she's in real trouble.

THOSE IN PERIL

Margaret Mayhew

In 1940, free-living artist Louis Duval decides to leave his studio in Brittany and, in his small motor boat, make the perilous journey to England. His aim is to offer his services in the continuing fight, and to help liberate his beloved France from the enemy. He reaches Dartmouth, where he finds lodgings with a young widow, Barbara Hillyard. Lieutenant Commander Alan Powell of the Royal Navy has been assigned the task of forming an undercover organisation to make clandestine boat trips across the channel to gather vital information. He enlists Louis Duval, who agrees to return to France to establish a Resistance network there. Alan falls deeply in love with Barbara, but she seems to have eyes only for the attractive Frenchman . . .